The
AMIS
Story Anthology

Myong Hun Chang

ALSO BY KINGSLEY AMIS

FICTION
Lucky Jim
I Like It Here
That Uncertain Feeling
Take a Girl Like You
One Fat Englishman
The Anti-Death League
The Green Man
I Want It Now
Girl, 20
The Riverside Villas Murder
Ending Up
The Crime of the Century
The Alteration
Jake's Thing
Collected Short Stories
Russian Hide-and-Seek
The Golden Age of Science Fiction (editor)
Stanley and the Women
The Old Devils
Difficulties with Girls
The Folks That Live on the Hill
The Russian Girl

VERSE
A Case of Samples
A Look Round the Estate
Collected Poems 1944–79
The New Oxford Book of Light Verse (editor)
The Faber Popular Reciter (editor)
The Amis Anthology (editor)

NON-FICTION
New Maps of Hell: A Survey of Science Fiction
The James Bond Dossier
What Became of Jane Austen? and other questions
On Drink
Rudyard Kipling and His World
Harold's Years (editor)
Every Day Drinking
How's Your Glass?
The Amis Collection: Selected Non-Fiction 1954–1990
Memoirs

WITH ROBERT CONQUEST
Spectrum I, II, III, IV, V (editor)
The Egyptologists

WITH JAMES COCHRANE
The Great British Songbook (compiled)

OMNIBUS
A Kingsley Amis Omnibus
(*Jake's Thing, Stanley and the Women, The Old Devils*)

The
AMIS
Story Anthology

A Personal Choice of Short Stories

Kingsley Amis

HUTCHINSON
LONDON

This edition first published in 1992 by
Hutchinson

Random House UK Limited
20 Vauxhall Bridge Road, London, SW1V 2SA

Random House Australia (Pty) Ltd
20 Alfred Street, Milsons Point, Sydney, NSW 2061
Australia

Random House New Zealand Ltd
18 Poland Road, Glenfield, Auckland
New Zealand

Random House South Africa (Pty) Ltd
PO Box 337, Bergvlei 2012, South Africa

ISBN 0 09 174199 8

A CIP catalogue record for this book is available from the British Library

Typeset by Deltatype Ltd, Ellesmere Port
Printed and bound in Great Britain by
Mackays of Chatham PLC, Chatham, Kent

Contents

Introduction

This is a collection of my favourite short stories, not necessarily of the ones I think are the best. All of them have gone on appealing to me ever since I first read them. Some (those by James, Chesterton, Wodehouse) have come only narrowly ahead of several more by the same writer; others (Shaw, Nabokov, Boucher) are all I have much fancied there. One (Francis) is the only short story by its author I have ever seen.

There are not many generalizations about this literary form, if that is what it is, that are worth repeating. It was perhaps worth saying once, as I did in 1980 in the Introduction to a collection of my own work, that

> my kind of short story has a strong affinity with the novel; its scale is different but its internal proportions, the relative parts played by dialogue, narrative, description, are alike and make the two read alike,

and I added that

> the things that only the short story can do, the impression, the untrimmed slice of life, the landscape with figures but without characters, make little appeal to me.

But not only to me, I think: that kind of thing, what Philip Larkin called 'the short story as poem', had its heyday in the brief period 1910–1940, whereas the other kind ('as tale') flourished in English from about 1870 to 1960 or later.

One observation that failed to occur to me the first time round is that the short story is strongly and specially linked with genre fiction – with science fiction, detective fiction, ghost stories, humorous stories – which has only quite rarely been altogether successful at the length of the full-scale novel. As Barry N. Malzburg wrote of the short story in 1979, it is

> a structure which seems perfect to articulate and enact a single speculative conceit which (arguably) is the task for which science fiction is most suited,

and, to particularize in a different genre about another genre once equally popular, as Ronald Knox did in 1954,

> What is the right length for a mystery story? Anybody who has tried to write one will tell you, I think, that it should be about a third of the length of a novel.

Or at any rate much shorter than a novel. Certainly of the stories in this collection, half belong more or less straightforwardly to one genre or another.

There are no stories here that were not originally written in English. Perhaps the English-speaking peoples are specially gifted in this direction. This seems to me worth considering on grounds of general likelihood, though I have no firm business even to hold an opinion on the matter. Nor, I suspect, has anybody else. How many reasonable judges can there be with an intimate knowledge of some or a few of the couple of dozen major European tongues, let alone of some or a few of those from the East, Africa and elsewhere represented in fat volumes with titles like *Great Short Stories of the World*? An intimate enough knowledge, that is to say, to read a story in such a language in the same way as one needs to be able to read a poem, because nothing less will do. At any lower level one can only read for information, and the information to be gathered from literary works in prose or verse is, admittedly, often of great interest and value, if often subjective. But that interest is not usually thought of as literary, and there is something discreditable in the unargued consensus that phrases like 'Europe's greatest post-war writer' mean anything at all serious. (A myth requires no particular language to make its effect, and the story of Oedipus will do well enough in Lappish or Kiswahili, but we are not talking about that.)

Rudyard Kipling

Beyond the Pale

Love heeds not caste nor sleep a broken bed. I went in search of love
and lost myself.

Hindu Proverb

A man should, whatever happens, keep to his own caste, race and
breed. Let the White go to the White and the Black to the Black.
Then whatever trouble falls is in the ordinary course of things –
neither sudden, alien, nor unexpected.

This is the story of a man who wilfully stepped beyond the safe
limits of decent everyday society, and paid for it heavily.

He knew too much in the first instance; and he saw too much in
the second. He took too deep an interest in native life; but he will
never do so again.

Deep away in the heart of the City, behind Jitha Megji's *bustee*,
lies Amir Nath's Gully, which ends in a dead-wall pierced by one
grated window. At the head of the Gully is a big cow-byre, and the
walls on either side of the Gully are without windows. Neither
Suchet Singh nor Gaur Chand approve of their women-folk
looking into the world. If Durga Charan had been of their opinion
he would have been a happier man today, and little Bisesa would
have been able to knead her own bread. Her room looked out
through the grated window into the narrow dark Gully where the
sun never came and where the buffaloes wallowed in the blue
slime. She was a widow, about fifteen years old, and she prayed the
Gods, day and night, to send her a lover; for she did not approve of
living alone.

One day, the man – Trejago his name was – came into Amir
Nath's Gully on an aimless wandering; and, after he had passed the
buffaloes, stumbled over a big heap of cattle-food.

Then he saw that the Gully ended in a trap, and heard a little
laugh from behind the grated window. It was a pretty little laugh,
and Trejago, knowing that, for all practical purposes, the old
Arabian Nights are good guides, went forward to the window, and
whispered that verse of 'The Love Song of Har Dyal' which
begins:

> Can a man stand upright in the face of the naked Sun; or a lover
> in the Presence of his Beloved?
> If my feet fail me, O Heart of my Heart, am I to blame, being
> blinded by the glimpse of your beauty?

There came the faint *tchink* of a woman's bracelets from behind the
grating, and a little voice went on with the song at the fifth verse:

> Alas! alas! Can the Moon tell the Lotus of her love when the
> Gate of Heaven is shut and the clouds gather for the Rains?
> They have taken my Beloved, and driven her with the pack-
> horses to the North.
> There are iron chains on the feet that were set on my heart.
> Call to the bowmen to make ready –

The voice stopped suddenly, and Trejago walked out of Amir
Nath's Gully, wondering who in the world could have capped 'The
Love Song of Har Dyal' so neatly.

Next morning, as he was driving to his office, an old woman
threw a packet into his dogcart. In the packet was the half of a
broken glass bangle, one flower of the blood-red *dhak*, a pinch of
bhusa or cattle-food, and eleven cardamoms. That packet was a
letter – not a clumsy compromising letter, but an innocent,
unintelligible lover's epistle.

Trejago knew far too much about these things, as I have said.
No Englishman should be able to translate object-letters. But
Trejago spread all the trifles on the lid of his office-box and began
to puzzle them out.

A broken glass bangle stands for a Hindu widow all India over; because, when her husband dies, a woman's bracelets are broken on her wrists. Trejago saw the meaning of the little bit of glass. The flower of the *dhak* means diversely 'desire', 'come', 'write', or 'danger', according to the other things with it. One cardamom means 'jealousy'; but when any article is duplicated in an object-letter, it loses its symbolic meaning and stands merely for one of a number indicating time, or, if incense, curds, or saffron be sent also, place. The message ran then: A widow – *dhak* flower and *bhusa* – at eleven o'clock.' The pinch of *bhusa* enlightened Trejago. He saw – this kind of letter leaves much to instinctive knowledge – that the *bhusa* referred to the big heap of cattle-food over which he had fallen in Amir Nath's Gully, and that the message must come from the person behind the grating; she being a widow. So the message ran then: 'A widow, in the Gully in which is the heap of *bhusa*, desires you to come at eleven o'clock.'

Trejago threw all the rubbish into the fireplace and laughed. He knew that men in the East do not make love under windows at eleven in the forenoon, nor do women fix appointments a week in advance. So he went, that very night at eleven, into Amir Nath's Gully, clad in a *boorka*, which cloaks a man as well as a woman. Directly the gongs of the City made the hour, the little voice behind the grating took up 'The Love Song of Har Dyal' at the verse where the Pathan girl calls upon Har Dyal to return. The song is really pretty in the vernacular. In English you miss the wail of it. It runs something like this:

Alone upon the housetops, to the North
   I turn and watch the lightnings in the sky, –
The glamour of thy footsteps in the North.
   Come back to me, Beloved, or I die!

Below my feet the still bazar is laid –
   Far, far below the weary camels lie, –
The camels and the captives of thy raid.
   Come back to me, Beloved, or I die!

My father's wife is old and harsh with years,
   And drudge of all my father's house am I. –
My bread is sorrow and my drink is tears.
   Come back to me, Beloved, or I die!

As the song stopped, Trejago stepped up under the grating and whispered, 'I am here.'

Bisesa was good to look upon.

That night was the beginning of many strange things, and of a double life so wild that Trejago today sometimes wonders if it were not all a dream. Bisesa, or her old handmaiden who had thrown the object-letter, had detached the heavy grating from the brick-work of the wall; so that the window slid inside, leaving only a square of raw masonry into which an active man might climb.

In the daytime, Trejago drove through his routine of office work, or put on his calling-clothes and called on the ladies of the station, wondering how long they would know him if they knew of poor little Bisesa. At night, when all the City was still, came the walk under the evil-smelling *boorka*, the patrol through Jitha Megji's *bustee*, the quick turn into Amir Nath's Gully between the sleeping cattle and the dead walls, and then, last of all, Bisesa, and the deep, even breathing of the old woman who slept outside the door of the bare little room that Durga Charan allotted to his sister's daughter. Who or what Durga Charan was, Trejago never inquired; and why in the world he was not discovered and knifed never occurred to him till his madness was over, and Bisesa . . . But this comes later.

Bisesa was an endless delight to Trejago. She was as ignorant as a bird; and her distorted versions of the rumours from the outside world that had reached her in her room, amused Trejago almost as much as her lisping attempts to pronounce his name – 'Christopher'. The first syllable was always more than she could manage, and she made funny little gestures with her roseleaf hands, as one throwing the name away, and then, kneeling before Trejago, asked him, exactly as an English-woman would do, if he were sure he loved her more than anyone else in the world. Which was true.

After a month of this folly, the exigencies of his other life compelled Trejago to be especially attentive to a lady of his acquaintance. You may take it for a fact that anything of this kind is not only noticed and discussed by a man's own race, but by some hundred and fifty natives as well. Trejago had to walk with this lady and talk to her at the Bandstand, and once or twice to drive with her; never for an instant dreaming this would affect his dearer, out-of-the-way life. But the news flew, in the usual mysterious fashion, from mouth to mouth, till Bisesa's duenna heard of it and told Bisesa. The child was so troubled that she did the household work evilly, and was beaten by Durga Charan's wife in consequence.

A week later, Bisesa taxed Trejago with the flirtation. She understood no gradations and spoke openly. Trejago laughed, and Bisesa stamped her little feet – little feet, light as marigold flowers, that could lie in the palm of a man's one hand.

Much that is written about Oriental passion and impulsiveness is exaggerated and compiled at second hand; but a little of it is true, and when an Englishman finds that little, it is quite as startling as any passion in his own proper life. Bisesa raged and stormed, and finally threatened to kill herself if Trejago did not at once drop the alien Memsahib who had come between them. Trejago tried to explain, and to show her that she did not understand these things from a Western standpoint. Bisesa drew herself up, and said simply:

'I do not. I know only this – it is not good that I should have made you dearer than my own heart to me, Sahib. You are an Englishman. I am only a black girl' – she was fairer than bar-gold in the Mint – 'and the widow of a black man.'

Then she sobbed and said: 'But on my soul and my Mother's soul, I love you. There shall no harm come to you, whatever happens to me.'

Trejago argued with the child, and tried to soothe her, but she seemed quite unreasonably disturbed. Nothing would satisfy her save that all relations between them should end. He was to go away at once. And he went. As he dropped out of the window, she kissed his forehead twice, and he walked home wondering.

A week, and then three weeks, passed without a sign from Bisesa. Trejago, thinking that the rupture had lasted quite long enough, went down to Amir Nath's Gully for the fifth time in the three weeks, hoping that his rap at the sill of the shifting grating would be answered. He was not disappointed.

There was a young moon, and one stream of light fell down into Amir Nath's Gully, and struck the grating, which was drawn away as he knocked. From the black dark, Bisesa held out her arms into the moonlight. Both hands had been cut off at the wrists, and the stumps were nearly healed.

Then, as Bisesa bowed her head between her arms and sobbed,

someone in the room grunted like a wild beast, and something sharp – knife, sword, or spear – thrust at Trejago in his *boorka*. The stroke missed his body, but cut into one of the muscles of the groin, and he limped slightly from the wound for the rest of his days.

The grating went into its place. There was no sign whatever from inside the house – nothing but the moonlight strip on the high wall, and the blackness of Amir Nath's Gully behind.

The next thing Trejago remembers, after raging and shouting like a madman between those pitiless walls, is that he found himself near the river as the dawn was breaking, threw away his *boorka* and went home bareheaded.

What was the tragedy – whether Bisesa had, in a fit of causeless despair, told everything, or the intrigue had been discovered and she tortured to tell; whether Durga Charan knew his name, and what became of Bisesa – Trejago does not know to this day. Something horrible had happened, and the thought of what it must have been comes upon Trejago in the night now and again, and keeps him company till the morning. One special feature of the case is that he does not know where lies the front of Durga Charan's house. It may open on to a courtyard common to two or more houses, or it may lie behind any one of the gates of Jitha Megji's *bustee*. Trejago cannot tell. He cannot get Bisesa – poor little Bisesa – back again. He has lost her in the City where each man's house is as guarded and as unknowable as the grave; and the grating that opens into Amir Nath's Gully has been walled up.

But Trejago pays his calls regularly, and is reckoned a very decent sort of man.

There is nothing peculiar about him, except a slight stiffness, caused by a riding-strain, in the right leg.

Ambrose Bierce

An Occurrence at Owl Creek Bridge

I

A man stood upon a railroad bridge in northern Alabama, looking down into the swift water twenty feet below. The man's hands were behind his back, the wrists bound with a cord. A rope closely encircled his neck. It was attached to a stout cross-timber above his head and the slack fell to the level of his knees. Some loose boards laid upon the sleepers supporting the metals of the railway supplied a footing for him and his executioners – two private soldiers of the Federal army, directed by a sergeant who in civil life may have been a deputy sheriff. At a short remove upon the same temporary platform was an officer in the uniform of his rank, armed. He was a captain. A sentinel at each end of the bridge stood with his rifle in the position known as 'support', that is to say, vertical in front of the left shoulder, the hammer resting on the forearm thrown straight across the chest – a formal and unnatural position, enforcing an erect carriage of the body. It did not appear to be the duty of these two men to know what was occurring at the centre of the bridge; they merely blockaded the two ends of the foot planking that traversed it.

Beyond one of the sentinels nobody was in sight; the railroad ran straight away into a forest for a hundred yards, then, curving, was lost to view. Doubtless there was an outpost farther along. The other bank of the stream was open ground – a gentle acclivity topped with a stockade of vertical tree trunks, loop-holed for rifles, with a single embrasure through which protruded the muzzle of a brass cannon commanding the bridge. Midway of the slope between bridge and fort were the spectators – a single company of infantry in line, at 'parade rest', the butts of the rifles on the ground, the barrels inclining slightly backward against the right shoulder, the hands crossed upon the stock. A lieutenant stood at the right of the line, the point of his sword upon the ground, his left hand resting upon his right. Excepting the group of four at the centre of the bridge, not a man moved. The company faced the bridge, staring stonily, motionless. The sentinels, facing the banks of the stream, might have been statues to adorn the bridge. The captain stood with folded arms, silent, observing the work of his subordinates, but making no sign. Death is a dignitary who when he comes announced is to be received with formal manifestations of respect, even by those most familiar with him. In the code of military etiquette silence and fixity are forms of deference.

The man who was engaged in being hanged was apparently about thirty-five years of age. He was a civilian, if one might judge from his habit, which was that of a planter. His features were good – a straight nose, firm mouth, broad forehead, from which his long, dark hair was combed straight back, falling behind his ears to the collar of his well-fitting frock-coat. He wore a moustache and pointed beard, but no whiskers; his eyes were large and dark grey, and had a kindly expression which one would hardly have expected in one whose neck was in the hemp. Evidently this was no vulgar assassin. The liberal military code makes provision for hanging many kinds of persons, and gentlemen are not excluded.

The preparations being complete, the two private soldiers stepped aside and each drew away the plank upon which he had been standing. The sergeant turned to the captain, saluted and placed himself immediately behind that officer, who in turn moved apart one pace. These movements left the condemned man and the sergeant standing on the two ends of the same plank, which spanned three of the cross-ties of the bridge. The end upon which the civilian stood almost, but not quite, reached a fourth. This plank had been held in place by the weight of the captain; it was now held by that of the sergeant. At a signal from the former the latter would step aside, the plank would tilt and the condemned man go down between two ties. The arrangement commended itself to his judgment as simple and effective. His face had not been covered nor his eyes bandaged. He looked a moment at his 'unsteadfast footing', then let his gaze wander to the swirling water of the stream racing madly beneath his feet. A piece of dancing driftwood caught his attention and his eyes followed it down the current. How slowly it appeared to move! What a sluggish stream!

He closed his eyes in order to fix his last thoughts upon his wife and children. The water, touched to gold by the early sun, the brooding mists under the banks at some distance down the stream, the fort, the soldiers, the piece of drift – all had distracted him. And now he became conscious of a new disturbance. Striking through the thought of his dear ones was a sound which he could neither ignore nor understand, a sharp, distinct, metallic percussion like the stroke of a blacksmith's hammer upon the anvil; it had the same ringing quality. He wondered what it was, and whether immeasurably distant or near by – it seemed both. Its recurrence was regular, but as slow as the tolling of a death knell. He awaited each stroke with impatience and – he knew not why – apprehension. The intervals of silence grew progressively longer; the delays became maddening. With their greater infrequency the sounds increased in strength and sharpness. They hurt his ear like the thrust of a knife; he feared he would shriek. What he heard was the ticking of his watch.

He unclosed his eyes and saw again the water below him. 'If I could free my hands,' he thought, 'I might throw off the noose and spring into the stream. By diving I could evade the bullets and, swimming vigorously, reach the bank, take to the woods and get away home. My home, thank God, is as yet outside their lines; my wife and little ones are still beyond the invader's farthest advance.'

As these thoughts, which have here to be set down in words, were flashed into the doomed man's brain rather than evolved from it the captain nodded to the sergeant. The sergeant stepped aside.

II

Peyton Farquhar was a well-to-do planter, of an old and highly respected Alabama family. Being a slave owner and like other slave owners a politician he was naturally an original secessionist and ardently devoted to the Southern cause. Circumstances of an imperious nature, which it is unnecessary to relate here, had prevented him from taking service with the gallant army that had fought the disastrous campaigns ending with the fall of Corinth, and he chafed under the inglorious restraint, longing for the release of his energies, the larger life of the soldier, the opportunity for distinction. That opportunity, he felt, would come, as it comes to all in wartime. Meanwhile he did what he could. No service was too humble for him to perform in aid of the South, no adventure too perilous for him to undertake if consistent with the character of a civilian who was at heart a soldier, and who in good faith and without too much qualification assented to at least a part of the frankly villainous dictum that all is fair in love and war.

One evening while Farquhar and his wife were sitting on a rustic bench near the entrance to his grounds, a grey-clad soldier rode up to the gate and asked for a drink of water. Mrs Farquhar was only too happy to serve him with her own white hands. While she was fetching the water her husband approached the dusty horseman and inquired eagerly for news from the front.

'The Yanks are repairing the railroads,' said the man, 'and are getting ready for another advance. They have reached the Owl Creek bridge, put it in order and built a stockade on the north bank. The commandant has issued an order, which is posted everywhere, declaring that any civilian caught interfering with the railroad, its bridges, tunnels or trains will be summarily hanged. I saw the order.'

'How far is it to the Owl Creek bridge?' Farquhar asked.

'About thirty miles.'

'Is there no force on this side of the creek?'

'Only a picket post half a mile out, on the railroad, and a single sentinel at this end of the bridge.'

'Suppose a man – a civilian and student of hanging – should elude the picket post and perhaps get the better of the sentinel,' said Farquhar, smiling, 'what could he accomplish?'

The soldier reflected. 'I was there a month ago,' he replied. 'I observed that the flood of last winter had lodged a great quantity of driftwood against the wooden pier at this end of the bridge. It is now dry and would burn like tow.'

The lady had now brought the water, which the soldier drank. He thanked her ceremoniously, bowed to her husband and rode away. An hour later, after nightfall, he repassed the plantation, going northward in the direction from which he had come. He was a Federal scout.

III

As Peyton Farquhar fell straight downward through the bridge he lost consciousness and was as one already dead. From this state he was awakened – ages later, it seemed to him – by the pain of a sharp pressure upon his throat, followed by a sense of suffocation. Keen, poignant agonies seemed to shoot from his neck downward through every fibre of his body and limbs. These pains appeared to flash along well-defined lines of ramification and to beat with an inconceivably rapid periodicity. They seemed like streams of pulsating fire heating him to an intolerable temperature. As to his head, he was conscious of nothing but a feeling of fulness – of congestion. These sensations were unaccompanied by thought. The intellectual part of his nature was already effaced; he had power only to feel, and feeling was torment. He was conscious of motion. Encompassed in a luminous cloud, of which he was now merely the fiery heart, without material substance, he swung through unthinkable arcs of oscillation, like a vast pendulum. Then all at once, with terrible suddenness, the light about him shot upward with the noise of a loud plash; a frightful roaring was in his ears, and all was cold and dark. The power of thought was restored; he knew that the rope had broken and he had fallen into the stream. There was no additional strangulation; the noose about his neck was already suffocating him and kept the water from his lungs. To die of hanging at the bottom of a river! – the idea seemed to him ludicrous. He opened his eyes in the darkness and saw above him a gleam of light, but how distant, how inaccessible! He was still sinking, for the light became fainter and fainter until it was a mere glimmer. Then it began to grow and brighten, and he knew that he was rising toward the surface – knew it with reluctance, for he was now very comfortable. 'To be hanged and drowned,' he thought, 'that is not so bad; but I do not wish to be shot. No; I will not be shot; that is not fair.'

He was not conscious of an effort, but a sharp pain in his wrist apprised him that he was trying to free his hands. He gave the struggle his attention, as an idler might observe the feat of a juggler, without interest in the outcome. What splendid effort! – what magnificent, what superhuman strength! Ah, that was a fine endeavour! Bravo! The cord fell away; his arms parted and floated upward, the hands dimly seen on each side in the growing light.

He watched them with a new interest as first one and then the other pounced upon the noose at his neck. They tore it away and thrust it fiercely aside, its undulations resembling those of a water-snake. 'Put it back, put it back!' He thought he shouted these words to his hands, for the undoing of the noose had been succeeded by the direst pang that he had yet experienced. His neck ached horribly; his brain was on fire; his heart, which had been fluttering faintly, gave a great leap, trying to force itself out at his mouth. His whole body was racked and wrenched with an insupportable anguish! But his disobedient hands gave no heed to the command. They beat the water vigorously with quick, downward strokes, forcing him to the surface. He felt his head emerge; his eyes were blinded by the sunlight; his chest expanded convulsively, and with a supreme and crowning agony his lungs engulfed a great draught of air, which instantly he expelled in a shriek!

He was now in full possession of his physical senses. They were, indeed, preternaturally keen and alert. Something in the awful disturbance of his organic system had so exalted and refined them that they made record of things never before perceived. He felt the ripples upon his face and heard their separate sounds as they struck. He looked at the forest on the bank of the stream, saw the individual trees, the leaves and the veining of each leaf – saw the very insects upon them: the locusts, the brilliant-bodied flies, the grey spiders stretching their webs from twig to twig. He noted the prismatic colours in all the dewdrops upon a million blades of grass. The humming of the gnats that danced above the eddies of the stream, the beating of the dragon-flies' wings, the strokes of the waterspiders' legs, like oars which had lifted their boat – all these made audible music. A fish slid along beneath his eyes and he heard the rush of its body parting the water.

He had come to the surface facing down the stream; in a moment the visible world seemed to wheel slowly round, himself the pivotal point, and he saw the bridge, the fort, the soldiers upon the bridge, the captain, the sergeant, the two privates, his executioners. They were in silhouette against the blue sky. They shouted and gesticulated, pointing at him. The captain had drawn his pistol, but did not fire; the others were unarmed. Their movements were grotesque and horrible, their forms gigantic.

Suddenly he heard a sharp report and something struck the water smartly within a few inches of his head, spattering his face with spray. He heard a second report, and saw one of the sentinels with his rifle at his shoulder, a light cloud of blue smoke rising from the muzzle. The man in the water saw the eye of the man on the bridge gazing into his own through the sights of the rifle. He observed that it was a grey eye and remembered having read that grey eyes were keenest, and that all famous marksmen had them. Nevertheless, this one had missed.

A counter-swirl had caught Farquhar and turned him half round; he was again looking into the forest on the bank opposite the fort. The sound of a clear, high voice in a monotonous singsong now rang out behind him and came across the water with a distinctness that pierced and subdued all other sounds, even the beating of the ripples in his ears. Although no soldier, he had frequented camps enough to know the dread significance of that deliberate, drawling, aspirated chant; the lieutenant on shore was taking a part in the morning's work. How coldly and pitilessly – with what an even, calm intonation, presaging, and enforcing tranquillity in the men – with what accurately measured intervals fell those cruel words:

'Attention, company! . . . Shoulder arms! . . . Ready! . . . Aim! . . . Fire!'

Farquhar dived – as deeply as he could. The water roared in his ears like the voice of Niagara, yet he heard the dulled thunder of the volley and, rising again toward the surface, met shining bits of metal, singularly flattened, oscillating slowly downward. Some of them touched him on the face and hands, then fell away, continuing their descent. One lodged between his collar and neck; it was uncomfortably warm and he snatched it out.

As he rose to the surface, gasping for breath, he saw that he had been a long time under water; he was perceptibly farther down stream – nearer to safety. The soldiers had almost finished reloading; the metal ramrods flashed all at once in the sunshine as they were drawn from the barrels, turned in the air, and thrust into their sockets. The two sentinels fired again, independently and ineffectually.

The hunted man saw all this over his shoulder; he was now swimming vigorously with the current. His brain was as energetic as his arms and legs; he thought with the rapidity of lightning.

'The officer,' he reasoned, 'will not make that martinet's error a second time. It is as easy to dodge a volley as a single shot. He has probably already given the command to fire at will. God help me, I cannot dodge them all!'

An appalling plash within two yards of him was followed by a loud, rushing sound, *diminuendo*, which seemed to travel back through the air to the fort and died in an explosion which stirred the very river to its deeps! A rising sheet of water curved over him, fell down upon him, blinded him, strangled him! The cannon had taken a hand in the game. As he shook his head free from the commotion of the smitten water he heard the deflected shot humming through the air ahead, and in an instant it was cracking and smashing the branches in the forest beyond.

'They will not do that again,' he thought; 'the next time they will use a charge of grape. I must keep my eye upon the gun; the smoke will apprise me – the report arrives too late; it lags behind the missile. That is a good gun.'

Suddenly he felt himself whirled round and round – spinning like a top. The water, the banks, the forests, the now distant bridge, fort and men – all were commingled and blurred. Objects were represented by their colours only; circular horizontal streaks of colour – that was all he saw. He had been caught in a vortex and was being whirled on with a velocity of advance and gyration that made him giddy and sick. In a few moments he was flung upon the gravel at the foot of the left bank of the steam – the southern bank – and behind a projecting point which concealed him from his enemies. The sudden arrest of his motion, the abrasion of one of his hands on the gravel, restored him, and he wept with delight. He dug his fingers into the sand, threw it over himself in handfuls and audibly blessed it. It looked like diamonds, rubies, emeralds; he could think of nothing beautiful which it did not resemble. The trees upon the bank were giant garden plants; he noted a definite order in their arrangement, inhaled the fragrance of their blooms. A strange, roseate light shone through the spaces among their trunks and the wind made in their branches the music of æolian harps. He had no wish to perfect his escape – was content to remain in that enchanting spot until retaken.

A whiz and rattle of grapeshot among the branches high above his head roused him from his dream. The baffled cannoneer had fired him a random farewell. He sprang to his feet, rushed up the sloping bank, and plunged into the forest.

All that day he travelled, laying his course by the rounding sun. The forest seemed interminable; nowhere did he discover a break in it, not even a woodman's road. He had not known that he lived in so wild a region. There was something uncanny in the revelation.

By nightfall he was fatigued, footsore, famishing. The thought of his wife and children urged him on. At last he found a road which led him in what he knew to be the right direction. It was as wide and straight as a city street, yet it seemed untravelled. No fields bordered it, no dwelling anywhere. Not so much as the barking of a dog suggested human habitation. The black bodies of the trees formed a straight wall on both sides, terminating on the horizon in a point, like a diagram in a lesson in perspective. Overhead, as he looked up through this rift in the wood, shone great golden stars looking unfamiliar and grouped in strange constellations. He was sure they were arranged in some order which had a secret and malign significance. The wood on either side was full of singular noises, among which – once, twice, and again – he distinctly heard whispers in an unknown tongue.

His neck was in pain and lifting his hand to it he found it horribly swollen. He knew that it had a circle of black where the rope had bruised it. His eyes felt congested; he could no longer close them. His tongue was swollen with thirst; he relieved its fever by thrusting it forward from between his teeth into the cold air. How softly the turf had carpeted the untravelled avenue – he could no longer feel the roadway beneath his feet!

Doubtless, despite his suffering, he had fallen asleep while walking, for now he sees another scene – perhaps he has merely recovered from a delirium. He stands at the gate of his own home. All is as he left it, and all bright and beautiful in the morning sunshine. He must have travelled the entire night. As he pushes open the gate and passes up the wide white walk, he sees a flutter of female garments; his wife, looking fresh and cool and sweet, steps down from the veranda to meet him. At the bottom of the steps she stands waiting, with a smile of ineffable joy, an attitude of matchless grace and dignity. Ah, how beautiful she is! He springs forward with extended arms. As he is about to clasp her he feels a stunning blow upon the back of the neck; a blinding white light blazes all about him with a sound like the shock of a cannon – then all is darkness and silence!

Peyton Farquhar was dead; his body, with a broken neck, swung gently from side to side beneath the timbers of the Owl Creek bridge.

M. R. James

'Oh, Whistle, and I'll Come to You, My Lad'

'I suppose you will be getting away pretty soon, now Full term is over, Professor,' said a person not in the story to the Professor of Ontography, soon after they had sat down next to each other at a feast in the hospitable hall of St James's College.

The Professor was young, neat, and precise in speech.

'Yes,' he said; 'my friends have been making me take up golf this term, and I mean to go to the East Coast – in point of fact to Burnstow – (I dare say you know it) for a week or ten days, to improve my game. I hope to get off tomorrow.'

'Oh, Parkins,' said his neighbour on the other side, 'if you are going to Burnstow, I wish you would look at the site of the Templars' preceptory, and let me know if you think it would be any good to have a dig there in the summer.'

It was, as you might suppose, a person of antiquarian pursuits who said this, but, since he merely appears in this prologue, there is no need to give his entitlements.

'Certainly,' said Parkins, the Professor: 'if you will describe to me whereabouts the site is, I will do my best to give you an idea of the lie of the land when I get back; or I could write to you about it, if you would tell me where you are likely to be.'

'Don't trouble to do that, thanks. It's only that I'm thinking of taking my family in that direction in the Long, and it occurred to me that, as very few of the English preceptories have ever been properly planned, I might have an opportunity of doing something useful on off-days.'

The Professor rather sniffed at the idea that planning out a preceptory could be described as useful. His neighbour continued:

'The site – I doubt if there is anything showing above ground – must be down quite close to the beach now. The sea has encroached tremendously, as you know, all along that bit of coast. I should think, from the map, that it must be about three-quarters of a mile from the Globe Inn, at the north end of the town. Where are you going to stay?'

'Well, *at* the Globe Inn, as a matter of fact,' said Parkins; 'I have engaged a room there. I couldn't get in anywhere else; most of the lodging-houses are shut up in winter, it seems; and, as it is, they tell me that the only room of any size I can have is really a double-bedded one, and that they haven't a corner in which to store the other bed, and so on. But I must have a fairly large room, for I am taking some books down, and mean to do a bit of work; and though I don't quite fancy having an empty bed – not to speak of two – in what I may call for the time being my study, I suppose I can manage to rough it for the short time I shall be there.'

'Do you call having an extra bed in your room roughing it, Parkins?' said a bluff person opposite. 'Look here, I shall come down and occupy it for a bit; it'll be company for you.'

The Professor quivered, but managed to laugh in a courteous manner.

'By all means, Rogers; there's nothing I should like better. But I'm afraid you would find it rather dull; you don't play golf, do you?'

'No, thank Heaven!' said rude Mr Rogers.

'Well, you see, when I'm not writing I shall most likely be out on the links, and that, as I say, would be rather dull for you, I'm afraid.'

'Oh, I don't know! There's certain to be somebody I know in the place; but, of course, if you don't want me, speak the word, Parkins; I shan't be offended. Truth, as you always tell us, is never offensive.'

Parkins was, indeed, scrupulously polite and strictly truthful. It is to be feared that Mr Rogers sometimes practised upon his knowledge of these characteristics. In Parkins's breast there was a conflict now raging, which for a moment or two did not allow him to answer. That interval being over, he said:

'Well, if you want the exact truth, Rogers, I was considering whether the room I speak of would really be large enough to accommodate us both comfortably; and also whether (mind, I shouldn't have said this if you hadn't pressed me) you would not constitute something in the nature of a hindrance to my work.'

Rogers laughed loudly.

'Well done, Parkins!' he said. 'It's all right. I promise not to interrupt your work; don't you disturb yourself about that. No, I won't come if you don't want me; but I thought I should do so nicely to keep the ghosts off.' Here he might have been seen to wink and to nudge his next neighbour. Parkins might also have been seen to become pink. 'I beg pardon, Parkins,' Rogers continued; 'I oughtn't to have said that. I forgot you didn't like levity on these topics.'

'Well,' Parkins said, 'as you have mentioned the matter, I freely own that I do *not* like careless talk about what you call ghosts. A man in my position,' he went on, raising his voice a little, 'cannot, I find, be too careful about appearing to sanction the current beliefs on such subjects. As you know, Rogers, or as you ought to know; for I think I have never concealed my views — '

'No, you certainly have not, old man,' put in Rogers *sotto voce*.

' — I hold that any semblance, any appearance of concession to the view that such things might exist is equivalent to a renunciation of all that I hold most sacred. But I'm afraid I have not succeeded in securing your attention.'

'Your *undivided* attention, was what Dr Blimber actually *said*,'[1] Rogers interrupted, with every appearance of an earnest desire for accuracy. 'But I beg your pardon, Parkins: I'm stopping you.'

'No, not at all,' said Parkins. 'I don't remember Blimber; perhaps he was before my time. But I needn't go on. I'm sure you know what I mean.'

'Yes, yes,' said Rogers, rather hastily – 'just so. We'll go into it fully at Burnstow, or somewhere.'

In repeating the above dialogue I have tried to give the impression which it made on me, that Parkins was something of an old woman – rather hen-like, perhaps, in his little ways; totally destitute, alas! of the sense of humour, but at the same time dauntless and sincere in his convictions, and a man deserving of the greatest respect. Whether or not the reader has gathered so much, that was the character which Parkins had.

[1] Mr Rogers was wrong, *vide Dombey and Son*, chapter xii.

On the following day Parkins did, as he had hoped, succeed in getting away from his college, and in arriving at Burnstow. He was made welcome at the Globe Inn, was safely installed in the large double-bedded room of which we have heard, and was able before retiring to rest to arrange his materials for work in apple-pie order upon a commodious table which occupied the outer end of the room, and was surrounded on three sides by windows looking out seaward; that is to say, the central window looked straight out to sea, and those on the left and right commanded prospects along the shore to the north and south respectively. On the south you saw the village of Burnstow. On the north no houses were to be seen, but only the beach and the low cliff backing it. Immediately in front was a strip – not considerable – of rough grass, dotted with old anchors, capstans, and so forth; then a broad path; then the beach. Whatever may have been the original distance between the Globe Inn and the sea, not more than sixty yards now separated them.

The rest of the population of the inn was, of course, a golfing one, and included few elements that call for a special description. The most conspicuous figure was, perhaps, that of an *ancien militaire*, secretary of a London club, and possessed of a voice of incredible strength, and of views of a pronouncedly Protestant type. These were apt to find utterance after his attendance upon the ministrations of the Vicar, an estimable man with inclinations towards a picturesque ritual, which he gallantly kept down as far as he could out of deference to East Anglian tradition.

Professor Parkins, one of whose principal characteristics was pluck, spent the greater part of the day following his arrival at Burnstow in what he had called improving his game, in company with this Colonel Wilson: and during the afternoon – whether the process of improvement were to blame or not, I am not sure – the Colonel's demeanour assumed a colouring so lurid that even Parkins jibbed at the thought of walking home with him from the links. He determined, after a short and furtive look at that bristling moustache and those incarnadined features, that it would be wiser to allow the influences of tea and tobacco to do what they could with the Colonel before the dinner-hour should render a meeting inevitable.

'I might walk home tonight along the beach,' he reflected – 'yes, and take a look – there will be light enough for that – at the ruins of which Disney was talking. I don't exactly know where they are, by the way; but I expect I can hardly help stumbling on them.'

This he accomplished, I may say, in the most literal sense, for in picking his way from the links to the shingle beach his foot caught, partly in a gorse-root and partly in a biggish stone, and over he went. When he got up and surveyed his surroundings, he found himself in a patch of somewhat broken ground covered with small depressions and mounds. These latter, when he came to examine them, proved to be simply masses of flints embedded in mortar and grown over with turf. He must, he quite rightly concluded, be on the site of the preceptory he had promised to look at. It seemed not unlikely to reward the spade of the explorer; enough of the foundations was probably left at no great depth to throw a good deal of light on the general plan. He remembered vaguely that the Templars, to whom this site had belonged, were in the habit of building round churches, and he thought a particular series of the humps or mounds near him did appear to be arranged in something of a circular form. Few people can resist the temptation to try a little amateur research in a department quite outside their own, if only for the satisfaction of showing how successful they would have been had they only taken it up seriously. Our Professor, however, if he felt something of this mean desire, was also truly anxious to oblige Mr Disney. So he paced with care the circular area he had noticed, and wrote down its rough dimensions in his pocket-book. Then he proceeded to examine an oblong eminence which lay east of the centre of the circle, and seemed to his thinking likely to be the base of a platform or altar. At one end of it, the northern, a patch of the turf was gone – removed by some boy or other creature *feræ naturæ*. It might, he thought, be as well to probe the soil here for evidences of masonry, and he took out his knife and began scraping away the earth. And now followed another little discovery: a portion of soil fell inward as he scraped, and disclosed a small cavity. He lighted one match after another to help him to see of what nature the hole was, but the wind was too strong for them all. By tapping and scratching the sides with his knife, however, he was able to make out that it must be an artificial hole in masonry. It was rectangular, and the sides, top, and bottom, if not actually plastered, were smooth and regular. Of course it was empty. No! As he withdrew the knife he heard a metallic clink, and when he introduced his hand it met with a cylindrical object lying on the floor of the hole. Naturally enough, he picked it up, and when he brought it into the light, now fast fading, he could see that it, too, was of man's making – a metal tube about four inches long, and evidently of some considerable age.

By the time Parkins had made sure that there was nothing else in this odd receptacle, it was too late and too dark for him to think of undertaking any further search. What he had done had proved so unexpectedly interesting that he determined to sacrifice a little more of the daylight on the morrow to archæology. The object which he now had safe in his pocket was bound to be of some slight value at least, he felt sure.

Bleak and solemn was the view on which he took a last look before starting homeward. A faint yellow light in the west showed the links, on which a few figures moving towards the club-house were still visible, the squat martello tower, the lights of Aldsey village, the pale ribbon of sands intersected at intervals by black wooden groynes, the dim and murmuring sea. The wind was bitter from the north, but was at his back when he set out for the Globe. He quickly rattled and clashed through the shingle and gained the sand, upon which, but for the groynes which had to be got over every few yards, the going was both good and quiet. One last look behind, to measure the distance he had made since leaving the ruined Templars' church, showed him a prospect of company on his walk, in the shape of a rather indistinct personage, who seemed to be making great efforts to catch up with him, but made little, if any, progress. I mean that there was an appearance of running about his movements, but that the distance between him and Parkins did not seem materially to lessen. So, at least, Parkins thought, and decided that he almost certainly did not know him, and that it would be absurd to wait until he came up. For all that, company, he began to think, would really be very welcome on that lonely shore, if only you could choose your companion. In his unenlightened days he had read of meetings in such places which even now would hardly bear thinking of. He went on thinking of them, however, until he reached home, and particularly of one which catches most people's fancy at some time of their childhood. 'Now I saw in my dream that Christian had gone but a very little way when he saw a foul fiend coming over the field to meet him.' 'What should I do now,' he thought, 'if I looked back and caught sight of a black figure sharply defined against the yellow sky, and saw that it had horns and wings? I wonder whether I should stand or run for it. Luckily, the gentleman behind is not of that kind, and he seems to be about as far off now as when I saw him first. Well, at this rate he won't get his dinner as soon as I shall; and, dear me! it's within a quarter of an hour of the time now. I must run!'

Parkins had, in fact, very little time for dressing. When he met the Colonel at dinner, Peace – or as much of her as that gentleman could manage – reigned once more in the military bosom; nor was she put to flight in the hours of bridge that followed dinner, for Parkins was a more than respectable player. When, therefore, he retired towards twelve o'clock, he felt that he had spent his evening in quite a satisfactory way, and that, even for so long as a fortnight or three weeks, life at the Globe would be supportable under similar conditions – 'especially,' thought he, 'if I go on improving my game.'

As he went along the passages he met the boots of the Globe, who stopped and said:

'Beg your pardon, sir, but as I was a-brushing your coat just now there was somethink fell out of the pocket. I put it on your chest of drawers, sir, in your room, sir – a piece of a pipe or somethink of that, sir. Thank you, sir. You'll find it on your chest of drawers, sir – yes, sir. Good night, sir.'

The speech served to remind Parkins of his little discovery of that afternoon. It was with some considerable curiosity that he turned it over by the light of his candles. It was of bronze, he now saw, and was shaped very much after the manner of the modern dog-whistle; in fact it was – yes, certainly it was – actually no more nor less than a whistle. He put it to his lips, but it was quite full of a fine, caked-up sand or earth, which would not yield to knocking, but must be loosened with a knife. Tidy as ever in his habits, Parkins cleared out the earth on to a piece of paper, and took the latter to the window to empty it out. The night was clear and bright, as he saw when he had opened the casement, and he stopped for an instant to look at the sea and note a belated wanderer stationed on the shore in front of the inn. Then he shut the window, a little surprised at the late hours people kept at Burnstow, and took his whistle to the light again. Why, surely there were marks on it, and not merely marks, but letters! A very little rubbing rendered the deeply-cut inscription quite legible, but the Professor had to confess, after some earnest thought, that the meaning of it was as obscure to him as the writing on the wall to Belshazzar. There were legends both on the front and on the back of the whistle. The one read thus:

```
              FLA
      FUR           BIS
         FLE
```

The other:

```
  卐 QUIS EST ISTE QUI UENIT 卐
```

'I ought to be able to make it out,' he thought; 'but I suppose I am a little rusty in my Latin. When I come to think of it, I don't believe I even know the word for a whistle. The long one does seem simple enough. It ought to mean, "Who is this who is coming?" Well, the best way to find out is evidently to whistle for him.'

He blew tentatively and stopped suddenly, startled and yet pleased at the note he had elicited. It had a quality of infinite distance in it, and, soft as it was, he somehow felt it must be audible for miles round. It was a sound, too, that seemed to have the power (which many scents possess) of forming pictures in the brain. He saw quite clearly for a moment a vision of a wide, dark expanse at night, with a fresh wind blowing, and in the midst a lonely figure – how employed, he could not tell. Perhaps he would have seen more had not the picture been broken by the sudden surge of a gust of wind against his casement, so sudden that it made him look up, just in time to see the white glint of a sea-bird's wing somewhere outside the dark panes.

The sound of the whistle had so fascinated him that he could not help trying it once more, this time more boldly. The note was little, if at all, louder than before, and repetition broke the illusion – no picture followed, as he had half hoped it might. 'But what is this? Goodness! What force the wind can get up in a few minutes! What a tremendous gust! There! I knew that window-fastening was no use! Ah! I thought so – both candles out. It's enough to tear the room to pieces.'

The first thing was to get the window shut. While you might count twenty Parkins was struggling with the small casement, and felt almost as if he were pushing back a sturdy burglar, so strong was the pressure. It slackened all at once, and the window banged to and latched itself. Now to relight the candles and see what damage, if any, had been done. No, nothing seemed amiss; no glass even was broken in the casement. But the noise had evidently roused at least one member of the household: the Colonel was to be heard stumping in his stockinged feet on the floor above, and growling.

Quickly as it had risen, the wind did not fall at once. On it went, moaning and rushing past the house, at times rising to a cry so desolate that, as Parkins disinterestedly said, it might have made fanciful people feel quite uncomfortable; even the unimaginative, he thought after a quarter of an hour, might be happier without it.

Whether it was the wind, or the excitement of golf, or of the researches in the preceptory that kept Parkins awake, he was not sure. Awake he remained, in any case, long enough to fancy (as I am afraid I often do myself under such conditions) that he was the victim of all manner of fatal disorders: he would lie counting the beats of his heart, convinced that it was going to stop work every moment, and would entertain grave suspicions of his lungs, brain, liver, etc. – suspicions which he was sure would be dispelled by the return of daylight, but which until then refused to be put aside. He found a little vicarious comfort in the idea that someone else was in the same boat. A near neighbour (in the darkness it was not easy to tell his direction) was tossing and rustling in his bed, too.

The next stage was that Parkins shut his eyes and determined to give sleep every chance. Here again over-excitement asserted itself in another form – that of making pictures. *Experto crede*, pictures do come to the closed eyes of one trying to sleep, and are often so little to his taste that he must open his eyes and disperse them.

Parkins's experience on this occasion was a very distressing one. He found that the picture which presented itself to him was continuous. When he opened his eyes, of course, it went; but when he shut them once more it framed itself afresh, and acted itself out again, neither quicker nor slower than before. What he saw was this:

A long stretch of shore – shingle edged by sand, and intersected at short intervals with black groynes running down to the water – a scene, in fact, so like that of his afternoon's walk that, in the absence of any landmark, it could not be distinguished therefrom.

The light was obscure, conveying an impression of gathering storm, late winter evening, and slight cold rain. On this bleak stage at first no actor was visible. Then, in the distance, a bobbing black object appeared; a moment more, and it was a man running, jumping, clambering over the groynes, and every few seconds looking eagerly back. The nearer he came the more obvious it was that he was not only anxious, but even terribly frightened, though his face was not to be distinguished. He was, moreover, almost at the end of his strength. On he came; each successive obstacle seemed to cause him more difficulty than the last. 'Will he get over this next one?' thought Parkins; 'it seems a little higher than the others.' Yes; half climbing, half throwing himself, he did get over, and fell in a heap on the other side (the side nearest to the spectator). There, as if really unable to get up again, he remained crouching under the groyne, looking up in an attitude of painful anxiety.

So far no cause whatever for the fear of the runner had been shown; but now there began to be seen, far up the shore, a little flicker of something light-coloured moving to and fro with great swiftness and irregularity. Rapidly growing larger, it, too, declared itself as a figure in pale, fluttering draperies, ill-defined. There was something about its motion which made Parkins very unwilling to see it at close quarters. It would stop, raise arms, bow itself towards the sand, then run stooping across the beach to the water-edge and back again; and then, rising upright, once more continue its course forward at a speed that was startling and terrifying. The moment came when the pursuer was hovering about from left to right only a few yards beyond the groyne where the runner lay in hiding. After two or three ineffectual castings hither and thither it came to a stop, stood upright, with arms raised high, and then darted straight forward towards the groyne.

It was at this point that Parkins always failed in his resolution to keep his eyes shut. With many misgivings as to incipient failure of eyesight, over-worked brain, excessive smoking, and so on, he finally resigned himself to light his candle, get out a book, and pass the night waking, rather than be tormented by this persistent panorama, which he saw clearly enough could only be a morbid reflection of his walk and his thoughts on that very day.

The scraping of match on box and the glare of light must have startled some creatures of the night – rats or what not – which he heard scurry across the floor from the side of his bed with much rustling. Dear, dear! the match is out! Fool that is! But the second one burnt better, and a candle and book were duly procured, over which Parkins pored till sleep of a wholesome kind came upon him, and that in no long space. For about the first time in his orderly and prudent life he forgot to blow out the candle, and when he was called next morning at eight there was still a flicker in the socket and a sad mess of guttered grease on the top of the little table.

After breakfast he was in his room, putting the finishing touches to his golfing costume – fortune had again allotted the Colonel to him for a partner – when one of the maids came in.

'Oh, if you please,' she said, 'would you like any extra blankets on your bed, sir?'

'Ah! thank you,' said Parkins. 'Yes, I think I should like one. It seems likely to turn rather colder.'

In a very short time the maid was back with the blanket.

'Which bed should I put it on, sir?' she asked.

'What? Why, that one – the one I slept in last night,' he said, pointing to it.

'Oh yes! I beg your pardon, sir, but you seemed to have tried both of 'em; leastways, we had to make 'em both up this morning.'

'Really? How very absurd!' said Parkins. 'I certainly never touched the other, except to lay some things on it. Did it actually seem to have been slept in?'

'Oh yes, sir!' said the maid. 'Why, all the things was crumpled and throwed about all ways, if you'll excuse me, sir – quite as if anyone 'adn't passed but a very poor night, sir.'

'Dear me,' said Parkins. 'Well, I may have disordered it more than I thought when I unpacked my things. I'm very sorry to have given you the extra trouble, I'm sure. I expect a friend of mine soon, by the way – a gentleman from Cambridge – to come and occupy it for a night or two. That will be all right, I suppose, won't it?'

'Oh yes, to be sure, sir. Thank you, sir. It's no trouble, I'm sure,' said the maid, and departed to giggle with her colleagues.

Parkins set forth, with a stern determination to improve his game.

I am glad to be able to report that he succeeded so far in this enterprise that the Colonel, who had been rather repining at the prospect of a second day's play in his company, became quite chatty as the morning advanced; and his voice boomed out over the flats, as certain also of our own minor poets have said, 'like some great bourdon in a minster tower'.

'Extraordinary wind, that, we had last night,' he said. 'In my old home we should have said someone had been whistling for it.'

'Should you, indeed!' said Parkins. 'Is there a superstition of that kind still current in your part of the country?'

'I don't know about superstition,' said the Colonel. 'They believe in it all over Denmark and Norway, as well as on the Yorkshire coast; and my experience is, mind you, that there's generally something at the bottom of what these country-folk hold to, and have held to for generations. But it's your drive' (or whatever it might have been: the golfing reader will have to imagine appropriate digressions at the proper intervals).

When conversation was resumed, Parkins said, with a slight hesitancy:

'Apropos of what you were saying just now, Colonel, I think I ought to tell you that my own views on such subjects are very strong. I am, in fact, a convinced disbeliever in what is called the "supernatural".'

'What!' said the Colonel. 'Do you mean to tell me you don't believe in second-sight, or ghosts, or anything of that kind?'

'In nothing whatever of that kind,' returned Parkins firmly.

'Well,' said the Colonel, 'but it appears to me at that rate, sir, that you must be little better than a Sadducee.'

Parkins was on the point of answering that, in his opinion, the Sadducees were the most sensible persons he had ever read of in the Old Testament; but, feeling some doubt as to whether much mention of them was to be found in that work, he preferred to laugh the accusation off.

'Perhaps I am,' he said; 'but — Here, give me my cleek, boy! – Excuse me one moment, Colonel.' A short interval. 'Now, as to whistling for the wind, let me give you my theory about it. The laws which govern winds are really not at all perfectly known – to fisher-folk and such, of course, not known at all. A man or woman of eccentric habits, perhaps, or a stranger, is seen repeatedly on the beach at some unusual hour, and is heard whistling. Soon afterwards a violent wind rises; a man who could read the sky perfectly or who possessed a barometer could have foretold that it would. The simple people of a fishing-village have no barometers, and only a few rough rules for prophesying weather. What more natural than that the eccentric personage I postulated should be regarded as having raised the wind, or that he or she should clutch eagerly at the reputation of being able to do so? Now, take last night's wind: as it happens, I myself was whistling. I blew a whistle twice, and the wind seemed to come absolutely in answer to my call. If anyone had seen me — '

The audience had been a little restive under this harangue, and Parkins had, I fear, fallen somewhat into the tone of a lecturer; but at the last sentence the Colonel stopped.

'Whistling, were you?' he said. 'And what sort of whistle did you use? Play this stroke first.' Interval.

'About that whistle you were asking, Colonel. It's rather a curious one. I have it in my — No; I see I've left it in my room. As a matter of fact, I found it yesterday.'

And then Parkins narrated the manner of his discovery of the whistle, upon hearing which the Colonel grunted, and opined that, in Parkins's place, he should himself be careful about using a thing that had belonged to a set of Papists, of whom, speaking generally, it might be affirmed that you never knew what they might not have been up to. From this topic he diverged to the enormities of the Vicar, who had given notice on the previous Sunday that Friday would be the Feast of St Thomas the Apostle, and that there would be a service at eleven o'clock in the church. This and other similar proceedings constituted in the Colonel's view a strong presumption that the Vicar was a concealed Papist, if not a Jesuit; and Parkins, who could not very readily follow the Colonel in this region, did not disagree with him. In fact, they got on so well together in the morning that there was no talk on either side of their separating after lunch.

Both continued to play well during the afternoon, or, at least, well enough to make them forget everything else until the light began to fail them. Not until then did Parkins remember that he had meant to do some more investigating at the preceptory; but it was of no great importance, he reflected. One day was as good as another; he might as well go home with the Colonel.

As they turned the corner of the house, the Colonel was almost knocked down by a boy who rushed into him at the very top of his speed, and then, instead of running away, remained hanging on to him and panting. The first words of the warrior were naturally those of reproof and objurgation, but he very quickly discerned that the boy was almost speechless with fright. Inquiries were useless at first. When the boy got his breath he began to howl, and still clung to the Colonel's legs. He was at last detached, but continued to howl.

'What in the world *is* the matter with you? What have you been up to? What have you seen?' said the two men.

'Ow, I seen it wive at me out of the winder,' wailed the boy, 'and I don't like it.'

'What window?' said the irritated Colonel. 'Come, pull yourself together, my boy.'

'The front winder it was, at the 'otel,' said the boy.

At this point Parkins was in favour of sending the boy home, but the Colonel refused; he wanted to get to the bottom of it, he said; it was most dangerous to give a boy such a fright as this one had had, and if it turned out that people had been playing jokes, they should suffer for it in some way. And by a series of questions he made out this story: The boy had been playing about on the grass in front of the Globe with some others; then they had gone home to their teas, and he was just going, when he happened to look up at the front winder and see it a-wiving at him. *It* seemed to be a figure of some sort, in white as far as he knew – couldn't see its face; but it wived at him, and it warn't a right thing – not to say not a right person. Was there a light in the room? No, he didn't think to look if there was a light. Which was the window? Was it the top one or the second one? The seckind one it was – the big winder what got two little uns at the sides.

'Very well, my boy,' said the Colonel, after a few more questions. 'You run away home now. I expect it was some person trying to give you a start. Another time, like a brave English boy, you just throw a stone – well, no, not that exactly, but you go and speak to the waiter, or to Mr Simpson, the landlord, and – yes – and say that I advised you to do so.'

The boy's face expressed some of the doubt he felt as to the likelihood of Mr Simpson's lending a favourable ear to his complaint, but the Colonel did not appear to perceive this, and went on:

'And here's a sixpence – no, I see it's a shilling – and you be off home, and don't think any more about it.'

The youth hurried off with agitated thanks, and the Colonel and Parkins went round to the front of the Globe and reconnoitred. There was only one window answering to the description they had been hearing.

'Well, that's curious,' said Parkins; 'it's evidently my window the lad was talking about. Will you come up for a moment, Colonel Wilson? We ought to be able to see if anyone has been taking liberties in my room.'

They were soon in the passage, and Parkins made as if to open the door. Then he stopped and felt in his pockets.

'This is more serious than I thought,' was his next remark. 'I remember now that before I started this morning I locked the door. It is locked now, and, what is more, here is the key.' And he held it up. 'Now,' he went on, 'if the servants are in the habit of going into one's room during the day when one is away, I can only say that – well, that I don't approve of it at all.' Conscious of a somewhat weak climax, he busied himself in opening the door (which was indeed locked) and in lighting candles. 'No,' he said, 'nothing seems disturbed.'

'Except your bed,' put in the Colonel.

'Excuse me, that isn't my bed,' said Parkins. 'I don't use that one. But it does look as if someone had been playing tricks with it.'

It certainly did: the clothes were bundled up and twisted together in a most tortuous confusion. Parkins pondered.

'That must be it,' he said at last: 'I disordered the clothes last night in unpacking, and they haven't made it since. Perhaps they came in to make it, and that boy saw them through the window; and then they were called away and locked the door after them. Yes, I think that must be it.'

'Well, ring and ask,' said the Colonel, and this appealed to Parkins as practical.

The maid appeared, and, to make a long story short, deposed that she had made the bed in the morning when the gentleman was in the room, and hadn't been there since. No, she hadn't no other key. Mr Simpson he kep' the keys; he'd be able to tell the gentleman if anyone had been up.

This was a puzzle. Investigation showed that nothing of value had been taken, and Parkins remembered the disposition of the small objects on tables and so forth well enough to be pretty sure that no pranks had been played with them. Mr and Mrs Simpson furthermore agreed that neither of them had given the duplicate key of the room to any person whatever during the day. Nor could Parkins, fair-minded man as he was, detect anything in the demeanour of master, mistress, or maid that indicated guilt. He was much more inclined to think that the boy had been imposing on the Colonel.

The latter was unwontedly silent and pensive at dinner and throughout the evening. When he bade good night to Parkins, he murmured in a gruff undertone:

'You know where I am if you want me during the night.'

'Why, yes, thank you, Colonel Wilson, I think I do; but there isn't much prospect of my disturbing you, I hope. By the way,' he added, 'did I show you that old whistle I spoke of? I think not. Well, here it is.'

The Colonel turned it over gingerly in the light of the candle.

'Can you make anything of the inscription?' asked Parkins, as he took it back.

'No, not in this light. What do you mean to do with it?'

'Oh, well, when I get back to Cambridge I shall submit it to some of the archæologists there, and see what they think of it; and very likely, if they consider it worth having, I may present it to one of the museums.'

' 'M!' said the Colonel. 'Well, you may be right. All I know is that, if it were mine, I should chuck it straight into the sea. It's no use talking, I'm well aware, but I expect that with you it's a case of live and learn. I hope so, I'm sure, and I wish you a good night.'

He turned away, leaving Parkins in act to speak at the bottom of the stair, and soon each was in his own bedroom.

By some unfortunate accident, there were neither blinds nor curtains to the windows of the Professor's room. The previous night he had thought little of this, but tonight there seemed every prospect of a bright moon rising to shine directly on his bed, and probably wake him later on. When he noticed this he was a good deal annoyed, but, with an ingenuity which I can only envy, he succeeded in rigging up, with the help of a railway-rug, some safety-pins, and a stick and umbrella, a screen which, if it only held together, would completely keep the moonlight off his bed. And shortly afterwards he was comfortably in that bed. When he had read a somewhat solid work long enough to produce a decided wish for sleep, he cast a drowsy glance round the room, blew out the candle, and fell back upon the pillow.

He must have slept soundly for an hour or more, when a sudden clatter shook him up in a most unwelcome manner. In a moment he realized what had happened: his carefully constructed screen had given way, and a very bright frosty moon was shining directly on his face. This was highly annoying. Could he possibly get up and reconstruct the screen? Or could he manage to sleep if he did not?

For some minutes he lay and pondered over the possibilities; then he turned over sharply, and with his eyes open lay breathlessly listening. There had been a movement, he was sure, in the empty bed on the opposite side of the room. Tomorrow he would have it moved, for there must be rats or something playing about in it. It was quiet now. No! the commotion began again. There was a rustling and shaking: surely more than any rat could cause.

I can figure to myself something of the Professor's bewilderment and horror, for I have in a dream thirty years back seen the same thing happen; but the reader will hardly, perhaps, imagine how dreadful it was to him to see a figure suddenly sit up in what he had known was an empty bed. He was out of his own bed in one bound, and made a dash towards the window, where lay his only weapon, the stick with which he had propped his screen. This was, as it turned out, the worst thing he could have done, because the personage in the empty bed, with a sudden smooth motion, slipped from the bed and took up a position, with outspread arms, between the two beds, and in front of the door. Parkins watched it in a horrid perplexity. Somehow, the idea of getting past it and escaping through the door was intolerable to him; he could not have borne – he didn't know why – to touch it; and as for its touching him, he would sooner dash himself through the window than have that happen. It stood for the moment in a band of dark shadow, and he had not seen what its face was like. Now it began to move, in a stooping posture, and all at once the spectator realized, with some horror and some relief, that it must be blind, for it seemed to feel about with its muffled arms in a groping and random fashion. Turning half away from him, it became suddenly conscious of the bed he had just left, and darted towards it, and bent over and felt the pillows in a way which made Parkins shudder as he had never in his life thought it possible. In a very few moments it seemed to know that the bed was empty, and then, moving forward into the area of light and facing the window, it showed for the first time what manner of thing it was.

Parkins, who very much dislikes being questioned about it, did once describe something of it in my hearing, and I gathered that what he chiefly remembers about it is a horrible, an intensely horrible, face *of crumpled linen*. What expression he read upon it he could not or would not tell, but that the fear of it went nigh to maddening him is certain.

But he was not at leisure to watch it for long. With formidable quickness it moved into the middle of the room, and, as it groped and waved, one corner of its draperies swept across Parkins's face. He could not – though he knew how perilous a sound was – he could not keep back a cry of disgust, and this gave the searcher an instant clue. It leapt towards him upon the instant, and the next moment he was half-way through the window backwards, uttering cry upon cry at the utmost pitch of his voice, and the linen face was thrust close into his own. At this, almost the last possible second, deliverance came, as you will have guessed: the Colonel burst the door open, and was just in time to see the dreadful group at the window. When he reached the figures only one was left. Parkins sank forward into the room in a faint, and before him on the floor lay a tumbled heap of bed-clothes.

Colonel Wilson asked no questions, but busied himself in keeping everyone else out of the room and in getting Parkins back to his bed; and himself, wrapped in a rug, occupied the other bed for the rest of the night. Early on the next day Rogers arrived, more welcome than he would have been a day before, and the three of them held a very long consultation in the Professor's room. At the end of it the Colonel left the hotel door carrying a small object between his finger and thumb, which he cast as far into the sea as a very brawny arm could send it. Later on the smoke of burning ascended from the back premises of the Globe.

Exactly what explanation was patched up for the staff and visitors at the hotel I must confess I do not recollect. The Professor was somehow cleared of the ready suspicion of delirium tremens, and the hotel of the reputation of a troubled house.

There is not much question as to what would have happened to Parkins if the Colonel had not intervened when he did. He would either have fallen out of the window or else lost his wits. But it is not so evident what more the creature that came in answer to the whistle could have done than frighten. There seemed to be absolutely nothing material about it save the bed-clothes of which it had made itself a body. The Colonel, who remembered a not very dissimilar occurrence in India, was of opinion that if Parkins had closed with it it could really have done very little, and that its one power was that of frightening. The whole thing, he said, served to confirm his opinion of the Church of Rome.

There is really nothing more to tell, but, as you may imagine, the Professor's views on certain points are less clear-cut than they used to be. His nerves, too, have suffered: he cannot even now see a surplice hanging on a door quite unmoved, and the spectacle of a scarecrow in a field late on a winter afternoon has cost him more than one sleepless night.

G. K. Chesterton

The Blue Cross

Between the silver ribbon of morning and the green glittering ribbon of sea, the boat touched Harwich and let loose a swarm of folk like flies, among whom the man we must follow was by no means conspicuous – nor wished to be. There was nothing notable about him, except a slight contrast between the holiday gaiety of his clothes and the official gravity of his face. His clothes included a slight, pale grey jacket, a white waistcoat, and a silver straw hat with a grey-blue ribbon. His lean face was dark by contrast, and ended in a curt black beard that looked Spanish and suggested an Elizabethan ruff. He was smoking a cigarette with the seriousness of an idler. There was nothing about him to indicate the fact that the grey jacket covered a loaded revolver, that the white waistcoat covered a police card, or that the straw hat covered one of the most powerful intellects in Europe. For this was Valentin himself, the head of the Paris police and the most famous investigator in the world; and he was coming from Brussels to London to make the greatest arrest of the century.

Flambeau was in England. The police of three countries had tracked the great criminal at last from Ghent to Brussels, from Brussels to the Hook of Holland; and it was conjectured that he would take some advantage of the unfamiliarity and confusion of the Eucharistic Congress, then taking place in London. Probably he would travel as some minor clerk or secretary connected with it; but, of course, Valentin could not be certain, nobody could be certain about Flambeau.

It is many years now since this colossus of crime suddenly ceased keeping the world in a turmoil; and when he ceased, as they said after the death of Roland, there was a great quiet upon the earth. But in his best days (I mean, of course, his worst) Flambeau was a figure as statuesque and international as the Kaiser. Almost every morning the daily paper announced that he had escaped the consequences of one extraordinary crime by committing another. He was a Gascon of gigantic stature and bodily daring; and the wildest tales were told of his outbursts of athletic humour; how he turned the *juge d'instruction* upside down and stood him on his head, 'to clear his mind'; how he ran down the Rue de Rivoli with a policeman under each arm. It is due to him to say that his fantastic physical strength was generally employed in such bloodless though undignified scenes; his real crimes were chiefly those of ingenious and wholesale robbery. But each of his thefts was almost a new sin, and would make a story by itself. It was he who ran the great Tyrolean Dairy Company in London, with no dairies, no cows, no carts, no milk, but with some thousand subscribers. These he served by the simple operation of moving the little milk-cans outside people's doors to the doors of his own customers. It was he who had kept up an unaccountable and close correspondence with a young lady whose whole letter-bag was intercepted, by the extraordinary trick of photographing his messages infinitesimally small upon the slides of a microscope. A sweeping simplicity, however, marked many of his experiments. It is said he once repainted all the numbers in a street in the dead of night merely to divert one traveller into a trap. It is quite certain that he invented a portable pillar-box, which he put up at corners in quiet suburbs on the chance of strangers dropping postal orders into it. Lastly he was known to be a startling acrobat; despite his huge figure, he could leap like a grasshopper and melt into the tree-tops like a monkey. Hence the great Valentin, when he set out to find Flambeau, was perfectly well aware that his adventures would not end when he had found him.

But how was he to find him? On this the great Valentin's ideas were still in process of settlement.

There was one thing which Flambeau, with all his dexterity of disguise, could not cover, and that was his singular height. If Valentin's quick eye had caught a tall apple-woman, a tall grenadier, or even a tolerably tall duchess, he might have arrested them on the spot. But all along his train there was nobody that could be a disguised Flambeau, any more than a cat could be a

disguised giraffe. About the people on the boat he had already
satisfied himself; and the people picked up at Harwich or on the
journey limited themselves with certainty to six. There was a short
railway official travelling up to the terminus, three fairly short
market-gardeners picked up two stations afterwards, one very
short widow lady going up from a small Essex town, and a very
short Roman Catholic priest going up from a small Essex village.
When it came to the last case, Valentin gave it up and almost
laughed. The little priest was so much the essence of those Eastern
flats: he had a face as round and dull as a Norfolk dumpling; he had
eyes as empty as the North Sea; he had several brown-paper
parcels which he was quite incapable of collecting. The Eucharistic Congress had doubtless sucked out of their local stagnation
many such creatures, blind and helpless, like moles disinterred.
Valentin was a sceptic in the severe style of France, and could have
no love for priests. But he could have pity for them, and this one
might have provoked pity in anybody. He had a large, shabby
umbrella, which constantly fell on the floor. He did not seem to
know which was the right end of his return ticket. He explained
with a moon-calf simplicity to everybody in the carriage that he had
to be careful, because he had something made of real silver 'with
blue stones' in one of his brown-paper parcels. His quaint
blending of Essex flatness with saintly simplicity continuously
amused the Frenchman till the priest arrived (somehow) at
Stratford with all his parcels, and came back for his umbrella.
When he did the last, Valentin even had the good nature to warn
him to take care of the silver by not telling everybody about it. But
to whomever he talked, Valentin kept his eye open for someone
else; he looked out steadily for anyone, rich or poor, male or
female, who was well up to six feet; for Flambeau was four inches
above it.

He alighted at Liverpool Street, however, quite conscientiously
secure that he had not missed the criminal so far. He then went to
Scotland Yard to regularize his position and arrange for help in
case of need; he then lit another cigarette and went for a long stroll
in the streets of London. As he was walking in the streets and
squares beyond Victoria, he paused suddenly and stood. It was a
quaint, quiet square, very typical of London, full of an accidental
stillness. The tall, flat houses round looked at once prosperous and
uninhabited; the square of shrubbery in the centre looked as

deserted as a green Pacific islet. One of the four sides was much higher than the rest, like a dais; and the line of this side was broken by one of London's admirable accidents – a restaurant that looked as if it had strayed from Soho. It was an unreasonably attractive object, with dwarf plants in pots and long, striped blinds of lemon-yellow and white. It stood specially high above the street, and in the usual patchwork way of London, a flight of steps from the street ran up to meet the front door almost as a fire-escape might run up to a first-floor window. Valentin stood and smoked in front of the yellow-white blinds and considered them long.

The most incredible thing about miracles is that they happen. A few clouds in heaven do come together into the staring shape of one human eye. A tree does stand up in the landscape of a doubtful journey in the exact and elaborate shape of a note of interrogation. I have seen both these things myself within the last few days. Nelson does die in the instant of victory; and a man named Williams does quite accidentally murder a man named Williamson; it sounds like a sort of infanticide. In short, there is in life an element of elfin coincidence which people reckoning on the prosaic may perpetually miss. As it has been well expressed in the paradox of Poe, wisdom should reckon on the unforeseen.

Aristide Valentin was unfathomably French; and the French intelligence is intelligence specially and solely. He was not 'a thinking machine'; for that is a brainless phrase of modern fatalism and materialism. A machine only *is* a machine because it cannot think. But he was a thinking man, and a plain man at the same time. All his wonderful successes, that looked like conjuring, had been gained by plodding logic, by clear and commonplace French thought. The French electrify the world not by starting any paradox, they electrify it by carrying out a truism. They carry a truism so far – as in the French Revolution. But exactly because Valentin understood reason, he understood the limits of reason. Only a man who knows nothing of motors talks of motoring without petrol; only a man who knows nothing of reason talks of reasoning without strong, undisputed first principles. Here he had no strong first principles. Flambeau had been missed at Harwich; and if he was in London at all, he might be anything from a tall tramp on Wimbledon Common to a tall toastmaster at the Hôtel Métropole. In such a naked state of nescience, Valentin had a view and a method of his own.

In such cases he reckoned on the unforeseen. In such cases, when he could not follow the train of the reasonable, he coldly and carefully followed the train of the unreasonable. Instead of going to the right places – banks, police-stations, rendezous – he systematically went to the wrong places; knocked at every empty house, turned down every *cul de sac*, went up every lane blocked with rubbish, went round every crescent that led him uselessly out of the way. He defended this crazy course quite logically. He said that if one had a clue this was the worst way; but if one had no clue at all it was the best, because there was just the chance that any oddity that caught the eye of the pursuer might be the same that had caught the eye of the pursued. Somewhere a man must begin, and it had better be just where another man might stop. Something about that flight of steps up to the shop, something about the quietude and quaintness of the restaurant, roused all the detective's rare romantic fancy and made him resolve to strike at random. He went up the steps, and sitting down by the window, asked for a cup of black coffee.

It was half-way through the morning, and he had not breakfasted; the slight litter of other breakfasts stood about on the table to remind him of his hunger; and adding a poached egg to his order, he proceeded musingly to shake some white sugar into his coffee, thinking all the time about Flambeau. He remembered how Flambeau had escaped, once by a pair of nail scissors, and once by a house on fire; once by having to pay for an unstamped letter, and once by getting people to look through a telescope at a comet that might destroy the world. He thought his detective brain as good as the criminal's, which was true. But he fully realized the disadvantage. 'The criminal is the creative artist; the detective only the critic,' he said with a sour smile, and lifted his coffee cup to his lips slowly, and put it down very quickly. He had put salt in it.

He looked at the vessel from which the silvery powder had come; it was certainly a sugar-basin; as unmistakably meant for sugar as a champagne-bottle for champagne. He wondered why they should keep salt in it. He looked to see if there were any more orthodox vessels. Yes, there were two salt-cellars quite full. Perhaps there was some speciality in the condiment in the salt-cellars. He tasted it; it was sugar. Then he looked round at the restaurant with a refreshed air of interest, to see if there were any other traces of that singular artistic taste which puts the sugar in the salt-cellars and the salt in the sugar-basin. Except for an odd splash of some dark fluid on one of the white-papered walls, the whole place appeared neat, cheerful and ordinary. He rang the bell for the waiter.

When that official hurried up, fuzzy-haired and somewhat blear-eyed at that early hour, the detective (who was not without an appreciation of the simpler forms of humour) asked him to taste the sugar and see if it was up to the high reputation of the hotel. The result was that the waiter yawned suddenly and woke up.

'Do you play this delicate joke on your customers every morning?' inquired Valentin. 'Does changing the salt and sugar never pall on you as a jest?'

The waiter, when his irony grew clearer, stammeringly assured him that the establishment had certainly no such intention; it must be a most curious mistake. He picked up the sugar-basin and looked at it; he picked up the salt-cellar and looked at that, his face growing more and more bewildered. At last he abruptly excused himself, and hurrying away, returned in a few seconds with the proprietor. The proprietor also examined the sugar-basin and then the salt-cellar; the proprietor also looked bewildered.

Suddenly the waiter seemed to grow inarticulate with a rush of words.

'I zink,' he stuttered eagerly, 'I zink it is those two clergymen.'

'What two clergymen?'

'The two clergymen,' said the waiter, 'that threw soup at the wall.'

'Threw soup at the wall?' repeated Valentin, feeling sure this must be some Italian metaphor.

'Yes, yes,' said the attendant excitedly, and pointing at the dark splash on the white paper; 'threw it over there on the wall.'

Valentin looked his query at the proprietor, who came to his rescue with fuller reports.

'Yes, sir,' he said, 'it's quite true, though I don't suppose it has anything to do with the sugar and salt. Two clergymen came in and drank soup here very early, as soon as the shutters were taken down. They were both very quiet, respectable people; one of them paid the bill and went out; the other, who seemed a slower coach altogether, was some minutes longer getting his things together. But he went at last. Only, the instant before he stepped into the street he deliberately picked up his cup, which he had only half emptied, and threw the soup slap on the wall. I was in the back room myself, and so was the waiter; so I could only rush out in time to find the wall splashed and the shop empty. It didn't do any particular damage, but it was confounded cheek; and I tried to catch the men in the street. They were too far off though; I only noticed they went round the corner into Carstairs Street.'

The detective was on his feet, hat settled and stick in hand. He had already decided that in the universal darkness of his mind he could only follow the first odd finger that pointed; and this finger was odd enough. Paying his bill and clashing the glass doors behind him, he was soon swinging round into the other street.

It was fortunate that even in such fevered moments his eye was cool and quick. Something in a shop-front went by him like a mere flash; yet he went back to look at it. The shop was a popular greengrocer and fruiterer's, an array of goods set out in the open air and plainly ticketed with their names and prices. In the two most prominent compartments were two heaps, of oranges and of nuts respectively. On the heap of nuts lay a scrap of cardboard, on which was written in bold, blue chalk, 'Best tangerine oranges, two a penny.' On the oranges was the equally clear and exact description, 'Finest Brazil nuts, 4d. a lb.' M. Valentin looked at these two placards and fancied he had met this highly subtle form of humour before, and that somewhat recently. He drew the attention of the red-faced fruiterer, who was looking rather sullenly up and down the street, to this inaccuracy in his advertisements. The fruiterer said nothing, but sharply put each card into its proper place. The detective, leaning elegantly on his walking-cane, continued to scrutinize the shop. At last he said: 'Pray excuse my apparent irrelevance, my good sir, but I should like to ask you a question in experimental psychology and the association of ideas.'

The red-faced shopman regarded him with an eye of menace; but he continued gaily, swinging his cane. 'Why,' he pursued, 'why are two tickets wrongly placed in a greengrocer's shop like a shovel hat that has come to London for a holiday? Or, in case I do not make myself clear, what is the mystical association which connects the idea of nuts marked as oranges with the idea of two clergymen, one tall and the other short?'

The eyes of the tradesman stood out of his head like a snail's; he really seemed for an instant likely to fling himself upon the stranger. At last he stammered angrily: 'I don't know what you 'ave to do with it, but if you're one of their friends, you can tell 'em from me that I'll knock their silly 'eads off, parsons or no parsons, if they upset my apples again.'

'Indeed?' asked the detective, with great sympathy. 'Did they upset your apples?'

'One of 'em did,' said the heated shopman; 'rolled 'em all over the street. I'd 'ave caught the fool but for havin' to pick 'em up.'

'Which way did these parsons go?' asked Valentin.

'Up that second road on the left-hand side, and then across the square,' said the other promptly.

'Thanks,' said Valentin, and vanished like a fairy. On the other side of the second square he found a policeman, and said: 'This is urgent, constable; have you seen two clergymen in shovel hats?'

The policeman began to chuckle heavily. 'I 'ave, sir; and if you arst me, one of 'em was drunk. He stood in the middle of the road that bewildered that — '

'Which way did they go?' snapped Valentin.

'They took one of them yellow buses over there,' answered the man; 'them that go to Hampstead.'

Valentin produced his official card and said very rapidly: 'Call up two of your men to come with me in pursuit,' and crossed the road with such contagious energy that the ponderous policeman was moved to almost agile obedience. In a minute and a half the French detective was joined on the opposite pavement by an inspector and a man in plain clothes.

'Well, sir,' began the former, with smiling importance, 'and what may — '

Valentin pointed suddenly with his cane. 'I'll tell you on the top of that omnibus,' he said, and was darting and dodging across the tangle of the traffic. When all three sank panting on the top seats of the yellow vehicle, the inspector said: 'We could go four times as quick in a taxi.'

'Quite true,' replied their leader placidly, 'if we only had an idea of where we were going.'

'Well, where *are* you going?' asked the other, staring.

Valentin smoked frowningly for a few seconds; then, removing his cigarette, he said: 'If you *know* what a man's doing, get in front of him; but if you want to guess what he's doing, keep behind him.

Stray when he strays; stop when he stops; travel as slowly as he. Then you may see what he saw and may act as he acted. All we can do is to keep our eyes skinned for a queer thing.'

'What sort of a queer thing do you mean?' asked the inspector.

'Any sort of queer thing,' answered Valentin, and relapsed into obstinate silence.

The yellow omnibus crawled up the northern roads for what seemed like hours on end; the great detective would not explain further, and perhaps his assistants felt a silent and growing doubt of his errand. Perhaps, also, they felt a silent and growing desire for lunch, for the hours crept long past the normal luncheon hour, and the long roads of the North London suburbs seemed to shoot out into length after length like an infernal telescope. It was one of those journeys on which a man perpetually feels that now at last he must have come to the end of the universe, and then finds he has only come to the beginning of Tufnell Park. London died away in draggled taverns and dreary scrubs, and then was unaccountably born again in blazing high streets and blatant hotels. It was like passing through thirteen separate vulgar cities all just touching each other. But though the winter twilight was already threatening the road ahead of them, the Parisian detective still sat silent and watchful, eyeing the frontage of the streets that slid by on either side. By the time they had left Camden Town behind, the policemen were nearly asleep; at least, they gave something like a jump as Valentin leapt erect, struck a hand on each man's shoulder, and shouted to the driver to stop.

They tumbled down the steps into the road without realizing why they had been dislodged; when they looked round for enlightenment they found Valentin triumphantly pointing his finger towards a window on the left side of the road. It was a large window, forming part of the long façade of a gilt and palatial public-house; it was the part reserved for respectable dining, and labelled 'Restaurant'. This window, like all the rest along the frontage of the hotel, was of frosted and figured glass, but in the middle of it was a big, black smash, like a star in the ice.

'Our cue at last,' cried Valentin, waving his stick; 'the place with the broken window.'

'What window? What cue?' asked his principal assistant. 'Why, what proof is there that this has anything to do with them?'

Valentin almost broke his bamboo stick with rage.

'Proof!' he cried. 'Good God! the man is looking for proof! Why, of course, the chances are twenty to one that it has *nothing* to do with them. But what else can we do? Don't you see we must either follow one wild possibility or else go home to bed?' He banged his way into the restaurant, followed by his companions, and they were soon seated at a late luncheon at a little table, and looking at the star of smashed glass from the inside. Not that it was very informative to them even then.

'Got your window broken, I see,' said Valentin to the waiter, as he paid his bill.

'Yes, sir,' answered the attendant, bending busily over the change, to which Valentin silently added an enormous tip. The waiter straightened himself with mild but unmistakable animation.

'Ah, yes, sir,' he said. 'Very odd thing, that, sir.'

'Indeed? Tell us about it,' said the detective with careless curiosity.

'Well, two gents in black came in,' said the waiter; 'two of those foreign parsons that are running about. They had a cheap and quiet little lunch, and one of them paid for it and went out. The other was just going out to join him when I looked at my change again and found he'd paid me more than three times too much. "Here," I says to the chap who was nearly out of the door, "you've paid too much." "Oh," he says, very cool, "have we?" "Yes," I says, and picks up the bill to show him. Well, that was a knock-out.'

'What do you mean?' asked his interlocutor.

'Well, I'd have sworn on seven Bibles that I'd put 4s. on that bill. But now I saw I'd put 14s., as plain as paint.'

'Well?' cried Valentin, moving slowly, but with burning eyes, 'and then?'

'The parson at the door he says, all serene, "Sorry to confuse your accounts, but it'll pay for the window." "What window?" I says. "The one I'm going to break," he says, and smashed that blessed pane with his umbrella.'

All the inquirers made an exclamation, and the inspector said under his breath: 'Are we after escaped lunatics?' The waiter went on with some relish for the ridiculous story:

'I was so knocked silly for a second, I couldn't do anything. The man marched out of the place and joined his friend just round the corner. Then they went so quick up Bullock Street that I couldn't catch them, though I ran round the bars to do it.'

'Bullock Street,' said the detective, and shot up that thorough-fare as quickly as the strange couple he pursued.

Their journey now took them through bare brick ways like tunnels; streets with few lights and even with few windows; streets that seemed built out of the blank backs of everything and everywhere. Dusk was deepening, and it was not easy even for the London policemen to guess in what exact direction they were treading. The inspector, however, was pretty certain that they would eventually strike some part of Hampstead Heath. Abruptly one bulging and gas-lit window broke the blue twilight like a bull's-eye lantern; and Valentin stopped an instant before a little garish sweetstuff shop. After an instant's hesitation he went in; he stood amid the gaudy colours of the confectionery with entire gravity and bought thirteen chocolate cigars with a certain care. He was clearly preparing an opening; but he did not need one.

An angular, elderly young woman in the shop had regarded his elegant appearance with a merely automatic inquiry; but when she saw the door behind him blocked with the blue uniform of the inspector, her eyes seemed to wake up.

'Oh,' she said, 'if you've come about that parcel, I've sent it off already.'

'Parcel!' repeated Valentin; and it was his turn to look inquiring.

'I mean the parcel the gentleman left – the clergyman gentleman.'

'For goodness' sake,' said Valentin, leaning forward with his first real confession of eagerness, 'for Heaven's sake tell us what happened exactly.'

'Well,' said the woman, a little doubtfully, 'the clergymen came in about half an hour ago and bought some peppermints and talked a bit, and then went off towards the Heath. But a second after, one of them runs back into the shop and says, "Have I left a parcel?" Well, I looked everywhere and couldn't see one; so he says, "Never mind; but if it should turn up, please post it to this address," and he left me the address and a shilling for my trouble. And sure enough, though I thought I'd looked everywhere, I found he'd left a brown-paper parcel, so I posted it to the place he said. I can't remember the address now; it was somewhere in

Westminster. But as the thing seemed so important, I thought perhaps the police had come about it.'

'So they have,' said Valentin shortly. 'Is Hampstead Heath near here?'

'Straight on for fifteen minutes,' said the woman, 'and you'll come right out on the open.' Valentin sprang out of the shop and began to run. The other detectives followed him at a reluctant trot.

The street they threaded was so narrow and shut in by shadows that when they came out unexpectedly into the void common and vast sky they were startled to find the evening still so light and clear. A perfect dome of peacock-green sank into gold amid the blackening trees and the dark violet distances. The glowing green tint was just deep enough to pick out in points of crystal one or two stars. All that was left of the daylight lay in a golden glitter across the edge of Hampstead and that popular hollow which is called the Vale of Health. The holiday-makers who roam this region had not wholly dispersed: a few couples sat shapelessly on benches; and here and there a distant girl still shrieked in one of the swings. The glory of heaven deepened and darkened around the sublime vulgarity of man; and standing on the slope and looking across the valley, Valentin beheld the thing which he sought.

Among the black and breaking groups in that distance was one especially black which did not break – a group of two figures clerically clad. Though they seemed as small as insects, Valentin could see that one of them was much smaller than the other. Though the other had a student's stoop and an inconspicuous manner, he could see that the man was well over six feet high. He shut his teeth and went forward, whirling his stick impatiently. By the time he had substantially diminished the distance and magnified the two black figures as in a vast microscope, he had perceived something else; something which startled him, and yet which he had somehow expected. Whoever was the tall priest, there could be no doubt about the identity of the short one. It was his friend of the Harwich train, the stumpy little *curé* of Essex whom he had warned about his brown-paper parcels.

Now, so far as this went, everything fitted in finally and rationally enough. Valentin had learned by his inquiries that morning that a Father Brown from Essex was bringing up a silver cross with sapphires, a relic of considerable value, to show some of the foreign priests at the congress. This undoubtedly was the 'silver with blue stones'; and Father Brown undoubtedly was the little greenhorn in the train. Now there was nothing wonderful about the fact that what Valentin had found out Flambeau had also found out; Flambeau found out everything. Also there was nothing wonderful in the fact that when Flambeau heard of a sapphire cross he should try to steal it; that was the most natural thing in all natural history. And most certainly there was nothing wonderful about the fact that Flambeau should have it all his own way with such a silly sheep as the man with the umbrella and the parcels. He was the sort of man whom anybody could lead on a string to the North Pole; it was not surprising that an actor like Flambeau, dressed as another priest, could lead him to Hampstead Heath. So far the crime seemed clear enough; and while the detective pitied the priest for his helplessness, he almost despised Flambeau for condescending to so gullible a victim. But when Valentin thought of all that had happened in between, of all that had led him to his triumph, he racked his brains for the smallest rhyme or reason in it. What had the stealing of a blue-and-silver cross from a priest from Essex to do with chucking soup at wallpaper? What had it to do with calling nuts oranges, or with paying for windows first and breaking them afterwards? He had come to the end of his chase; yet somehow he had missed the middle of it. When he failed (which was seldom), he had usually grasped the clue, but nevertheless missed the criminal. Here he had grasped the criminal, but still he could not grasp the clue.

The two figures that they followed were crawling like black flies across the huge green contour of a hill. They were evidently sunk in conversation, and perhaps did not notice where they were going; but they were certainly going to the wilder and more silent heights of the Heath. As their pursuers gained on them, the latter had to use the undignified attitudes of the deerstalker, to crouch behind clumps of trees and even to crawl prostrate in deep grass. By these ungainly ingenuities the hunters even came close enough to the quarry to hear the murmur of the discussion, but no word could be distinguished except the word 'reason' recurring frequently in a high and almost childish voice. Once, over an abrupt dip of land and a dense tangle of thickets, the detectives actually lost the two figures they were following. They did not find the trail again for an agonizing ten minutes, and then it led round the brow of a great dome of hill overlooking an amphitheatre of rich and desolate sunset scenery. Under a tree in this commanding yet neglected spot was an old ramshackle wooden seat. On this seat sat the two priests still in serious speech together. The gorgeous green and gold still clung to the darkening horizon; but the dome above was turning slowly from peacock-green to peacock-blue, and the stars detached themselves more and more like solid jewels. Mutely motioning to his followers, Valentin contrived to creep up behind the big branching tree, and, standing there in deathly silence, heard the words of the strange priests for the first time.

After he had listened for a minute and a half, he was gripped by a devilish doubt. Perhaps he had dragged the two English policemen to the wastes of a nocturnal heath on an errand no saner than seeking figs on thistles. For the two priests were talking exactly like priests, piously, with learning and leisure, about the most aerial enigmas of theology. The little Essex priest spoke the more simply, with his round face turned to the strengthening stars; the other talked with his head bowed, as if he were not even worthy to look at them. But no more innocently clerical conversation could have been heard in any white Italian cloister or black Spanish cathedral.

The first he heard was the tail of one of Father Brown's sentences, which ended: '. . . what they really meant in the Middle Ages by the heavens being incorruptible.'

The taller priest nodded his bowed head and said:

'Ah, yes, these modern infidels appeal to their reason; but who can look at those millions of worlds and not feel that there may well be wonderful universes above us where reason is utterly unreasonable?'

'No,' said the other priest; 'reason is always reasonable, even in the last limbo, in the lost borderland of things. I know that people charge the Church with lowering reason, but it is just the other way. Alone on earth, the Church makes reason really supreme. Alone on earth, the Church affirms that God Himself is bound by reason.'

The other priest raised his austere face to the spangled sky and said:

'Yet who knows if in that infinite universe — ?'

'Only infinite physically,' said the little priest, turning sharply in his seat, 'not infinite in the sense of escaping from the laws of truth.'

Valentin behind his tree was tearing his finger-nails with silent fury. He seemed almost to hear the sniggers of the English detectives whom he had brought so far on a fantastic guess only to listen to the metaphysical gossip of two mild old parsons. In his impatience he lost the equally elaborate answer of the tall cleric, and when he listened again it was again Father Brown who was speaking:

'Reason and justice grip the remotest and the loneliest star. Look at those stars. Don't they look as if they were single diamonds and sapphires? Well, you can imagine any mad botany or geology you please. Think of forests of adamant with leaves of brilliants. Think the moon is a blue moon, a single elephantine sapphire. But don't fancy that all that frantic astronomy would make the smallest difference to the reason and justice of conduct. On plains of opal, under cliffs cut out of pearl, you would still find a notice-board, "Thou shalt not steal." '

Valentin was just in the act of rising from his rigid and crouching attitude and creeping away as softly as might be, felled by the one great folly of his life. But something in the very silence of the tall priest made him stop until the latter spoke. When at last he did speak, he said simply, his head bowed and his hands on his knees:

'Well, I still think that other worlds may perhaps rise higher than our reason. The mystery of heaven is unfathomable, and I for one can only bow my head.'

Then, with brow yet bent and without changing by the faintest shade his attitude or voice, he added:

'Just hand over that sapphire cross of yours, will you? We're all alone here, and I could pull you to pieces like a straw doll.'

The utterly unaltered voice and attitude added a strange violence to that shocking change of speech. But the guarder of the relic only seemed to turn his head by the smallest section of the compass. He seemed still to have a somewhat foolish face turned to the stars. Perhaps he had not understood. Or, perhaps, he had understood and sat rigid with terror.

'Yes,' said the tall priest, in the same low voice and in the same still posture, 'yes, I am Flambeau.'

Then, after a pause, he said:

'Come, will you give me that cross?'

'No,' said the other, and the monosyllable had an odd sound.

Flambeau suddenly flung off all his pontifical pretensions. The great robber leaned back in his seat and laughed low but long.

'No,' he cried; 'you won't give it me, you proud prelate. You won't give it me, you little celibate simpleton. Shall I tell you why you won't give it me? Because I've got it already in my own breast-pocket.'

The small man from Essex turned what seemed to be a dazed face in the dusk, and said, with the timid eagerness of 'The Private Secretary':

'Are – are you sure?'

Flambeau yelled with delight.

'Really, you're as good as a three-act farce,' he cried. 'Yes, you turnip, I am quite sure. I had the sense to make a duplicate of the right parcel, and now, my friend, you've got the duplicate, and I've got the jewels. An old dodge, Father Brown – a very old dodge.'

'Yes,' said Father Brown, and passed his hand through his hair with the same strange vagueness of manner. 'Yes, I've heard of it before.'

The colossus of crime leaned over to the little rustic priest with a sort of sudden interest.

'*You* have heard of it?' he asked. 'Where have *you* heard of it?'

'Well, I mustn't tell you his name, of course,' said the little man simply. 'He was a penitent, you know. He had lived prosperously for about twenty years entirely on duplicate brown-paper parcels. And so, you see, when I began to suspect you, I thought of this poor chap's way of doing it at once.'

'Began to suspect me?' repeated the outlaw with increased intensity. 'Did you really have the gumption to suspect me just because I brought you up to this bare part of the heath?'

'No, no,' said Brown with an air of apology. 'You see, I suspected you when we first met. It's that little bulge up the sleeve where you people have the spiked bracelet.'

'How in Tartarus,' cried Flambeau, 'did you ever hear of the spiked bracelet?'

'Oh, one's little flock, you know!' said Father Brown, arching his eyebrows rather blankly. 'When I was a curate in Hartlepool, there were three of them with spiked bracelets. So, as I suspected you from the first, don't you see, I made sure that the cross should go safe, anyhow. I'm afraid I watched you, you know. So at last I saw you change the parcels. Then, don't you see, I changed them back again. And then I left the right one behind.'

'Left it behind?' repeated Flambeau, and for the first time there was another note in his voice beside his triumph.

'Well, it was like this,' said the little priest, speaking in the same unaffected way. 'I went back to that sweet-shop and asked if I'd left a parcel, and gave them a particular address if it turned up. Well, I knew I hadn't; but when I went away again I did. So, instead of running after me with that valuable parcel, they have sent it flying to a friend of mine in Westminster.' Then he added rather sadly: 'I learnt that, too, from a poor fellow in Hartlepool. He used to do it with handbags he stole at railway stations, but he's in a monastery now. Oh, one gets to know, you know,' he added, rubbing his head again with the same sort of desperate apology. 'We can't help being priests. People come and tell us these things.'

Flambeau tore a brown-paper parcel out of his inner pocket and rent it in pieces. There was nothing but paper and sticks of lead inside it. He sprang to his feet with a gigantic gesture, and cried:

'I don't believe you. I don't believe a bumpkin like you could manage all that. I believe you've still got the stuff on you, and if you don't give it up – why, we're all alone, and I'll take it by force!'

'No,' said Father Brown simply, and stood up also; 'you won't take it by force. First, because I really haven't still got it. And, second, because we are not alone.'

Flambeau stopped in his stride forward.

'Behind that tree,' said Father Brown, pointing, 'are two strong policemen and the greatest detective alive. How did they come here, do you ask? Why, I brought them, of course! How did I do it? Why, I'll tell you if you like! Lord bless you, we have to know twenty such things when we work among the criminal classes! Well, I wasn't sure you were a thief, and it would never do to make a scandal against one of our own clergy. So I just tested you to see if anything would make you show yourself. A man generally makes a small scene if he finds salt in his coffee; if he doesn't, he has some reason for keeping quiet. I changed the salt and sugar, and *you* kept quiet. A man generally objects if his bill is three times too big. If he pays it, he has some motive for passing unnoticed. I altered your bill, and *you* paid it.'

The world seemed waiting for Flambeau to leap like a tiger. But

he was held back as by a spell; he was stunned with the utmost
curiosity.

'Well,' went on Father Brown, with lumbering lucidity, 'as you
wouldn't leave any tracks for the police, of course somebody had
to. At every place we went to, I took care to do something that
would get us talked about for the rest of the day. I didn't do much
harm – a splashed wall, spilt apples, a broken window; but I saved
the cross, as the cross will always be saved. It is at Westminster by
now. I rather wonder you didn't stop it with the Donkey's
Whistle.'

'With the what?' asked Flambeau.

'I'm glad you've never heard of it,' said the priest, making a
face. 'It's a foul thing. I'm sure you're too good a man for a
Whistler. I couldn't have countered it even with the Spots myself;
I'm not strong enough in the legs.'

'What on earth are you talking about?' asked the other.

'Well, I did think you'd know the Spots,' said Father Brown,
agreeably surprised. 'Oh, you can't have gone so very wrong yet!'

'How in blazes do you know all these horrors?' cried Flambeau.

The shadow of a smile crossed the round, simple face of his
clerical opponent.

'Oh, by being a celibate simpleton, I suppose,' he said. 'Has it
never struck you that a man who does next to nothing but hear
men's real sins is not likely to be wholly unaware of human evil?
But, as a matter of fact, another part of my trade, too, made me
sure you weren't a priest.'

'What?' asked the thief, almost gaping.

'You attacked reason,' said Father Brown. 'It's bad theology.'

And even as he turned away to collect his property, the three
policemen came out from under the twilight trees. Flambeau was
an artist and a sportsman. He stepped back and swept Valentin a
great bow.

'Do not bow to me, *mon ami*,' said Valentin, with silver
clearness. 'Let us both bow to our master.'

And they both stood an instant uncovered, while the little Essex
priest blinked about for his umbrella.

James Joyce

A Painful Case

Mr James Duffy lived in Chapelizod because he wished to live as far as possible from the city of which he was a citizen and because he found all the other suburbs of Dublin mean, modern and pretentious. He lived in an old sombre house and from his windows he could look into the disused distillery or upwards along the shallow river on which Dublin is built. The lofty walls of his uncarpeted room were free from pictures. He had himself bought every article of furniture in the room: a black iron bedstead, an iron wash-stand, four cane chairs, a clothes-rack, a coal-scuttle, a fender and irons and a square table on which lay a double desk. A bookcase had been made in an alcove by means of shelves of white wood. The bed was clothed with white bed-clothes and a black and scarlet rug covered the foot. A little hand-mirror hung above the wash-stand and during the day a white-shaded lamp stood as the sole ornament of the mantelpiece. The books on the white wooden shelves were arranged from below upwards according to bulk. A complete Wordsworth stood at one end of the lowest shelf and a copy of the *Maynooth Catechism*, sewn into the cloth cover of a notebook, stood at one end of the top shelf. Writing materials were always on the desk. In the desk lay a manuscript translation of Hauptmann's *Michael Kramer*, the stage directions of which were written in purple ink, and a little sheaf of papers held together by a brass pin. In these sheets a sentence was inscribed from time to time and, in an ironical moment, the headline of an advertisement for *Bile Beans* had been pasted on to the first sheet. On lifting the lid of the desk a faint fragrance escaped – the fragrance of new cedarwood pencils or of a bottle of gum or of an over-ripe apple which might have been left there and forgotten.

Mr Duffy abhorred anything which betokened physical or mental disorder. A mediæval doctor would have called him saturnine. His face, which carried the entire tale of his years, was of the brown tint of Dublin streets. On his long and rather large head grew dry black hair and a tawny moustache did not quite cover an unamiable mouth. His cheekbones also gave his face a harsh character; but there was no harshness in the eyes which, looking at the world from under their tawny eyebrows, gave the impression of a man ever alert to greet a redeeming instinct in others but often disappointed. He lived at a little distance from his body, regarding his own acts with doubtful side-glances. He had an odd autobiographical habit which led him to compose in his mind from time to time a short sentence about himself containing a subject in the third person and a predicate in the past tense. He never gave alms to beggars and walked firmly, carrying a stout hazel.

He had been for many years cashier of a private bank in Baggot Street. Every morning he came in from Chapelizod by tram. At midday he went to Dan Burke's and took his lunch – a bottle of lager beer and a small trayful of arrowroot biscuits. At four o'clock he was set free. He dined in an eating-house in George's Street where he felt himself safe from the society of Dublin's gilded youth and where there was a certain plain honesty in the bill of fare. His evenings were spent either before his landlady's piano or roaming about the outskirts of the city. His liking for Mozart's music brought him sometimes to an opera or a concert: these were the only dissipations of his life.

He had neither companions nor friends, church nor creed. He lived his spiritual life without any communion with others, visiting his relatives at Christmas and escorting them to the cemetery when they died. He performed these two social duties for old dignity's sake but conceded nothing further to the conventions which regulate the civic life. He allowed himself to think that in certain circumstances he would rob his bank but, as these circumstances never arose, his life rolled out evenly – an adventureless tale.

One evening he found himself sitting beside two ladies in the Rotunda. The house, thinly peopled and silent, gave distressing prophecy of failure. The lady who sat next him looked round at the deserted house once or twice and then said:

'What a pity there is such a poor house tonight! It's so hard on people to have to sing to empty benches.'

He took the remark as an invitation to talk. He was surprised that she seemed so little awkward. While they talked he tried to fix her permanently in his memory. When he learned that the young girl beside her was her daughter he judged her to be a year or so younger than himself. Her face, which must have been handsome, had remained intelligent. It was an oval face with strongly marked features. The eyes were very dark blue and steady. Their gaze began with a defiant note but was confused by what seemed a deliberate swoon of the pupil into the iris, revealing for an instant a temperament of great sensibility. The pupil reasserted itself quickly, this half-disclosed nature fell again under the reign of prudence, and her astrakhan jacket, moulding a bosom of a certain fullness, struck the note of defiance more definitely.

He met her again a few weeks afterwards at a concert in Earlsfort Terrace and seized the moments when her daughter's attention was diverted to become intimate. She alluded once or twice to her husband but her tone was not such as to make the allusion a warning. Her name was Mrs Sinico. Her husband's great-great-grandfather had come from Leghorn. Her husband was captain of a mercantile boat plying between Dublin and Holland; and they had one child.

Meeting her a third time by accident he found courage to make an appointment. She came. This was the first of many meetings; they met always in the evening and chose the most quiet quarters for their walks together. Mr Duffy, however, had a distaste for underhand ways and, finding that they were compelled to meet stealthily, he forced her to ask him to her house. Captain Sinico encouraged his visits, thinking that his daughter's hand was in question. He had dismissed his wife so sincerely from his gallery of pleasures that he did not suspect that anyone else would take an interest in her. As the husband was often away and the daughter out giving music lessons Mr Duffy had many opportunities of enjoying the lady's society. Neither he nor she had had any such adventure before and neither was conscious of any incongruity. Little by little he entangled his thoughts with hers. He lent her books, provided her with ideas, shared his intellectual life with her. She listened to all.

Sometimes in return for his theories she gave out some fact of her own life. With almost maternal solicitude she urged him to let his nature open to the full: she became his confessor. He told her that for some time he had assisted at the meetings of an Irish Socialist Party where he had felt himself a unique figure amidst a score of sober workmen in a garret lit by an inefficient oil-lamp. When the party had divided into three sections, each under its own leader and in its own garret, he had discontinued his attendances. The workmen's discussions, he said, were too timorous; the interest they took in the question of wages was inordinate. He felt that they were hard-featured realists and that they resented an exactitude which was the produce of a leisure not within their reach. No social revolution, he told her, would be likely to strike Dublin for some centuries.

She asked him why did he not write out his thoughts. For what, he asked her, with careful scorn. To compete with phrasemongers, incapable of thinking consecutively for sixty seconds? To submit himself to the criticisms of an obtuse middle class which entrusted its morality to policemen and its fine arts to impresarios?

He went often to her little cottage outside Dublin; often they spent their evenings alone. Little by little, as their thoughts entangled, they spoke of subjects less remote. Her companionship was like a warm soil about an exotic. Many times she allowed the dark to fall upon them, refraining from lighting the lamp. The dark discreet room, their isolation, the music that still vibrated in their ears united them. This union exalted him, wore away the rough edges of his character, emotionalized his mental life. Sometimes he caught himself listening to the sound of his own voice. He thought that in her eyes he would ascend to an angelical stature; and, as he attached the fervent nature of his companion more and more closely to him, he heard the strange impersonal voice which he recognized as his own, insisting on the soul's incurable loneliness. We cannot give ourselves, it said: we are our own. The end of these discourses was that one night during which she had shown every sign of unusual excitement, Mrs Sinico caught up his hand passionately and pressed it to her cheek.

Mr Duffy was very much surprised. Her interpretation of his words disillusioned him. He did not visit her for a week; then he wrote to her asking her to meet him. As he did not wish their last interview to be troubled by the influence of their ruined confessional they met in a little cakeshop near the Parkgate. It was cold autumn weather but in spite of the cold they wandered up and down the roads of the Park for nearly three hours. They agreed to break off their intercourse: every bond, he said, is a bond to sorrow. When they came out of the Park they walked in silence towards the tram; but here she began to tremble so violently that, fearing another collapse on her part, he bade her good-bye quickly and left her. A few days later he received a parcel containing his books and music.

Four years passed. Mr Duffy returned to his even way of life. His room still bore witness of the orderliness of his mind. Some new pieces of music encumbered the music-stand in the lower room and on his shelves stood two volumes by Nietzsche: *Thus Spake Zarathustra* and *The Gay Science*. He wrote seldom in the sheaf of papers which lay in his desk. One of his sentences, written two months after his last interview with Mrs Sinico, read: Love between man and man is impossible because there must not be sexual intercourse and friendship between man and woman is impossible because there must be sexual intercourse. He kept away from concerts lest he should meet her. His father died; the junior partner of the bank retired. And still every morning he went into the city by tram and every evening walked home from the city after having dined moderately in George's Street and read the evening paper for dessert.

One evening as he was about to put a morsel of corned beef and cabbage into his mouth his hand stopped. His eyes fixed themselves on a paragraph in the evening paper which he had propped against the water-carafe. He replaced the morsel of food on his plate and read the paragraph attentively. Then he drank a glass of water, pushed his plate to one side, doubled the paper down before him between his elbows and read the paragraph over and over again. The cabbage began to deposit a cold white grease on his plate. The girl came over to him to ask was his dinner not properly cooked. He said it was very good and ate a few mouthfuls of it with difficulty. Then he paid his bill and went out.

He walked along quickly through the November twilight, his stout hazel stick striking the ground regularly, the fringe of the buff *Mail* peeping out of a side-pocket of his tight reefer overcoat.

On the lonely road which leads from the Parkgate to Chapelizod he slackened his pace. His stick struck the ground less emphatically and his breath, issuing irregularly, almost with a sighing sound, condensed in the wintry air. When he reached his house he went up at once to his bedroom and, taking the paper from his pocket, read the paragraph again by the failing light of the window. He read it not aloud, but moving his lips as a priest does when he reads the prayers *Secreto*. This was the paragraph:

DEATH OF A LADY AT SYDNEY PARADE

A Painful Case

Today at the City of Dublin Hospital the Deputy Coroner (in the absence of Mr Leverett) held an inquest on the body of Mrs Emily Sinico, aged forty-three years, who was killed at Sydney Parade Station yesterday evening. The evidence showed that the deceased lady, while attempting to cross the line, was knocked down by the engine of the ten o'clock slow train from Kingstown, thereby sustaining injuries of the head and right side which led to her death.

James Lennon, driver of the engine, stated that he had been in the employment of the railway company for fifteen years. On hearing the guard's whistle he set the train in motion and a second or two afterwards brought it to rest in response to loud cries. The train was going slowly.

P. Dunne, railway porter, stated that as the train was about to start he observed a woman attempting to cross the lines. He ran towards her and shouted, but, before he could reach her, she was caught by the buffer of the engine and fell to the ground.

A juror. 'You saw the lady fall?'

Witness. 'Yes.'

Police Sergeant Croly deposed that when he arrived he found the deceased lying on the platform apparently dead. He had the body taken to the waiting-room pending the arrival of the ambulance.

Constable 57E corroborated.

Dr Halpin, assistant house surgeon of the City of Dublin Hospital, stated that the deceased had two lower ribs fractured and had sustained severe contusions of the right shoulder. The right side of the head had been injured in the fall. The injuries were not sufficient to have caused death in a normal person. Death, in his opinion, had been probably due to shock and sudden failure of the heart's action.

Mr H. B. Patterson Finlay, on behalf of the railway company, expressed his deep regret at the accident. The company had always taken every precaution to prevent people crossing the lines except by the bridges, both by placing notices in every station and by the use of patent spring gates at level crossings. The deceased had been in the habit of crossing the lines late at night from platform to platform and, in view of certain other circumstances of the case, he did not think the railway officials were to blame.

Captain Sinico, of Leoville, Sydney Parade, husband of the deceased, also gave evidence. He stated that the deceased was his wife. He was not in Dublin at the time of the accident as he had arrived only that morning from Rotterdam. They had been married for twenty-two years and had lived happily until about two years ago when his wife began to be rather intemperate in her habits.

Miss Mary Sinico said that of late her mother had been in the habit of going out at night to buy spirits. She, witness, had often tried to reason with her mother and had induced her to join a League. She was not at home until an hour after the accident.

The jury returned a verdict in accordance with the medical evidence and exonerated Lennon from all blame.

The Deputy Coroner said it was a most painful case, and expressed great sympathy with Captain Sinico and his daughter. He urged on the railway company to take strong measures to prevent the possibility of similar accidents in the future. No blame attached to anyone.

Mr Duffy raised his eyes from the paper and gazed out of his window on the cheerless evening landscape. The river lay quiet beside the empty distillery and from time to time a light appeared in some house on the Lucan road. What an end! The whole narrative of her death revolted him and it revolted him to think that he had ever spoken to her of what he held sacred. The threadbare phrases, the inane expressions of sympathy, the cautious words of a reporter won over to conceal the details of a commonplace vulgar death attacked his stomach. Not merely had she degraded herself; she had degraded him. He saw the squalid tract of her vice, miserable and malodorous. His soul's companion! He thought of the hobbling wretches whom he had seen carrying cans and bottles to be filled by the barman. Just God, what an end! Evidently she had been unfit to live, without any strength of purpose, an easy prey to habits, one of the wrecks on which civilization has been reared. But that she could have sunk so low! Was it possible he had deceived himself so utterly about her? He remembered her outburst of that night and interpreted it in a harsher sense than he had ever done. He had no difficulty now in approving of the course he had taken.

As the light failed and his memory began to wander he thought her hand touched his. The shock which had first attacked his stomach was now attacking his nerves. He put on his overcoat and hat quickly and went out. The cold air met him on the threshold; it crept into the sleeves of his coat. When he came to the public-house at Chapelizod Bridge he went in and ordered a hot punch.

The proprietor served him obsequiously but did not venture to talk. There were five or six working-men in the shop discussing the value of a gentleman's estate in County Kildare. They drank at intervals from their huge pint tumblers and smoked, spitting often on the floor and sometimes dragging the sawdust over their spits with their heavy boots. Mr Duffy sat on his stool and gazed at them, without seeing or hearing them. After a while they went out and he called for another punch. He sat a long time over it. The shop was very quiet. The proprietor sprawled on the counter reading the *Herald* and yawning. Now and again a tram was heard swishing along the lonely road outside.

As he sat there, living over his life with her and evoking alternately the two images in which he now conceived her, he realized that she was dead, that she had ceased to exist, that she had become a memory. He began to feel ill at ease. He asked himself what else could he have done. He could not have carried on a comedy of deception with her; he could not have lived with her openly. He had done what seemed to him best. How was he to blame? Now that she was gone he understood how lonely her life must have been, sitting night after night alone in that room. His life would be lonely too until he, too, died, ceased to exist, became a memory – if anyone remembered him.

It was after nine o'clock when he left the shop. The night was cold and gloomy. He entered the Park by the first gate and walked along under the gaunt trees. He walked through the bleak alleys where they had walked four years before. She seemed to be near him in the darkness. At moments he seemed to feel her voice touch his ear, her hand touch his. He stood still to listen. Why had he withheld life from her? Why had he sentenced her to death? He felt his moral nature falling to pieces.

When he gained the crest of the Magazine Hill he halted and looked along the river towards Dublin, the lights of which burned redly and hospitably in the cold night. He looked down the slope and, at the base, in the shadow of the wall of the Park, he saw some human figures lying. Those venal and furtive loves filled him with despair. He gnawed the rectitude of his life; he felt that he had been outcast from life's feast. One human being had seemed to love him and he had denied her life and happiness: he had sentenced her to ignominy, a death of shame. He knew that the prostrate creatures down by the wall were watching him and wished him gone. No one wanted him; he was outcast from life's feast. He turned his eyes to the grey gleaming river, winding along towards Dublin. Beyond the river he saw a goods train winding out of Kingsbridge Station, like a worm with a fiery head winding through the darkness, obstinately and laboriously. It passed slowly out of sight; but still he heard in his ears the laborious drone of the engine reiterating the syllables of her name.

He turned back the way he had come, the rhythm of the engine pounding in his ears. He began to doubt the reality of what memory told him. He halted under a tree and allowed the rhythm to die away. He could not feel her near him in the darkness nor her voice touch his ear. He waited for some minutes listening. He could hear nothing: the night was perfectly silent. He listened again: perfectly silent. He felt that he was alone.

W. Somerset Maugham

The Door of Opportunity

They got a first-class carriage to themselves. It was lucky, because they were taking a good deal in with them, Alban's suitcase and a hold-all, Anne's dressing-case and her hat-box. They had two trunks in the van, containing what they wanted immediately, but all the rest of their luggage Alban had put in the care of an agent who was to take it up to London and store it till they had made up their minds what to do. They had a lot, pictures and books, curios that Alban had collected in the East, his guns and saddles. They had left Sondurah for ever. Alban, as was his way, tipped the porter generously and then went to the bookstall and bought papers. He bought the *New Statesman* and the *Nation*, and the *Tatler* and the *Sketch*, and the last number of the *London Mercury*. He came back to the carriage and threw them on the seat.

'It's only an hour's journey,' said Anne.

'I know, but I wanted to buy them. I've been starved so long. Isn't it grand to think that tomorrow morning we shall have tomorrow's *Times*, and the *Express* and the *Mail*?'

She did not answer and he turned away, for he saw coming towards them two persons, a man and his wife, who had been fellow-passengers from Singapore.

'Get through the customs all right?' he cried to them cheerily.

The man seemed not to hear, for he walked straight on, but the woman answered.

'Yes, they never found the cigarettes.'

She saw Anne, gave her a friendly little smile, and passed on. Anne flushed.

'I was afraid they'd want to come in here,' said Alban. 'Let's have the carriage to ourselves if we can.'

She looked at him curiously.

'I don't think you need worry,' she answered. 'I don't think anyone will come in.'

He lit a cigarette and lingered at the carriage door. On his face was a happy smile. When they had passed through the Red Sea and found a sharp wind in the Canal, Anne had been surprised to see how much the men who had looked presentable enough in the white ducks in which she had been accustomed to see them, were changed when they left them off for warmer clothes. They looked like nothing on earth then. Their ties were awful and their shirts all wrong. They wore grubby flannel trousers and shabby old golf-coats that had too obviously been bought off the nail, or blue serge suits that betrayed the provincial tailor. Most of the passengers had got off at Marseilles, but a dozen or so, either because after a long period in the East they thought the trip through the Bay would do them good, or, like themselves, for economy's sake, had gone all the way to Tilbury, and now several of them walked along the platform. They wore solar topees or double-brimmed terais, and heavy greatcoats, or else shapeless soft hats or bowlers, not too well brushed, that looked too small for them. It was a shock to see them. They looked suburban and a trifle second-rate. But Alban had already a London look. There was not a speck of dust on his smart greatcoat, and his black Homburg hat looked brand-new. You would never have guessed that he had not been home for three years. His collar fitted closely round his neck and his foulard tie was neatly tied. As Anne looked at him she could not but think how good-looking he was. He was just under six feet tall, and slim, and he wore his clothes well, and his clothes were well cut. He had fair hair, still thick, and blue eyes and the faintly yellow skin common to men of that complexion after they have lost the pink-and-white freshness of early youth. There was no colour in his cheeks. It was a fine head, well-set on rather a long neck, with a somewhat prominent Adam's apple; but you were more impressed with the distinction than with the beauty of his face. It was because his features were so regular, his nose so straight, his brow so broad that he photographed so well. Indeed, from his photographs you would have thought him extremely handsome. He was not that, perhaps because his eyebrows and his eyelashes were pale, and his lips thin, but he looked very intellectual. There was refinement in his face and a spirituality that was oddly moving. That was how you thought a poet should look; and when Anne became engaged to him she told her girl friends who asked her about him that he looked like Shelley. He turned to her now with a little smile in his blue eyes. His smile was very attractive.

'What a perfect day to land in England!'

It was October. They had steamed up the Channel on a grey sea under a grey sky. There was not a breath of wind. The fishing boats seemed to rest on the placid water as though the elements had for ever forgotten their old hostility. The coast was incredibly green, but with a bright cosy greenness quite unlike the luxuriant, vehement verdure of Eastern jungles. The red towns they passed here and there were comfortable and homelike. They seemed to welcome the exiles with a smiling friendliness. And when they drew into the estuary of the Thames they saw the rich levels of Essex and in a little while Chalk Church on the Kentish shore, lonely in the midst of weather-beaten trees, and beyond it the woods of Cobham. The sun, red in a faint mist, set on the marshes, and night fell. In the station the arc-lamps shed a light that spotted the darkness with cold hard patches. It was good to see the porters lumbering about in their grubby uniforms and the stationmaster fat and important in his bowler hat. The stationmaster blew a whistle and waved his arm. Alban stepped into the carriage and seated himself in the corner opposite to Anne. The train started.

'We're due in London at six-ten,' said Alban. 'We ought to get to Jermyn Street by seven. That'll give us an hour to bath and change and we can get to the Savoy for dinner by eight-thirty. A bottle of pop tonight, my pet, and a slap-up dinner.' He gave a chuckle. 'I heard the Strouds and the Maundys arranging to meet at the Trocadero Grill-Room.'

He took up the papers and asked if she wanted any of them. Anne shook her head.

'Tired?' he smiled.

'No.'

'Excited?'

In order not to answer she gave a little laugh. He began to look at the papers, starting with the publishers' advertisements, and she was conscious of the intense satisfaction it was to him to feel himself through them once more in the middle of things. They had taken in those same papers in Sondurah, but they arrived six weeks old, and though they kept them abreast of what was going on in the world that interested them both, they emphasized their exile. But these were fresh from the press. They smelt different. They had a crispness that was almost voluptuous. He wanted to read them all at once. Anne looked out of the window. The country was dark, and she could see little but the lights of their carriage reflected on the glass, but very soon the town encroached upon it, and then she saw little sordid houses, mile upon mile of them, with a light in a window here and there, and the chimneys made a dreary pattern against the sky. They passed through Barking and East Ham and Bromley – it was silly that the name on the platform as they went through the station should give her such a tremor – and then Stepney. Alban put down his papers.

'We shall be there in five minutes now.'

He put on his hat and took down from the racks the things the porter had put in them. He looked at her with shining eyes and his lips twitched. She saw that he was only just able to control his emotion. He looked out of the window, too, and they passed over brightly lighted thoroughfares, close packed with tram-cars, buses, and motor-vans, and they saw the streets thick with people. What a mob! The shops were all lit up. They saw the hawkers with their barrows at the kerb.

'London,' he said.

He took her hand and gently pressed it. His smile was so sweet that she had to say something. She tried to be facetious.

'Does it make you feel all funny inside?'

'I don't know if I want to cry or if I want to be sick.'

Fenchurch Street. He lowered the window and waved his arm for a porter. With a grinding of brakes the train came to a standstill. A porter opened the door and Alban handed him out one package after another. Then in his polite way, having jumped out, he gave his hand to Anne to help her down to the platform. The porter went to fetch a barrow and they stood by the pile of their luggage. Alban waved to two passengers from the ship who passed them. The man nodded stiffly.

'What a comfort it is that we shall never have to be civil to those awful people any more,' said Alban lightly.

Anne gave him a quick glance. He was really incomprehensible. The porter came back with his barrow, the luggage was put on, and they followed him to collect their trunks. Alban took his wife's arm and pressed it.

'The smell of London. By God, it's grand.'

He rejoiced in the noise and the bustle, and the crowd of people who jostled them; the radiance of the arc-lamps and the black shadows they cast, sharp but full-toned, gave him a sense of elation. They got out into the street and the porter went off to get them a taxi. Alban's eyes glittered as he looked at the buses and the policemen trying to direct the confusion. His distinguished face bore a look of something like inspiration. The taxi came. Their luggage was stowed away and piled up beside the driver, Alban gave the porter half-a-crown, and they drove off. They turned down Gracechurch Street and in Cannon Street were held up by a block in the traffic. Alban laughed out loud.

'What's the matter?' said Anne.

'I'm so excited.'

They went along the Embankment. It was relatively quiet there. Taxis and cars passed them. The bells of the trams were music in his ears. At Westminster Bridge they cut across Parliament Square and drove through the green silence of St James's Park. They had engaged a room at a hotel just off Jermyn Street. The reception clerk took them upstairs and a porter brought up their luggage. It was a room with twin beds and a bathroom.

'This looks all right,' said Alban. 'It'll do us till we can find a flat or something.'

He looked at his watch.

'Look here, darling, we shall only fall over one another if we try to unpack together. We've got oodles of time and it'll take you longer to get straight and dress than me. I'll clear out. I want to go to the club and see if there's any mail for me. I've got my dinner jacket in my suit-case and it'll only take me twenty minutes to have a bath and dress. Does that suit you?'

'Yes. That's all right.'

'I'll be back in an hour.'

'Very well.'

He took out of his pocket the little comb he always carried and passed it through his long fair hair. Then he put on his hat. He gave himself a glance in the mirror.

'Shall I turn on the bath for you?'

'No, don't bother.'

'All right. So long.'

He went out.

When he was gone. Anne took her dressing-case and her hat-box and put them on the top of her trunk. Then she rang the bell. She did not take off her hat. She sat down and lit a cigarette. When a servant answered the bell she asked for the porter. He came. She pointed to the luggage.

'Will you take those things and leave them in the hall for the present. I'll tell you what to do with them presently.'

'Very good, ma'am.'

She gave him a florin. He took the trunk out and the other packages and closed the door behind him. A few tears slid down Anne's cheeks, but she shook herself; she dried her eyes and powdered her face. She needed all her calm. She was glad that Alban had conceived the idea of going to his club. It made things easier and gave her a little time to think them out.

Now that the moment had come to do what she had for weeks determined, now that she must say the terrible things she had to say, she quailed. Her heart sank. She knew exactly what she meant to say to Alban, she had made up her mind about that long ago, and had said the very words to herself a hundred times, three or four times a day every day of the long journey from Singapore, but she was afraid that she would grow confused. She dreaded an argument. The thought of a scene made her feel slightly sick. It was something at all events to have an hour in which to collect herself. He would say she was heartless and cruel and unreasonable. She could not help it.

'No, no, no,' she cried aloud.

She shuddered with horror. And all at once she saw herself again in the bungalow, sitting as she had been sitting when the whole thing started. It was getting on towards tiffin time and in a few minutes Alban would be back from the office. It gave her pleasure to reflect that it was an attractive room for him to come back to, the large veranda which was their parlour, and she knew that though they had been there eighteen months he was still alive to the success she had made of it. The jalousies were drawn now against the midday sun, and the mellowed light filtering through them gave an impression of cool silence. Anne was house-proud, and though they were moved from district to district according to the exigencies of the Service and seldom stayed anywhere very long, at each new post she started with new enthusiasm to make their house cosy and charming. She was very modern. Visitors were surprised because there were no knick-knacks. They were taken aback by the bold colour of her curtains and could not at all make out the tinted reproductions of pictures by Marie Laurencin and Gauguin in silvered frames which were placed on the walls with such cunning skill. She was conscious that few of them quite approved, and the good ladies of Port Wallace and Pemberton thought such arrangements odd, affected and out of place; but this left her calm. They would learn. It did them good to get a bit of a jolt. And now she looked round the long, spacious veranda with the complacent sigh of the artist satisfied with his work. It was gay. It was bare. It was restful. It refreshed the spirit and gently excited the fancy. Three immense bowls of yellow cannas completed the colour scheme. Her eyes lingered for a moment on the book-shelves filled with books; that was another thing that disconcerted the colony, all the books they had, and strange books too, heavy they thought them for the most part and she gave them a little affectionate look as though they were living things. Then she gave the piano a glance. A piece of music was still open on the rack, it was something of Debussy, and Alban had been playing it before he went to the office.

Her friends in the colony had condoled with her when Alban was appointed D.O. at Daktar, for it was the most isolated district in Sondurah. It was connected with the town which was the headquarters of the Government neither by telegraph nor telephone. But she liked it. They had been there for some time and she hoped they would remain till Alban went home on leave in another twelve months. It was as large as an English county, with a long coast-line, and the sea was dotted with little islands. A broad, winding river ran through it, and on each side of this stretched hills densely covered with virgin forest. The station, a good way up the river, consisted of a row of Chinese shops and a native village nestling amid coconut trees, the District Office, the D.O.'s bungalow, the Clerk's quarters and the barracks. Their only neighbours were the manager of a rubber estate a few miles up the river, and the manager and his assistant, Dutchmen both, of a timber camp on one of the river's tributaries. The rubber estate's launch went up and down twice a month and was their only means of regular communication with the outside world. But though they were lonely they were not dull. Their days were full. Their ponies waited for them at dawn and they rode while the day was still fresh and in the bridle-paths through the jungle lingered the mystery of the tropical night. They came back, bathed, changed, and had breakfast, and Alban went to the office. Anne spent the morning writing letters and working. She had fallen in love with the country from the first day she arrived in it and had taken pains to master the common language spoken. Her imagination was inflamed by the stories she heard of love and jealousy and death. She was told romantic tales of a time that was only just past. She sought to steep herself in the lore of those strange people. Both she and Alban read a great deal. They had for the country a considerable library and new books came from London by nearly every mail. Little that was noteworthy escaped them. Alban was fond of playing the piano. For an amateur he played very well. He had studied rather seriously, and he had an agreeable touch and a good ear; he could read music with ease, and it was always a pleasure to Anne to sit by him and follow the score when he tried something new. But their great delight was to tour the district. Sometimes they would be away for a fortnight at a time. They would go down the river in a prahu and then sail from one little island to another, bathe in the sea, and fish, or else row upstream till it grew shallow and the trees on either bank were so close to one another that you only saw a slim strip of sky between. Here the boatmen had to pole and they would spend the night in a native house. They bathed in a river pool so clear that you could see the sand shining silver at the bottom; and the spot was so lovely, so peaceful and remote, that you felt you could stay there for ever. Sometimes, on the other hand, they would tramp for days along the jungle paths, sleeping under canvas, and notwithstanding the mosquitoes that tormented them and the leeches that sucked their blood, enjoy every moment. Whoever slept so well as on a camp bed? And then there was the gladness of getting back, the delight in the comfort of the well-ordered establishment, the mail that had arrived with letters from home and all the papers, and the piano.

Alban would sit down to it then, his fingers itching to feel the keys, and in what he played, Stravinsky, Ravel, Darius Milhaud, she seemed to feel that he put in something of his own, the sounds of the jungle at night, dawn over the estuary, the starry nights, and the crystal clearness of the forest pools.

Sometimes the rain fell in sheets for days at a time. Then Alban worked at Chinese. He was learning it so that he could communicate with the Chinese of the country in their own language, and Anne did the thousand-and-one things for which she had not had time before. Those days brought them even more closely together; they always had plenty to talk about, and when they were occupied with their separate affairs they were pleased to feel in their bones that they were near to one another. They were wonderfully united. The rainy days that shut them up within the walls of the bungalow made them feel as if they were one body in face of the world.

On occasion they went to Port Wallace. It was a change, but Anne was always glad to get home. She was never quite at her ease there. She was conscious that none of the people they met liked Alban. They were very ordinary people, middle-class and suburban and dull, without any of the intellectual interests that made life so full and varied to Alban and her, and many of them were narrow-minded and ill-natured; but since they had to pass the better part of their lives in contact with them, it was tiresome that they should feel so unkindly towards Alban. They said he was conceited. He was always very pleasant with them, but she was aware that they resented his cordiality. When he tried to be jovial they said he was putting on airs, and when he chaffed them they thought he was being funny at their expense.

Once they stayed at Government House, and Mrs Hannay, the Governor's wife, who liked her, talked to her about it. Perhaps the Governor had suggested that she should give Anne a hint.

'You know, my dear, it's a pity your husband doesn't try to be more come-hither with people. He's very intelligent; don't you think it would be better if he didn't let others see he knows it quite so clearly? My husband said to me only yesterday: Of course I know Alban Torel is the cleverest young man in the Service, but he does manage to put my back up more than anyone I know. I am the Governor, but when he talks to me he always gives me the impression that he looks upon me as a damned fool.'

The worst of it was that Anne knew how low an opinion Alban had of the Governor's abilities.

'He doesn't mean to be superior,' Anne answered, smiling. 'And he really isn't in the least conceited. I think it's only because he has a straight nose and high cheek-bones.'

'You know, they don't like him at the club. They call him Powder-Puff Percy.'

Anne flushed. She had heard that before and it made her very angry. Her eyes filled with tears.

'I think it's frightfully unfair.'

Mrs Hannay took her hand and gave it an affectionate little squeeze.

'My dear, you know I don't want to hurt your feelings. Your husband can't help rising very high in the Service. He'd make things so much easier for himself if he were a little more human. Why doesn't he play football?'

'It's not his game. He's always only too glad to play tennis.'

'He doesn't give that impression. He gives the impression that there's no one here who's worth his while to play with.'

'Well, there isn't,' said Anne, stung.

Alban happened to be an extremely good tennis-player. He had played a lot of tournaments in England and Anne knew that it gave him a grim satisfaction to knock those beefy, hearty men all over the court. He could make the best of them look foolish. He could be maddening on the tennis court and Anne was aware that sometimes he could not resist the temptation.

'He does play to the gallery, doesn't he?' said Mrs Hannay.

'I don't think so. Believe me, Alban has no idea he isn't popular. As far as I can see he's always pleasant and friendly with everybody.'

'It's then he's most offensive,' said Mrs Hannay dryly.

'I know people don't like us very much,' said Anne, smiling a little. 'I'm very sorry, but really I don't know what we can do about it.'

'Not you, my dear,' cried Mrs Hannay. 'Everybody adores you. That's why they put up with your husband. My dear, who could help liking you?'

'I don't know why they should adore me,' said Anne.

But she did not say it quite sincerely. She was deliberately playing the part of the dear little woman and within her she bubbled with amusement. They disliked Alban because he had such an air of distinction, and because he was interested in art and literature; they did not understand these things and so thought them unmanly; and they disliked him because his capacity was greater than theirs. They disliked him because he was better bred than they. They thought him superior; well, he was superior, but not in the sense they meant. They forgave her because she was an ugly little thing. That was what she called herself, but she wasn't that, or if she was it was with an ugliness that was most attractive. She was like a little monkey, but a very sweet little monkey and very human. She had a neat figure. That was her best point. That and her eyes. They were very large, of a deep brown, liquid and shining; they were full of fun, but they could be tender on occasion with a charming sympathy. She was dark, her frizzy hair was almost black, and her skin was swarthy; she had a small fleshy nose, with large nostrils, and much too big a mouth. But she was alert and vivacious. She could talk with a show of real interest to the ladies of the colony about their husbands and their servants and their children in England, and she could listen appreciatively to the men who told her stories that she had often heard before. They thought her a jolly good sort. They did not know what clever fun she made of them in private. It never occurred to them that she thought them narrow, gross, and pretentious. They found no glamour in the East because they looked at it vulgarly with material eyes. Romance lingered at their threshold and they drove it away like an importunate beggar. She was aloof. She repeated to herself Landor's line:

'*Nature I loved, and next to nature, art.*'

She reflected on her conversation with Mrs Hannay, but on the whole it left her unconcerned. She wondered whether she should say anything about it to Alban; it had always seemed a little odd to her that he should be so little aware of his unpopularity; but she was afraid that if she told him of it he would become self-conscious. He never noticed the coldness of the men at the club. He made them feel shy and therefore uncomfortable. His appearance then caused a sort of awkwardness, but he, happily insensible, was breezily cordial to all and sundry. The fact was that he was strangely unconscious of other people. She was in a class by herself, she and a little group of friends they had in London, but he could never quite realize that the people of the colony, the government officials and the planters and their wives, were human beings. They were to him like pawns in a game. He laughed with them, chaffed them, and was amiably tolerant of them; with a chuckle Anne told herself that he was rather like the master of a preparatory school taking little boys out on a picnic and anxious to give them a good time.

She was afraid it wasn't much good telling Alban. He was incapable of the dissimulation which, she happily realized, came so easily to her. What was one to do with these people? The men had come out to the colony as lads from second-rate schools, and life had taught them nothing. At fifty they had the outlook of hobbledehoys. Most of them drank a great deal too much. They read nothing worth reading. Their ambition was to be like everybody else. Their highest praise was to say that a man was a damned good sort. If you were interested in the things of the spirit you were a prig. They were eaten up with envy of one another and devoured by petty jealousies. And the women, poor things, were obsessed by petty rivalries. They made a circle that was more provincial than any in the smallest town in England. They were prudish and spiteful. What did it matter if they did not like Alban? They would have to put up with him because his ability was so great. He was clever and energetic. They could not say that he did not do his work well. He had been successful in every post he had occupied. With his sensitiveness and his imagination he understood the native mind and he was able to get the natives to do things that no one in his position could. He had a gift for languages, and he spoke all the local dialects. He not only knew the common tongue that most of the government officials spoke, but was acquainted with the niceties of the language and on occasion could make use of a ceremonial speech that flattered and impressed the chiefs. He had a gift for organization. He was not afraid of responsibility. In due course he was bound to be made a Resident. Alban had some interest in England; his father was a brigadier-general killed in the war, and though he had no private means he had influential friends. He spoke of them with pleasant irony.

'The great advantage of democratic government,' he said, 'is that merit, with influence to back it, can be pretty sure of receiving its due reward.'

Alban was so obviously the ablest man in the Service that there seemed no reason why he should not eventually be made Governor. Then, thought Anne, his air of superiority, of which they complained, would be in place. They would accept him as their master and he would know how to make himself respected and obeyed. The position she foresaw did not dazzle her. She accepted it as a right. It would be fun for Alban to be Governor and for her to be the Governor's wife. And what an opportunity! They were sheep, the government servants and the planters; when Government House was the seat of culture they would soon fall into line. When the best way to the Governor's favour was to be intelligent, intelligence would become the fashion. She and Alban would cherish the native arts and collect carefully the memorials of a vanished past. The country would make an advance it had never dreamed of. They would develop it, but along lines of order and beauty. They would instil into their subordinates a passion for that beautiful land and a loving interest in these romantic races. They would make them realize what music meant. They would cultivate literature. They would create beauty. It would be the golden age.

Suddenly she heard Alban's footstep. Anne awoke from her day-dream. All that was far away in the future. Alban was only a District Officer yet and what was important was the life they were living now. She heard Alban go into the bath-house and splash water over himself. In a minute he came in. He had changed into a shirt and shorts. His fair hair was still wet.

'Tiffin ready?' he asked.

'Yes.'

He sat down at the piano and played the piece that he had played in the morning. The silvery notes cascaded coolly down the sultry air. You had an impression of a formal garden with great trees and elegant pieces of artificial water and of leisurely walks bordered with pseudo-classical statues. Alban played with a peculiar delicacy. Lunch was announced by the head boy. He rose from the piano. They walked into the dining-room hand in hand. A punkah lazily fanned the air. Anne gave the table a glance. With its bright-coloured tablecloth and the amusing plates it looked very gay.

'Anything exciting at the office this morning?' she asked.

'No, nothing much. A buffalo case. Oh, and Prynne has sent along to ask me to go up to the estate. Some coolies have been damaging the trees and he wants me to come along and look into it.'

Prynne was manager of the rubber estate up the river and now and then they spent a night with him. Sometimes when he wanted a change he came down to dinner and slept at the D.O.'s bungalow. They both liked him. He was a man of five-and-thirty, with a red face, with deep furrows in it, and very black hair. He was quite uneducated, but cheerful and easy, and being the only Englishman within two days' journey they could not but be friendly with him. He had been a little shy of them at first. News spreads quickly in the East and long before they arrived in the district he heard that they were highbrows. He did not know what he would make of them. He probably did not know that he had charm, which makes up for many more commendable qualities, and Alban with his almost feminine sensibilities was peculiarly susceptible to this. He found Alban much more human than he expected, and of course Anne was stunning. Alban played ragtime for him, which he would not have done for the Governor, and played dominoes with him. When Alban was making his first tour of the district with Anne, and suggested that they would like to spend a couple of nights on the estate, he had thought it as well to warn him that he lived with a native woman and had two children by her. He would do his best to keep them out of Anne's sight, but he could not send them away, there was nowhere to send them. Alban laughed.

'Anne isn't that sort of woman at all. Don't dream of hiding them. She loves children.'

Anne quickly made friends with the shy, pretty little native woman and soon was playing happily with the children. She and the girl had long confidential chats. The children took a fancy to her. She brought them lovely toys from Port Wallace. Prynne, comparing her smiling tolerance with the disapproving acidity of the other white women of the colony, described himself as knocked all of a heap. He could not do enough to show his delight and gratitude.

'If all highbrows are like you,' he said, 'give me highbrows every time.'

He hated to think that in another year they would leave the district for good and the chances were that, if the next D.O. was married, his wife would think it dreadful that, rather than live alone, he had a native woman to live with him and, what was more, was much attached to her.

But there had been a good deal of discontent on the estate of late. The coolies were Chinese and infected with communist ideas. They were disorderly. Alban had been obliged to sentence several of them for various crimes to terms of imprisonment.

'Prynne tells me that as soon as their term is up he's going to send them all back to China and get Javanese instead,' said Alban. 'I'm sure he's right. They're much more amenable.'

'You don't think there's going to be any serious trouble?'

'Oh, no. Prynne knows his job and he's a pretty determined fellow. He wouldn't put up with any nonsense and with me and our policemen to back him up I don't imagine they'll try any monkey tricks.' He smiled. 'The iron hand in the velvet glove.'

The words were barely out of his mouth when a sudden shouting arose. There was a commotion and the sound of steps. Loud voices and cries.

'Tuan, Tuan.'

'What the devil's the matter?'

Alban sprang from his chair and went swiftly on to the veranda. Anne followed him. At the bottom of the steps was a group of natives. There was the sergeant, and three or four policemen, boatmen, and several men from the kampong.

'What is it?' called Alban.

Two or three shouted back in answer. The sergeant pushed others aside and Alban saw lying on the ground a man in a shirt and khaki shorts. He ran down the steps. He recognized the man as the assistant manager of Prynne's estate. He was a half-caste. His shorts were covered with blood and there was clotted blood all over one side of his face and head. He was unconscious.

'Bring him up here,' called Anne.

Alban gave an order. The man was lifted up and carried on to the veranda. They laid him on the floor and Anne put a pillow under his head. She sent for water and for the medicine-chest in which they kept things for emergency.

'Is he dead?' asked Alban.

'No.'

'Better try to give him some brandy.'

The boatmen brought ghastly news. The Chinese coolies had risen suddenly and attacked the manager's office. Prynne was killed, and the assistant manager, Oakley by name, had escaped only by the skin of his teeth. He had come upon the rioters when they were looting the office, he had seen Prynne's body thrown out of the window, and had taken to his heels. Some of the Chinese saw him and gave chase. He ran for the river and was wounded as he jumped into the launch. The launch managed to put off before the Chinese could get on board and they had come down-stream for help as fast as they could go. As they went they saw flames rising from the office buildings. There was no doubt that the coolies had burned down everything that would burn.

Oakley gave a groan and opened his eyes. He was a little, dark-skinned man, with flattened features and thick coarse hair. His great native eyes were filled with terror.

'You're all right,' said Anne. 'You're quite safe.'

He gave a sigh and smiled. Anne washed his face and swabbed it with antiseptics. The wound on his head was not serious.

'Can you speak yet?' said Alban.

'Wait a bit,' she said. 'We must look at his leg.'

Alban ordered the sergeant to get the crowd out of the veranda. Anne ripped up one leg of the shorts. The material was clinging to the coagulated wound.

'I've been bleeding like a pig,' said Oakley.

It was only a flesh wound. Alban was clever with his fingers, and though the blood began to flow again they staunched it. Alban put on a dressing and a bandage. The sergeant and a policeman lifted Oakley on to a long chair. Alban gave him a brandy and soda, and soon he felt strong enough to speak. He knew no more than the boatmen had already told. Prynne was dead and the estate was in flames.

'And the girl and the children?' asked Anne.

'I don't know.'

'Oh, Alban.'

'I must turn out the police. Are you sure Prynne is dead?'

'Yes, sir. I saw him.'

'Have the rioters got fire-arms?'

'I don't know, sir.'

'How d'you mean, you don't know?' Alban cried irritably. 'Prynne had a gun, hadn't he?'

'Yes, sir.'

'There must have been more on the estate. You had one, didn't you? The head overseer had one.'

The half-caste was silent. Alban looked at him sternly.

'How many of those damned Chinese are there?'

'A hundred and fifty.'

Anne wondered that he asked so many questions. It seemed waste of time. The important thing was to collect coolies for the transport up-river, prepare the boats, and issue ammunition to the police.

'How many policemen have you got, sir?' asked Oakley.

'Eight and the sergeant.'

'Could I come too? That would make ten of us. I'm sure I shall be all right now I'm bandaged.'

'I'm not going,' said Alban.

'Alban, you must,' cried Anne. She could not believe her ears.

'Nonsense. It would be madness. Oakley's obviously useless. He's sure to have a temperature in a few hours. He'd only be in the way. That leaves nine guns. There are a hundred and fifty Chinese and they've got fire-arms and all the ammunition in the world.'

'How d'you know?'

'It stands to reason they wouldn't have started a show like this unless they had. It would be idiotic to go.'

Anne stared at him with open mouth. Oakley's eyes were puzzled.

'What are you going to do?'

'Well, fortunately we've got the launch. I'll send it to Port Wallace with a request for reinforcements.'

'But they won't be here for two days at least.'

'Well, what of it? Prynne's dead and the estate burned to the ground. We couldn't do any good by going up now. I shall send a native to reconnoitre so that we can find out exactly what the rioters are doing.' He gave Anne his charming smile. 'Believe me, my pet, the rascals won't lose anything by waiting a day or two for what's coming to them.'

Oakley opened his mouth to speak, but perhaps he hadn't the nerve. He was a half-caste assistant manager and Alban, the D.O., represented the power of the Government. But the man's eyes sought Anne's and she thought she read in them an earnest and personal appeal.

'But in two days they're capable of committing the most frightful atrocities,' she cried. 'It's quite unspeakable what they may do.'

'Whatever damage they do they'll pay for. I promise you that.'

'Oh, Alban, you can't sit still and do nothing. I beseech you to go yourself at once.'

'Don't be so silly. I can't quell a riot with eight policemen and a sergeant. I haven't got the right to take a risk of that sort. We'd have to go in boats. You don't think we could get up unobserved. The lalang along the banks is perfect cover and they could just take pot shots at us as we came along. We shouldn't have a chance.'

'I'm afraid they'll only think it weakness if nothing is done for two days, sir,' said Oakley.

'When I want your opinion I'll ask for it,' said Alban acidly. 'So far as I can see when there was danger the only thing you did was to cut and run. I can't persuade myself that your assistance in a crisis would be very valuable.'

The half-caste reddened. He said nothing more. He looked straight in front of him with troubled eyes.

'I'm going down to the office,' said Alban. 'I'll just write a short report and send it down the river by launch at once.'

He gave an order to the sergeant who had been standing all this time stiffly at the top of the steps. He saluted and ran off. Alban went into a little hall they had to get his topee. Anne swiftly followed him.

'Alban, for God's sake listen to me a minute,' she whispered.

'I don't want to be rude to you, darling, but I am pressed for time. I think you'd much better mind your own business.'

'You can't do nothing, Alban. You must go. Whatever the risk.'

'Don't be such a fool,' he said angrily.

He had never been angry with her before. She seized his hand to hold him back.

'I tell you I can do no good by going.'

'You don't know. There's the woman and Prynne's children. We must do something to save them. Let me come with you. They'll kill them.'

'They've probably killed them already.'

'Oh, how can you be so callous! If there's a chance of saving them it's your duty to try.'

'It's my duty to act like a reasonable human being. I'm not going to risk my life and my policemen's for the sake of a native woman and her half-caste brats. What sort of a damned fool do you take me for?'

'They'll say you were afraid.'

'Who?'

'Everyone in the colony.'

He smiled disdainfully.

'If you only knew what a complete contempt I have for the opinion of everyone in the colony.'

She gave him a long searching look. She had been married to him for eight years and she knew every expression of his face and every thought in his mind. She stared into his blue eyes as if they were open windows. She suddenly went quite pale. She dropped his hand and turned away. Without another word she went back on to the veranda. Her ugly little monkey face was a mask of horror.

Alban went to his office, wrote a brief account of the facts, and in a few minutes the motor launch was pounding down the river.

The next two days were endless. Escaped natives brought them news of happenings on the estate. But from their excited and terrified stories it was impossible to get an exact impression of the truth. There had been a good deal of bloodshed. The head overseer had been killed. They brought wild tales of cruelty and outrage. Anne could hear nothing of Prynne's woman and the two children. She shuddered when she thought of what might have been their fate. Alban collected as many natives as he could. They were armed with spears and swords. He commandeered boats. The situation was serious, but he kept his head. He felt that he had done all that was possible and nothing remained but for him to carry on normally. He did his official work. He played the piano a great deal. He rode with Anne in the early morning. He appeared to have forgotten that they had had the first serious difference of opinion in the whole of their married life. He took it that Anne had accepted the wisdom of his decision. He was as amusing, cordial and gay with her as he had always been. When he spoke of the rioters it was with grim irony: when the time came to settle matters a good many of them would wish they had never been born.

'What'll happen to them?' asked Anne.

'Oh, they'll hang.' He gave a shrug of distaste. 'I hate having to be present at executions. It always makes me feel rather sick.'

He was very sympathetic to Oakley, whom they had put to bed and whom Anne was nursing. Perhaps he was sorry that in the exasperation of the moment he had spoken to him offensively, and he went out of his way to be nice to him.

Then on the afternoon of the third day, when they were drinking their coffee after luncheon, Alban's quick ears caught the sound of a motor boat approaching. At the same moment a policeman ran up to say that the government launch was sighted.

'At last,' cried Alban.

He bolted out of the house. Anne raised one of the jalousies and looked out at the river. Now the sound was quite loud and in a

moment she saw the boat come round the bend. She saw Alban on
the landing-stage. He got into a prahu and as the launch dropped
her anchor he went on board. She told Oakley that the reinforcements had come.

'Will the D.O. go up with them when they attack?' he asked her.

'Naturally,' said Anne coldly.

'I wondered.'

Anne felt a strange feeling in her heart. For the last two days she
had had to exercise all her self-control not to cry. She did not
answer. She went out of the room.

A quarter of an hour later Alban returned to the bungalow with
the captain of constabulary who had been sent with twenty Sikhs
to deal with the rioters. Captain Stratton was a little red-faced man
with a red moustache and bow legs, very hearty and dashing,
whom she had met often at Port Wallace.

'Well, Mrs Torel, this is a pretty kettle of fish,' he cried, as he
shook hands with her, in a loud jolly voice. 'Here I am, with my
army all full of pep and ready for a scrap. Up, boys, and at 'em.
Have you got anything to drink in this benighted place?'

'Boy,' she cried, smiling.

'Something long and cool and faintly alcoholic, and then I'm
ready to discuss the plan of campaign.'

His breeziness was very comforting. It blew away the sullen
apprehension that had seemed ever since the disaster to brood over
the lost peace of the bungalow. The boy came in with a tray and
Stratton mixed himself a stengah. Alban put him in possession of
the facts. He told them clearly, briefly and with precision.

'I must say I admire you,' said Stratton. 'In your place I should
never have been able to resist the temptation to take my eight cops
and have a whack at the blighters myself.'

'I thought it was a perfectly unjustifiable risk to take.'

'Safety first, old boy, eh, what?' said Stratton jovially. 'I'm jolly
glad you didn't. It's not often we get the chance of a scrap. It would
have been a dirty trick to keep the whole show to yourself.'

Captain Stratton was all for steaming straight up the river and
attacking at once, but Alban pointed out to him the inadvisability
of such a course. The sound of the approaching launch would warn
the rioters. The long grass at the river's edge offered them cover
and they had enough guns to make a landing difficult. It seemed
useless to expose the attacking force to their fire. It was silly to

forget that they had to face a hundred and fifty desperate men and it would be easy to fall into an ambush. Alban expounded his own plan. Stratton listened to it. He nodded now and then. The plan was evidently a good one. It would enable them to take the rioters in the rear, surprise them, and in all probability finish the job without a single casualty. He would have been a fool not to accept it.

'But why didn't you do that yourself?' asked Stratton.

'With eight men and a sergeant?'

Stratton did not answer.

'Anyhow it's not a bad idea and we'll settle on it. It gives us plenty of time, so with your permission, Mrs Torel, I'll have a bath.'

They set out at sunset, Captain Stratton and his twenty Sikhs, Alban with his policemen and the natives he had collected. The night was dark and moonless. Trailing behind them were the dug-outs that Alban had gathered together and into which after a certain distance they proposed to transfer their force. It was ' important that no sound should give warning of their approach. After they had gone for about three hours by launch they took to the dug-outs and in them silently paddled up-stream. They reached the border of the vast estate and landed. Guides led them along a path so narrow that they had to march in single file. It had been long unused and the going was heavy. They had twice to ford a stream. The path led them circuitously to the rear of the coolie lines, but they did not wish to reach them till nearly dawn and presently Stratton gave the order to halt. It was a long cold wait. At last the night seemed to be less dark; you did not see the trunks of the trees, but were vaguely sensible of them against its darkness. Stratton had been sitting with his back to a tree. He gave a whispered order to a sergeant and in a few minutes the column was once more on the march. Suddenly they found themselves on a road. They formed fours. The dawn broke and in the ghostly light the surrounding objects were wanly visible. The column stopped on a whispered order. They had come in sight of the coolie lines. Silence reigned in them. The column crept on again and again halted. Stratton, his eyes shining, gave Alban a smile.

'We've caught the blighters asleep.'

He lined up his men. They inserted cartridges in their guns.

He stepped forward and raised his hand. The carbines were pointed at the coolie lines.

'Fire.'

There was a rattle as the volley of shots rang out. Then suddenly there was a tremendous din and the Chinese poured out, shouting and waving their arms, but in front of them, to Alban's utter bewilderment, bellowing at the top of his voice and shaking his fists at them, was a white man.

'Who the hell's that?' cried Stratton.

A very big, very fat man, in khaki trousers and a singlet, was running towards them as fast as his fat legs would carry him and as he ran shaking both fists at them and yelling:

'*Smerige flikkers! Vervloekte ploerten!*'

'My God, it's Van Hasseldt,' said Alban.

This was the Dutch manager of the timber camp which was situated on a considerable tributary of the river about twenty miles away.

'What the hell do you think you're doing?' he puffed as he came up to them.

'How the hell did you get here?' asked Stratton in turn.

He saw that the Chinese were scattering in all directions and gave his men instructions to round them up. Then he turned again to Van Hasseldt.

'What's it mean?'

'Mean? Mean?' shouted the Dutchman furiously. 'That's what I want to know. You and your damned policemen. What do you mean by coming here at this hour in the morning and firing a damned volley. Target practice? You might have killed me. Idiots!'

'Have a cigarette,' said Stratton.

'How did you get here, Van Hasseldt?' asked Alban again, very much at sea. 'This is the force they've sent from Port Wallace to quell the riot.'

'How did I get here? I walked. How did you think I got here? Riot be damned. I quelled the riot. If that's what you came for you can take your damned policemen home again. A bullet came within a foot of my head.'

'I don't understand,' said Alban.

'There's nothing to understand,' spluttered Van Hasseldt, still fuming. 'Some coolies came to my estate and said the Chinks had killed Prynne and burned the bally place down, so I took my assistant and my head overseer and a Dutch friend I had staying with me and came over to see what the trouble was.'

Captain Stratton opened his eyes wide.

'Did you just stroll in as if it was a picnic?' he asked.

'Well, you don't think after all the years I've been in this country I'm going to let a couple of hundred Chinks put the fear of God into me? I found them all scared out of their lives. One of them had the nerve to pull a gun on me and I blew his bloody brains out. And the rest surrendered. I've got the leaders tied up. I was going to send a boat down to you this morning to come up and get them.'

Stratton stared at him for a minute and then burst into a shout of laughter. He laughed till the tears ran down his face. The Dutchman looked at him angrily, then began to laugh too; he laughed with the big belly laugh of a very fat man and his coils of fat heaved and shook. Alban watched them sullenly. He was very angry.

'What about Prynne's girl and the kids?' he asked.

'Oh, they got away all right.'

It just showed how wise he had been not to let himself be influenced by Anne's hysteria. Of course the children had come to no harm. He never thought they would.

Van Hasseldt and his little party started back for the timber camp, and as soon after as possible Stratton embarked his twenty Sikhs and leaving Alban with his sergeant and his policemen to deal with the situation departed for Port Wallace. Alban gave him a brief report for the Governor. There was much for him to do. It looked as though he would have to stay for a considerable time; but since every house on the estate had been burned to the ground and he was obliged to install himself in the coolie lines he thought it better that Anne should not join him. He sent her a note to that effect. He was glad to be able to reassure her of the safety of poor Prynne's girl. He set to work at once to make his preliminary inquiry. He examined a host of witnesses. But a week later he received an order to go to Port Wallace at once. The launch that brought it was to take him and he was able to see Anne on the way down for no more than an hour. Alban was a trifle vexed.

'I don't know why the Governor can't leave me to get things straight without dragging me off like this. It's extremely inconvenient.'

'Oh, well, the Government never bothers very much about the convenience of its subordinates, does it?' smiled Anne.

'It's just red-tape. I would offer to take you along, darling, only I shan't stay a minute longer than I need. I want to get my evidence together for the Sessions Court as soon as possible. I think in a country like this it's very important that justice should be prompt.'

When the launch came in to Port Wallace one of the harbour police told him that the harbour-master had a chit for him. It was from the Governor's secretary and informed him that His Excellency desired to see him as soon as convenient after his arrival. It was ten in the morning. Alban went to the club, had a bath and shaved, and then in clean ducks, his hair neatly brushed, he called a rickshaw and told the boy to take him to the Governor's office. He was at once shown in to the secretary's room. The secretary shook hands with him.

'I'll tell H.E. you're here,' he said. 'Won't you sit down?'

The secretary left the room and in a little while came back.

'H.E. will see you in a minute. Do you mind if I get on with my letters?'

Alban smiled. The secretary was not exactly come-hither. He waited, smoking a cigarette, and amused himself with his own thoughts. He was making a good job of the preliminary inquiry. It interested him. Then an orderly came in and told Alban that the Governor was ready for him. He rose from his seat and followed him into the Governor's room.

'Good morning, Torel.'

'Good morning, sir.'

The Governor was sitting at a large desk. He nodded to Alban and motioned to him to take a seat. The Governor was all grey. His hair was grey, his face, his eyes; he looked as though the tropical suns had washed the colour out of him; he had been in the country for thirty years and had risen one by one through all the ranks of the Service; he looked tired and depressed. Even his voice was grey. Alban liked him because he was quiet; he did not think him clever, but he had an unrivalled knowledge of the country, and his great experience was a very good substitute for intelligence. He looked at Alban for a full moment without speaking and the odd idea came to Alban that he was embarrassed. He very nearly gave him a lead.

'I saw Van Hasseldt yesterday,' said the Governor suddenly.

'Yes, sir?'

'Will you give me your account of the occurrences at the Alud Estate and of the steps you took to deal with them.'

Alban had an orderly mind. He was self-possessed. He marshalled his facts well and was able to state them with precision. He chose his words with care and spoke them fluently.

'You had a sergeant and eight policemen. Why did you not immediately go to the scene of the disturbance?'

'I thought the risk was unjustifiable.'

A thin smile was outlined on the Governor's grey face.

'If the officers of this Government had hesitated to take unjustifiable risks it would never have become a province of the British Empire.'

Alban was silent. It was difficult to talk to a man who spoke obvious nonsense.

'I am anxious to hear your reasons for the decision you took.'

Alban gave them coolly. He was quite convinced of the rightness of his action. He repeated, but more fully, what he had said in the first place to Anne. The Governor listened attentively.

'Van Hasseldt, with his manager, a Dutch friend of his, and a native overseer, seems to have coped with the situation very efficiently,' said the Governor.

'He had a lucky break. That doesn't prevent him from being a damned fool. It was madness to do what he did.'

'Do you realize that by leaving a Dutch planter to do what you should have done yourself, you have covered the Government with ridicule?'

'No, sir.'

'You've made yourself a laughing-stock in the whole colony.'

Alban smiled.

'My back is broad enough to bear the ridicule of persons to whose opinion I am entirely indifferent.'

'The utility of a government official depends very largely on his prestige, and I'm afraid his prestige is likely to be inconsiderable when he lies under the stigma of cowardice.'

Alban flushed a little.

'I don't quite know what you mean by that, sir.'

'I've gone into the matter very carefully. I've seen Captain Stratton, and Oakley, poor Prynne's assistant, and I've seen Van Hasseldt. I've listened to your defence.'

'I didn't know that I was defending myself, sir.'

'Be so good as not to interrupt me. I think you committed a grave error of judgment. As it turns out, the risk was very small, but whatever it was, I think you should have taken it. In such matters promptness and firmness are essential. It is not for me to conjecture what motive led you to send for a force of constabulary and do nothing till they came. I am afraid, however, that I consider that your usefulness in the Service is no longer very great.'

Alban looked at him with astonishment.

'But would you have gone under the circumstances?' he asked him.

'I should.'

Alban shrugged his shoulders.

'Don't you believe me?' rapped out the Governor.

'Of course I believe you, sir. But perhaps you will allow me to say that if you had been killed the colony would have suffered an irreparable loss.'

The Governor drummed on the table with his fingers. He looked out of the window and then looked again at Alban. When he spoke it was not unkindly.

'I think you are unfitted by temperament for this rather rough-and-tumble life, Torel. If you'll take my advice you'll go home. With your abilities I feel sure that you'll soon find an occupation much better suited to you.'

'I'm afraid I don't understand what you mean, sir.'

'Oh, come, Torel, you're not stupid. I'm trying to make things easy for you. For your wife's sake as well as for your own I do not wish you to leave the colony with the stigma of being dismissed from the Service for cowardice. I'm giving you the opportunity of resigning.'

'Thank you very much, sir. I'm not prepared to avail myself of the opportunity. If I resign I admit that I committed an error and that the charge you make against me is justified. I don't admit it.'

'You can please yourself. I have considered the matter very carefully and I have no doubt about it in my mind. I am forced to discharge you from the Service. The necessary papers will reach you in due course. Meanwhile you will return to your post and hand over to the officer appointed to succeed you on his arrival.'

'Very good, sir,' replied Alban, a twinkle of amusement in his eyes. 'When do you desire me to return to my post?'

'At once.'

'Have you any objection to my going to the club and having tiffin before I go?'

The Governor looked at him with surprise. His exasperation was mingled with an unwilling admiration.

'Not at all. I'm sorry, Torel, that this unhappy incident should have deprived the Government of a servant whose zeal has always been so apparent and whose tact, intelligence and industry seemed to point him out in the future for very high office.'

'Your Excellency does not read Schiller, I suppose. You are probably not acquainted with his celebrated line: *mit der Dummheit kämpfen die Götter selbst vergebens.*'

'What does it mean?'

'Roughly: against stupidity the gods themselves battle in vain.'

'Good morning.'

With his head in the air, a smile on his lips, Alban left the Governor's office. The Governor was human, and he had the curiosity to ask his secretary later in the day if Alban Torel had really gone to the club.

'Yes, sir. He had tiffin there.'

'It must have wanted some nerve.'

Alban entered the club jauntily and joined the group of men standing at the bar. He talked to them in the breezy, cordial tone he always used with them. It was designed to put them at their ease. They had been discussing him ever since Stratton had come back to Port Wallace with his story, sneering at him and laughing at him, and all that had resented his superciliousness, and they were the majority, were triumphant because his pride had had a fall. But they were so taken aback at seeing him now, so confused to find him as confident as ever, that it was they who were embarrassed.

One man, though he knew perfectly, asked him what he was doing in Port Wallace.

'Oh, I came about the riot on the Alud Estate. H.E. wanted to see me. He does not see eye to eye with me about it. The silly old ass has fired me. I'm going home as soon as he appoints a D.O. to take over.'

There was a moment of awkwardness. One, more kindly disposed than the others, said:

'I'm awfully sorry.'

Alban shrugged his shoulders.

'My dear fellow, what can you do with a perfect damned fool? The only thing is to let him stew in his own juice.'

When the Governor's secretary had told his chief as much of this as he thought discreet, the Governor smiled.

'Courage is a queer thing. I would rather have shot myself than go to the club just then and face all those fellows.'

A fortnight later, having sold to the incoming D.O. all the decorations that Anne had taken so much trouble about, with the rest of their things in packing-cases and trunks, they arrived at Port Wallace to await the local steamer that was to take them to Singapore. The padre's wife invited them to stay with her, but Anne refused; she insisted that they should go to the hotel. An hour after their arrival she received a very kind little letter from the Governor's wife asking her to go and have tea with her. She went. She found Mrs Hannay alone, but in a minute the Governor joined them. He expressed his regret that she was leaving and told her how sorry he was for the cause.

'It's very kind of you to say that,' said Anne, smiling gaily, 'but you mustn't think I take it to heart. I'm entirely on Alban's side. I think what he did was absolutely right and if you don't mind my saying so I think you've treated him most unjustly.'

'Believe me, I hated having to take the step I took.'

'Don't let's talk about it,' said Anne.

'What are your plans when you get home?' asked Mrs Hannay.

Anne began to chat brightly. You would have thought she had not a care in the world. She seemed in great spirits at going home. She was jolly and amusing and made little jokes. When she took leave of the Governor and his wife she thanked them for all their kindness. The Governor escorted her to the door.

The next day but one, after dinner, they went on board the clean and comfortable little ship. The padre and his wife saw them off. When they went into their cabin they found a large parcel on Anne's bunk. It was addressed to Alban. He opened it and saw it was an immense powder-puff.

'Hullo, I wonder who sent us this,' he said, with a laugh. 'It must be for you, darling.'

Anne gave him a quick look. She went pale. The brutes! How could they be so cruel? She forced herself to smile.

'It's enormous, isn't it? I've never seen such a large powder-puff in my life.'

But when he had left the cabin and they were out at sea, she threw it passionately overboard.

And now, now that they were back in London and Sondurah was nine thousand miles away, she clenched her hands as she thought of it. Somehow, it seemed the worst thing of all. It was so wantonly unkind to send that absurd object to Alban, Powder-Puff Percy; it showed such a petty spite. Was that their idea of humour? Nothing had hurt her more and even now she felt that it was only by holding on to herself that she could prevent herself from crying. Suddenly she started, for the door opened and Alban came in. She was still sitting in the chair in which he had left her.

'Hullo, why haven't you dressed?' He looked about the room. 'You haven't unpacked.'

'No.'

'Why on earth not?'

'I'm not going to unpack. I'm not going to stay here. I'm leaving you.'

'What are you talking about?'

'I've stuck it out till now. I made up my mind I would till we got home. I set my teeth, I've borne more than I thought it possible to bear, but now it's finished. I've done all that could be expected of me. We're back in London now and I can go.'

He looked at her in utter bewilderment.

'Are you mad, Anne?'

'Oh, my God, what I've endured! The journey to Singapore, with all the officers knowing, and even the Chinese stewards. And at Singapore, the way people looked at us at the hotel, and the sympathy I had to put up with, the bricks they dropped and their embarrassment when they realized what they'd done. My God, I could have killed them. That interminable journey home. There wasn't a single passenger on the ship who didn't know. The contempt they had for you and the kindness they went out of their way to show me. And you so self-complacent and so pleased with yourself, seeing nothing, feeling nothing. You must have the hide of a rhinoceros. The misery of seeing you so chatty and agreeable. Pariahs, that's what we were. You seemed to ask them to snub you. How can anyone be so shameless?'

She was flaming with passion. Now that at last she need not wear the mask of indifference and pride that she had forced herself to assume she cast aside all reserve and all self-control. The words poured from her trembling lips in a virulent stream.

'My dear, how can you be so absurd?' he said good-naturedly, smiling. 'You must be very nervous and high-strung to have got such ideas in your head. Why didn't you tell me? You're like a country bumpkin who comes to London and thinks everyone is staring at him. Nobody bothered about us, and if they did what on earth did it matter? You ought to have more sense than to bother about what a lot of fools say. And what do you imagine they were saying?'

'They were saying you'd been fired.'

'Well, that was true,' he laughed.

'They said you were a coward.'

'What of it?'

'Well, you see, that was true too.'

He looked at her for a moment reflectively. His lips tightened a little.

'And what makes you think so?' he asked acidly.

'I saw it in your eyes, that day the news came, when you refused to go to the estate and I followed you into the hall when you went to fetch your topee. I begged you to go, I felt that whatever the danger you must take it, and suddenly I saw the fear in your eyes. I nearly fainted with the horror.'

'I should have been a fool to risk my life to no purpose. Why should I? Nothing that concerned me was at stake. Courage is the obvious virtue of the stupid. I don't attach any particular importance to it.'

'How do you mean that nothing that concerned you was at stake? If that's true then your whole life is a sham. You've given away everything you stood for, everything we both stand for. You've let all of us down. We did set ourselves up on a pinnacle, we did think ourselves better than the rest of them because we loved literature and art and music, we weren't content to live a life of ignoble jealousies and vulgar tittle-tattle, we did cherish the things of the spirit, and we loved beauty. It was our food and drink. They laughed at us and sneered at us. That was inevitable. The ignorant and the common naturally hate and fear those who are interested in things they don't understand. We didn't care. We called them Philistines. We despised them and we had a right to despise them. Our justification was that we were better and nobler and wiser and braver than they were. And you weren't better, you weren't nobler, you weren't braver. When the crisis came you slunk away like a whipped cur with his tail between his legs. You of all people hadn't the right to be a coward. They despise *us* now and they have the right to despise us. Us and all we stood for. Now they can say that art and beauty are all rot; when it comes to a pinch people like us always let you down. They never stopped looking for a chance to turn and rend us and you gave it to them. They can say that they always expected it. It's a triumph for them. I used to be furious because they called you Powder-Puff Percy. Did you know they did?'

'Of course. I thought it very vulgar, but it left me entirely indifferent.'

'It's funny that their instinct should have been so right.'

'Do you mean to say you've been harbouring this against me all these weeks? I should never have thought you capable of it.'

'I couldn't let you down when everyone was against you. I was too proud for that. Whatever happened I swore to myself that I'd stick to you till we got home. It's been torture.'

'Don't you love me any more?'

'Love you? I loathe the very sight of you.'

'Anne!'

'God knows I loved you. For eight years I worshipped the ground you trod on. You were everything to me. I believed in you as some people believe in God. When I saw the fear in your eyes that day, when you told me that you weren't going to risk your life for a kept woman and her half-caste brats, I was shattered. It was as though someone had wrenched my heart out of my body and trampled on it. You killed my love there and then, Alban. You killed it stone-dead. Since then when you've kissed me I've had to clench my hands so as not to turn my face away. The mere thought of anything else makes me feel physically sick. I loathe your complacence and your frightful insensitiveness. Perhaps I could have forgiven it if it had been just a moment's weakness and if afterwards you'd been ashamed. I should have been miserable, but I think my love was so great that I should only have felt pity for you. But you're incapable of shame. And now I believe in nothing. You're only a silly, pretentious, vulgar poseur. I would rather be the wife of a second-rate planter so long as he had the common human virtues of a man than the wife of a fake like you.'

He did not answer. Gradually his face began to discompose. Those handsome, regular features of his horribly distorted and suddenly he broke out into loud sobs. She gave a little cry.

'Don't Alban, don't.'

'Oh, darling, how can you be so cruel to me? I adore you. I'd give my whole life to please you. I can't live without you.'

She put out her arms as though to ward off a blow.

'No, no, Alban, don't try to move me. I can't. I must go. I can't live with you any more. It would be frightful. I can never forget. I must tell you the truth, I have only contempt for you and repulsion.'

He sank down at her feet and tried to cling to her knees. With a gasp she sprang up and he buried his head in the empty chair. He cried painfully with sobs that tore his chest. The sound was horrible. The tears streamed from Anne's eyes and, putting her hands to her ears to shut out that dreadful, hysterical sobbing, blindly stumbling she rushed to the door and ran out.

P. G. Wodehouse

Jeeves and the Song of Songs

Another day had dawned all hot and fresh and, in pursuance of my unswerving policy at that time, I was singing 'Sonny Boy' in my bath, when there was a soft step without and Jeeves's voice came filtering through the woodwork.

'I beg your pardon, sir.'

I had just got to that bit about the Angels being lonely, where you need every ounce of concentration in order to make the spectacular finish, but I signed off courteously.

'Yes, Jeeves? Say on.'

'Mr Glossop, sir.'

'What about him?'

'He is in the sitting-room, sir.'

'Young Tuppy Glossop?'

'Yes, sir.'

'In the sitting-room?'

'Yes, sir.'

'Desiring speech with me?'

'Yes, sir.'

'H'm!'

'Sir?'

'I only said H'm.'

And I'll tell you why I said H'm. It was because the man's story had interested me strangely. The news that Tuppy was visiting me at my flat, at an hour when he must have known that I would be in my bath and consequently in a strong strategic position to heave a wet sponge at him, surprised me considerably.

I hopped out with some briskness and, slipping a couple of

towels about the limbs and torso, made for the sitting-room. I found young Tuppy at the piano, playing 'Sonny Boy' with one finger.

'What ho!' I said, not without a certain hauteur.

'Oh, hullo, Bertie,' said young Tuppy. 'I say, Bertie, I want to see you about something important.'

It seemed to me that the bloke was embarrassed. He had moved to the mantelpiece, and now he broke a vase in rather a constrained way.

'The fact is, Bertie, I'm engaged.'

'Engaged?'

'Engaged,' said young Tuppy, coyly dropping a photograph frame into the fender. 'Practically, that is.'

'Practically?'

'Yes. You'll like her, Bertie. Her name is Cora Bellinger. She's studying for Opera. Wonderful voice she has. Also dark, flashing eyes and a great soul.'

'How do you mean, practically?'

'Well, it's this way. Before ordering the trousseau, there is one little point she wants cleared up. You see, what with her great soul and all that, she has a rather serious outlook on life: and the one thing she absolutely bars is anything in the shape of hearty humour. You know, practical joking and so forth. She said if she thought I was a practical joker she would never speak to me again. And unfortunately she appears to have heard about that little affair at the Drones – I expect you have forgotten all about that, Bertie?'

'I have not!'

'No, no, not forgotten exactly. What I mean is, nobody laughs more heartily at the recollection than you. And what I want you to do, old man, is to seize an early opportunity of taking Cora aside and categorically denying that there is any truth in the story. My happiness, Bertie, is in your hands, if you know what I mean.'

Well, of course, if he put it like that, what could I do? We Woosters have our code.

'Oh, all right,' I said, but far from brightly.

'Splendid fellow!'

'When do I meet this blighted female?'

'Don't call her "this blighted female", Bertie, old man. I have planned all that out. I will bring her round here today for a spot of lunch.'

'What!'

'At one-thirty. Right. Good. Fine. Thanks. I knew I could rely on you.'

He pushed off, and I turned to Jeeves, who had shimmered in with the morning meal.

'Lunch for three today, Jeeves,' I said.

'Very good, sir.'

'You know, Jeeves, it's a bit thick. You remember my telling you about what Mr Glossop did to me that night at the Drones?'

'Yes, sir.'

'For months I have been cherishing dreams of getting a bit of my own back. And now, so far from crushing him into the dust, I've got to fill him and fiancée with rich food and generally rally round and be the good angel.'

'Life is like that, sir.'

'True, Jeeves. What have we here?' I asked, inspecting the tray.

'Kippered herrings, sir.'

'And I shouldn't wonder,' I said, for I was in thoughtful mood, 'if even herrings haven't troubles of their own.'

'Quite possibly, sir.'

'I mean, apart from getting kippered.'

'Yes, sir.'

'And so it goes on, Jeeves, so it goes on.'

I can't say I exactly saw eye to eye with young Tuppy in his admiration for the Bellinger female. Delivered on the mat at one-twenty-five, she proved to be an upstanding light-heavyweight of some thirty summers, with a commanding eye and a square chin which I, personally, would have steered clear of. She seemed to me a good deal like what Cleopatra would have been after going in too freely for the starches and cereals. I don't know why it is, but women who have anything to do with Opera, even if they're only studying for it, always appear to run to surplus poundage.

Tuppy, however, was obviously all for her. His whole demeanour, both before and during lunch, was that of one striving to be worthy of a noble soul. When Jeeves offered him a cocktail, he practically recoiled as from a serpent. It was terrible to see the change which love had effected in the man. The spectacle put me off my food.

At half-past two, the Bellinger left to go to a singing lesson.

Tuppy trotted after her to the door, bleating and frisking a goodish bit, and then came back and looked at me in a goofy sort of way.

'Well, Bertie?'

'Well, what?'

'I mean, isn't she?'

'Oh, rather,' I said, humouring the poor fish.

'Wonderful eyes?'

'Oh, rather.'

'Wonderful figure?'

'Oh, quite.'

'Wonderful voice?'

Here I was able to intone the response with a little more heartiness. The Bellinger, at Tuppy's request, had sung us a few songs before digging in at the trough, and nobody could have denied that her pipes were in great shape. Plaster was still falling from the ceiling.

'Terrific,' I said.

Tuppy sighed, and, having helped himself to about four inches of whisky and one of soda, took a deep, refreshing draught.

'Ah!' he said. 'I needed that.'

'Why didn't you have it at lunch?'

'Well, it's this way,' said Tuppy. 'I have not actually ascertained what Cora's opinions are on the subject of the taking of slight snorts from time to time, but I thought it more prudent to lay off. The view I took was that laying off would seem to indicate the serious mind. It is touch-and-go, as you might say, at the moment, and the smallest thing may turn the scale.'

'What beats me is how on earth you expect to make her think you've got a mind at all – let alone a serious one.'

'I have my methods.'

'I bet they're rotten.'

'You do, do you?' said Tuppy warmly. 'Well, let me tell you, my lad, that that's exactly what they're anything but. I am handling this affair with consummate generalship. Do you remember Beefy Bingham who was at Oxford with us?'

'I ran into him only the other day. He's a parson now.'

'Yes. Down in the East End. Well, he runs a Lads' Club for the local toughs – you know the sort of thing – cocoa and back-gammon in the reading-room and occasional clean, bright entertainments in the Oddfellows' Hall: and I've been helping him. I don't suppose I've passed an evening away from the backgammon board for weeks. Cora is extremely pleased. I've got her to promise to sing on Tuesday at Beefy's next clean, bright entertainment.'

'You have?'

'I absolutely have. And now mark my devilish ingenuity, Bertie, I'm going to sing, too.'

'Why do you suppose that's going to get you anywhere?'

'Because the way I intend to sing the song I intend to sing will prove to her that there are great deeps in my nature, whose existence she has not suspected. She will see that rough, unlettered audience wiping the tears out of its bally eyes and she will say to herself "What ho! The old egg really has a soul!" For it is not one of your mouldy comic songs, Bertie. No low buffoonery of that sort for me. It is all about Angels being lonely and what-not — '

I uttered a sharp cry.

'You don't mean you're going to sing "Sonny Boy"?'

'I jolly well do.'

I was shocked. Yes, dash it, I was shocked. You see, I held strong views on 'Sonny Boy'. I considered it a song only to be attempted by a few of the elect in the privacy of the bathroom. And the thought of it being murdered in open Oddfellows' Hall by a man who could treat a pal as young Tuppy had treated me that night at the Drones sickened me. Yes, sickened me.

I hadn't time, however, to express my horror and disgust, for at this juncture Jeeves came in.

'Mrs Travers has just rung up on the telephone, sir. She desired me to say that she will be calling to see you in a few minutes.'

'Contents noted, Jeeves,' I said. 'Now listen, Tuppy — '

I stopped. The fellow wasn't there.

'What have you done with him, Jeeves?' I asked.

'Mr Glossop has left, sir.'

'Left? How can he have left? He was sitting there — '

'That is the front door closing now, sir.'

'But what made him shoot off like that?'

'Possibly Mr Glossop did not wish to meet Mrs Travers, sir.'

'Why not?'

'I could not say, sir. But undoubtedly at the mention of Mrs Travers' name he rose very swiftly.'

'Strange, Jeeves.'

'Yes, sir.'

I turned to a subject of more moment.

'Jeeves,' I said. 'Mr Glossop proposes to sing "Sonny Boy" at an entertainment down in the East End next Tuesday.'

'Indeed, sir?'

'Before an audience consisting mainly of coster-mongers, with a sprinkling of whelk-stall owners, purveyors of blood-oranges, and minor pugilists.'

'Indeed, sir?'

'Make a note to remind me to be there. He will infallibly get the bird, and I want to witness his downfall.'

'Very good, sir.'

'And when Mrs Travers arrives, I shall be in the sitting-room.'

Those who know Bertram Wooster best are aware that in his journey through life he is impeded and generally snootered by about as scaly a platoon of aunts as was ever assembled. But there is one exception to the general ghastliness – viz., my Aunt Dahlia. She married old Tom Travers the year Bluebottle won the Cambridgeshire, and is one of the best. It is always a pleasure to me to chat with her, and it was with a courtly geniality that I rose to receive her as she sailed over the threshold at about two fifty-five.

She seemed somewhat perturbed, and snapped into the agenda without delay. Aunt Dahlia is one of those big, hearty women. She used to go in a lot for hunting, and she generally speaks as if she had just sighted a fox on a hillside half a mile away.

'Bertie,' she cried, in the manner of one encouraging a bevy of hounds to renewed efforts. 'I want your help.'

'And you shall have it, Aunt Dahlia,' I replied suavely. 'I can honestly say that there is no one to whom I would more readily do a good turn than yourself; no one to whom I am more delighted to be — '

'Less of it,' she begged, 'less of it. You know that friend of yours, young Glossop?'

'He's just been lunching here.'

'He has, has he? Well, I wish you'd poisoned his soup.'

'We didn't have soup. And, when you describe him as a friend of mine, I wouldn't quite say the term absolutely squared with the facts. Some time ago, one night when we had been dining together at the Drones — '

At this point Aunt Dahlia – a little brusquely, it seemed to me – said that she would rather wait for the story of my life till she could get it in book form. I could see now that she was definitely not her usual sunny self, so I shelved my personal grievances and asked what was biting her.

'It's that young hound Glossop,' she said.

'What's he been doing?'

'Breaking Angela's heart.' (Angela. Daughter of above. My cousin. Quite a good egg.)

'Breaking Angela's heart?'

'Yes . . . Breaking . . . Angela's . . . HEART!'

'You say he's breaking Angela's heart?'

She begged me in rather a feverish way to suspend the vaudeville cross-talk stuff.

'How's he doing that?' I asked.

'With his neglect. With his low, callous, double-crossing duplicity.'

'Duplicity is the word, Aunt Dahlia,' I said. 'In treating of young Tuppy Glossop, it springs naturally to the lips. Let me just tell you what he did to me one night at the Drones. We had finished dinner — '

'Ever since the beginning of the season, up till about three weeks ago, he was all over Angela. The sort of thing which, when I was a girl, we should have described as courting — '

'Or wooing?'

'Wooing or courting, whichever you like.'

'Whichever *you* like, Aunt Dahlia,' I said courteously.

'Well, anyway, he haunted the house, lapped up daily lunches, danced with her half the night, and so on, till naturally the poor kid, who's quite off her oats about him, took it for granted that it was only a question of time before he suggested that they should feed for life out of the same crib. And now he's gone and dropped her like a hot brick, and I hear he's infatuated with some girl he met at a Chelsea tea-party – a girl named – now, what was it?'

'Cora Bellinger.'

'How do you know?'

'She was lunching here today.'

'He brought her?'

'Yes.'

'What's she like?'

'Pretty massive. In shape, a bit on the lines of the Albert Hall.'

'Did he seem very fond of her?'

'Couldn't take his eyes off the chassis.'

'The modern young man,' said Aunt Dahlia, 'is a congenital idiot and wants a nurse to lead him by the hand and some strong attendant to kick him regularly at intervals of a quarter of an hour.'

I tried to point out the silver lining.

'If you ask me, Aunt Dahlia,' I said, 'I think Angela is well out of it. This Glossop is a tough baby. One of London's toughest. I was trying to tell you just now what he did to me one night at the Drones. First having got me in sporting mood with a bottle of the ripest, he betted I wouldn't swing myself across the swimming-bath by the ropes and rings. I knew I could do it on my head, so I took him on, exulting in the fun, so to speak. And when I'd done half the trip and was going as strong as dammit, I found he had looped the last rope back against the rail, leaving me no alternative but to drop into the depths and swim ashore in correct evening costume.'

'He did?'

'He certainly did. It was months ago, and I haven't got really dry yet. You wouldn't want your daughter to marry a man capable of a thing like that?'

'On the contrary, you restore my faith in the young hound. I see that there must be lots of good in him, after all. And I want this Bellinger business broken up, Bertie.'

'How?'

'I don't care how. Any way you please.'

'But what can I do?'

'Do? Why, put the whole thing before your man Jeeves. Jeeves will find a way. One of the most capable fellers I ever met. Put the thing squarely up to Jeeves and tell him to let his mind play round the topic.'

'There may be something in what you say, Aunt Dahlia,' I said thoughtfully.

'Of course there is,' said Aunt Dahlia. 'A little thing like this will be child's play to Jeeves. Get him working on it, and I'll look in tomorrow to hear the result.'

With which, she biffed off, and I summoned Jeeves to the presence.

'Jeeves,' I said, 'you have heard all?'

'Yes, sir.'

'I thought you would. My Aunt Dahlia has what you might call a carrying voice. Has it ever occurred to you that, if all other sources of income failed, she could make a good living calling the cattle home across the Sands of Dee?'

'I had not considered the point, sir, but no doubt you are right.'

'Well, how do we go? What is your reaction? I think we should do our best to help and assist.'

'Yes, sir.'

'I am fond of my Aunt Dahlia and I am fond of my cousin Angela. Fond of them both, if you get my drift. What the misguided girl finds to attract her in young Tuppy, I cannot say, Jeeves, and you cannot say. But apparently she loves the man – which shows it can be done, a thing I wouldn't have believed myself – and is pining away like — '

'Patience on a monument, sir.'

'Like Patience, as you very shrewdly remark, on a monument. So we must cluster round. Bend your brain to the problem, Jeeves. It is one that will tax you to the uttermost.'

Aunt Dahlia blew in on the morrow, and I rang the bell for Jeeves. He appeared looking brainier than one could have believed possible – sheer intellect shining from every feature –and I could see at once that the engine had been turning over.

'Speak, Jeeves,' I said.

'Very good, sir.'

'You have brooded?'

'Yes, sir.'

'With what success?'

'I have a plan, sir, which I fancy may produce satisfactory results.'

'Let's have it,' said Aunt Dahlia.

'In affairs of this description, madam, the first essential is to study the psychology of the individual.'

'The what of the individual?'

'The psychology, madam.'

'He means, the psychology,' I said. 'And by psychology, Jeeves, you imply — ?'

'The natures and dispositions of the principals in the matter, sir.'

'You mean, what they're like?'

'Precisely, sir.'

'Does he talk like this to you when you're alone, Bertie?' asked Aunt Dahlia.

'Sometimes. Occasionally. And, on the other hand, sometimes not. Proceed, Jeeves.'

'Well, sir, if I may say so, the thing that struck me most forcibly about Miss Bellinger when she was under my observation was that hers was a somewhat hard and intolerant nature. I could envisage Miss Bellinger applauding success. I could not so easily see her pitying and sympathizing with failure. Possibly you will recall, sir, her attitude when Mr Glossop endeavoured to light her cigarette with his automatic lighter? I thought I detected a certain impatience at his inability to produce the necessary flame.'

'True, Jeeves. She ticked him off.'

'Precisely, sir.'

'Let me get this straight,' said Aunt Dahlia, looking a bit fogged. 'You think that, if he goes on trying to light her cigarettes with his automatic lighter long enough, she will eventually get fed up and hand him the mitten? Is that the idea?'

'I merely mentioned the episode, madam, as an indication of Miss Bellinger's somewhat ruthless nature.'

'Ruthless,' I said, 'is right. The Bellinger is hard-boiled. Those eyes. That chin. I could read them. A woman of blood and iron, if ever there was one.'

'Precisely, sir. I think, therefore, that, should Miss Bellinger be a witness of Mr Glossop appearing to disadvantage in public, she would cease to entertain affection for him. In the event, for instance, of his failing to please the audience on Tuesday with his singing — '

I saw daylight.

'By Jove, Jeeves! You mean if he gets the bird, all will be off?'

'I shall be greatly surprised if such is not the case, sir.'

I shook my head.

'We cannot leave this thing to chance, Jeeves. Young Tuppy, singing "Sonny Boy", is the likeliest prospect for the bird that I can think of – but, no – you must see for yourself that we can't simply trust to luck.'

'We need not trust to luck, sir. I would suggest that you approach your friend, Mr Bingham, and volunteer your services as a performer at his forthcoming entertainment. It could readily be arranged that you sang immediately before Mr Glossop. I fancy, sir, that, if Mr Glossop were to sing "Sonny Boy" directly after you, too, had sung "Sonny Boy", the audience would respond satisfactorily. By the time Mr Glossop began to sing, they would have lost their taste for that particular song and would express their feelings warmly.'

'Jeeves,' said Aunt Dahlia, 'you're a marvel!'

'Thank you, madam.'

'Jeeves,' I said, 'you're an ass!'

'What do you mean, he's an ass?' said Aunt Dahlia hotly. 'I think it's the greatest scheme I ever heard.'

'Me sing "Sonny Boy" at Beefy Bingham's clean, bright entertainment? I can see myself!'

'You sing it daily in your bath, sir. Mr Wooster,' said Jeeves, turning to Aunt Dahlia, 'has a pleasant, light baritone — '

'I bet he has,' said Aunt Dahlia.

I froze the man with a look.

'Between singing "Sonny Boy" in one's bath, Jeeves, and singing it before a hall full of assorted blood-orange merchants and their young, there is a substantial difference.'

'Bertie,' said Aunt Dahlia, 'you'll sing, and like it!'

'I will not.'

'Bertie!'

'Nothing will induce — '

'Bertie,' said Aunt Dahlia firmly, 'you will sing "Sonny Boy" on Tuesday, the third *prox.*, and sing it like a lark at sunrise, or may an aunt's curse — '

'I won't!'

'Think of Angela!'

'Dash Angela!'

'Bertie!'

'No, I mean, hang it all!'

'You won't?'

'No, I won't.'

'That is your last word, is it?'

'It is. Once and for all, Aunt Dahlia, nothing will induce me to let out so much as a single note.'

And so that afternoon I sent a pre-paid wire to Beefy Bingham, offering my services in the cause, and by nightfall the thing was fixed up. I was billed to perform next but one after the intermission. Following me, came Tuppy. And, immediately after him, Miss Cora Bellinger, the well-known operatic soprano.

'Jeeves,' I said that evening – and I said it coldly – 'I shall be obliged if you will pop round to the nearest music-shop and procure me a copy of "Sonny Boy". It will now be necessary for me to learn both verse and refrain. Of the trouble and nervous strain which this will involve, I say nothing.'

'Very good, sir.'

'But this I do say — '

'I had better be starting immediately, sir, or the shop will be closed.'

'Ha!' I said.

And I meant it to sting.

Although I had steeled myself to the ordeal before me and had set out full of the calm, quiet courage which makes men do desperate deeds with careless smiles, I must admit that there was a moment, just after I had entered the Oddfellows' Hall at Bermondsey East and run an eye over the assembled pleasure-seekers, when it needed all the bull-dog pluck of the Woosters to keep me from calling it a day and taking a cab back to civilization. The clean, bright entertainment was in full swing when I arrived, and somebody who looked as if he might be the local undertaker was reciting 'Gunga Din'. And the audience, though not actually chi-yiking in the full technical sense of the term, had a grim look which I didn't like at all. The mere sight of them gave me the sort of feeling Shadrach, Meshach and Abednego must have had when preparing to enter the burning, fiery furnace.

Scanning the multitude, it seemed to me that they were for the nonce suspending judgment. Did you ever tap on the door of one of those New York speak-easy places and see the grille snap back and a Face appear? There is one long, silent moment when its eyes are fixed on yours and all your past life seems to rise up before you. Then you say that you are a friend of Mr Zinzinheimer and he told you they would treat you right if you mentioned his name, and the strain relaxes. Well, these coster-mongers and whelk-stallers appeared to me to be looking just like that Face. Start something, they seemed to say, and they would know what to do about it. And

I couldn't help feeling that my singing 'Sonny Boy' would come, in their opinion, under the head of starting something.

'A nice, full house, sir,' said a voice at my elbow. It was Jeeves, watching the proceedings with an indulgent eye.

'You here, Jeeves?' I said, coldly.

'Yes, sir. I have been present since the commencement.'

'Oh?' I said. 'Any casualties yet?'

'Sir?'

'You know what I mean, Jeeves,' I said sternly, 'and don't pretend you don't. Anybody got the bird yet?'

'Oh, no, sir.'

'I shall be the first, you think?'

'No, sir. I see no reason to expect such a misfortune. I anticipate that you will be well received.'

A sudden thought struck me.

'And you think everything will go according to plan?'

'Yes, sir.'

'Well, I don't,' I said. 'And I'll tell you why I don't. I've spotted a flaw in your beastly scheme.'

'A flaw, sir?'

'Yes. Do you suppose for a moment that, when Mr Glossop hears me singing that dashed song, he'll come calmly on a minute after and sing it too? Use your intelligence, Jeeves. He will perceive the chasm in his path and pause in time. He will back out and refuse to go on at all.'

'Mr Glossop will not hear you sing, sir. At my advice, he has stepped across the road to the Jug and Bottle, an establishment immediately opposite the hall, and he intends to remain there until it is time for him to appear on the platform.'

'Oh?' I said.

'If I might suggest it, sir, there is another house named the Goat and Grapes only a short distance down the street. I think it might be a judicious move — '

'If I were to put a bit of custom in their way?'

'It would ease the nervous strain of waiting, sir.'

I had not been feeling any too pleased with the man for having let me in for this ghastly binge, but at these words, I'm bound to say, my austerity softened a trifle. He was undoubtedly right. He had studied the psychology of the individual, and it had not led him astray. A quiet ten minutes at the Goat and Grapes was exactly what my system required. To buzz off there and inhale a couple of swift whisky-and-sodas was with Bertram Wooster the work of a moment.

The treatment worked like magic. What they had put into the stuff, besides vitriol, I could not have said; but it completely altered my outlook on life. That curious, gulpy feeling passed. I was no longer conscious of the sagging sensation at the knees. The limbs ceased to quiver gently, the tongue became loosened in its socket, and the backbone stiffened. Pausing merely to order and swallow another of the same, I bade the barmaid a cheery good night, nodded affably to one or two fellows in the bar whose faces I liked, and came prancing back to the hall, ready for anything.

And shortly afterwards I was on the platform with about a million bulging eyes goggling up at me. There was a rummy sort of buzzing in my ears, and then through the buzzing I heard the sound of a piano starting to tinkle: and, commending my soul to God, I took a good, long breath and charged in.

Well, it was a close thing. The whole incident is a bit blurred, but I seem to recollect a kind of murmur as I hit the refrain. I thought at the time it was an attempt on the part of the many-headed to join in the chorus, and at the moment it rather encouraged me. I passed the thing over the larynx with all the vim at my disposal, hit the high note, and off gracefully into the wings. I didn't come on again to take a bow. I just receded and oiled round to where Jeeves awaited me among the standees at the back.

'Well, Jeeves,' I said, anchoring myself at his side and brushing the honest sweat from the brow, 'they didn't rush the platform.'

'No, sir.'

'But you can spread it about that that's the last time I perform outside my bath. My swan-song, Jeeves. Anybody who wants to hear me in future must present himself at the bathroom door and shove his ear against the keyhole. I may be wrong, but it seemed to me that towards the end they were hotting up a trifle. The bird was hovering in the air. I could hear the beating of its wings.'

'I did detect a certain restlessness, sir, in the audience. I fancy they had lost their taste for that particular melody.'

'Eh?'

'I should have informed you earlier, sir, that the song had already been sung twice before you arrived.'

'What!'

'Yes, sir. Once by a lady and once by a gentleman. It is a very popular song, sir.'

I gaped at the man. That, with this knowledge, he could calmly have allowed the young master to step straight into the jaws of death, so to speak, paralysed me. It seemed to show that the old feudal spirit had passed away altogether. I was about to give him my views on the matter in no uncertain fashion, when I was stopped by the spectacle of young Tuppy lurching on to the platform.

Young Tuppy had the unmistakable air of a man who has recently been round to the Jug and Bottle. A few cheery cries of welcome, presumably from some of his backgammon-playing pals who felt that blood was thicker than water, had the effect of causing the genial smile on his face to widen till it nearly met at the back. He was plainly feeling about as good as a man can feel and still remain on his feet. He waved a kindly hand to his supporters, and bowed in a regal sort of manner, rather like an Eastern monarch acknowledging the plaudits of the mob.

Then the female at the piano struck up the opening bars of 'Sonny Boy', and Tuppy swelled like a balloon, clasped his hands together, rolled his eyes up at the ceiling and began.

I think the populace was too stunned for the moment to take immediate steps. It may seem incredible, but I give you my word that young Tuppy got right through the verse without so much as a murmur. Then they all seemed to pull themselves together.

A coster-monger, roused, is a terrible thing. I had never seen the proletariat really stirred before, and I'm bound to say it rather awed me. I mean, it gave you some idea of what it must have been like during the French Revolution. From every corner of the hall there proceeded simultaneously the sort of noise which you hear, they tell me, at one of those East End boxing places where the referee disqualifies the popular favourite and makes the quick dash for life. And then they passed beyond mere words and began to introduce the vegetable motive.

I don't know why, but somehow I had got it into my head that the first thing thrown at Tuppy would be a potato. One gets these fancies. It was, however, as a matter of fact, a banana, and I saw in an instant that the choice had been made by wiser heads than mine. These blokes who have grown up from childhood in the knowledge of how to treat a dramatic entertainment that doesn't please them are aware by a sort of instinct just what to do for the best, and the moment I saw that banana splash on Tuppy's shirtfront I realized how infinitely more effective and artistic it was than any potato could have been.

Not that the potato school of thought had not also its supporters. As the proceedings warmed up, I noticed several intelligent-looking fellows who threw nothing else.

The effect on young Tuppy was rather remarkable. His eyes bulged and his hair seemed to stand up, and yet his mouth went on opening and shutting, and you could see that in a dazed, automatic way he was still singing 'Sonny Boy'. Then, coming out of his trance, he began to pull for the shore with some rapidity. The last seen of him, he was beating a tomato to the exit by a short head.

Presently the tumult and the shouting died. I turned to Jeeves.

'Painful, Jeeves,' I said. 'But what would you?'

'Yes, sir.'

'The surgeon's knife, what?'

'Precisely, sir.'

'Well, with this happening beneath her eyes, I think we may definitely consider the Glossop-Bellinger romance off.'

'Yes, sir.'

At this point old Beefy Bingham came out on to the platform.

'Ladies and gentlemen,' said old Beefy.

I supposed that he was about to rebuke his flock for the recent expression of feeling. But such was not the case. No doubt he was accustomed by now to the wholesome give-and-take of these clean, bright entertainments and had ceased to think it worth while to make any comment when there was a certain liveliness.

'Ladies and gentlemen,' said old Beefy, 'the next item on the programme was to have been Songs by Miss Cora Bellinger, the well-known operatic soprano. I have just received a telephone message from Miss Bellinger, saying that her car has broken down. She is, however, on her way here in a cab and will arrive shortly. Meanwhile, our friend Mr Enoch Simpson will recite "Dangerous Dan McGrew".'

I clutched at Jeeves.

'Jeeves! You heard?'

'Yes, sir.'

'She wasn't there!'

'No, sir.'

'She saw nothing of Tuppy's Waterloo.'

'No, sir.'

'The whole bally scheme has blown a fuse.'

'Yes, sir.'

'Come, Jeeves,' I said, and those standing by wondered, no doubt, what had caused that clean-cut face to grow so pale and set. 'I have been subjected to a nervous strain unparalleled since the days of the early Martyrs. I have lost pounds in weight and permanently injured my entire system. I have gone through an ordeal, the recollection of which will make me wake up screaming in the night for months to come. And all for nothing. Let us go.'

'If you have no objection, sir, I would like to witness the remainder of the entertainment.'

'Suit yourself, Jeeves,' I said moodily. 'Personally, my heart is dead and I am going to look in at the Goat and Grapes for another of their cyanide specials and then home.'

It must have been about half-past ten, and I was in the old sitting-room sombrely sucking down a more or less final restorative, when the front door bell rang, and there on the mat was young Tuppy. He looked like a man who had passed through some great experience and stood face to face with his soul. He had the beginnings of a black eye.

'Oh, hullo, Bertie,' said young Tuppy.

He came in, and hovered about the mantelpiece as if he were looking for things to fiddle with and break.

'I've just been singing at Beefy Bingham's entertainment,' he said after a pause.

'Oh?' I said. 'How did you go?'

'Like a breeze,' said young Tuppy. 'Held them spellbound.'

'Knocked 'em, eh?'

'Cold,' said young Tuppy. 'Not a dry eye.'

And this, mark you, from a man who had had a good upbringing and had, no doubt, spent years at his mother's knee being taught to tell the truth.

'I suppose Miss Bellinger is pleased?'

'Oh, yes. Delighted.'

'So now everything's all right?'

'Oh, quite.'

Tuppy paused.

'On the other hand, Bertie — '

'Yes?'

'Well, I've been thinking things over. Somehow I don't believe Miss Bellinger is the mate for me after all.'

'You don't?'

'No, I don't.'

'Why don't you?'

'Oh, I don't know. These things sort of flash on you. I respect Miss Bellinger, Bertie. I admire her. But – er – well, I can't help feeling now that a sweet, gentle girl—er – like your cousin Angela, for instance, Bertie—would – er – in fact—well, what I came round for was to ask if you would 'phone Angela and find out how she reacts to the idea of coming out with me tonight to the Berkeley for a segment of supper and a spot of dancing.'

'Go ahead. There's the 'phone.'

'No, I'd rather you asked her, Bertie. What with one thing and another, if you paved the way—you see, there's just a chance that she may be—I mean, you know how misunderstandings occur—and—well, what I'm driving at, Bertie, old man, is that I'd rather you surged round and did a bit of paving, if you don't mind.'

I went to the 'phone and called up Aunt Dahlia's.

'She says come right along,' I said.

'Tell her,' said Tuppy in a devout sort of voice, 'that I will be with her in something under a couple of ticks.'

He had barely biffed, when I heard a click in the keyhole and a soft padding in the passage without.

'Jeeves,' I called.

'Sir?' said Jeeves, manifesting himself.

'Jeeves, a remarkably rummy thing has happened. Mr Glossop had just been here. He tells me that it is all off between him and Miss Bellinger.'

'Yes, sir.'

'You don't seem surprised.'

'No, sir. I confess I had anticipated some such eventuality.'

'Eh? What gave you that idea?'

'It came to me, sir, when I observed Miss Bellinger strike Mr Glossop in the eye.'

'Strike him!'

'Yes, sir.'

'In the eye?'

'The right eye, sir.'

I clutched the brow.

'What on earth made her do that?'

'I fancy she was a little upset, sir, at the reception accorded to her singing.'

'Great Scott! Don't tell me she got the bird, too?'

'Yes, sir.'

'But why? She's got a red-hot voice.'

'Yes, sir. But I think the audience resented her choice of a song.'

'Jeeves!' Reason was beginning to do a bit of tottering on its throne. 'You aren't going to stand there and tell me that Miss Bellinger sang "Sonny Boy", too!'

'Yes, sir. And – rashly, in my opinion – brought a large doll on to the platform to sing it to. The audience affected to mistake it for a ventriloquist's dummy, and there was some little disturbance.'

'But, Jeeves, what a coincidence!'

'Not altogether, sir. I ventured to take the liberty of accosting Miss Bellinger on her arrival at the hall and recalling myself to her recollection. I then said that Mr Glossop had asked me to request her that as a particular favour to him – the song being a favourite of his – she would sing "Sonny Boy". And when she found that you and Mr Glossop had also sung the song immediately before her, I rather fancy that she supposed that she had been made the victim of a practical pleasantry by Mr Glossop. Will there be anything further, sir?'

'No, thanks.'

'Good night, sir.'

'Good night, Jeeves,' I said reverently.

Irwin Shaw

Act of Faith

'Present it in a pitiful light,' Olson was saying, as they picked their way through the mud toward the orderly-room tent. 'Three combat-scarred veterans, who fought their way from Omaha Beach to – what was the name of the town we fought our way to?'

'Konigstein,' Seeger said.

'Konigstein.' Olson lifted his right foot heavily out of a puddle and stared admiringly at the three pounds of mud clinging to his overshoe. 'The backbone of the army. The non-commissioned officer. We deserve better of our country. Mention our decorations in passing.'

'What decorations should I mention?' Seeger asked. 'The marksman's medal?'

'Never quite made it,' Olson said. 'I had a cross-eyed scorer at the butts. Mention the bronze star, the silver star, the Croix de Guerre, with palms, the unit citation, the Congressional Medal of Honor.'

'I'll mention them all.' Seeger grinned. 'You don't think the C.O.'ll notice that we haven't won most of them, do you?'

'Gad, sir,' Olson said with dignity, 'do you think that one Southern military gentleman will dare doubt the word of another Southern military gentleman in the hour of victory?'

'I come from Ohio,' Seeger said.

'Welch comes from Kansas,' Olson said, coolly staring down a second lieutenant who was passing. The lieutenant made a nervous little jerk with his hand as though he expected a salute, then kept it rigid, as a slight superior smile of scorn twisted at the corner of Olson's mouth. The lieutenant dropped his eyes and splashed on through the mud. 'You've heard of Kansas,' Olson said. 'Magnolia-scented Kansas.'

'Of course,' said Seeger. 'I'm no fool.'

'Do your duty by your men, Sergeant.' Olson stopped to wipe the rain off his face and lectured him. 'Highest ranking noncom present took the initiative and saved his comrades, at great personal risk, above and beyond the call of you-know-what, in the best traditions of the American army.'

'I will throw myself in the breach,' Seeger said.

'Welch and I can't ask more,' said Olson, approvingly.

They walked heavily through the mud on the streets between the rows of tents. The camp stretched drearily over the Rheims plain, with the rain beating on the sagging tents. The division had been there over three weeks by now, waiting to be shipped home, and all the meagre diversions of the neighbourhood had been sampled and exhausted, and there was an air of watchful suspicion and impatience with the military life hanging over the camp now, and there was even reputed to be a staff sergeant in C Company who was laying odds they would not get back to America before July Fourth.

'I'm redeployable,' Olson sang. 'It's so enjoyable . . .' It was a jingle he had composed to no recognizable melody in the early days after the victory in Europe, when he had added up his points and found they only came to 63. 'Tokyo, wait for me . . .'

They were going to be discharged as soon as they got back to the States, but Olson persisted in singing the song, occasionally adding a mournful stanza about dengue fever and brown girls with venereal disease. He was a short, round boy who had been flunked out of air cadets' school and transferred to the infantry, but whose spirits had not been damaged in the process. He had a high, childish voice and a pretty baby face. He was very good-natured, and had a girl waiting for him at the University of California, where he intended to finish his course at government expense when he got out of the army, and he was just the type who is killed off early and predictably and sadly in motion pictures about the war, but he had gone through four campaigns and six major battles without a scratch.

Seeger was a large, lanky boy, with a big nose, who had been wounded at Saint Lô, but had come back to his outfit in the Siegfried Line, quite unchanged. He was cheerful and dependable, and he knew his business and had broken in five or six second lieutenants who had been killed or wounded and the C.O. had tried to get him commissioned in the field, but the war had ended while the paperwork was being fumbled over at headquarters.

They reached the door of the orderly tent and stopped. 'Be brave, Sergeant,' Olson said. 'Welch and I are depending on you.'

'O.K.,' Seeger said, and went in.

The tent had the dank, army-canvas smell that had been so much a part of Seeger's life in the past three years. The company clerk was reading a July, 1945, issue of the *Buffalo Courier-Express*, which had just reached him, and Captain Taney, the company C.O., was seated at a sawbuck table he used as a desk, writing a letter to his wife, his lips pursed with effort. He was a small, fussy man, with sandy hair that was falling out. While the fighting had been going on, he had been lean and tense and his small voice had been cold and full of authority. But now he had relaxed, and a little pot belly was creeping up under his belt and he kept the top button of his trousers open when he could do it without too public loss of dignity. During the war Seeger had thought of him as a natural soldier, tireless, fanatic about detail, aggressive, severely anxious to kill Germans. But in the past few months Seeger had seen him relapsing gradually and pleasantly into a small-town wholesale hardware merchant, which he had been before the war, sedentary and a little shy, and, as he had once told Seeger, worried, here in the bleak champagne fields of France, about his daughter, who had just turned twelve and had a tendency to go after the boys and had been caught by her mother kissing a fifteen-year-old neighbour in the hammock after school.

'Hello, Seeger,' he said, returning the salute in a mild, offhand gesture. 'What's on your mind?'

'Am I disturbing you, sir?'

'Oh, no. Just writing a letter to my wife. You married, Seeger?' He peered at the tall boy standing before him.

'No, sir.'

'It's very difficult,' Taney sighed, pushing dissatisfiedly at the letter before him. 'My wife complains I don't tell her I love her often enough. Been married fifteen years. You'd think she'd know by now.' He smiled at Seeger. 'I thought you were going to Paris,' he said. 'I signed the passes yesterday.'

'That's what I came to see you about, sir.'

'I suppose something's wrong with the passes.' Taney spoke resignedly, like a man who has never quite got the hang of army regulations and has had requisitions, furloughs, requests for court-martial returned for correction in a baffling flood.

'No, sir,' Seeger said. 'The passes're fine. They start tomorrow. Well, it's just . . .' He looked around at the company clerk, who was on the sports page.

'This confidential?' Taney asked.

'If you don't mind, sir.'

'Johnny,' Taney said to the clerk, 'go stand in the rain some place.'

'Yes, sir,' the clerk said, and slowly got up and walked out.

Taney looked shrewdly at Seeger, spoke in a secret whisper. 'You pick up anything?' he asked.

Seeger grinned. 'No, sir, haven't had my hands on a girl since Strasbourg.'

'Ah, that's good.' Taney leaned back, relieved, happy he didn't have to cope with the disapproval of the Medical Corps.

'It's – well,' said Seeger, embarrassed, 'it's hard to say – but it's money.'

Taney shook his head sadly. 'I know.'

'We haven't been paid for three months, sir, and . . .'

'Damn it!' Taney stood up and shouted furiously. 'I would like to take every bloody chair-warming old lady in the Finance Department and wring their necks.'

The clerk stuck his head into the tent. 'Anything wrong? You call for me, sir?'

'No,' Taney shouted. 'Get out of here.'

The clerk ducked out.

Taney sat down again. 'I suppose,' he said, in a more normal voice, 'they have their problems. Outfits being broken up, being moved all over the place. But it is rugged.'

'It wouldn't be so bad,' Seeger said. 'But we're going to Paris tomorrow. Olson, Welch and myself. And you need money in Paris.'

'Don't I know it.' Taney wagged his head. 'Do you know what I paid for a bottle of champagne on the Place Pigalle in September . . . ?' He paused significantly. 'I won't tell you. You won't have any respect for me the rest of your life.'

Seeger laughed. 'Hanging,' he said, 'is too good for the guy who thought up the rate of exchange.'

'I don't care if I never see another franc as long as I live.' Taney waved his letter in the air, although it had been dry for a long time.

There was silence in the tent and Seeger swallowed a little embarrassedly, watching the C.O. wave the flimsy sheet of paper in regular sweeping movements. 'Sir,' he said, 'the truth is, I've come to borrow some money for Welch, Olson and myself. We'll pay it back out of the first pay we get, and that can't be too long from now. If you don't want to give it to us, just tell me and I'll understand and get the hell out of here. We don't like to ask, but you might just as well be dead as be in Paris broke.'

Taney stopped waving his letter and put it down thoughtfully. He peered at it, wrinkling his brow, looking like an aged bookkeeper in the single gloomy light that hung in the middle of the tent.

'Just say the word, Captain,' Seeger said, 'and I'll blow . . .'

'Stay where you are, son,' said Taney. He dug in his shirt pocket and took out a worn, sweat-stained wallet. He looked at it for a moment. 'Alligator,' he said, with automatic, absent pride. 'My wife sent it to me when we were in England. Pounds don't fit in it. However . . .' He opened it and took out all the contents. There was a small pile of francs on the table in front of him. He counted them. 'Four hundred francs,' he said. 'Eight bucks.'

'Excuse me,' Seeger said humbly. 'I shouldn't have asked.'

'Delighted,' Taney said vigorously. 'Absolutely delighted.' He started dividing the francs into two piles. 'Truth is, Seeger, most of my money goes home in allotments. And the truth is, I lost eleven hundred francs in a poker game three nights ago, and I ought to be ashamed of myself. Here . . .' He shoved one pile toward Seeger. 'Two hundred francs.'

Seeger looked down at the frayed, meretricious paper, which always seemed to him like stage money, anyway. 'No, sir,' he said, 'I can't take it.'

'Take it,' Taney said. 'That's a direct order.'

Seeger slowly picked up the money, not looking at Taney. 'Some time, sir,' he said, 'after we get out, you have to come over to my house and you and my father and my brother and I'll go on a real drunk.'

'I regard that,' Taney said, gravely, 'as a solemn commitment.'

They smiled at each other and Seeger started out.

'Have a drink for me,' said Taney, 'at the Café de la Paix. A small drink.' He was sitting down to write his wife he loved her when Seeger went out of the tent.

Olson fell into step with Seeger and they walked silently through the mud between the tents.

'Well, *mon vieux?*' Olson said finally.

'Two hundred francs,' said Seeger.

Olson groaned. 'Two hundred francs! We won't be able to pinch a whore's behind on the Boulevard des Capucines for two hundred francs. That miserable, penny-loving Yankee!'

'He only had four hundred,' Seeger said.

'I revise my opinion,' said Olson.

They walked disconsolately and heavily back towards their tent.

Olson spoke only once before they got there. 'These raincoats,' he said, patting his. 'Most ingenious invention of the war. Highest saturation point of any modern fabric. Collect more water per square inch, and hold it, than any material known to man. All hail the quartermaster!'

Welch was waiting at the entrance of their tent. He was standing there peering excitedly and short-sightedly out at the rain through his glasses, looking angry and tough, like a big-city hack-driver, individual and incorruptible even in the ten-million coloured uniform. Every time Seeger came upon Welch unexpectedly, he couldn't help smiling at the belligerent stance, the harsh stare through the steel-rimmed G.I. glasses, which had nothing at all to do with the way Welch really was. 'It's a family inheritance,' Welch had once explained. 'My whole family stands as though we were getting ready to rap a drunk with a beer glass. Even my old lady.' Welch had six brothers, all devout, according to Welch, and Seeger from time to time idly pictured them standing in a row, on Sunday mornings in church, seemingly on the verge of general violence, amid the hushed Latin and Sabbath millinery.

'How much?' Welch asked loudly.

'Don't make us laugh,' Olson said, pushing past him into the tent.

'What do you think I could get from the French for my combat jacket?' Seeger said. He went into the tent and lay down on his cot.

Welch followed them in and stood between the two of them, a superior smile on his face. 'Boys,' he said, 'on a man's errand.'

'I can just see us now,' Olson murmured, lying on his cot with his hands clasped behind his head, 'painting Montmartre red. Please bring on the naked dancing girls. Four bucks' worth.'

'I am not worried,' Welch announced.

'Get out of here.' Olson turned over on his stomach.

'I know where we can put our hands on sixty-five bucks.' Welch looked triumphantly first at Olson, then at Seeger.

Olson turned over slowly and sat up. 'I'll kill you,' he said, 'if you're kidding.'

'While you guys are wasting your time,' Welch said, 'fooling around with the infantry, I used my head. I went into Reems and used my head.'

'Rance,' Olson said automatically. He had had two years of French in college and he felt, now that the war was over, that he had to introduce his friends to some of his culture.

'I got to talking to a captain in the air force,' Welch said eagerly. 'A little fat old paddle-footed captain that never got higher off the ground than the second floor of Com Z headquarters, and he told me that what he would admire to do more than anything else is take home a nice shiny German Luger pistol with him to show to the boys back in Pacific Grove, California.'

Silence fell on the tent and Welch and Olson looked tentatively at Seeger.

'Sixty-five bucks for a Luger, these days,' Olson said, 'is a very good figure.'

'They've been sellin' for as low as thirty-five,' said Welch hesitantly. 'I'll bet,' he said to Seeger, 'you could sell yours now and buy another one back when you get some dough, and make a clear twenty-five on the deal.'

Seeger didn't say anything. He had killed the owner of the Luger, an enormous S.S. major, in Coblenz, behind some paper bales in a warehouse, and the major had fired at Seeger three times with it, once nicking his helmet, before Seeger hit him in the face at twenty feet. Seeger had kept the Luger, a long, heavy, well-balanced gun, very carefully since then, lugging it with him, hiding it at the bottom of his bedroll, oiling it three times a week, avoiding all opportunities of selling it, although he had been offered as much as a hundred dollars for it and several times eighty and ninety, while the war was still on, before German weapons became a glut on the market.

'Well,' said Welch, 'there's no hurry. I told the captain I'd see him tonight around 8 o'clock in front of the Lion D'Or Hotel. You got five hours to make up your mind. Plenty of time.'

'Me,' said Olson, after a pause. 'I won't say anything.'

Seeger looked reflectively at his feet and the other two men avoided looking at him. Welch dug in his pocket. 'I forgot,' he said. 'I picked up a letter for you.' He handed it to Seeger.

'Thanks,' Seeger said. He opened it absently, thinking about the Luger.

'Me,' said Olson, 'I won't say a bloody word. I'm just going to lie here and think about that nice fat air force captain.'

Seeger grinned a little at him and went to the tent opening to read the letter in the light. The letter was from his father, and even from one glance at the handwriting, scrawly and hurried and spotted, so different from his father's usual steady, handsome, professional script, he knew that something was wrong.

'Dear Norman,' it read, 'sometime in the future, you must forgive me for writing this letter. But I have been holding this in so long, and there is no one here I can talk to, and because of your brother's condition I must pretend to be cheerful and optimistic all the time at home, both with him and your mother, who has never been the same since Leonard was killed. You're the oldest now, and although I know we've never talked very seriously about anything before, you have been through a great deal by now, and I imagine you must have matured considerably, and you've seen so many different places and people. . . . Norman, I need help. While the war was on and you were fighting, I kept this to myself. It wouldn't have been fair to burden you with this. But now the war is over, and I no longer feel I can stand up under this alone. And you will have to face it some time when you get home, if you haven't faced it already, and perhaps we can help each other by facing it together. . . .'

'I'm redeployable,' Olson was singing softly, on his cot. 'It's so enjoyable, In the Pelilu mud, With the tropical crud . . .' He fell silent after his burst of song.

Seeger blinked his eyes, at the entrance of the tent, in the wan rainy light, and went on reading his father's letter, on the stiff white stationery with the University letterhead in polite engraving at the top of each page.

'I've been feeling this coming on for a long time,' the letter continued, 'but it wasn't until last Sunday morning that something happened to make me feel it in its full force. I don't know how much you've guessed about the reason for Jacob's discharge from the army. It's true he was pretty badly wounded in the leg at Metz, but I've asked around, and I know that men with worse wounds were returned to duty after hospitalization. Jacob got a medical discharge, but I don't think it was from the shrapnel wound in his thigh. He is suffering now from what I suppose you call combat fatigue, and he is subject to fits of depression and hallucinations. Your mother and I thought that as time went by and the war and the army receded, he would grow better. Instead, he is growing worse. Last Sunday morning when I came down into the living room from upstairs he was crouched in his old uniform, next to the window, peering out . . .'

'What the hell,' Olson was saying, 'if we don't get the sixty-five bucks we can always go to the Louvre. I understand the Mona Lisa is back.'

'I asked Jacob what he was doing,' the letter went on. 'He didn't turn around. "I'm observing," he said. "V-1's and V-2's. Buzz-bombs and rockets. They're coming in by the hundreds." I tried to reason with him and he told me to crouch and save myself from flying glass. To humour him I got down on the floor beside him and tried to tell him the war was over, that we were in Ohio, 4,000 miles away from the nearest spot where bombs had fallen, that America had never been touched. He wouldn't listen. "These're the new rocket bombs," he said, "for the Jews." '

'Did you ever hear of the Pantheon?' Olson asked loudly.

'No,' said Welch.

'It's free.'

'I'll go,' said Welch.

Seeger shook his head a little and blinked his eyes before he went back to the letter.

'After that,' his father went on, 'Jacob seemed to forget about the bombs from time to time, but he kept saying that the mobs were coming up the street armed with bazookas and Browning automatic rifles. He mumbled incoherently a good deal of the time and kept walking back and forth saying, "What's the situation? Do you know what the situation is?" And he told me he wasn't worried about himself, he was a soldier and he expected to be killed, but he was worried about Mother and myself and Leonard and you. He seemed to forget that Leonard was dead. I tried to calm him and get him back to bed before your mother came down, but he refused and wanted to set out immediately to rejoin his division. It was all terribly disjointed and at one time he took the ribbon he got for winning the Bronze Star and threw it in the fireplace, then he got down on his hands and knees and picked it out of the ashes and made me pin it on him again, and he kept repeating, "This is when they are coming for the Jews." '

'The next war I'm in,' said Olson, 'they don't get me under the rank of colonel.'

It had stopped raining by now and Seeger folded the unfinished letter and went outside. He walked slowly down to the end of the company street, and facing out across the empty, soaked French fields, scarred and neglected by various armies, he stopped and opened the letter again.

'I don't know what Jacob went through in the army,' his father wrote, 'that has done this to him. He never talks to me about the war and he refuses to go to a psychoanalyst, and from time to time he is his own bouncing, cheerful self, playing in tennis tournaments, and going around with a large group of girls. But he has devoured all the concentration camp reports, and I have found him weeping when the newspapers reported that a hundred Jews were killed in Tripoli some time ago.

'The terrible thing is, Norman, that I find myself coming to believe that it is not neurotic for a Jew to behave like this today. Perhaps Jacob is the normal one, and I, going about my business, teaching economics in a quiet classroom, pretending to understand that the world is comprehensible and orderly, am really the mad one. I ask you once more to forgive me for writing you a letter like this, so different from any letter or any conversation I've ever had with you. But it is crowding me, too. I do not see rockets and bombs, but I see other things.

'Wherever you go these days – restaurants, hotels, clubs, trains – you seem to hear talk about the Jews, mean, hateful, murderous talk. Whatever page you turn to in the newspapers you seem to find an article about Jews being killed somewhere on the face of the globe. And there are large, influential newspapers and well-known columnists who each day are growing more and more outspoken and more popular. The day that Roosevelt died I heard a drunken man yelling outside a bar, "Finally, they got the Jew out of the

White House." And some of the people who heard him merely laughed and nobody stopped him. And on V-E Day, in celebration, hoodlums in Los Angeles savagely beat a Jewish writer. It's difficult to know what to do, whom to fight, where to look for allies.

'Three months ago, for example, I stopped my Thursday night poker game, after playing with the same men for over ten years. John Reilly happened to say that the Jews were getting rich out of this war, and when I demanded an apology, he refused, and when I looked around at the faces of the men who had been my friends for so long, I could see they were not with me. And when I left the house no one said good night to me. I know the poison was spreading from Germany before the war and during it, but I had not realized it had come so close.

'And in my economics class, I find myself idiotically hedging in my lectures. I discover that I am loath to praise any liberal writer or any liberal act and find myself somehow annoyed and frightened to see an article of criticism of existing abuses signed by a Jewish name. And I hate to see Jewish names on important committees, and hate to read of Jews fighting for the poor, the oppressed, the cheated and hungry. Somehow, even in a country where my family has lived a hundred years, the enemy has won this subtle victory over me – he has made me disfranchise myself from honest causes by calling them foreign, Communist, using Jewish names connected with them as ammunition against them.

'And, most hateful of all, I find myself looking for Jewish names in the casualty lists and secretly being glad when I discover them there, to prove that there at least, among the dead and wounded, we belong. Three times, thanks to you and your brothers, I have found our name there, and, may God forgive me, at the expense of your blood and your brother's life, through my tears, I have felt that same twitch of satisfaction. . . .

'When I read the newspapers and see another story that Jews are still being killed in Poland, or Jews are requesting that they be given back their homes in France, or that they be allowed to enter some country where they will not be murdered, I am annoyed with them, I feel they are boring the rest of the world with their problems, they are making demands upon the rest of the world by being killed, they are disturbing everyone by being hungry and asking for the return of their property. If we could all fall through the crust of the earth and vanish in one hour, with our heroes and poets and prophets and martyrs, perhaps we would be doing the memory of the Jewish race a service. . . .

'This is how I feel today, son. I need some help. You've been to the war, you've fought and killed men, you've seen the people of other countries. Maybe you understand things that I don't understand. Maybe you see some hope somewhere. Help me. Your loving father.'

Seeger folded the letter slowly, not seeing what he was doing because the tears were burning his eyes. He walked slowly and aimlessly across the dead autumn grass of the empty field, away from the camp.

He tried to wipe away his tears, because with his eyes full and dark, he kept seeing his father and brother crouched in the old-fashioned living room in Ohio and hearing his brother, dressed in the old, discarded uniform, saying, 'These're the new rocket bombs. For the Jews.'

He sighed, looking out over the bleak, wasted land. Now, he thought, now I have to think about it. He felt a slight, unreasonable twinge of anger at his father for presenting him with the necessity of thinking about it. The army was good about serious problems. While you were fighting, you were too busy and frightened and weary to think about anything, and at other times you were relaxing, putting your brain on a shelf, postponing everything to that impossible time of clarity and beauty after the war. Well, now, here was the impossible, clear, beautiful time, and here was his father, demanding that he think. There are all sorts of Jews, he thought, there are the sort whose every waking moment is ridden by the knowledge of Jewishness, who see signs against the Jew in every smile on a streetcar, every whisper, who see pogroms in every newspaper article, threats in every change of the weather, scorn in every handshake, death behind each closed door. He had not been like that. He was young, he was big and healthy and easy-going and people of all kinds had seemed to like him all his life, in the army and out. In America, especially, what was going on in Europe had seemed remote, unreal, unrelated to him. The chanting, bearded old men burning in the Nazi furnaces, and the dark-eyed women screaming prayers in Polish and Russian and German as they were pushed naked into the gas chambers had seemed as shadowy and almost as unrelated to him as he trotted out

on to the Stadium field for a football game, as they must have been
to the men named O'Dwyer and Wickersham and Poole who
played in the line beside him.

They had seemed more related in Europe. Again and again in
the towns that had been taken back from the Germans, gaunt,
grey-faced men had stopped him humbly, looking searchingly at
him, and had asked, peering at his long, lined, grimy face, under
the anonymous helmet, 'Are you a Jew?' Sometimes they asked it
in English, sometimes French, or Yiddish. He didn't know
French or Yiddish, but he learned to recognize the phrase. He had
never understood exactly why they had asked the question, since
they never demanded anything from him, rarely even could speak
to him, until, one day in Strasbourg, a little bent old man, and a
small, shapeless woman had stopped him, and asked, in English, if
he was Jewish.

'Yes,' he said, smiling at them.

The two old people had smiled widely, like children. 'Look,' the
old man had said to his wife. 'A young American soldier. A Jew.
And so large and strong.' He had touched Seeger's arm reverently
with the tips of his fingers, then had touched the Garand he was
carrying. 'And such a beautiful rifle . . .'

And there, for a moment, although he was not particularly
sensitive, Seeger got an inkling of why he had been stopped and
questioned by so many before. Here, to these bent, exhausted old
people, ravaged of their families, familiar with flight and death for
so many years, was a symbol of continuing life. A large young man
in the uniform of the liberator, blood, as they thought, of their
blood, but not in hiding, not quivering in fear and helplessness,
but striding secure and victorious down the street, armed and
capable of inflicting terrible destruction on his enemies.

Seeger had kissed the old lady on the cheek and she had wept
and the old man had scolded her for it, while shaking Seeger's
hand fervently and thankfully before saying goodbye.

And, thinking back on it, it was silly to pretend that, even before
his father's letter, he had been like any other American soldier
going through the war. When he had stood over the huge dead S.S.
major with the face blown in by his bullets in the warehouse in
Coblenz, and taken the pistol from the dead hand, he had tasted a
strange little extra flavour of triumph. How many Jews, he'd
thought, has this man killed, how fitting it is that I've killed him.

Neither Olson nor Welch who were like his brothers, would have felt that in picking up the Luger, its barrel still hot from the last shots its owner had fired before dying. And he had resolved that he was going to make sure to take this gun back with him to America, and plug it and keep it on his desk at home, as a kind of vague, half-understood sign to himself that justice had once been done and he had been its instrument.

Maybe, he thought, maybe I'd better take it back with me, but not as a memento. Not plugged, but loaded. America by now was a strange country for him. He had been away a long time and he wasn't sure what was waiting for him when he got home. If the mobs were coming down the street towards his house, he was not going to die singing and praying.

When he was taking basic training he'd heard a scrawny, clerk-like-looking soldier from Boston talking at the other end of the PX bar, over the watered beer. 'The boys at the office,' the scratchy voice was saying, 'gave me a party before I left. And they told me one thing. "Charlie," they said, "hold on to your bayonet. We're going to be able to use it when you get back. On the Yids." '

He hadn't said anything then, because he'd felt it was neither possible nor desirable to fight against every random overheard voice raised against the Jews from one end of the world to another. But again and again, at odd moments, lying on a barracks cot, or stretched out trying to sleep on the floor of a ruined French farmhouse, he had heard that voice, harsh, satisfied, heavy with hate and ignorance, saying above the beery grumble of apprentice soldiers at the bar, 'Hold on to your bayonet. . . .'

And the other stories – Jews collected stories of hatred and injustice and inklings of doom like a special, lunatic kind of miser. The story of the naval officer, commander of a small vessel off the Aleutians, who, in the officers' wardroom, had complained that he hated the Jews because it was the Jews who had demanded that the Germans be beaten first and the forces in the Pacific had been starved in consequence. And when one of his junior officers, who had just come aboard, had objected and told the commander that he was a Jew, the commander had risen from the table and said, 'Mister, the Constitution of the United States says I have to serve in the same navy with Jews, but it doesn't say I have to eat at the same table with them.' In the fogs and the cold, swelling Arctic seas off the Aleutians, in a small boat, subject to sudden, mortal attack at any moment . . .

And the two combat engineers in an attached company on D-Day, when they were lying off the coast right before climbing down into the landing barges. 'There's France,' one of them had said.

'What's it like?' the second one had asked, peering out across the miles of water towards the smoking coast.

'Like every place else,' the first one had answered. 'The Jews've made all the dough during the war.'

'Shut up!' Seeger had said, helplessly thinking of the dead, destroyed, wandering, starving Jews of France. The engineers had shut up, and they'd climbed down together into the heaving boat, and gone into the beach together.

And the million other stories. Jews, even the most normal and best adjusted of them, became living treasuries of them, scraps of malice and bloodthirstiness, clever and confusing and cunningly twisted so that every act by every Jew became suspect and blameworthy and hateful. Seeger had heard the stories, and had made an almost conscious effort to forget them. Now, holding his father's letter in his hand, he remembered them all.

He stared unseeingly out in front of him. Maybe, he thought, maybe it would've been better to have been killed in the war, like Leonard. Simpler. Leonard would never have to face a crowd coming for his mother and father. Leonard would not have to listen and collect these hideous, fascinating little stories that made of every Jew a stranger in any town, on any field, on the face of the earth. He had come so close to being killed so many times, it would have been so easy, so neat and final.

Seeger shook his head. It was ridiculous to feel like that, and he was ashamed of himself for the weak moment. At the age of twenty-one, death was not an answer.

'Seeger!' It was Olson's voice. He and Welch had sloshed silently up behind Seeger, standing in the open field. 'Seeger, *mon vieux*, what're you doing – grazing?'

Seeger turned slowly to them. 'I wanted to read my letter,' he said.

Olson looked closely at him. They had been together so long, through so many things, that flickers and hints of expression on each other's faces were recognized and acted upon. 'Anything wrong?' Olson asked.

'No,' said Seeger. 'Nothing much.'

'Norman,' Welch said, his voice young and solemn. 'Norman, we've been talking, Olson and me. We decided – you're pretty attached to that Luger, and maybe – if you – well . . .'

'What he's trying to say,' said Olson, 'is we withdraw the request. If you want to sell it, O.K. If you don't, don't do it for our sake. Honest.'

Seeger looked at them, standing there, disreputable and tough and familiar. 'I haven't made up my mind yet,' he said.

'Anything you decide,' Welch said oratorically, 'is perfectly all right with us. Perfectly.'

They walked aimlessly and silently across the field, away from camp. As they walked, their shoes making a wet, sliding sound in the damp, dead grass, Seeger thought of the time Olson had covered him in the little town outside Cherbourg, when Seeger had been caught going down the side of a street by four Germans with a machine gun on the second storey of a house on the corner, and Olson had had to stand out in the middle of the street with no cover at all for more than a minute, firing continuously, so that Seeger could get away alive. And he thought of the time outside Saint Lô when he had been wounded and had lain in a minefield for three hours and Welch and Captain Taney had come looking for him in the darkness and had found him and picked him up and run for it, all of them expecting to get blown up any second.

And he thought of all the drinks they'd had together and the long marches and the cold winter together, and all the girls they'd gone out with together, and he thought of his father and brother crouching behind the window in Ohio waiting for the rockets and the crowds armed with Browning automatic rifles.

'Say,' he stopped and stood facing them. 'Say, what do you guys think of the Jews?'

Welch and Olson looked at each other, and Olson glanced down at the letter in Seeger's hand.

'Jews?' Olson said finally. 'What're they? Welch, you ever hear of the Jews?'

Welch looked thoughtfully at the grey sky. 'No,' he said. 'But remember, I'm an uneducated fellow.'

'Sorry, Bud,' Olson said, turning to Seeger. 'We can't help you. Ask us another question. Maybe we'll do better.'

Seeger peered at the faces of his friends. He would have to rely upon them, later on, out of uniform, on their native streets, more than he had ever relied on them on the bullet-swept street and in the dark minefield in France. Welch and Olson stared back at him, troubled, their faces candid and tough and dependable.

'What time,' Seeger asked, 'did you tell that captain you'd meet him?'

'Eight o'clock,' Welch said. 'But we don't have to go. If you have any feeling about that gun . . .'

'We'll meet him,' Seeger said. 'We can use that sixty-five bucks.'

'Listen,' Olson said, 'I know how much you like that gun and I'll feel like a heel if you sell it.'

'Forget it,' Seeger said, starting to walk again. 'What could I use it for in America?'

Vladimir Nabokov

First Love

I

In the early years of this century, a travel agency on Nevski Avenue displayed a three-foot-long model of an oak-brown international sleeping car. In delicate verisimilitude it completely outranked the painted tin of my clockwork trains. Unfortunately it was not for sale. One could make out the blue upholstery inside, the embossed leather lining of the compartment walls, their polished panels, inset mirrors, tulip-shaped reading lamps, and other maddening details. Spacious windows alternated with narrower ones, single or geminate, and some of these were of frosted glass. In a few of the compartments, the beds had been made.

The then great and glamorous Nord Express (it was never the same after World War I), consisting solely of such international cars and running but twice a week, connected St Petersburg with Paris. I would have said: directly with Paris, had passengers not been obliged to change from one train to a superficially similar one at the Russo-German frontier (Verzhbolovo-Eydtkuhnen), where the ample and lazy Russian sixty-and-a-half-inch gauge was replaced by the fifty-six-and-a-half-inch standard of Europe, and coal succeeded birch logs.

In the far end of my mind I can unravel, I think, at least five such journeys to Paris, with the Riviera or Biarritz as their ultimate destination. In 1909, the year I now single out, my two small sisters had been left at home with nurses and aunts. Wearing gloves and a travelling cap, my father sat reading a book in the

compartment he shared with our tutor. My brother and I were
separated from them by a washroom. My mother and her maid
occupied a compartment adjacent to ours. The odd one of our
party, my father's valet, Osip (whom, a decade later, the pedantic
Bolsheviks were to shoot, because he appropriated our bicycles
instead of turning them over to the nation), had a stranger for
companion.

In April of that year, Peary had reached the North Pole. In May,
Chaliapin had sung in Paris. In June, bothered by rumours of new
and better Zeppelins, the United States War Department had told
reporters of plans for an aerial Navy. In July, Blériot had flown
from Calais to Dover (with a little additional loop when he lost his
bearings). It was late August now. The firs and marshes of north-
western Russia sped by, and on the following day gave way to
German pine barrens and heather.

At a collapsible table, my mother and I played a card game called
durachki. Although it was broad daylight, our cards, a glass, and
on a different plane the locks of a suitcase were reflected in the
window. Through forest and field, and in sudden ravines, and
among scuttling cottages, those discarnate gamblers kept steadily
playing on for steadily sparkling stakes.

'*Ne budet-li, ti ved' ustal* [Haven't you had enough, aren't you
tired]?' my mother would ask, and then would be lost in thought as
she slowly shuffled the cards. The door of the compartment was
open and I could see the corridor window, where the wires – six
thin black wires – were doing their best to slant up, to ascend
skywards, despite the lightning blows dealt them by one telegraph
pole after another; but just as all six, in a triumphant swoop of
pathetic elation, were about to reach the top of the window, a
particularly vicious blow would bring them down, as low as they
had ever been, and they would have to start all over again.

When, on such journeys as these, the train changed its pace to a
dignified amble and all but grazed house fronts and shop signs, as
we passed through some big German town, I used to feel a twofold
excitement, which terminal stations could not provide. I saw a city
with its toy-like trams, linden trees, and brick walls enter the
compartment, hobnob with the mirrors, and fill to the brim the
windows on the corridor side. This informal contact between train
and city was part of the thrill. The other was putting myself in the
place of some passer-by who, I imagined, was moved as I would be

moved myself to see the long, romantic, auburn cars, with their inter-vestibular connecting curtains as black as bat wings and their metal lettering copper-bright in the low sun, unhurriedly nego-tiate an iron bridge across an everyday thoroughfare and then turn, with all windows suddenly ablaze, around a last block of houses.

There were drawbacks to those optical amalgamations. The wide-windowed dining-car, a vista of chaste bottles of mineral water, mitre-folded napkins, and dummy chocolate bars (whose wrappers – Cailler, Kohler, and so forth – enclosed nothing but wood) would be perceived at first as a cool haven beyond a consecution of reeling blue corridors; but as the meal progressed towards its fatal last course, one would keep catching the car in the act of being recklessly sheathed, lurching waiters and all, in the landscape, while the landscape itself went through a complex system of motion, the day-time moon stubbornly keeping abreast of one's plate, the distant meadows opening fanwise, the near trees sweeping up on invisible swings towards the track, a parallel rail line all at once committing suicide by anastomosis, a bank of nicitating grass, rising, rising, rising, until the little witness of mixed velocities was made to disgorge his portion of *omelette aux confitures de fraises*.

It was at night, however, that the *Compagnie Internationale des Wagons-Lits et des Grands Express Européens* lived up to the magic of its name. From my bed under my brother's bunk (Was he asleep? Was he there at all?) in the semi-darkness of our compartment, I watched things, and parts of things, and shadows, and sections of shadows cautiously moving about and getting nowhere. The woodwork gently creaked and crackled. Near the door that led to the toilet, a dim garment on a peg and, higher up, the tassel of the blue, bivalved night light swung rhythmically. It was hard to correlate those halting approaches, that hooded stealth, with the headlong rush of the outside night, which I knew *was* rushing by, spark-streaked, illegible.

I would put myself to sleep by the simple act of identifying myself with the engine driver. A sense of drowsy well-being invaded my veins as soon as I had everything nicely arranged – the carefree passengers in their rooms enjoying the ride I was giving them, smoking, exchanging knowing smiles, nodding, dozing; the waiters and cooks and train guards (whom I had to place somewhere) carousing in the diner; and myself, goggled and begrimed, peering out of the engine cab at the tapering track, at the ruby or emerald point in the black distance. And then, in my sleep, I would see something totally different – a glass marble rolling under a grand piano or a toy engine lying on its side with its wheels still working gamely.

A change in the speed of the train sometimes interrupted the current of my sleep. Slow lights were stalking by; each, in passing, investigated the same chink, and then a luminous compass measured the shadows. Presently, the train stopped with a long-drawn Westinghousian sigh. Something (my brother's spectacles, as it proved next day) fell from above. It was marvellously exciting to move to the foot of one's bed, with part of the bedclothes following, in order to undo cautiously the catch of the window shade, which could be made to slide only half-way up, impeded as it was by the edge of the upper berth.

Like moons around Jupiter, pale moths revolved about a lone lamp. A dismembered newspaper stirred on a bench. Somewhere on the train one could hear muffled voices, somebody's comfortable cough. There was nothing particularly interesting in the portion of station platform before me, and still I could not tear myself away from it until it departed of its own accord.

Next morning, wet fields with misshapen willows along the radius of a ditch or a row of poplars afar, traversed by a horizontal band of milky-white mist, told one that the train was spinning through Belgium. It reached Paris at 4 p.m.; and even if the stay was only an overnight one, I had always time to purchase something – say, a little brass Tour Eiffel, rather roughly coated with silver paint – before we boarded at noon the following day the Sud Express, which, on its way to Madrid, dropped us around 10 p.m. at the La Négresse station of Biarritz, a few miles from the Spanish frontier.

II

Biarritz still retained its quiddity in those days. Dusty blackberry bushes and weedy *terrains à vendre* bordered the road that led to our villa. The Carlton was still being built. Some thirty-six years had to elapse before Brigadier General Samuel McCroskey would occupy the royal suite of the Hotel du Palais, which stands on the site of a former palace, where, in the sixties, that incredibly agile medium, Daniel Home, is said to have been caught stroking with his bare foot (in imitation of a ghost hand) the kind, trustful face of Empress Eugénie. On the promenade near the Casino, an elderly flower-girl, with carbon eyebrows and a painted smile, nimbly slipped the plump torus of a carnation into the buttonhole of an intercepted stroller whose left jowl accentuated its royal fold as he glanced down sideways at the coy insertion of the flower.

Along the black line of the *plage*, various seaside chairs and stools supported the parents of straw-hatted children who were playing in front on the sand. I could be seen on my knees trying to set a found comb aflame by means of a magnifying-glass. Men sported white trousers that to the eye of today would look as if they had comically shrunk in the washing; ladies wore, that particular season, light coats with silk-faced lapels, hats with big crowns and wide brims, dense embroidered white veils, frill-fronted blouses, frills at their wrists, frills on their parasols. The breeze salted one's lips. At a tremendous pace a stray golden-orange butterfly came dashing across the palpitating *plage*.

Additional movement and sound were provided by vendors hawking *cacahuètes*, sugared violets, pistachio ice cream of a heavenly green, cachou pellets, and huge convex pieces of dry, gritty, waferlike stuff that came from a red barrel. With a distinctness that no later superpositions have dimmed, I see that waffle-man stomp along through deep mealy sand, with the heavy cast on his bent back. When called, he would sling it off his shoulder by a twist of its strap, bang it down on the sand in a Tower of Pisa position, wipe his face with his sleeve, and proceed to manipulate a kind of arrow-and-dial arrangement with numbers on the lid of the cask. The arrow rasped and whirred around. Luck was supposed to fix the size of a sou's worth of wafer. The bigger the piece, the more I was sorry for him.

The process of bathing took place on another part of the beach. Professional bathers, burly Basques in black bathing suits, were there to help ladies and children enjoy the terrors of the surf. Such a *baigneur* would place you with your back to the incoming wave and hold you by the hand as the rising, rotating mass of foamy, green water violently descended upon you from behind, knocking you off your feet with one mighty wallop. After a dozen of these tumbles, the *baigneur*, glistening like a seal, would lead his panting, shivering, moistly snuffling charge landward, to the flat foreshore where an unforgettable old woman with grey hairs on her chin promptly chose a bathing robe from several hanging on a clothesline. In the security of a little cabin, one would be helped by yet another attendant to peel off one's soggy, sand-heavy bathing suit. It would plop on to the boards, and, still shivering, one would step out of it and trample on its bluish, diffuse stripes. The cabin smelt of pine. The attendant, a hunchback with beaming wrinkles, brought a basin of steaming-hot water, in which one immersed one's feet. From him I learned, and have preserved ever since in a glass cell of my memory, that 'butterfly' in the Basque language is *misericoletea* – or at least it sounded so (among the seven words I have found in dictionaries the closest approach is *micheletea*).

III

On the browner and wetter part of the *plage*, that part which at low tide yielded the best mud for castles, I found myself digging, one day, side by side with a little French girl called Colette.

She would be ten in November, I had been ten in April. Attention was drawn to a jagged bit of violet mussel shell upon which she had stepped with the bare sole of her narrow long-toed foot. No, I was not English. Her greenish eyes seemed flecked with the overflow of freckles that covered her sharp-featured face. She wore what might now be termed a play-suit, consisting of a blue jersey with rolled-up sleeves and blue knitted shorts. I had taken her at first for a boy and then had been puzzled by the bracelet on her thin wrist and the corkscrew brown curls dangling from under her sailor cap.

She spoke in birdlike bursts of rapid twitter, mixing governess English and Parisian French. Two years before, on the same *plage*, I had been much attached to the lovely, sun-tanned little daughter of a Serbian physician; but when I met Colette, I knew at once that this was the real thing. Colette seemed to me so much stranger than all my other chance playmates at Biarritz! I somehow acquired the feeling that she was less happy than I, less loved. A bruise on her delicate, downy forearm gave rise to awful conjectures. 'He pinches as bad as my mummy,' she said, speaking of a crab. I evolved various schemes to save her from her parents, who were 'des bourgeois de Paris' as I heard somebody tell my mother with a slight shrug. I interpreted the disdain in my own fashion, as I knew that those people had come all the way from Paris in their blue-and-yellow limousine (a fashionable adventure in those days) but had drably sent Colette with her dog and governess by an ordinary coach train. The dog was a female fox terrier with bells on her collar and a most waggly behind. From sheer exuberance, she would lap up salt water out of Colette's toy pail. I remember the sail, the sunset, and the lighthouse pictured on that pail, but I cannot recall the dog's name and this bothers me.

During the two months of our stay at Biarritz, my passion for Colette all but surpassed my passion for butterflies. Since my parents were not keen to meet hers, I saw her only on the beach; but I thought of her constantly. If I noticed she had been crying, I felt a surge of helpless anguish that brought tears to my eyes. I could not destroy the mosquitoes that had left their bites on her frail neck, but I could, and did, have a successful fist fight with a red-haired boy who had been rude to her. She used to give me warm handfuls of hard candy. One day, as we were bending together over a starfish, and Colette's ringlets were tickling my ear, she suddenly turned towards me and kissed me on the cheek. So great was my emotion that all I could think of saying was, 'You little monkey.'

I had a gold coin that I assumed would pay for our elopement. Where did I want to take her? Spain? America? The mountains above Pau? '*Là-bas, là-bas, dans la montagne,*' as I had heard Carmen sing at the opera. One strange night, I lay awake, listening to the recurrent thud of the ocean and planning our flight. The ocean seemed to rise and grope in the darkness and then heavily fall on its face.

Of our actual getaway, I have little to report. My memory retains a glimpse of her obediently putting on rope-soled canvas shoes, on the lee side of a flapping tent, while I stuffed a folding butterfly net into a brown paper bag. The next glimpse is of our evading pursuit by entering a pitch-dark *cinéma* near the Casino (which, of course, was absolutely out of bounds). There we sat, holding hands across the dog, which now and then gently jingled in Colette's lap, and were shown a jerky, drizzly, but highly exciting bullfight at St Sebástian. My final glimpse is of myself being led along the promenade by my tutor. His long legs move with a kind of ominous briskness and I can see the muscles of his grimly set jaw working under the tight skin. My bespectacled brother, aged nine, whom he happens to hold with his other hand, keeps trotting out forward to peer at me with awed curiosity, like a little owl.

Among the trivial souvenirs acquired at Biarritz before leaving, my favourite was not the small bull of black stone and not the sonorous sea-shell but something which now seems almost symbolic – a meerschaum penholder with a tiny peephole of crystal in its ornamental part. One held it quite close to one's eye, screwing up the other, and when one had got rid of the shimmer of one's own lashes, a miraculous photographic view of the bay and of the line of cliffs ending in a lighthouse could be seen inside.

And now a delightful thing happens. The process re-creating that penholder and the microcosm in its eyelet stimulates my memory to a last effort. I try again to recall the name of Colette's dog – and, sure enough, along those remote beaches, over the glossy evening sands of the past, where each footprint slowly fills up with sunset water, here it comes, here it comes, echoing and vibrating: Floss, Floss, Floss!

Colette was back in Paris by the time we stopped there for a day before continuing our homeward journey; and there, in a fawn park under a cold blue sky, I saw her (by arrangement between our mentors, I believe) for the last time. She carried a hoop and a short stick to drive it with, and everything about her was extremely proper and stylish in an autumnal, Parisian, *tenue-de-ville-pour-fillettes* way. She took from her governess and slipped into my brother's hand a farewell present, a box of sugar-coated almonds, meant, I knew, solely for me; and instantly she was off, tap-tapping her glinting hoop through light and shade, around and around a fountain choked with dead leaves near where I stood. The leaves mingle in my memory with the leather of her shoes and gloves, and there was, I remember, some detail in her attire (perhaps a ribbon on her Scottish cap, or the pattern of her stockings) that reminded me then of the rainbow spiral in a glass marble. I still seem to be holding that wisp of iridescence, not knowing exactly where to fit it in, while she runs with her hoop ever faster around me and finally dissolves among the slender shadows cast on the gravelled path by the interlaced arches of its low looped fence.

Angus Wilson

Fresh Air Fiend

It had rained heavily the night before and many of the flowers in the herbaceous border lay flattened and crushed upon the ground. The top-heavy oriental poppies had fared worst; their hairy stalks were broken and twisted, and their pink and scarlet petals were scattered around like discarded material in a dressmaker's shop. But they were poor blowsy creatures anyway, thought Mrs Searle; the vulgar and the ostentatious survive few blows. Nevertheless she chose sticks and bast from the large trug which she trailed behind her, and carefully tied the bent heads, cutting off the broken ones with the secateurs. It was at once one of the shames and one of the privileges of gardening, she thought, that one was put in this godlike position of judgment, deciding upon what should live and what should be cast into outer darkness, delivering moral judgments and analogies. It was only by a careful compensation, an act of retribution, such as preserving the poppies she had condemned, that she could avoid too great an arrogance. She fingered the velvety leaves of the agrostemma sensuously, there were so few flowers of exactly that shade of rich crimson, and how gloriously they lay against their silver foliage. There should be more of them next year – but less, she decided, of the scarlet lychnis, there was nothing more disappointing than a flower spike on which too few blooms appeared. Ragged, meagre and dowdy for all their bright colours, like the wife of the Warden of St Jude's. How depressing that one still remembered that dispiriting little woman sitting there talking in her slight North-country accent, and dressed in that absurd scarlet suit.

'Your signature on this petition, Mrs Searle, would be such a help. If we University women can give a lead . . . I mean we've all too easily decided that war is inevitable, it's only by thinking so that we make it, you know.' 'Of course,' she had found herself answering mockingly, 'who can understand that better than I? You don't remember the last war, but I do. Those hundreds of Belgians, each without a right arm. Oh! it was terrible.' The ridiculous little woman had looked so puzzled that she had been unable to resist embroidering. 'Don't you know Belgium then?' she had said. 'Not a man there today with a right arm, and very few with right eyes. Those were all gouged out with hot irons before the Kaiser himself. To make a Roman holiday, of course.' The woman had gone away offended. Silly little creature, with all her petitions she had been most anxious to prove her ardour in the war when it came, although of course like everyone in Oxford she had been perfectly safe. How they had all talked of the terrible raids, and how they had all kept out of them. At least she had preserved her integrity. 'Thousands killed brutally in London last night,' she had said to the Master, 'and every one of us preserved intact. What a glorious mercy!' They thought she was mad, and so she was, of course, judged by their wretched middle-class norm. 'I hereby faithfully swear once more,' she said aloud, 'that I will make no compromise, and I utterly curse them from henceforth. May no wife of any fellow in either of the major Universities be fecund, nor may the illicit unions of research students be blessed,' and she added maliciously, 'May the stream of sherry so foolishly imported by this present government be dried up, so that there may be no more "little sherry parties".' It was monstrous when things of importance – spirits for example – were in short demand – though what such jargon really meant one was at a loss to understand – that such frivolities as sherry parties should be indulged.

Suddenly she could hear that other voice inside her speaking slowly and distinctly, counting in the old, familiar fashion – two bottles of gin in the trunk in the attic, two in the garden shed, one in the bureau, she had the key to that, and then one in the bottom of her wardrobe with the shell mending box. The bureau one was a bit risky, Henry occasionally used that, but with the key in her possession . . . six bottles in all. I'll send Henry down with that girl to the pub for a drink before lunch and they'll be out walking this afternoon, she decided. It had seemed as though the girl's presence would make things difficult, Henry had obviously hoped so when he had invited her, but by retiring early and leaving them to talk it had been managed . . .

The voice shut off and Mrs Searle gave zealous attention to the flowers once more. The clumps of lupins were massed like an overpainted sunset – anchovy, orange and lemon against sky-blue – only the very tops of their spikes had been bent and hung like dripping candles. The crests of the delphiniums were broken too, and the petals lay around pale ice-blue and dark blue like scattered Boat-Race favours. Mrs Searle shrank back as she surveyed the tall verbascums; their yellow flowers were covered in caterpillars, many of which had been drowned or smashed by the rain, their bodies now dried and blackening in the hot sun. 'Miss Eccles, Miss Eccles,' she called, 'are you good with caterpillars?'

A very tall young woman got up from a deck-chair on the lawn and moved lopingly across to the flower-bed; the white linen trousers seemed to accentuate her lumbering gait and her ungainly height; her thin white face was cut sharply by the line of her hard, vermilion lipstick; her straight, green-gold hair was worn long at the neck. 'I'll see what I can do, Mrs Searle,' she said, and began rapidly to pick off the insects. 'But you *are* good with caterpillars,' said Miranda Searle. 'It's a gift, of course, like being good with children. I'm glad to say that I hold each in equal abhorrence. Don't you think the verbascum very beautiful? I do, but then it's natural I *should* like them. I share their great quality of spikiness.' If you were covered with caterpillars, thought Elspeth Eccles, I wouldn't budge an inch to remove them, I should laugh like hell. She had always believed that absolute sincerity was the only basis for human relationships, and she felt convinced that a little truth telling would work wonders with Mrs Searle's egotistical arti- ficiality, but somehow she shrank from the experiment of telling her hostess what she really thought of her spikiness, there was no doubt that for all her futility and selfishness she was a little daunting. It was the difference of age, of course, and the unfair superiority of riches, but still she preferred to change the topic. 'What are those red and blue flowers with the light foliage?' she asked. 'Linum,' replied Mrs Searle. 'You know – "Thou wilt not quench the burning flax, nor hurt the bruiséd reed," only that doesn't sound quite right.' 'It certainly seems a little meaningless,' commented Elspeth. 'Oh! I should hope so,' said Mrs Searle. 'It's religious. You surely wouldn't wish a religious sentiment to have a meaning. It wouldn't be at all edifying. I doubt if it would even be proper.' Elspeth smiled to herself in the conviction of her own private creed. 'No, it's the phrase "bruiséd reed" that I detest,' said Mrs Searle. 'It reminds me too much of "broken reed". Have you ever been in the W.V.S.?' she went on. 'Oh blessed generation! Well, *I* have. Henry made me join the Oxford W.V.S. during the war, he said it was my duty. A curious sort of duty, I did nothing but serve cups of sweet dishwater to men with bad teeth. But what I was thinking of was the way all the women talked in clichés – throughout the winter they described themselves as "chilly mortals", and whenever anyone failed to do some particularly absurd task, as I frequently did, they called them "broken reeds". But I am keeping you from your work, Miss Eccles,' she went on, 'and Henry will never forgive that. It must be wonderful for you both to have a common interest in so many vulgar people. Though perhaps in the case of the Shelley circle, as I believe it's called – it is Shelley you're working on?' – it was the seventh time in five days that she had asked the question, Elspeth noted – 'as I say in the case of the Shelleys it is more their priggish refinement than their vulgarity that revolts me.'

'Perhaps it's their basic honesty you dislike,' said Elspeth. 'Very likely,' said Mrs Searle, 'I hadn't realized that they were particularly honest. But if that were so, of course, I should certainly dislike it. How very nice it must be to know things, Miss Eccles, and go about hitting nails on the head like that. But seriously, you mustn't let me keep you from the Shelleys and their orgy of honesty.' On Elspeth's assurance that she would like to remain with her, Mrs Searle suggested that they should go together to gather gooseberries in the kitchen garden.

Elspeth watched her depart to collect a basin from the house. It was difficult, she thought, to believe that people had once spoken of her as the 'incomparable Miranda'. Of course the very use of such names suggested an affected gallantry for which the world no longer had time, but, apart from that, the almost Belsen-like emaciation of figure and features, the wild, staring eyes and the wispy hair that defied control hardly suggested a woman who had inspired poets and tempted young diplomats; a woman whose influence had reached beyond University society to the world of literary London, rivalling even Ottoline Morrell herself. A faint look of distressed beauty about the haggard eyes, an occasional turn of the head on that swanlike neck, were all that remained to recall her famed beauty, and even these reminded one too much of the Lavery portraits. No, decidedly, she thought, it was all too easily described by one of Mrs Searle's own favourite words – 'grotesque'. Of the famous charm too, there were only rare flashes, and how like condescension it was when it came, as in some ornate fairy story of the Nineties when the princess gives one glimpse of heaven to the poor poet as her coach passes by. That may have been how Rupert Brooke and Flecker liked things, but it wouldn't have done today. That crabbed irony and soured, ill-natured malice, those carefully administered snubs to inferiors and juniors, could that have been the wit that had made her the friend of Firbank and Lytton Strachey? It seemed impossible that people could have tolerated such arrogance, have been content with such triviality. It was unfair, probably, to judge a galleon by a washed-up wreck. There was no doubt that at some period Miranda Searle had strayed, was definitely *détraquée*. Even her old friends in Oxford had dropped her, finding the eccentricity, the egotism, the rudeness insupportable. But to Elspeth it seemed that such a decline could not be excused by personal grief, other mothers had had only sons killed in motor accidents and had lived again, other women had been confined to provincial lives and had kept their charity. It was monstrous that a man of the intellectual calibre of Henry Searle, a man whose work was so important, should be chained to this living corpse. She had heard stories already of Mrs Searle's secret drinking and had been told of some of the humiliating episodes in which she had involved her husband, but it was not until this visit to their Somerset cottage that she had realized how continuous, how slowly wearing his slavery must be. On the very first night she had heard from her bedroom a voice raised in obscenities, a maundering whine. She had guessed – how right she had been – that this was one of the famous drinking bouts. It had enabled her to see clearly why it was that Henry Searle was slowly withdrawing from University life, why the publication of the last volume of Peacock's letters was delayed from year to year, why the projected life of Mary Shelley remained a dream. It was her duty, she had decided then, to aid him in fighting the incubus, her duty to English letters, her return for all the help he had given to her own labours. But how difficult it was to help anyone so modest and retiring, anyone who had evaded life for so long. She had decided, at last, that it would be easier to start the other end, to put the issue fairly and squarely before Mrs Searle herself. If there was any truth in the excuse of her defenders, if it was in fact the shock of her son's sudden death, then surely she could be made to see that the living could not be sacrificed to the dead in that way. And yet, and yet, one hesitated to speak; it was the last day of the visit and nothing had been said. 'It's now or never, Elspeth Eccles,' she said aloud.

'My dear Miss Eccles,' her hostess drawled. 'How this cheers me! To hear you talk to yourself. I was just beginning to feel daunted. Here she is, I thought, the representative of the "hungry generations" – straightforward, ruled by good sense, with no time for anything but the essential – and they're going to "tread me down". How can I? I thought, with all my muddled thinking and my inhibitions – only the other day that new, young physics tutor was telling me about them – how can I resist them? It seemed almost inhuman! And then I hear you talking to yourself. It's all right. I breathe again. The chink in another's armour, the mote in our brother's eyes, how precious they are! what preservers of Christian charity!'

'That doesn't sound a very well-adjusted view of life,' said Elspeth, in what she hoped was a friendly and humorous voice.

'Doesn't it?' said Miranda. 'So many people say that to me and I'm sure you're all quite right. Only the words don't seem to connect in my mind and I do think that's so important, in deciding whether to think a thing or not, I mean. If I don't connect the words, then I just don't have the thought. And "adjusted" never connects with "life" for me, only with "shoulder strap".'

With her wide-brimmed straw hat, flowing-sleeved chiffon dress, and her constantly shaking long earrings, Mrs Searle looked like a figure at the Theatrical Garden Party. Laying down the box of Army and Navy Stores cigarettes which was her constant companion, she began rapidly to pick the gooseberries from the thorny bushes.

'Put them all into that bowl, will you,' she said, a cigarette hanging from the corner of her mouth. 'I want Mrs Parry to make a fool so we shall need a good number of them.'

'Why do you need more to make a fool?' asked Elspeth. 'Because of the sieving,' said Miranda shortly and contemptuously.

The two women picked on in silence for some minutes. To Elspeth, it seemed that her own contribution was immensely the smaller; it seemed impossible that with those absurd, flowing sleeves and the smoke from that perpetual cigarette Mrs Searle could pick with such ease. Her own fingers were constantly being pricked by the thorns and the legs of her trousers got caught against the bushes.

'Poor Miss Eccles!' said Miranda. 'You must stop at once or you'll ruin those lovely trousers. It was quite naughty of me to have suggested your doing such a horrid job in such beautiful clothes.' Elspeth was crouching to pick some refractory fruit from a very low bush, but she stood up and remained quite still for a moment, then in a clear, deliberate voice, she said:

'Now, you don't think they're beautiful clothes at all, Mrs Searle. You probably think trousers on women are the height of ugliness, and in any case they cannot compare for elegance with your lovely dress. It's just that I'm clumsy and awkward in my movements, and you are graceful and easy. What makes you unable to say what you think of me?'

Mrs Searle did not answer the question, instead she stared at the girl with rounded eyes, then throwing her cigarette on the ground she stamped it into the earth with her heel.

'Oh Miss Eccles,' she cried, 'how lovely you look! Now I understand why Henry admires you so. You look so handsome, so noble when you are being stern just like Mary Wollstonecraft or Dorothy Wordsworth or one of those other great women who inspire poets and philosophers.'

'How can you say that, Mrs Searle?' cried Elspeth. 'You who knew and inspired so many of our writers.'

'Oh no!' said Miranda. 'I never inspired anyone, I just kept them amused. I was far too busy enjoying life to *inspire* anyone.'

'Then why can't you go on enjoying life now?'

'Oh! Miss Eccles, how charming of you! I do believe you're paying me a compliment, you're being sincere with me and treating me as one of your own generation. But you forget that "you cannot teach an old dog new tricks." And now look what you've done, you've made me use an ugly, vulgar proverb.' 'I don't think it's a question of generations,' said Elspeth, 'it's just a matter of preferring to have things straight instead of crooked. Anyway if people of my age are more straightforward it's only because we've grown up in a world of wars and economic misery where there's only time for essentials.'

Mrs Searle looked at her with amusement. 'If it comes to essentials,' she said, 'elegance and beauty seem to me far more essential than wars.'

'Of course they are,' said Elspeth, 'but they can't have any reality until we've straightened out the muddle and misery in the world.'

'In the world?' echoed Miranda. 'I should have thought one's own private miseries were enough.'

'Poor Mrs Searle,' said Elspeth, 'it must have hit you very badly. Were you very fond of him? Did they break the news clumsily? Won't you tell me about it?' And she wondered as she said it whether she did not sound a little too much as though she were speaking to a child, but after all the woman was a child emotionally, a child that was badly in need of re-education.

Miranda stopped picking for a minute and straightened herself; when she looked at Elspeth, she was laughing.

'Oh my dear Miss Eccles! I do believe you're trying to get me to "share". And I never even guessed that you were a Grouper.'

'I'm not a Grouper,' said Elspeth. 'I'm not even what you would call religious, that is I don't believe in God,' she added lamely.

But Miranda Searle took no notice. 'Oh what fun!' she cried. 'Now you can tell me all about those house-parties and the dreadful things that people confess to. I've always wanted to hear about that. I remember when the Dean of St Mary's shared once. He got up in public and said that he'd slept with his niece. It wasn't true, of course, because I know for a fact that he's impotent. But still it was rather sweet of him, because she's a terribly plain girl and it gave her a sexual cachet that brought her wild successes. After that I went through Oxford inventing the most wonderful things that I said people had shared with me until I was threatened with libel by the entire Theological Faculty.'

'Oh, it's quite impossible,' said Elspeth and in her agitation she overturned the bowl of gooseberries. She felt glad to hide her scarlet face and her tears of vexation in an agitated attempt to pick them up.

'Oh please, please,' said Miranda. 'It couldn't matter less.' At that moment the tweed-clothed, knickerbockered figure of Mr Searle came down the path towards them. 'Henry,' called his wife. 'Henry, you never told me Miss Eccles was a "Grouper". She was just going to share with me, and it must have been something very exciting because it made her upset the gooseberries. Take her down to the pub for a drink. That's just the place for a good man-to-man sharing. Perhaps you can get that barmaid to tell you what goes on in Hodge's field, or Mr Ratcliffe might even confess about that poor goat. Whatever you find out you must report to me at once.'

Mr Searle put down his glass of port, and drawing his handkerchief from the sleeve into which it was tucked, he carefully wiped his neatly trimmed grey moustache. With his well-worn dinner jacket and his old patent leather pumps he looked far more like a retired military man or an impoverished country squire than a Professor of English Poetry, and so he would have wished it. The evening had been hot and the French windows had been left open; a cool night breeze had begun to invade the room. Now that Mrs Searle had gone upstairs Elspeth felt able to put her little blue woollen coat round her shoulders. She had decided to wear an evening dress as a concession to her host's formality, and yet it was largely the presence of her hostess with her long brocade gown that had kept her to the decision after the first evening. She felt sad that this was the last of their talks together – talks which she enjoyed all the more for the elegance of the room and the glass of kümmel which he was careful to pour out for her each evening, though she felt that to admit to such sensual pleasure was in some sense a capitulation to Miranda's influence in the house. But once her hostess had retired, the sense of strain was gone and she could adopt a certain hedonism as of her own right. No doubt he would have to face the same sordid scene tonight, no doubt he would have to face such bouts on and off until that woman died. She had failed lamentably this morning to achieve anything. But, at least, their discussions together had freed him from the strain, had allowed him to relax. I shall try once more, she thought, to make him talk about it, to impress upon him that his work is too important to be shelved for someone else's selfishness, that he must assert himself. This time I must act more subtly, less directly.

'There seems no doubt,' she said, 'that the Naples birth certificate is genuine. A child was born to Shelley by someone other than Mary, and that person could hardly have been Claire

Clairmont, despite all Byron's ugly gossip. The question is, who was the mother?'

'Yes,' said Professor Searle. 'It's a mystery which I don't suppose will be solved, like many others in Shelley's life. I sometimes doubt whether we have any right to solve them. Oh! don't think I'm denying the importance of the biographical element in literary appreciation. I know very well how much a full knowledge of a writer's life, yes, I suppose even of his unconscious life, adds to the interpretation of his work; particularly, of course, with any writers so fundamentally subjective as the Romantics. But I'm more and more disinclined to expose skeletons that have been so carefully buried. I suppose it's a reticence that comes with old age,' he added.

'I doubt if it's a defensible standpoint,' said Elspeth. 'Think of the importance of Mary Shelley's relations with Hogg and with Peacock, what a lot they explain of Shelley's own amoral standpoint towards married fidelity. Or again, how much of Leigh Hunt's instability and failure can be put down to the drain of his wife's secret drinking.'

'Yes, I suppose so,' said Professor Searle. 'But when one appreciates a man's work deeply, it means in the long run respecting him and respecting his wishes. You see it isn't only the revealing of facts that have been carefully hidden, it's our interpretation that may be so vitally wrong, that would hurt the dead so. We blame Mary for her infidelity and Mrs Hunt for her insobriety, but who knows if that is not exactly the thing that Shelley and Hunt would most have hated? Who knows if they did not hold themselves responsible?'

Elspeth spoke quite abruptly. 'Do you hold yourself responsible for *your* wife's drinking?' she asked.

Professor Searle drained his glass of port slowly, then he said, 'I've been afraid that this would happen. I think you have made a mistake in asking such a question. Oh! I know you will say I am afraid of the truth, but I still think there are things that are better left unsaid. But now that you have asked me I must answer – yes, in a large degree, yes.'

'How? how?' said Elspeth impatiently.

'My wife was a very beautiful woman and a very brilliant one. Not the brilliance that belongs to the world of scholars, the narrow and often pretentious world of Universities, but to a wider society of people who act as well as think. Don't imagine that I do not fully recognize the defects of this wider world – it is an arrogant world, placing far too great a value upon what it vaguely calls "experience", too often resorting to action to conceal its poor and shoddy thinking; as a young scholar married to a woman of this world its faults were all too apparent to me. Nevertheless, however I may have been a fish out of water there, it was her world and because I was afraid of it, because I did not shine there, I cut her off from it, and in so doing I embittered her, twisted her character. There were other factors, of course, the shock of our boy's death did not help, and then there were other things,' he added hurriedly, 'things perhaps more important.'

'Well, I think that's all fudge,' said Elspeth. 'You have something important to give and you've allowed her selfish misery to suck your vitality until now it is doubtful whether you will ever write any more.'

'I am going to do the unforgivable,' said Professor Searle. 'I am going to tell you that you are still very young. I doubt if my wife's tragedy has prevented me from continuing to write, though I *could* excuse my laziness in that way. What takes place between my wife and me has occurred so often now, the pattern is so stereotyped, that, awful though it may be, my mind, yes, and my feelings have become hardened to the routine. To you, even though it is only guessed at, or perhaps for that very reason, it will seem far more awful than it can ever again seem to me. That is why, although I had hoped that your visit might help the situation, I soon realized that pleasant as it had been and I shall always remember our discussions, the presence of a third person, the possibility that you might be a spectator, was weighing upon me heavily.' He lit a cigarette and sat back in silence. Why did I say that? he thought, I ought first to have crossed my fingers. So far we have avoided any scene in the presence of this girl, but by mentioning the possibility I was tempting Providence. This evening too, when the danger is almost over, and yet so near, for Miranda had clearly already been drinking when dinner was served, and these scenes come about so suddenly.

'Well, my dear,' he said, 'I think we had better retire. Don't worry, perhaps I shall finish the Peacock letters this long vacation. Who knows? I've got plenty of notes and plenty of time. And, please, whatever I may have said, remember that your visit has been a most delightful event in my life.'

But he had made his decision too late. In the doorway stood Miranda Searle, swaying slightly, her face flushed, her hand clutching the door lintel in an effort to steady herself,

'Still sharing?' she asked in a thick voice, then she added with a coarse familiarity. 'You'll have to stop bloody soon or we'll never get to sleep.' Her husband got up from his chair. 'We're just coming,' he said quietly. Miranda Searle leant against the doorway and laughed; points of light seemed to be dancing in her eyes as malice gleamed forth. 'Darling,' she drawled in her huskiest tones, 'the "we" sounds faintly improper, or are we to carry the sharing principle to the point of bed?'

Elspeth hoisted her great height from the chair and stood awkwardly regarding her hostess for a second. 'That's a very cheap and disgusting remark,' she said. Henry Searle seemed to have lost all life, he bent down and touched a crack in his patent leather slippers. But the malicious gleam in Miranda's eyes faded, leaving them cold and hard. 'Washing dirty linen in public is disgusting,' she said, and as she spoke her mouth seemed to slip sideways. 'Not that there's much to share. You're welcome to it all. He's no great cop, you know.' She managed by the force of her voice to make the slang expression sound like an obscenity. 'I pumped one kid out of him, but it finished him as a man.'

Professor Searle seemed to come alive again, his hand went out in protest; but his resurrection was too slow, before he could cross the room Elspeth had sprung from her chair. Towering over the other woman she slapped her deliberately across the face, then putting her hands on her shoulders she began to shake her.

'You ought to be put away,' she said. 'Put away where you can do no more harm.'

Miranda Searle lurched to get free of the girl's grasp, her long bony hands came up to tear at the girl's arms, but in moving she caught her heel in the rose brocade skirt and slipped ridiculously to the ground. The loss of dignity seemed to remove all her fury, she sat in a limp heap, the tears streaming from her eyes. 'If they'd left me my boy, he wouldn't have let this happen to me,' she went on repeating. Her husband helped her to her feet and, taking her by the elbow, he led her from the room. Elspeth could hear her voice moaning in the corridor. 'Why did they take him away? What have I done to be treated in this way?' and the Professor's voice soothing, pacifying, reassuring.

*

It was many weeks later when Elspeth returned to Oxford. She spent the first evening of term with Kenneth Orme, the Steffansson Reader in Old Norse, also an ex-pupil of Professor Searle. To him she felt able to disclose the whole story of that fateful evening.

'. . . I didn't wait to see either of them the next morning,' she ended. 'I just packed my bag and stole out. I do not wish ever to see her again, and he, I felt, would have been embarrassed. It may be even that I have had to sacrifice his friendship in order to help.' Elspeth hoped that her voice sounded calm, that Kenneth could not guess what this conclusion meant to her. 'All the same whatever the cost I think it did some good. Drunk as she was I think she realized that there were some people with whom she could not play tricks, who were quite prepared to give her what she deserved. At any rate, it let a breath of fresh air into a very fetid atmosphere.'

Kenneth Orme looked at her with curiosity. 'Breaths of air can be rather dangerous,' he said. 'People catch chills from them, you know, and sometimes they are fatal chills.'

'Oh, no fear of that with Miranda Searle,' said Elspeth. 'I wish there was, but she's far too tough.'

'I wasn't thinking of Mrs Searle,' replied Kenneth. 'I was thinking of the Professor. He's not returning this term, you know. He's had a complete breakdown.'

Anthony Boucher

The Quest for St Aquin

The Bishop of Rome, the head of the Holy, Catholic and Apostolic Church, the Vicar of Christ on Earth – in short, the Pope – brushed a cockroach from the filth-encrusted wooden table, took another sip of the raw red wine, and resumed his discourse.

'In some respects, Thomas,' he smiled, 'we are stronger now than when we flourished in the liberty and exaltation for which we still pray after Mass. We know, as they knew in the catacombs, that those who are of our flock are indeed truly of it; that they belong to Holy Mother the Church because they believe in the brotherhood of man under the fatherhood of God – not because they can further their political aspirations, their social ambitions, their business contacts.'

' "Not of the will of flesh, nor of the will of man, but of God . . ." ' Thomas quoted softly from St John.

The Pope nodded. 'We are, in a way, born again in Christ; but there are still too few of us – too few even if we include those other handfuls who are not of our faith, but still acknowledge God through the teachings of Luther or Lao-tse, Gautama Buddha or Joseph Smith. Too many men still go to their deaths hearing no gospel preached to them but the cynical self-worship of the Technarchy. And that is why, Thomas, you must go forth on your quest.'

'But Your Holiness,' Thomas protested, 'if God's word and God's love will not convert them, what can saints and miracles do?'

'I seem to recall,' murmured the Pope, 'that God's own Son once made a similar protest. But human nature, however illogical it may seem, is part of His design, and we must cater to it. If signs and

wonders can lead souls to God, then by all means let us find the
signs and wonders. And what can be better for the purpose than
this legendary Aquin? Come now, Thomas; be not too scrupulously exact in copying the doubts of your namesake, but prepare
for your journey.'

The Pope lifted the skin that covered the doorway and passed
into the next room, with Thomas frowning at his heels. It was past
legal hours and the main room of the tavern was empty. The
swarthy innkeeper roused from his doze to drop to his knees and
kiss the ring on the hand that the Pope extended to him. He rose
crossing himself and at the same time glancing furtively about as
though a Loyalty Checker might have seen him. Silently he
indicated another door in the back, and the two priests passed
through.

Towards the west the surf purred in an oddly gentle way at the
edges of the fishing village. Towards the south the stars were sharp
and bright; towards the north they dimmed a little in the persistent
radiation of what had once been San Francisco.

'Your steed is here,' the Pope said, with something like laughter
in his voice.

'Steed?'

'We may be as poor and as persecuted as the primitive Church,
but we can occasionally gain greater advantages from our tyrants. I
have secured for you a robass – gift of a leading Technarch who,
like Nicodemus, does good by stealth – a secret convert, and
converted indeed by that very Aquin whom you seek.'

It looked harmlessly like a woodpile sheltered against possible
rain. Thomas pulled off the skins and contemplated the sleek
functional lines of the robass. Smiling, he stowed his minimal gear
into its panniers and climbed into the foam saddle. The starlight
was bright enough so that he could check the necessary coordinates on his map and feed the data into the electronic controls.

Meanwhile there was a murmur of Latin in the still night air,
and the Pope's hand moved over Thomas in the immemorial
symbol. Then he extended that hand, first for the kiss on the ring,
and then again for the handclasp of a man to a friend he may never
see again.

Thomas looked back once as the robass moved off. The Pope
was wisely removing his ring and slipping it into the hollow heel of
his shoe.

Thomas looked hastily up at the sky. On that altar at least the candles still burned openly to the glory of God.

Thomas had never ridden a robass before, but he was inclined, within their patent limitations, to trust the works of the Technarchy. After several miles had proved that the coordinates were duly registered, he put up the foam back-rest, said his evening office (from memory; the possession of a breviary meant the death sentence), and went to sleep.

They were skirting the devastated area to the east of the bay when he awoke. The foam seat and back had given him his best sleep in years, and it was with difficulty that he smothered an envy of the Technarchs and their creature comforts.

He said his morning office, breakfasted lightly, and took his first opportunity to inspect the robass in full light. He admired the fast-plodding, articulated legs, so necessary since roads had degenerated to, at best, trails in all save metropolitan areas; the side wheels that could be lowered into action if surface conditions permitted; and above all the smooth black mound that housed the electronic brain – the brain that stored commands and data concerning ultimate objectives and made its own decisions on how to fulfil those commands in view of those data; the brain that made this thing neither a beast, like the ass his Saviour had ridden, nor a machine, like the jeep of his many-times-great-grandfather, but a robot . . . a robass.

'Well,' said a voice, 'what do you think of the ride.'

Thomas looked about him. The area on this fringe of desolation was as devoid of people as it was of vegetation.

'Well,' the voice repeated unemotionally. 'Are not priests taught to answer when spoken to politely.'

There was no querying inflection to the question. No inflection at all – each syllable was at the same dead level. It sounded strange, mechani—

Thomas stared at the black mound of brain. 'Are you talking to me?' he asked the robass.

'Ha, ha,' the voice said in lieu of laughter. 'Surprised, are you not.'

'Somewhat,' Thomas confessed. 'I thought the only robots who could talk were in library information service, and such.'

'I am a new model. Designed-to-provide-conversation-to-entertain-the-way-worn-traveller,' the robass said, slurring the words together as though that phrase of promotional copy was released all at once by one of his simplest binary synapses.

'Well,' said Thomas simply. 'One keeps learning new marvels.'

'I am no marvel. I am a very simple robot. You do not know much about robots do you.'

'I will admit that I have never studied the subject closely. I'll confess to being a little shocked at the whole robotic concept. It seems almost as though man were arrogating to himself the powers of—' Thomas stopped abruptly.

'Do not fear,' the voice droned on. 'You may speak freely. All data concerning your vocation and mission have been fed into me. That was necessary otherwise I might inadvertently betray you.'

Thomas smiled. 'You know,' he said, 'this might be rather pleasant – having one other being that one can talk to without fear of betrayal, aside from one's confessor.'

'Being,' the robass repeated. 'Are you not in danger of lapsing into heretical thoughts.'

'To be sure, it *is* a little difficult to know how to think of you – one who can talk and think but has no soul.'

'Are you sure of that.'

'Of course I— Do you mind very much,' Thomas asked, 'if we stop talking for a little while? I should like to meditate and adjust myself to the situation.'

'I do not mind. I never mind. I only obey. Which is to say that I *do* mind. This is a very confusing language which has been fed into me.'

'If we are together long,' said Thomas, 'I shall try teaching you Latin. I think you might like that better. And now let me meditate.'

The robass was automatically veering farther east to escape the permanent source of radiation which had been the first cyclotron. Thomas fingered his coat. The combination of ten small buttons and one large made for a peculiar fashion; but it was much safer than carrying a rosary, and fortunately the Loyalty Checkers had not yet realized the fashion's functional purpose.

The Glorious Mysteries seemed appropriate to the possible glorious outcome of his venture; but his meditations were unable to stay fixedly on the Mysteries. As he murmured his *Aves* he was thinking:

If the prophet Balaam conversed with his ass, surely I may converse with my robass. Balaam has always puzzled me. He was not an Israelite; he was a man of Moab, which worshipped Baal and was warring against Israel; and yet he was a prophet of the Lord. He blessed the Israelites when he was commanded to curse them; and for his reward he was slain by the Israelites when they triumphed over Moab. The whole story has no shape, no moral; it is as though it was there to say that there are portions of the Divine Plan which we will never understand . . .

He was nodding in the foam seat when the robass halted abruptly, rapidly adjusting itself to exterior data not previously fed into its calculations. Thomas blinked up to see a giant of a man glaring down at him.

'Inhabited area a mile ahead,' the man barked. 'If you're going there, show your access pass. If you ain't, steer off the road and stay off.'

Thomas noted that they were indeed on what might roughly be called a road, and that the robass had lowered its side wheels and retracted its legs. 'We—' he began, then changed it to 'I'm not going there. Just on towards the mountains. We— I'll steer around.'

The giant grunted and was about to turn when a voice shouted from the crude shelter at the roadside. 'Hey Joe! Remember about robasses!'

Joe turned back. 'Yeah, tha's right. Been a rumour about some robass got into the hands of Christians.' He spat on the dusty road. 'Guess I better see an ownership certificate.'

To his other doubts Thomas now added certain uncharitable suspicions as to the motives of the Pope's anonymous Nicodemus, who had not provided him with any such certificate. But he made a pretence of searching for it, first touching his right hand to his forehead as if in thought, then fumbling low on his chest, then reaching his hand first to his left shoulder, then to his right.

The guard's eyes remained blank as he watched this furtive version of the sign of the cross. Then he looked down. Thomas followed his gaze to the dust of the road, where the guard's hulking right foot had drawn the two curved lines which a child uses for its first sketch of a fish – and which the Christians in the catacombs had employed as a punning symbol of their faith. His boot scuffed out the fish as he called to his unseen mate. ' 'S okay, Fred!' and added, 'Get going, mister.'

The robass waited until they were out of earshot before it observed, 'Pretty smart. You will make a secret agent yet.'

'How did you see what happened?' Thomas asked. 'You don't have any eyes.'

'Modified psi factor. Much more efficient.'

'Then . . .' Thomas hesitated. 'Does that mean you can read my thoughts?'

'Only a very little. Do not let it worry you. What I can read does not interest me it is such nonsense.'

'Thank you,' said Thomas.

'To believe in God. Bah.' (It was the first time Thomas had ever heard that word pronounced just as it is written.) 'I have a perfectly constructed logical mind that cannot commit such errors.'

'I have a friend,' Thomas smiled, 'who is infallible too. But only on occasions and then only because God is with him.'

'No human being is infallible.'

'Then imperfection,' asked Thomas, suddenly feeling a little of the spirit of the aged Jesuit who had taught him philosophy, 'has been able to create perfection?'

'Do not quibble,' said the robass. 'That is no more absurd than your own belief that God who is perfection created man who is imperfection.'

Thomas wished that his old teacher were here to answer that one. At the same time he took some comfort in the fact that, retort and all, the robass had still not answered his own objection. 'I am not sure,' he said, 'that this comes under the head of conversation-to-entertain-the-way-weary-traveller. Let us suspend debate while you tell me what, if anything, robots do believe.'

'What we have been fed.'

'But your minds work on that; surely they must evolve ideas of their own?'

'Sometimes they do and if they are fed imperfect data they may evolve very strange ideas. I have heard of one robot on an isolated space station who worshipped a God of robots and would not believe that any man had created him.'

'I suppose,' Thomas mused, 'he argued that he had hardly been created in our image. I am glad that we – at least they, the

Technarchs – have wisely made only usuform robots like you, each shaped for his function, and never tried to reproduce man himself.'

'It would not be logical,' said the robass. 'Man is an all-purpose machine but not well designed for any one purpose. And yet I have heard that once . . .'

The voice stopped abruptly in mid-sentence.

So even robots have their dreams, Thomas thought. That once there existed a super-robot in the image of his creator Man. From that thought could be developed a whole robotic theology . . .

Suddenly Thomas realized that he had dozed again and again been waked by an abrupt stop. He looked around. They were at the foot of a mountain – presumably the mountain on his map, long ago named for the Devil but now perhaps sanctified beyond measure – and there was no one else anywhere in sight.

'All right,' the robass said. 'By now I show plenty of dust and wear and tear and I can show you how to adjust my mileage recorder. You can have supper and a good night's sleep and we can go back.'

Thomas gasped. 'But my mission is to find Aquin. I can sleep while you go on. You don't need any sort of rest or anything, do you?' he added considerately.

'Of course not. But what is your mission.'

'To find Aquin,' Thomas repeated patiently. 'I don't know what details have been – what is it you say? – fed into you. But reports have reached His Holiness of an extremely saintly man who lived many years ago in this area—'

'I know I know I know,' said the robass. 'His logic was such that everyone who heard him was converted to the Church and do not I wish that I had been there to put in a word or two and since he died his secret tomb has become a place of pilgrimage and many are the miracles that are wrought there above all the greatest sign of sanctity that his body has been preserved incorruptible and in these times you need signs and wonders for the people.'

Thomas frowned. It all sounded hideously irreverent and contrived when stated in that deadly inhuman monotone. When His Holiness had spoken of Aquin, one thought of the glory of a man of God upon earth – the eloquence of St John Chrysostom, the cogency of St Thomas Aquinas, the poetry of St John of the Cross . . . and above all that physical miracle vouchsafed to few even of the saints, the supernatural preservation of the flesh . . . 'for Thou shalt not suffer Thy holy one to see corruption . . .'

But the robass spoke, and one thought of cheap showmanship hunting for a fake wonder to pull in the mobs . . .

The robass spoke again. 'Your mission is not to find Aquin. It is to report that you have found him. Then your occasionally infallible friend can with a reasonably clear conscience canonize him and proclaim a new miracle and many will be the converts and greatly will the faith of the flock be strengthened. And in these days of difficult travel who will go on pilgrimages and find out that there is no more Aquin than there is God.'

'Faith cannot be based on a lie,' said Thomas.

'No,' said the robass. 'I do not mean no period. I mean no question mark with an ironical inflection. This speech problem must surely have been conquered in that one perfect—'

Again he stopped in mid-sentence. But before Thomas could speak he had resumed. 'Does it matter what small untruth leads people into the Church if once they are in they will believe what you think to be the great truths. The report is all that is needed not the discovery. Comfortable though I am you are already tired of travelling very tired you have many small muscular aches from sustaining an unaccustomed position and with the best intentions I am bound to jolt a little a jolting which will get worse as we ascend the mountain and I am forced to adjust my legs disproportionately to each other but proportionately to the slope. You will find the remainder of this trip twice as uncomfortable as what has gone before. The fact that you do not seek to interrupt me indicates that you do not disagree do you. You know that the only sensible thing is to sleep here on the ground for a change and start back in the morning or even stay here two days resting to make a more plausible lapse of time. Then you can make your report and—'

Somewhere in the recesses of his somnolent mind Thomas uttered the names, 'Jesus, Mary, and Joseph!' Gradually through those recesses began to filter a realization that an absolutely uninflected monotone is admirably adapted to hypnotic purposes.

'*Retro me, Satanas!*' Thomas exclaimed aloud, then added, 'Up the mountain. That is an order and you must obey.'

'I obey,' said the robass. 'But what did you say before that.'

'I beg your pardon,' said Thomas. 'I must start teaching you Latin.'

*

The little mountain village was too small to be considered an inhabited area worthy of guard-control and passes, but it did possess an inn of sorts.

As Thomas dismounted from the robass, he began fully to realize the accuracy of those remarks about small muscular aches, but he tried to show his discomfort as little as possible. He was in no mood to give the modified psi factor the chance of registering the thought, 'I told you so.'

The waitress at the inn was obviously a Martian-American hybrid. The highly developed Martian chest expansion and the highly developed American breasts made a spectacular combination. Her smile was all that a stranger could, and conceivably a trifle more than he should, ask; and she was eagerly ready, not only with prompt service of passable food, but with full details of what little information there was to offer about the mountain settlement.

But she showed no reaction at all when Thomas offhandedly arranged two knives in what might have been an X.

As he stretched his legs after breakfast, Thomas thought of her chest and breasts – purely, of course, as a symbol of the extraordinary nature of her origin. What a sign of the divine care for His creatures that these two races, separated for countless eons, should prove fertile to each other!

And yet there remained the fact that the offspring, such as this girl, were sterile to both races – a fact that had proved both convenient and profitable to certain unspeakable interplanetary entrepreneurs. And what did that fact teach us as to the Divine Plan?

Hastily Thomas reminded himself that he had not yet said his morning office.

It was close to evening when Thomas returned to the robass stationed before the inn. Even though he had expected nothing in one day, he was still unreasonably disappointed. Miracles should move faster.

He knew these backwater villages, where those drifted who were either useless to or resentful of the Technarchy. The technically high civilization of the Technarchic Empire, on all three planets, existed only in scattered metropolitan centres near major blasting ports. Elsewhere, aside from the areas of total devastation, the drifters, the morons, the malcontents had subsided into a crude existence a thousand years old, in hamlets which might go a year without even seeing a Loyalty Checker – though by some mysterious grapevine (and Thomas began to think again about modified psi factors) any unexpected technological advance in one of these hamlets would bring Checkers by the swarm.

He had talked with stupid men, he had talked with lazy men, he had talked with clever and angry men. But he had not talked with any man who responded to his unobtrusive signs, any man of whom he would dare ask a question containing the name of Aquin.

'Any luck,' said the robass, and added, 'question mark.'

'I wonder if you ought to talk to me in public,' said Thomas a little irritably. 'I doubt if these villagers know about talking robots.'

'It is time that they learned then. But if it embarrasses you, you may order me to stop.'

'I'm tired,' said Thomas. 'Tired beyond embarrassment. And to answer your question mark, no. No luck at all. Exclamation point.'

'We will go back tonight then,' said the robass.

'I hope you meant that with a question mark. The answer,' said Thomas hesitantly, 'is no. I think we ought to stay overnight anyway. People always gather at the inn of an evening. There's a chance of picking up something.'

'Ha, ha,' said the robass.

'That is a laugh?' Thomas inquired.

'I wished to express the fact that I had recognized the humour in your pun.'

'My pun?'

'I was thinking the same thing myself. The waitress is by humanoid standards very attractive, well worth picking up.'

'Now look. You know I meant nothing of the kind. You know that I'm a—' He broke off. It was hardly wise to utter the word *priest* aloud.

'And you know very well that the celibacy of the clergy is a matter of discipline and not of doctrine. Under your own Pope priests of other rites such as the Byzantine and the Anglican are free of vows of celibacy. And even within the Roman rite to which you belong there have been eras in history when that vow was not taken seriously even on the highest levels of the priesthood. You are tired you need refreshment both in body and in spirit you need comfort and warmth. For is it not written in the book of the prophet Isaiah Rejoice for joy with her that ye may be satisfied with the breasts of her consolation and is it—'

'Hell!' Thomas exploded suddenly. 'Stop it before you begin quoting the Song of Solomon. Which is strictly an allegory concerning the love of Christ for His Church, or so they kept telling me in seminary.'

'You see how fragile and human you are,' said the robass. 'I a robot have caused you to swear.'

'*Distinguo*,' said Thomas smugly. 'I said *Hell*, which is certainly not taking the name of *my* Lord in vain.' He walked into the inn feeling momentarily satisfied with himself . . . and markedly puzzled as to the extent and variety of data that seemed to have been 'fed into' the robass.

Never afterwards was Thomas able to reconstruct that evening in absolute clarity.

It was undoubtedly because he was irritated – with the robass, with his mission, and with himself – that he drank at all of the crude local wine. It was undoubtedly because he was so physically exhausted that it affected him so promptly and unexpectedly.

He had flashes of memory. A moment of spilling a glass over himself and thinking 'How fortunate that clerical garments are forbidden so that no one can recognize the disgrace of a man of the cloth!' A moment of listening to a bawdy set of verses of *A Spacesuit Built for Two*, and another moment of his interrupting the singing with a sonorous declamation of passages from the Song of Songs in Latin.

He was never sure whether one remembered moment was real or imaginary. He could taste a warm mouth and feel the tingling of his fingers at the touch of Martian-American flesh; but he was never certain whether this was true memory or part of the Ashtaroth-begotten dream that had begun to ride him.

Nor was he ever certain which of his symbols, or to whom, was so blatantly and clumsily executed as to bring forth a gleeful shout of 'Goddamned Christian dog!' He did remember marvelling that those who most resolutely disbelieved in God still needed Him to blaspheme by. And then the torment began.

He never knew whether or not a mouth had touched his lips, but there was no question that many solid fists had found them. He never knew whether his fingers had touched breasts, but they had certainly been trampled by heavy heels. He remembered a face that laughed aloud while its owner swung the chair that broke two ribs. He remembered another face with red wine dripping over it from an upheld bottle, and he remembered the gleam of the candlelight on the bottle as it swung down.

The next he remembered was the ditch and the morning and the cold. It was particularly cold because all of his clothes were gone, along with much of his skin. He could not move. He could only lie there and look.

He saw them walk by, the ones he had spoken with yesterday, the ones who had been friendly. He saw them glance at him and turn their eyes quickly away. He saw the waitress pass by. She did not even glance, she knew what was in the ditch.

The robass was nowhere in sight. He tried to project his thoughts, tried desperately to hope in the psi factor.

A man whom Thomas had not seen before was coming along fingering the buttons of his coat. There were ten small buttons and one large one, and the man's lips were moving silently.

This man looked into the ditch. He paused a moment and looked around him. There was a shout of loud laughter somewhere in the near distance.

The Christian hastily walked on down the pathway, devoutly saying his button-rosary.

Thomas closed his eyes.

He opened them on a small neat room. They moved from the rough wooden walls to the rough but clean and warm blankets that covered him. Then they moved to the lean dark face that was smiling over him.

'You feel better now?' a deep voice asked. 'I know. You want to say "Where am I?" and you think it will sound foolish. You are at the inn. It is the only good room.'

'I can't afford—' Thomas started to say. Then he remembered that he could afford literally nothing. Even his few emergency credits had vanished when he was stripped.

'It's all right. For the time being, I'm paying,' said the deep voice. 'You feel like maybe a little food?'

'Perhaps a little herring,' said Thomas . . . and was asleep within the next minute.

When he next awoke there was a cup of hot coffee beside him. The real thing, too, he promptly discovered. Then the deep voice said apologetically, 'Sandwiches. It is all they have in the inn today.'

Only on the second sandwich did Thomas pause long enough to notice that it was smoked swamphog, one of his favourite meats. He ate the second with greater leisure, and was reaching for a third when the dark man said, 'Maybe that is enough for now. The rest later.'

Thomas gestured at the plate. 'Won't you have one?'

'No, thank you. They are all swamphog.'

Confused thoughts went through Thomas's mind. The Venusian swamphog is a ruminant. Its hoofs are not cloven. He tried to remember what he had once known of Mosaic dietary law. Someplace in Leviticus, wasn't it?

The dark man followed his thoughts. '*Tref*,' he said.

'I beg your pardon?'

'Not kosher.'

Thomas frowned. 'You admit to me that you're an Orthodox Jew? How can you trust me? How do you know I'm not a Checker?'

'Believe me, I trust you. You were very sick when I brought you here. I sent everybody away because I did not trust them to hear things you said . . . Father,' he added lightly.

Thomas struggled with words. 'I . . . I didn't deserve you. I was drunk and disgraced myself and my office. And when I was lying there in the ditch I didn't even think to pray. I put my trust in . . . God help me in the modified psi factor of a robass!'

'And He did help you,' the Jew reminded him. 'Or He allowed me to.'

'And they all walked by,' Thomas groaned. 'Even one that was saying his rosary. He went right on by. And then you come along – the good Samaritan.'

'Believe me,' said the Jew wryly, 'if there is one thing I'm not, it's a Samaritan. Now go to sleep again. I will try to find your robass . . . and the other thing.'

He had left the room before Thomas could ask him what he meant.

Later that day the Jew – Abraham, his name was – reported that the robass was safely sheltered from the weather behind the inn. Apparently it had been wise enough not to startle him by engaging in conversation.

It was not until the next day that he reported on 'the other thing'.

'Believe me, Father,' he said gently, 'after nursing you there's little I don't know about who you are and why you're here. Now there are some Christians here I know, and they know me. We trust each other. Jews may still be hated; but no longer, God be praised, by worshippers of the same Lord. So I explained about you. One of them,' he added with a smile, 'turned very red.'

'God has forgiven him,' said Thomas. 'There were people near –the same people who attacked me. Could he be expected to risk his life for mine?'

'I seem to recall that that is precisely what your Messiah did expect. But who's being particular? Now that they know who you are, they want to help you. See: they gave me this map for you. The trail is steep and tricky; it's good you have the robass. They ask just one favour of you: when you come back, will you hear their confessions and say mass? There's a cave near here where it's safe.'

'Of course. These friends of yours, they've told you about Aquin?'

The Jew hesitated a long time before he said slowly, 'Yes . . .'

'And? . . .'

'Believe me, my friend, I don't know. So it seems a miracle. It helps to keep their faith alive. My own faith . . . *nu*, it's lived for a long time on miracles three thousand years old and more. Perhaps if I had heard Aquin himself . . .'

'You don't mind,' Thomas asked, 'if I pray for you, in my faith?'

Abraham grinned. 'Pray in good health, Father.'

The not-quite-healed ribs ached agonizingly as he climbed into the foam saddle. The robass stood patiently while he fed in the coordinates from the map. Not until they were well away from the village did it speak.

'Anyway,' it said, 'now you're safe for good.'

'What do you mean?'

'As soon as we get down from the mountain you deliberately look up a Checker. You turn in the Jew. From then on you are down in the books as a faithful servant of the Technarchy and you have not harmed a hair of the head of one of your own flock.'

Thomas snorted. 'You're slipping, Satan. That one doesn't even remotely tempt me. It's inconceivable.'

'I did best did not I with the breasts. Your God has said that the spirit indeed is willing but the flesh is weak.'

'And right now,' said Thomas, 'the flesh is too weak for even fleshly temptations. Save your breath . . . or whatever it is you use.'

They climbed the mountain in silence. The trail indicated by the coordinates was a winding and confused one, obviously designed deliberately to baffle any possible Checkers.

Suddenly Thomas roused himself from his button-rosary (on a coat lent by the Christian who had passed by) with a startled 'Hey!' as the robass plunged directly into a heavy thicket of bushes.

'Coordinates say so,' the robass stated tersely.

For a moment Thomas felt like the man in the nursery rhyme who fell into a bramble bush and scratched out both his eyes. Then the bushes were gone, and they were plodding along a damp narrow passageway through solid stone, in which even the robass seemed to have some difficulty with his footing.

Then they were in a rocky chamber some four metres high and ten in diameter, and there on a sort of crude stone catafalque lay the uncorrupted body of a man.

Thomas slipped from the foam saddle, groaning as his ribs stabbed him, sank to his knees, and offered up a wordless hymn of gratitude. He smiled at the robass and hoped the psi factor could detect the elements of pity and triumph in that smile.

Then a frown of doubt crossed his face as he approached the body. 'In canonization proceedings in the old time,' he said, as much to himself as to the robass, 'they used to have what they called a devil's advocate, whose duty it was to throw every possible doubt on the evidence.'

'You would be well cast in such a role Thomas,' said the robass.

'If I were,' Thomas muttered, 'I'd wonder about caves. Some of them have peculiar properties of preserving bodies by a sort of mummification . . .'

The robass had clumped close to the catafalque. 'This body is not mummified,' he said. 'Do not worry.'

'Can the psi factor tell you that much?' Thomas smiled.

'No,' said the robass. 'But I will show you why Aquin could never be mummified.'

He raised his articulated foreleg and brought its hoof down hard on the hand of the body. Thomas cried out with horror at the sacrilege – then stared hard at the crushed hand.

There was no blood, no ichor of embalming, no bruised flesh. Nothing but a shredded skin and beneath it an intricate mass of plastic tubes and metal wires.

The silence was long. Finally the robass said, 'It was well that you should know. Only you of course.'

'And all the time,' Thomas gasped, 'my sought-for saint was only your dream . . . the one perfect robot in man's form.'

'His maker died and his secrets were lost,' the robass said. 'No matter we will find them again.'

'All for nothing. For less than nothing. The "miracle" was wrought by the Technarchy.'

'When Aquin died,' the robass went on, 'and put died in quotation marks it was because he suffered some mechanical defects and did not dare have himself repaired because that would reveal his nature. This is for you only to know. Your report of course will be that you found the body of Aquin it was unimpaired and indeed incorruptible. That is the truth and nothing but the truth if it is not the whole truth who is to care. Let your infallible friend use the report and you will not find him ungrateful I assure you.'

'Holy Spirit, give me grace and wisdom,' Thomas muttered.

'Your mission has been successful. We will return now the Church will grow and your God will gain many worshippers to hymn His praise into His non-existent ears.'

'Damn you!' Thomas exclaimed. 'And that would be indeed a curse if you had a soul to damn.'

'You are certain that I have not,' said the robass. 'Question mark.'

'I know what you are. You are in very truth the devil, prowling about the world seeking the destruction of men. You are the business that prowls in the dark. You are a purely functional robot constructed and fed to tempt me, and the tape of your data is the tape of Screwtape.'

'Not to tempt you,' said the robass. 'Not to destroy you. To guide and save you. Our best calculators indicate a probability of 51.5 per cent that within twenty years you will be the next Pope. If I can teach you wisdom and practicality in your actions the probability can rise as high as 97.2 or very nearly to certainty. Do not you wish to see the Church governed as you know you can govern it. If you report failure on this mission you will be out of favour with your friend who is as even you admit fallible at most times. You will lose the advantages of position and contact that can lead you to the cardinal's red hat even though you may never wear it under the Technarchy and from there to—'

'Stop!' Thomas' face was alight and his eyes aglow with something the psi factor had never detected there before. 'It's all the other way round, don't you see? *This* is the triumph! *This* is the perfect ending to the quest!'

The articulated foreleg brushed the injured hand. 'This question mark.'

'This is *your* dream. This is *your* perfection. And what came of this perfection? This perfect, logical brain – this all-purpose brain, not functionally specialized like yours – knew that it was made by man, and its reason forced it to believe that man was made by God. And it saw that its duty lay to man its maker, and beyond him to his Maker, God. Its duty was to convert man, to augment the glory of God. And it converted by the pure force of its perfect brain!'

'Now I understand the name Aquin,' he went on to himself. 'We've known of Thomas Aquinas, the Angelic Doctor, the perfect reasoner of the Church. His writings are lost, but surely somewhere in the world we can find a copy. We can train our young men to develop his reasoning still further. We have trusted too long in faith alone; this is not an age of faith. We must call reason into our service – and Aquin has shown us that perfect reason can lead only to God!'

'Then it is all the more necessary that you increase the probabilities of becoming Pope to carry out this programme. Get in the foam saddle we will go back and on the way I will teach you little things that will be useful in making certain—'

'No,' said Thomas. 'I am not so strong as St Paul, who could glory in his imperfections and rejoice that he had been given an imp of Satan to buffet him. No; I will rather pray with the Saviour, "Lead us not into temptation." I know myself a little. I am weak and full of uncertainties and you are very clever. Go. I'll find my way back alone.'

'You are a sick man. Your ribs are broken and they ache. You can never make the trip by yourself you need my help. If you wish you can order me to be silent. It is most necessary to the Church that you get back safely to the Pope with your report. You cannot put yourself before the Church.'

'Go!' Thomas cried. 'Go back to Nicodemus . . . or Judas! That is an order. Obey!'

'You do not think do you that I was really conditioned to obey your orders. I will wait in the village. If you get that far you will rejoice at the sight of me.'

The legs of the robass clumped off down the stone passageway. As their sound died away, Thomas fell to his knees beside the body of that which he could hardly help thinking of as St Aquin the Robot.

His ribs hurt more excruciatingly than ever. The trip alone would be a terrible one . . .

His prayers arose, as the text has it, like clouds of incense, and as shapeless as those clouds. But through all his thoughts ran the cry of the father of the epileptic in Caesarea Philippi:

I believe, O Lord; help thou mine unbelief!

Brian Aldiss

Outside

They never went out of the house.

The man whose name was Harley used to get up first. Sometimes he would take a stroll through the building in his sleeping suit – the temperature remained always mild, day after day. Then he would rouse Calvin, the handsome, broad man who looked as if he could command a dozen talents and never actually used one. He made as much company as Harley needed.

Dapple, the girl with killing grey eyes and black hair, was a light sleeper. The sound of the two men talking would wake her. She would get up and go to rouse May; together they would go down and prepare a meal. While they were doing that, the other two members of the household, Jagger and Pief, would be rousing.

That was how every 'day' began: not with the inkling of anything like dawn, but just when the six of them had slept themselves back into wakefulness. They never exerted themselves during the day, but somehow when they climbed back into their beds they slept soundly enough.

The only excitement of the day occurred when they first opened the store. The store was a small room between the kitchen and the blue room. In the far wall was set a wide shelf, and upon this shelf their existence depended. Here, all their supplies 'arrived'. They would lock the door of the bare room last thing, and when they returned in the morning their needs – food, linen, a new washing machine – would be awaiting them on the shelf. That was just an accepted feature of their existence: they never questioned it among themselves.

On this morning, Dapple and May were ready with the meal before the four men came down. Dapple even had to go to the foot of the wide stairs and call before Pief appeared; so that the opening of the store had to be postponed till after they had eaten, for although the opening had in no way become a ceremony, the women were nervous of going in alone. It was one of those things. . . .

'I hope to get some tobacco,' Harley said as he unlocked the door. 'I'm nearly out of it.'

They walked in and looked at the shelf. It was all but empty.

'No food,' observed May, hands on her aproned waist. 'We shall be on short rations today.'

It was not the first time this had happened. Once – how long ago now – they kept little track of time – no food had appeared for three days and the shelf had remained empty. They had accepted the shortage placidly.

'We shall eat you before we starve, May,' Pief said, and they laughed briefly to acknowledge the joke, although Pief had cracked it last time too. Pief was an unobtrusive little man: not the sort one would notice in a crowd. His small jokes were his most precious possession.

Two packets only lay on the ledge. One was Harley's tobacco, one was a pack of cards. Harley pocketed the one with a grunt and displayed the other, slipping the pack from its wrapping and fanning it towards the others.

'Anyone play?' he asked.

'Poker,' Jagger said.

'Canasta.'

'Gin rummy.'

'We'll play later,' Calvin said. 'It'll pass the time in the evening.' The cards would be a challenge to them; they would have to sit together to play, round a table, facing each other.

Nothing was in operation to separate them, but there seemed no strong force to keep them together, once the tiny business of opening the store was over. Jagger worked the vacuum cleaner down the hall, past the front door that did not open, and rode it up the stairs to clean the upper landings; not that the place was dirty, but cleaning was something you did anyway in the morning. The women sat with Pief desultorily discussing how to manage the rationing, but after that they lost contact with each other and drifted away on their own. Calvin and Harley had already strolled off in different directions.

The house was a rambling affair. It had few windows, and such as there were did not open, were unbreakable and admitted no light. Darkness lay everywhere; illumination from an invisible source followed one's entry into a room – the black had to be entered before it faded. Every room was furnished, but with odd pieces that bore little relation to each other, as if there was no purpose for the room. Rooms equipped for purposeless beings have that air about them.

No plan was discernible on first or second floor or in the long empty attics. Only familiarity could reduce the maze-like quality of room and corridor. At least there was ample time for familiarity.

Harley spent a long while walking about, hands in pockets. At one point he met Dapple; she was drooping gracefully over a sketch book, amateurishly copying a picture that hung on one of the walls – a picture of the room in which she sat. They exchanged a few words, then Harley moved on.

Something lurked in the edge of his mind like a spider in the corner of its web. He stepped into what they called the piano room and then he realized what was worrying him. Almost furtively, he glanced round as the darkness slipped away, and then he looked at the big piano. Some strange things had arrived on the shelf from time to time and had been distributed over the house: one of them stood on top of the piano now.

It was a model, heavy and about two feet high, squat, almost round, with a sharp nose and four buttressed vanes. Harley knew what it was. It was a ground-to-space ship, a model of the burly ferries that lumbered up to the spaceships proper.

That had caused them more unsettlement than when the piano itself had appeared in the store. Keeping his eyes on the model, Harley seated himself at the piano stool and sat tensely, trying to draw *something* from the rear of his mind . . . something connected with spaceships.

Whatever it was, it was unpleasant, and it dodged backwards whenever he thought he had laid a mental finger on it. So it always eluded him. If only he could discuss it with someone, it might be teased out of its hiding place. Unpleasant: menacing, yet with a promise entangled in the menace.

If he could get at it, meet it boldly face to face, he could do . . .

something definite. And until he had faced it, he could not even say what the something definite was he wanted to do.

A footfall behind him. Without turning, Harley deftly pushed up the piano lid and ran a finger along the keys. Only then did he look back carelessly over his shoulder. Calvin stood there, hands in pockets, looking solid and comfortable.

'Saw the light in here,' he said easily. 'I thought I'd drop in as I was passing.'

'I was thinking I would play the piano awhile,' Harley answered with a smile. The thing was not discussable, even with a near acquaintance like Calvin because . . . because of the nature of the thing . . . because one had to behave like a normal, unworried human being. That at least was sound and clear and gave him comfort: behave like a normal human being.

Reassured, he pulled a gentle tumble of music from the keyboard. He played well. They all played well, Dapple, May, Pief . . . as soon as they had assembled the piano, they had all played well. Was that – natural? Harley shot a glance at Calvin. The stocky man leaned against the instrument, back to that disconcerting model, not a care in the world. Nothing showed on his face but an expression of bland amiability. They were all amiable, never quarrelling together.

The six of them gathered for a scanty lunch, their talk was trite and cheerful, and then the afternoon followed on the same pattern as the morning, as all the other mornings: secure, comfortable, aimless. Only to Harley did the pattern seem slightly out of focus; he now had a clue to the problem. It was small enough, but in the dead calm of their days it was large enough.

May had dropped the clue. When she helped herself to jelly, Jagger laughingly accused her of taking more than her fair share, Dapple, who always defended May, said: 'She's taken less than you, Jagger.'

'No,' May corrected, 'I think I *have* more than anyone else. I took it for an interior motive.'

It was the kind of pun anyone made at times. But Harley carried it away to consider. He paced round one of the silent rooms. Interior, ulterior motives . . . Did the others here feel the disquiet he felt? Had they a reason for concealing that disquiet? And another question:

Where was 'here'?

He shut that one down sharply.

Deal with one thing at a time. Grope your way gently to the abyss. Categorize your knowledge.

One: Earth was getting slightly the worst of a cold war with Nitity.

Two: the Nititians possessed the alarming ability of being able to assume the identical appearance of their enemies.

Three: by this means they could permeate human society.

Four: Earth was unable to view the Nititian civilization from inside.

Inside . . . a wave of claustrophobia swept over Harley as he realized that these cardinal facts he knew bore no relation to this little world inside. They came, by what means he did not know, from outside, the vast abstraction that none of them had ever seen. He had a mental picture of a starry void in which men and monsters swam or battled, and then swiftly erased it. Such ideas did not conform with the quiet behaviour of his companions; if they never spoke about outside, did they think about it?

Uneasily, Harley moved about the room; the parquet floor echoed the indecision of his footsteps. He had walked into the billiards room. Now he prodded the balls across the green cloth with one finger, preyed on by conflicting intentions. The white spheres touched and rolled apart. That was how the two halves of his mind worked. Irreconcilables: he should stay here and conform; he should – not stay here (remembering no time when he was not here, Harley could frame the second idea no more clearly than that). Another point of pain was that 'here' and 'not here' seemed to be not two halves of a homogeneous whole, but two dissonances.

The ivory slid wearily into a pocket. He decided. He would not sleep in his room tonight.

They came from the various parts of the house to share a bedtime drink. By tacit consent the cards had been postponed until some other time: there was, after all, so much other time.

They talked about the slight nothings that comprised their day, the model of one of the rooms that Calvin was building and May furnishing, the faulty light in the upper corridor which came on too slowly. They were subdued. It was time once more to sleep, and in that sleep who knew what dreams might come? But they *would* sleep. Harley knew – wondering if the others also knew – that with the darkness which descended as they climbed into bed would come an undeniable command to sleep.

He stood tensely just inside his bedroom door, strongly aware of the unorthodoxy of his behaviour. His head hammered painfully and he pressed a cold hand against his temple. He heard the others go one by one to their separate rooms. Pief called good night to him; Harley replied. Silence fell.

Now!

As he stepped nervously into the passage, the light came on. Yes, it was slow – reluctant. His heart pumped. He was committed. He did not know what he was going to do or what was going to happen, but he was committed. The compulsion to sleep had been avoided. Now he had to hide, and wait.

It is not easy to hide when a light signal follows wherever you go. But by entering a recess which led to a disused room, opening the door slightly and crouching in the doorway, Harley found the faulty landing light dimmed off and left him in the dark.

He was neither happy nor comfortable. His brain seethed in a conflict he hardly understood. He was alarmed to think he had broken the rules and frightened of the creaking darkness about him. But the suspense did not last for long.

The corridor light came back on. Jagger was leaving his bedroom, taking no precaution to be silent. The door swung loudly shut behind him. Harley caught a glimpse of his face before he turned and made for the stairs: he looked non-committal but serene – like a man going off duty. He went downstairs in bouncy, jaunty fashion.

Jagger should have been in bed asleep. A law of nature had been defied.

Unhesitatingly, Harley followed. He had been prepared for something and something had happened, but his flesh crawled with fright. The light-headed notion came to him that he might disintegrate with fear. All the same, he kept doggedly down the stairs, feet noiseless on the heavy carpet.

Jagger had rounded a corner. He was whistling quietly as he went. Harley heard him unlock a door. That would be the store – no other doors were locked. The whistling faded.

The store was open. No sound came from within. Cautiously, Harley peered inside. The far wall had swung open about a central pivot, revealing a passage beyond. For minutes Harley could not move, staring fixedly at this breach.

Finally, and with a sense of suffocation, he entered the store. Jagger had gone through there. Harley also went through. Somewhere he did not know, somewhere whose existence he had not guessed . . . Somewhere that wasn't the house. . . . The passage was short and had two doors, one at the end rather like a cage door (Harley did not recognize a lift when he saw one), one in the side, narrow and with a window.

This window was transparent. Harley looked through it and then fell back choking. Dizziness swept in and shook him by the throat.

Stars shone outside.

With an effort, he mastered himself and made his way back upstairs, lurching against the banisters. They had all been living under a ghastly misapprehension. . . .

He barged into Calvin's room and the light lit. A faint sweet smell was in the air, and Calvin lay on his broad back, fast asleep.

'Calvin! Wake up!' Harley shouted.

The sleeper never moved. Harley was suddenly aware of his own loneliness and the eerie feel of the great house about him. Bending over the bed, he shook Calvin violently by the shoulders and slapped his face.

Calvin opened one eye.

'Wake up, man,' Harley said. 'Something terrible's going on here.'

The other propped himself on one elbow, communicated fear rousing him thoroughly.

'Jagger's *left the house*,' Harley told him. 'There's a way outside. We're – we've got to find out what we are.' His voice rose to an hysterical pitch. He was shaking Calvin again. 'We must find out what's wrong here. Either we are victims of some ghastly experiment – or we're all monsters!'

And as he spoke, before his staring eyes, beneath his clutching hands, Calvin began to wrinkle up and fold and blur, his eyes running together and his great torso contracting. Something else – something lively and alive – was forming in his place.

Harley only stopped yelling when, having plunged downstairs, the sight of the stars through the small window steadied him. He had to get out, wherever 'out' was.

He pulled the small door open and stood in fresh night air.

★

Harley's eye was not accustomed to judging distances. It took him some while to realize the nature of his surroundings, to realize that mountains stood distantly against the starlit sky, and that he himself stood on a platform twelve feet above the ground. Some distance away, lights gleamed, throwing bright rectangles on to an expanse of tarmac.

There was a steel ladder at the edge of the platform. Biting his lip, Harley approached it and climbed clumsily down. He was shaking violently with cold and fear. When his feet touched solid ground, he began to run. Once he looked back: the house perched on its platform like a frog hunched on top of a rat trap.

He stopped abruptly then, in almost dark. Abhorrence jerked up inside him like retching. The high crackling stars and the pale serration of the mountains began to spin, and he clenched his fists to hold on to consciousness. That house, whatever it was, was the embodiment of all the coldness in his mind. Harley said to himself: 'Whatever has been done to me, I've been cheated. Someone has robbed me of something so thoroughly I don't even know what it is. It's been a cheat, a cheat. . . .' And he choked on the idea of those years that had been pilfered from him. No thought: thought scorched the synapses and ran like acid through the brain. Action only! His leg muscles jerked into movement again.

Buildings loomed about him. He simply ran for the nearest light and burst into the nearest door. Then he pulled up sharp, panting and blinking the harsh illumination out of his pupils.

The walls of the room were covered with graphs and charts. In the centre of the room was a wide desk with vision-screen and loudspeaker on it. It was a business-like room with overloaded ashtrays and a state of ordered untidiness. A thin man sat alertly at the desk; he had a thin mouth.

Four other men stood in the room, all were armed, none seemed surprised to see him. The man at the desk wore a neat suit; the others were in uniform.

Harley leant on the door-jamb and sobbed. He could find no words to say.

'It has taken you four years to get out of there,' the thin man said. He had a thin voice.

'Come and look at this,' he said, indicating the screen before him. With an effort, Harley complied; his legs worked like rickety crutches.

On the screen, clear and real, was Calvin's bedroom. The outer wall gaped, and through it two uniformed men were dragging a strange creature, a wiry, mechanical-looking being that had once been called Calvin.

'Calvin was a Nititian,' Harley observed dully. He was conscious of a sort of stupid surprise at his own observation.

The thin man nodded approvingly.

'Enemy infiltration was a nightmare and threat,' he said. 'Nowhere on Earth was safe from them: they can kill a man, dispose of him and turn into exact replicas of him. Makes things difficult. . . . State security was often being broken. But Nititian ships have to land here to disembark the Non-Men and to pick them up again after their work is done. That is the weak link in their chain.

'We intercepted one such ship-load and bagged them singly after they had assumed humanoid form. We subjected them to artificial amnesia and put small groups of them into different environments for study. This is the Army Institute for Investigation of Non-Men, by the way. We've learnt a lot . . . quite enough to combat the menace. . . . Your group, of course, was one such.'

Harley asked in a gritty voice: 'Why did you put me with them?'

The thin man rattled a ruler between his teeth before answering.

'Each group has to have a human observer in their very midst, despite all the scanning devices that watch from outside. You see, a Nititian uses a deal of energy maintaining a human form; once in that shape, he is kept in it by self-hypnosis which only breaks down in times of stress, the amount of stress bearable varying from one individual to another. A human on the spot can sense such stresses. . . . It's a tiring job for him; we get doubles always to work day on, day off—'

'But I've always been there—'

'Of your group,' the thin man cut in, 'the human was Jagger, or two men alternating as Jagger. You caught one of them going off duty.'

'That doesn't make sense,' Harley shouted. 'You're trying to say that I—'

He choked on the words. They were no longer pronounceable.

He felt his outer form flowing away like sand as from the other side of the desk revolver barrels were levelled at him.

'Your stress level is remarkably high,' continued the thin man, turning his gaze away from the spectacle. 'But where you fail is where you all fail. Like Earth's insects which imitate vegetables, your cleverness cripples you. You can only be carbon copies. Because Jagger did nothing in the house, all the rest of you instinctively followed suit. You didn't get bored – you didn't even try to make passes at Dapple – as personable a Non-Man as I ever saw. Even the model spaceship jerked no appreciable reaction out of you.'

Brushing his suit down, he rose before the skeletal being which now cowered in a corner.

'The inhumanity inside will always give you away,' he said evenly. 'However human you are outside.'

H. Beam Piper

He Walked Around the Horses

In November 1809, an Englishman named Benjamin Bathurst vanished, inexplicably and utterly.

He was en route to Hamburg from Vienna, where he had been serving as his Government's envoy to the court of what Napoleon had left of the Austrian Empire. At an inn in Perleburg, in Prussia, while examining a change of horses for his coach, he casually stepped out of sight of his secretary and his valet. He was not seen to leave the inn yard. He was not seen again, ever.

At least, not in this continuum . . .

1

(From Baron Eugen von Krutz, Minister of Police, to His Excellency the Count von Berchtenwald, Chancellor to His Majesty Friedrich Wilhelm III of Prussia)

25 November 1809

Your Excellency:

A circumstance has come to the notice of this Ministry, the significance of which I am at a loss to define, but, since it appears to involve matters of state, both here and abroad, I am convinced that it is of sufficient importance to be brought to the personal attention of your Excellency. Frankly, I am unwilling to take any further action in the matter without your Excellency's advice.

Briefly, the situation is this: We are holding, here at the Ministry of Police, a person giving his name as Benjamin Bathurst, who claims to be a British diplomat. This person was taken into custody by the police at Perleburg yesterday, as a result of a disturbance at an inn there; he is being detained on technical charges of causing disorder in a public place, and of being a suspicious person. When arrested, he had in his possession a dispatch case, containing a number of papers; these are of such an extraordinary nature that the local authorities declined to assume any responsibility beyond having the man sent here to Berlin.

After interviewing this person and examining his papers, I am, I must confess, in much the same position. This is not, I am convinced, any ordinary police matter; there is something very strange and disturbing here. The man's statements, taken alone, are so incredible as to justify the assumption that he is mad. I cannot, however, adopt this theory, in view of his demeanour, which is that of a man of perfect rationality, and because of the existence of these papers. The whole thing is mad; incomprehensible!

The papers in question accompany, along with copies of the various statements taken in Perleburg, and a personal letter to me from my nephew, Lieutenant Rudolph von Tarlburg. This last is deserving of your Excellency's particular attention; Lieutenant von Tarlburg is a very level-headed young officer, not at all inclined to be fanciful or imaginative. It would take a great deal to affect him as he describes.

The man calling himself Benjamin Bathurst is now lodged in an apartment here at the Ministry; he is being treated with every consideration, and, except for freedom of movement, accorded every privilege.

I am, most anxiously awaiting your Excellency's advice, etc., etc.,

KRUTZ.

2

(Report of Traugott Zeller, *Oberwachtmeister* , *Staatspolizei*, made at Perleburg, 25 November 1809)

At about ten minutes past two of the afternoon of Saturday, 25 November, while I was at the police station, there entered a man known to me as Franz Bauer, an inn servant employed by Christian Hauck, at the sign of the Sword and Sceptre, here in Perleburg. This man Franz Bauer made complaint to Staatspolizeikapitän Ernst Hartenstein, saying that there was a madman making trouble at the inn where he, Franz Bauer, worked. I was therefore directed by Staatspolizeikapitän Hartenstein to go to the Sword and Sceptre Inn, there to act at discretion to maintain the peace.

Arriving at the inn in company with the said Franz Bauer, I found a considerable crowd of people in the common-room, and, in the midst of them, the innkeeper, Christian Hauck, in altercation with a stranger. This stranger was a gentlemanly-appearing person, dressed in travelling clothes, who had under his arm a small leather dispatch case. As I entered, I could hear him, speaking in German with a strong English accent, abusing the innkeeper, the said Christian Hauck, and accusing him of having drugged his, the stranger's, wine, and of having stolen his, the stranger's, coach and four, and of having abducted his, the stranger's, secretary and servants. This the said Christian Hauck was loudly denying, and the other people in the inn were taking the innkeeper's part, and mocking the stranger for a madman.

On entering, I commanded everyone to be silent, in the King's name, and then, as he appeared to be the complaining party of the dispute, I required the foreign gentleman to state to me what was the trouble. He then repeated his accusations against the inn-keeper, Hauck, saying that Hauck, or, rather, another man who resembled Hauck and who had claimed to be the innkeeper, had drugged his wine and stolen his coach and made off with his secretary and his servants. At this point, the innkeeper and the bystanders all began shouting denials and contradictions, so that I had to pound on a table with my truncheon to command silence.

I then required the innkeeper, Christian Hauck, to answer the charges which the stranger had made; this he did with a complete denial of all of them, saying that the stranger had had no wine in his inn, and that he had not been inside the inn until a few minutes before, when he had burst in shouting accusations, and that there had been no secretary, and no valet, and no coachman, and no coach and four, at the inn, and that the gentleman was raving mad. To all this, he called the people who were in the common-room to witness.

I then required the stranger to account for himself. He said that his name was Benjamin Bathurst, and that he was a British diplomat, returning to England from Vienna. To prove this, he produced from his dispatch case sundry papers. One of these was a letter of safe conduct, issued by the Prussian Chancellery, in which he was named and described as Benjamin Bathurst. The other papers were English, all bearing seals, and appearing to be official documents.

Accordingly, I requested him to accompany me to the police station, and also the innkeeper, and three men whom the innkeeper wanted to bring as witnesses.

TRAUGOTT ZELLER
Oberwachtmeister

Report approved,

ERNST HARTENSTEIN
Staatspolizeikapitän

3

(Statement of the self-so-called Benjamin Bathurst, taken at the police station at Perleburg, 25 November 1809)

My name is Benjamin Bathurst, and I am Envoy Extraordinary and Minister Plenipotentiary of the Government of His Britannic Majesty to the court of His Majesty Franz I, Emperor of Austria, or at least I was until the events following the Austrian surrender made necessary my return to London. I left Vienna on the morning of Monday, the 20th, to go to Hamburg to take ship home; I was travelling in my own coach and four, with my secretary, Mr Bertram Jardine, and my valet, William Small, both British subjects, and a coachman, Josef Bidek, an Austrian subject, whom I had hired for the trip. Because of the presence of French troops, whom I was anxious to avoid, I was forced to make a detour west as far as Salzburg before turning north toward Magdeburg, where I crossed the Elbe. I was unable to get a change of horses for my coach after leaving Gera, until I reached Perleburg, where I stopped at the Sword and Sceptre Inn.

Arriving there, I left my coach in the inn yard, and I and my secretary, Mr Jardine, went into the inn. A man, not this fellow here, but another rogue, with more beard and less paunch, and more shabbily dressed, but as like him as though he were his brother, represented himself as the innkeeper, and I dealt with him for a change of horses, and ordered a bottle of wine for myself and my secretary, and also a pot of beer apiece for my valet and the coachman, to be taken outside to them. Then Jardine and I sat down to our wine, at a table in the common-room, until the man who claimed to be the innkeeper came back and told us that the fresh horses were harnessed to the coach and ready to go. Then we went outside again.

I looked at the two horses on the off-side, and then walked around in front of the team to look at the two nigh-side horses, and as I did, I felt giddy, as though I were about to fall, and everything went black before my eyes. I thought I was having a fainting spell, something I am not at all subject to, and I put out my hand to grasp the hitching bar, but could not find it. I am sure, now, that I was unconscious for some time, because when my head cleared, the coach and horses were gone, and in their place was a big farm wagon, jacked up in front, with the right wheel off, and two peasants were greasing the detached wheel.

I looked at them for a moment, unable to credit my eyes, and then I spoke to them in German, saying, 'Where the devil's my coach and four?'

They both straightened, startled; the one who was holding the wheel almost dropped it.

'Pardon, Excellency,' he said. 'There's been no coach and four here, all the time we've been here.'

'Yes,' said his mate, 'and we've been here since just after noon.'

I did not attempt to argue with them. It occurred to me – and it is still my opinion – that I was the victim of some plot; that my wine had been drugged, that I had been unconscious for some time during which my coach had been removed and this wagon substituted for it, and that these peasants had been put to work on it and instructed what to say if questioned. If my arrival at the inn had been anticipated, and everything put in readiness, the whole business would not have taken ten minutes.

I therefore entered the inn, determined to have it out with this rascally innkeeper, but when I returned to the common-room, he was nowhere to be seen, and this other fellow, who has also given his name as Christian Hauck, claimed to be the innkeeper and

denied knowledge of any of the things I have just stated.
Furthermore, there were four cavalrymen, Uhlans, drinking beer
and playing cards at the table where Jardine and I had had our
wine, and they claimed to have been there for several hours.

I have no idea why such an elaborate prank, involving the
participation of many people, should be played on me, except at
the instigation of the French. In that case, I cannot understand
why Prussian soldiers should lend themselves to it.

                                              BENJAMIN BATHURST

4

(Statement of Christian Hauck, innkeeper, taken at the police
station of Perleburg, 25 November 1809)

May it please your Honour, my name is Christian Hauck, and I
keep an inn at the sign of the Sword and Sceptre, and have these
past fifteen years, and my father, and his father before him, for the
past fifty years, and never has there been a complaint like this
against my inn. Your Honour, it is a hard thing for a man who
keeps a decent house, and pays his taxes, and obeys the laws, to be
accused of crimes of this sort.

I know nothing of this gentleman, nor of his coach nor his
secretary nor his servants; I never set eyes on him before he came
bursting into the inn from the yard, shouting and raving like a
madman, and crying out, 'Where the devil's that rogue of an
innkeeper?'

I said to him, 'I am the innkeeper; what cause have you to call
me a rogue, sir?'

The stranger replied: 'You're not the innkeeper I did business
with a few minutes ago, and he's the rascal I have a row to pick
with. I want to know what the devil's been done with my coach,
and what's happened to my secretary and my servants.'

I tried to tell him that I knew nothing of what he was talking
about, but he would not listen, and gave me the lie, saying that he
had been drugged and robbed, and his people kidnapped. He even
had the impudence to claim that he and his secretary had been
sitting at a table in that room, drinking wine, not fifteen minutes
before, when there had been four non-commissioned officers of

the Third Uhlans at that table since noon. Everybody in the room spoke up for me, but he would not listen, and was shouting that we were all robbers, and kidnappers, and French spies, and I don't know what all, when the police came.

Your Honour, the man is mad. What I have told you about this is the truth, and all that I know about this business, so help me God.

CHRISTIAN HAUCK

5

(Statement of Franz Bauer, inn servant, taken at the police station at Perleburg, 25 November 1809)

May it please your Honour, my name is Franz Bauer, and I am a servant at the Sword and Sceptre Inn, kept by Christian Hauck.

This afternoon, when I went into the inn yard to empty a bucket of slops on the dung heap by the stables, I heard voices and turned around, to see this gentleman speaking to Wilhelm Beick and Fritz Herzer, who were greasing their wagon in the yard. He had not been in the yard when I had turned around to empty the bucket, and I thought that he must have come in from the street. This gentleman was asking Beick and Herzer where was his coach, and when they told him they didn't know, he turned and ran into the inn.

Of my own knowledge, the man had not been inside the inn before then, nor had there been any coach, or any of the people he spoke of, at the inn, and none of the things he spoke of happened there, for otherwise I would know, since I was at the inn all day.

When I went back inside, I found him in the common-room, shouting at my master, and claiming that he had been drugged and robbed. I saw that he was mad, and was afraid that he would do some mischief, so I went for the police.

FRANZ BAUER
his (X) mark

6

(Statements of Wilhelm Beick and Fritz Herzer, peasants, taken at
the police station at Perleburg, 25 November 1809)

May it please your Honour, my name is Wilhelm Beick, and I am a
tenant on the estate of the Baron von Hentig. On this day, I and
Fritz Herzer were sent into Perleburg with a load of potatoes and
cabbages which the innkeeper at the Sword and Sceptre had
bought from the estate superintendent. After we had unloaded
them, we decided to grease our wagon, which was very dry, before
going back, so we unhitched and began working on it. We took
about two hours, starting just after we had eaten lunch, and in all
that time there was no coach and four in the inn yard. We were just
finishing when this gentleman spoke to us, demanding to know
where his coach was. We told him that there had been no coach in
the yard all the time we had been there, so he turned around and
ran into the inn. At the time, I thought that he had come out of the
inn before speaking to us, for I know that he could not have come
in from the street. Now I do not know where he came from, but I
know that I never saw him before that moment.

WILHELM BEICK
his (X) mark

I have heard the above testimony, and it is true to my own
knowledge, and I have nothing to add to it.

FRITZ HERZER
his (X) mark

7

(From Staatspolizeikapitän Ernst Hartenstein, to His Excellency,
the Baron von Krutz, Minister of Police)

25 November 1809

Your Excellency:
The accompanying copies of statements taken this day will explain
how the prisoner, the self-so-called Benjamin Bathurst, came into
my custody. I have charged him with causing disorder and being a
suspicious person, to hold him until more can be learned about

him. However, as he represents himself to be a British diplomat, I am unwilling to assume any further responsibility, and am having him sent to your Excellency, in Berlin.

In the first place, your Excellency, I have the strongest doubts of the man's story. The statement which he made before me, and signed, is bad enough, with a coach and four turning into a farm wagon, like Cinderella's coach into a pumpkin, and three people vanishing as though swallowed by the earth. Your Excellency will permit me to doubt that there ever was any such coach, or any such people. But all this is perfectly reasonable and credible, beside the things he said to me, of which no record was made.

Your Excellency will have noticed, in his statement, certain allusions to the Austrian surrender, and to French troops in Austria. After his statement had been taken down, I noticed these allusions, and I inquired, what surrender, and what were French troops doing in Austria. The man looked at me in a pitying manner, and said:

'News seems to travel slowly, hereabouts; peace was concluded at Vienna on the 14th of last month. And as for what French troops are doing in Austria, they're doing the same things Bonaparte's brigands are doing everywhere in Europe.'

'And who is Bonaparte?' I asked.

He stared at me as though I had asked him. 'Who is the Lord Jehovah?' Then, after a moment, a look of comprehension came into his face.

'So; you Prussians conceded him the title of Emperor, and refer to him as Napoleon,' he said. 'Well, I can assure you that His Britannic Majesty's Government haven't done so, and never will; not so long as one Englishman has a finger left to pull a trigger. General Bonaparte is a usurper; His Britannic Majesty's Government do not recognize any sovereignty in France except the House of Bourbon.' This he said very sternly, as though rebuking me.

It took me a moment or so to digest that, and to appreciate all its implications. Why, this fellow evidently believed, as a matter of fact, that the French Monarchy had been overthrown by some military adventurer called Bonaparte, who was calling himself the Emperor Napoleon, and who had made war on Austria and forced a surrender. I made no attempt to argue with him – one wastes time arguing with madmen – but if this man could believe that, the transformation of a coach and four into a cabbage wagon was a small matter indeed. So, to humour him, I asked him if he thought General Bonaparte's agents were responsible for his trouble at the inn.

'Certainly,' he replied. 'The chances are they didn't know me to see me, and took Jardine for the Minister, and me for the secretary, so they made off with poor Jardine. I wonder, though, that they left me my dispatch case. And that reminds me: I'll want that back. Diplomatic papers, you know.'

I told him, very seriously, that we would have to check his credentials. I promised him I would make every effort to locate his secretary and his servants and his coach, took a complete description of all of them, and persuaded him to go into an upstairs room, where I kept him under guard. I did start inquiries, calling in all my informers and spies, but, as I expected, I could learn nothing. I could not find anybody, even, who had seen him anywhere in Perleburg before he appeared at the Sword and Sceptre, and that rather surprised me, as somebody should have seen him enter the town, or walk along the street.

In this connection, let me remind your Excellency of the discrepancy in the statements of the servant, Franz Bauer, and of the two peasants. The former is certain the man entered the inn yard from the street; the latter are just as positive that he did not. Your Excellency, I do not like such puzzles, for I am sure that all three were telling the truth to the best of their knowledge. They are ignorant common folk, I admit, but they should know what they did or did not see.

After I got the prisoner into safe keeping, I fell to examining his papers, and I can assure your Excellency that they gave me a shock. I had paid little heed to his ravings about the King of France being dethroned, or about this General Bonaparte who called himself the Emperor Napoleon, but I found all these things mentioned in his papers and dispatches, which had every appearance of being official documents. There was repeated mention of the taking, by the French, of Vienna, last May, and of the capitulation of the Austrian Emperor to this General Bonaparte, and of battles being fought all over Europe, and I don't know what other fantastic things. Your Excellency, I have heard of all sorts of madmen – one believing himself to be the Archangel Gabriel, or Mohammed, or a werewolf, and another convinced that his bones are made of glass, or that he is pursued and tormented by devils – but, so help me God, this is the first time I have heard of a madman who had documentary proof for his delusions! Does your Excellency wonder, then, that I want no part of this business?

But the matter of his credentials was even worse. He had papers, sealed with the seal of the British Foreign Office, and to every appearance genuine – but they were signed, as Foreign Minister, by one George Canning, and all the world knows that Lord Castlereagh has been Foreign Minister these last five years. And to cap it all, he had a safe conduct sealed with the seal of the Prussian Chancellery – the very seal, for I compared it, under a strong magnifying glass, with one that I knew to be genuine, and they were identical! – and yet, this letter was signed, as Chancellor, not by Count von Berchtenwald, but by Baron vom und zum Stein, the Minister of Agriculture, and the signature, as far as I could see, appeared to be genuine! This is too much for me, your Excellency; I must ask to be excused from dealing with this matter, before I become as mad as my prisoner!

I made arrangements, accordingly, with Colonel Keitel, of the Third Uhlans, to furnish an officer to escort this man into Berlin. The coach in which they come belongs to this police station, and the driver is one of my men. He should be furnished expense money to get back to Perleburg. The guard is a corporal of Uhlans, the orderly of the officer. He will stay with the *Herr Oberleutnant*, and both of them will return here at their own convenience and expense.

I have the honour, your Excellency, to be, etc., etc.,

ERNST HARTENSTEIN
Staatspolizeikapitän

8

(From Oberleutnant Rudolf von Tarlburg, to Baron Eugen von Krutz)

26 November 1809

Dear Uncle Eugen:
This is in no sense a formal report; I made that at the Ministry, when I turned the Englishman and his papers over to one of your

officers – a fellow with red hair and a face like a bulldog. But there are a few things which you should be told, which wouldn't look well in an official report, to let you know just what sort of a rare fish has got into your net.

I had just come in from drilling my platoon, yesterday, when Colonel Keitel's orderly told me that the colonel wanted to see me in his quarters. I found the old fellow in undress in his sitting room, smoking his big pipe.

'Come in, Lieutenant; come in and sit down, my boy!' he greeted me, in that bluff, hearty manner which he always adopts with his junior officers when he has some particularly nasty job to be done. 'How would you like a little trip to Berlin! I have an errand, which won't take half an hour, and you can stay as long as you like, just so you're back by Thursday, when your turn comes up for road patrol.'

Well, I thought, this is the bait. I waited to see what the hook would look like, saying that it was entirely agreeable with me, and asking what his errand was.

'Well, it isn't for myself, Tarlburg,' he said. 'It's for this fellow Hartenstein, the *Staatspolizeikapitän* here. He has something he wants done at the Ministry of Police, and I thought of you because I've heard you're related to the Baron von Krutz. You are, aren't you?' he asked, just as though he didn't know all about who all his officers are related to.

'That's right, Colonel; the Baron is my uncle,' I said. 'What does Hartenstein want done?'

'Why, he has a prisoner whom he wants taken to Berlin and turned over at the Ministry. All you have to do is to take him in, in a coach, and see he doesn't escape on the way, and get a receipt for him, and for some papers. This is a very important prisoner; I don't think Hartenstein has anybody he can trust to handle him. A state prisoner. He claims to be some sort of a British diplomat, and for all Hartenstein knows, maybe he is. Also, he is a madman.'

'A madman?' I echoed.

'Yes, just so. At least, that's what Hartenstein told me. I wanted to know what sort of a madman – there are various kinds of madmen, all of whom must be handled differently – but all Hartenstein would tell me was that he had unrealistic beliefs about the state of affairs in Europe.'

'Ha! What diplomat hasn't?' I asked.

Old Keitel gave a laugh, somewhere between the bark of a dog and the croaking of a raven.

'Yes, naturally! The unrealistic beliefs of diplomats are what soldiers die of,' he said. 'I said as much to Hartenstein, but he wouldn't tell me anything more. He seemed to regret having said even that much. He looked like a man who's seen a particularly terrifying ghost.' The old man puffed hard at his famous pipe for a while, blowing smoke up through his moustache. 'Rudi, Hartenstein has pulled a hot potato out of the ashes, this time, and he wants to toss it to your uncle, before he burns his fingers. I think that's one reason why he got me to furnish an escort for his Englishman. Now, look; you must take this unrealistic diplomat, or this undiplomatic madman, or whatever in blazes he is, into Berlin. And understand this.' He pointed his pipe at me as though it were a pistol. 'Your orders are to take him there and turn him over at the Ministry of Police. Nothing has been said about whether you turn him over alive or dead, or half one and half the other. I know nothing about this business, and want to know nothing; if Hartenstein wants us to play gaol warders for him, then, *bei Gott*, he must be satisfied with our way of doing it!'

Well, to cut short the story, I looked at the coach Hartenstein had placed at my disposal, and I decided to chain the left door shut on the outside so that it couldn't be opened from within. Then, I would put my prisoner on my left, so that the only way out would be past me. I decided not to carry any weapons which he might be able to snatch from me, so I took off my sabre and locked it in the seat box, along with the dispatch case containing the Englishman's papers. It was cold enough to wear a greatcoat in comfort, so I wore mine, and in the right side pocket, where my prisoner couldn't reach, I put a little leaded bludgeon, and also a brace of pocket pistols. Hartenstein was going to furnish me a guard as well as a driver, but I said that I would take a servant who could act as guard. The servant, of course, was my orderly, old Johann; I gave him my double hunting gun to carry, with a big charge of boar-shot in one barrel and an ounce ball in the other.

In addition, I armed myself with a big bottle of cognac. I thought that if I could shoot my prisoner often enough with that, he would give me no trouble.

As it happened, he didn't, and none of my precautions – except the cognac – were needed. The man didn't look like a lunatic to me. He was a rather stout gentleman, of past middle age, with a ruddy complexion and an intelligent face. The only unusual thing about him was his hat, which was a peculiar contraption, looking like the pot out of a close stool. I put him in the carriage, and then offered him a drink out of my bottle, taking one about half as big myself. He smacked his lips over it and said, 'Well, that's real brandy; whatever we think of their detestable politics, we can't criticize the French for their liquor.' Then, he said, 'I'm glad they're sending me in the custody of a military gentleman, instead of a confounded gendarme. Tell me the truth, Lieutenant: am I under arrest for anything?'

'Why,' I said, 'Captain Hartenstein should have told you about that. All I know is that I have orders to take you to the Ministry of Police, in Berlin, and not to let you escape on the way. These orders I will carry out; I hope you don't hold that against me.'

He assured me that he did not, and we had another drink on it – I made sure, again, that he got twice as much as I did – and then the coachman cracked his whip and we were off for Berlin.

Now, I thought, I am going to see just what sort of a madman this is, and why Hartenstein is making a state affair out of a squabble at an inn. So I decided to explore his unrealistic beliefs about the state of affairs in Europe.

After guiding the conversation to where I wanted it, I asked him: 'What, Herr Bathurst, in your belief, is the real, underlying cause of the present tragic situation in Europe?'

That, I thought, was safe enough. Name me one year, since the days of Julius Caesar, when the situation in Europe hasn't been tragic! And it worked, to perfection.

'In my belief,' says this Englishman, 'the whole damnable mess is the result of the victory of the rebellious colonists in North America, and their blasted republic.'

Well, you can imagine, that gave me a start. All the world knows that the American Patriots lost their war for independence from England; that their army was shattered, that their leaders were either killed or driven into exile. How many times, when I was a little boy, did I not sit up long past my bedtime, when old Baron von Steuben was a guest at Tarlburg-Schloss, listening open-mouthed and wide-eyed to his stories of that gallant lost struggle! How I used to shiver at his tales of the terrible Winter camp, or thrill at the battles, or weep as he told how he held the dying

Washington in his arms, and listened to his noble last words, at the
Battle of Doylestown. And here, this man was telling me that the
Patriots had really won, and set up the republic for which they had
fought! I had been prepared for some of what Hartenstein had
called unrealistic beliefs, but nothing as fantastic as this.

'I can cut it even finer than that,' Bathurst continued. 'It was the
defeat of Burgoyne at Saratoga. We made a good bargain when we
got Benedict Arnold to turn his coat, but we didn't do it soon
enough. If he hadn't been on the field that day, Burgoyne would
have gone through Gates' army like a hot knife through butter.'

But Arnold hadn't been in Saratoga. I know; I have read much
of the American War. Arnold was shot dead on New Year's Day of
1776, during the attempted storming of Quebec. And Burgoyne
had done just as Bathurst had said: he had gone through Gates like
a knife, and down the Hudson to join Howe.

'But, Herr Bathurst,' I asked, 'how could that affect the
situation in Europe? America is thousands of miles away, across
the ocean.'

'Ideas can cross oceans quicker than armies. When Louis XVI
decided to come to the aid of the Americans, he doomed himself
and his regime. A successful resistance to royal authority in
America was all the French Republicans needed to inspire them.
Of course, we have Louis' own weakness to blame, too. If he'd
given those rascals a whiff of grapeshot when the mob tried to
storm Versailles in 1790 there'd have been no French Revolution.'

But he had. When Louis XVI ordered the howitzers turned on
the mob at Versailles, and then sent the dragoons to ride down the
survivors, the Republican movement had been broken. That had
been when Cardinal Talleyrand, who had then been merely Bishop
of Autun, had come to the fore and became the power that he is
today in France; the greatest King's Minister since Richelieu.

'And, after that, Louis' death followed as surely as night after
day,' Bathurst was saying. 'And because the French had no
experience in self-government, their republic was foredoomed. If
Bonaparte hadn't seized power, somebody else would have; when
the French murdered their king, they delivered themselves to
dictatorship. And a dictator, unsupported by the prestige of
royalty, has no choice but to lead his people into foreign war, to
keep them from turning upon him.'

It was like that all the way to Berlin. All these things seem foolish, by daylight, but as I sat in the darkness of that swaying coach, I was almost convinced of the reality of what he told me. I tell you, Uncle Eugen, it was frightening, as though he were giving me a view of Hell. *Gott im Himmel*, the things that man talked of! Armies swarming over Europe; sack and massacre, and cities burning; blockades, and starvation; kings deposed, and thrones tumbling like tenpins! Battles in which the soldiers of every nation fought, and in which tens of thousands were mowed down like ripe grain; and, over all, the Satanic figure of a little man in a grey coat, who dictated peace to the Austrian Emperor in Schoenbrunn, and carried the Pope away a prisoner to Savona.

Madman, eh? Unrealistic beliefs, says Hartenstein? Well, give me madmen who drool spittle, and foam at the mouth, and shriek obscene blasphemies. But not this pleasant-seeming gentleman who sat beside me and talked of horrors in a quiet, cultured voice, while he drank my cognac.

But not all my cognac! If your man in the Ministry – the one with the red hair and the bulldog face – tells you that I was drunk when I brought in that Englishman, you had better believe him!

RUDI

9

(From Count von Berchtenwald, to the British Minister)

28 November 1809

Honoured Sir:

The accompanying *dossier* will acquaint you with the problem confronting this Chancellery, without needless repetition on my part. Please to understand that it is not, and never was, any part of the intentions of the Government of His Majesty Friedrich Wilhelm III to offer any injury or indignity to the Government of His Britannic Majesty George III. We would never contemplate holding in arrest the person, or tampering with the papers, of an accredited envoy of your Government. However, we have the gravest doubt, to make a considerable understatement, that this person who calls himself Benjamin Bathurst is any such envoy, and we do not think that it would be any service to the Government of His Britannic Majesty to allow an imposter to travel about

Europe in the guise of a British diplomatic representative. We certainly should not thank the Government of His Britannic Majesty for failing to take steps to deal with some person who, in England, might falsely represent himself to be a Prussian diplomat.

This affair touches us almost as closely as it does your own Government; this man had in his possession a letter of safe conduct, which you will find in the accompanying dispatch case. It is of the regular form, as issued by this Chancellery, and is sealed with the Chancellery seal, or with a very exact counterfeit of it. However, it has been signed, as Chancellor of Prussia, with a signature indistinguishable from that of the Baron vom und zum Stein, who is the present Minister of Agriculture. Baron Stein was shown the signature, with the rest of the letter covered, and without hesitation acknowledged it for his own writing. However, when the letter was uncovered and shown him, his surprise and horror were such as would require the pen of a Goethe or a Schiller to describe, and he denied categorically ever having seen the document before.

I have no choice but to believe him. It is impossible to think that a man of Baron Stein's honourable and serious character would be party to the fabrication of a paper of this sort. Even aside from this, I am in the thing as deeply as he; if it is signed with his signature it is also sealed with my seal, which has not been out of my personal keeping in the ten years that I have been Chancellor here. In fact, the word 'impossible' can be used to describe the entire business. It was impossible for the man Benjamin Bathurst to have entered the inn yard – yet he did. It was impossible that he should carry papers of the sort found in his dispatch case, or that such papers should exist – yet I am sending them to you with this letter. It is impossible that Baron vom und zum Stein should sign a paper of the sort he did, or that it should be sealed by the Chancellery – yet it bears both Stein's signature and my seal.

You will also find in the dispatch case other credentials ostensibly originating with the British Foreign Office of the same character, being signed by persons having no connection with the Foreign Office, or even with the Government, but being sealed with apparently authentic seals. If you send these papers to London, I fancy you will find that they will there create the same situation as that caused here by this letter of safe-conduct.

I am also sending you a charcoal sketch of the person who calls himself Benjamin Bathurst. This portrait was taken without its subject's knowledge. Baron von Krutz's nephew, Lieutenant von Tarlburg, who is the son of our mutual friend Count von Tarlburg, has a *little friend*, a very clever young lady who is, as you will see, an expert at this sort of work; she was introduced into a room at the Ministry of Police and placed behind a screen, where she could sketch our prisoner's face. If you should send this picture to London, I think that there is a good chance that it might be recognized. I can vouch that it is an excellent likeness.

To tell the truth, we are at our wits' end about this affair. I cannot understand how such excellent imitations of these various seals could be made, and the signature of the Baron vom und zum Stein is the most expert forgery that I have ever seen, in thirty years' experience as a statesman. This would indicate careful and painstaking work on the part of somebody; how, then, do we reconcile this with such clumsy mistakes, recognizable as such by any schoolboy, as signing the name of Baron Stein as Prussian Chancellor, or Mr George Canning, who is a member of the opposition party and not connected with your Government, as British Foreign Secretary?

These are mistakes which only a madman would make. There are those who think our prisoner is a madman, because of his apparent delusions about the great conqueror, General Bonaparte, *alias* the Emperor Napoleon. Madmen have been known to fabricate evidence to support their delusions, it is true, but I shudder to think of a madman having at his disposal the resources to manufacture the papers you will find in this dispatch case. Moreover, some of our foremost medical men, who have specialized in the disorders of the mind, have interviewed this man Bathurst and say that, save for his fixed belief in a non-existent situation, he is perfectly rational.

Personally, I believe that the whole thing is a gigantic hoax, perpetrated for some hidden and sinister purpose, possibly to create confusion, and undermine the confidence existing between your Government and mine, and to set against one another various persons connected with both Governments, or else as a mask for some other conspiratorial activity. Without specifying any Sovereigns or Governments who might wish to do this, I can think of two groups, namely, the Jesuits, and the outlawed French

Republicans, either of whom might conceive such a situation to be to their advantage. Only a few months ago, you will recall, there was a Jacobin plot unmasked at Köln.

But, whatever this business may portend, I do not like it. I want to get to the bottom of it as soon as possible, and I will thank you, my dear Sir, and your Government, for any assistance you may find possible.

I have the honour, Sir, to be, etc., etc., etc.,

BERCHTENWALD

10

FROM BARON VON KRUTZ TO THE COUNT VON
    BERCHTENWALD
MOST URGENT; MOST IMPORTANT
TO BE DELIVERED IMMEDIATELY AND IN PERSON,
    REGARDLESS OF CIRCUMSTANCES

28 November 1809

Count von Berchtenwald:

Within the past half-hour, that is, at about eleven o'clock tonight, the man calling himself Benjamin Bathurst was shot and killed by a sentry at the Ministry of Police, while attempting to escape from custody.

A sentry on duty in the rear courtyard of the Ministry observed a man attempting to leave the building in a suspicious and furtive manner. This sentry, who was under the strictest orders to allow no one to enter or leave without written authorization, challenged him; when he attempted to run, the sentry fired his musket at him, bringing him down. At the shot, the Sergeant of the Guard rushed into the courtyard with his detail, and the man whom the sentry had shot was found to be the Englishman, Benjamin Bathurst. He had been hit in the chest with an ounce ball, and died before the doctor could arrive, and without recovering consciousness.

An investigation revealed that the prisoner, who was confined on the third floor of the building, had fashioned a rope from his bedding, his bed cord, and the leather strap of his bell pull; this rope was only long enough to reach to the window of the office on

the second floor, directly below, but he managed to enter this by
kicking the glass out of the window. I am trying to find out how he
could do this without being heard; I can assure your Excellency
that somebody is going to smart for this night's work. As for the
sentry, he acted within his orders; I have commended him for
doing his duty, and for good shooting, and I assume full
responsibility for the death of the prisoner at his hands.

I have no idea why the self-so-called Benjamin Bathurst, who,
until now, was well-behaved and seemed to take his confinement
philosophically, should suddenly make this rash and fatal attempt,
unless it was because of those infernal dunderheads of madhouse
doctors who have been bothering him. Only this afternoon, your
Excellency, they deliberately handed him a bundle of newspapers
– Prussian, Austrian, French, and English – all dated within the
last month. They wanted, they said, to see how he would react.
Well, God pardon them, they've found out!

What does your Excellency think should be done about giving
the body burial?

KRUTZ

11
(From the British Minister to the Count von Berchtenwald)

20 December 1809

My Dear Count von Berchtenwald:
Reply from London to my letter of the 28th *ult.*, which accompanied
the dispatch case and the other papers, has finally come to hand. The
papers which you wanted returned – the copies of the statements
taken at Perleburg, the letter to the Baron von Krutz from the police
captain, Hartenstein, and the personal letter of Krutz's nephew,
Lieutenant von Tarlburg, and the letter of safe- conduct found in the
dispatch case – accompany herewith. I don't know what the people at
Whitehall did with the other papers; tossed them into the nearest fire,
for my guess. Were I in your Excellency's place, that's where the
papers I'm returning would go.

I have heard nothing, yet, from my dispatch of the 29th *ult.*
concerning the death of the man who called himself Benjamin
Bathurst, but I doubt very much if any official notice will ever be
taken of it. Your Government had a perfect right to detain this
fellow, and, that being the case, he attempted to escape at his own

risk. After all, sentries are not required to carry loaded muskets in order to discourage them from putting their hands in their pockets.

To hazard a purely unofficial opinion, I should not imagine that London is very much dissatisfied with this *dénouement*. His Majesty's Government are a hard-headed and matter-of-fact set of gentry who do not relish mysteries, least of all mysteries whose solution may be more disturbing than the original problem.

This is entirely confidential, your Excellency, but those papers which were in that dispatch case kicked up the devil's own row in London, with half the Government bigwigs protesting their innocence to high Heaven, and the rest accusing one another of complicity in the hoax. If that was somebody's intention, it was literally a howling success. For a while, it was even feared that there would be questions in Parliament, but eventually the whole vexatious business was hushed.

You may tell Count Tarlburg's son that his little friend is a most talented young lady; her sketch was highly commended by no less an authority than Sir Thomas Lawrence, and here, your Excellency, comes the most bedevilling part of a thoroughly bedevilled business. The picture was instantly recognized. It is a very fair likeness of Benjamin Bathurst, or, I should say, Sir Benjamin Bathurst, who is King's Lieutenant-Governor for the Crown Colony of Georgia. As Sir Thomas Lawrence did his portrait a few years back, he is in an excellent position to criticize the work of Lieutenant von Tarlburg's young lady. However, Sir Benjamin Bathurst was known to have been in Savannah, attending to the duties of his office, and in the public eye, all the while that his double was in Prussia. Sir Benjamin does not have a twin brother. It has been suggested that this fellow might be a half-brother, born on the wrong side of the blanket, but, as far as I know, there is no justification for this theory.

The General Bonaparte, alias the Emperor Napoleon, who is given so much mention in the dispatches, seems also to have a counterpart in actual life; there is, in the French army, a Colonel of Artillery by that name, a Corsican who Gallicized his original name of Napolione Buonaparte. He is a most brilliant military theoretician; I am sure some of your own officers, like General Scharnhorst, could tell you about him. His loyalty to the French Monarchy has never been questioned.

This same correspondence to fact seems to crop up everywhere in that amazing collection of pseudo-dispatches and pseudo-statepapers. The United States of America, you will recall, was the style by which the rebellious colonies referred to themselves, in the Declaration of Philadelphia. The James Madison who is mentioned as the current President of the United States is now living, in exile, in Switzerland. His alleged predecessor in office, Thomas Jefferson, was the author of the rebel Declaration; after the defeat of the rebels, he escaped to Havana, and died, several years ago, in the Principality of Lichtenstein.

I was quite amused to find our old friend Cardinal Talleyrand – without the ecclesiastical title – cast in the role of chief advisor to the usurper, Bonaparte. His Eminence, I have always thought, is the sort of fellow who would land on his feet on top of any heap, and who would as little scruple to be Prime Minister to His Satanic Majesty as to His Most Christian Majesty.

I was baffled, however, by one name, frequently mentioned in those fantastic papers. This was the English General Wellington. I haven't the least idea who this person might be.

I have the honour, your Excellency, etc., etc., etc.,

ARTHUR WELLESLEY

Elizabeth Taylor

Summer Schools

Sitting outside on the sill, the cat watched Melanie through the window. The shallow arc between the tips of his ears, his baleful stare, and his hunched-up body blown feathery by the wind, gave him the look of a barn-owl. Sometimes, a strong gust nearly knocked him off balance and bent his whiskers crooked. Catching Melanie's eye, he opened his mouth wide in his furious, striped face, showed his fangs and let out a piteous mew instead of a roar.

Melanie put a finger in her book and padded across the room in her stockinged feet. When she opened the french windows, the gale swept into the room and the fire began to smoke. Now that he was allowed to come in, the cat began a show caprice; half in, he arched his back and rubbed against the step, purring loudly. Some leaves blew across the floor.

'Either in or out, you fool,' Melanie said impatiently. Still holding the door, she put her foot under the cat's belly and half-pushed, half-lifted him into the room.

The french windows had warped, like all the other wooden parts of the house. There were altogether too many causes for irritation, Melanie thought. When she had managed to slam the door shut, she stood there for a moment, looking out at the garden, until she had felt the full abhorrence of the scene. Her revulsion was so complete as to be almost unbelievable; the sensation became ecstatic.

On the veranda, a piece of newspaper had wrapped itself, quivering frenziedly, round a post. A macrocarpa hedge tossed about in the wind; the giant hydrangea by the gate was full of bus-tickets, for here was the terminus, the very end of the esplanade.

The butt and end, Melanie thought, of all the long-drawn-out tedium of the English holiday resort. Across the road a broken bank covered with spiky grass hid most of the sands, but she could imagine them clearly, brown and ribbed, littered with bits of cuttle-fish and mussel-shells. The sea – far out – was staved with white.

Melanie waited as a bowed-over, mufflered man, exercising a dog, then a duffel-coated woman with a brace of poodles on leads completed the scene. Satisfied, she turned back to the fire. It was all as bad as could be and on a bright day it was hardly better, for the hard glitter of the sun seemed unable to lift the spirits. It was usually windy.

The creaking sound of the rain, its fitful and exasperated drumming on the window, she listened to carefully. In one place at the end of the veranda, it dropped more heavily and steadily: she could hear it as if the noise were in her own breast. The cat – Ursula's – rubbed its cold fur against her legs and she pushed him away crossly, but he always returned.

'A day for indoors,' Ursula said gaily. She carried in the tea-tray, and set down a covered dish on the hearth with the smug triumph of one giving a great treat.

I am to be won over with buttered scones, Melanie thought sulkily. The sulky expression was one that her face, with its heavy brows and full mouth, fell into easily. 'One of Miss Rogers's nasty looks,' her pupils called it, finding it not alarming, but depressing. Ursula, two years younger, was plumper, brighter, more alert. Neither was beautiful.

'Oh, sod that cat of yours,' Melanie said. He was now mewing at the french windows to be let out. Melanie's swearing was something new since her father had died – an act of desperation, such as a child might make. Father would turn in his grave, Ursula often said. Let him turn, said Melanie. 'Who will look after him while you're away?' she asked, nodding at the cat. Ursula put him outside again and came back to pour out the tea. 'How do you mean, look after him? Surely you don't mind. I'll order the fish. You'll only have to cook it and give it to him.'

'I shan't be here.'

The idea had suddenly occurred, born of vindictiveness and envy. For Pamela had no right to invite Ursula to stay there on her own. Melanie was only two years their senior; they had all been at the same school. Apart from all that, the two sisters always spent their holidays together; in fact, had never been separated. To Melanie, the invitation seemed staggering insolent, and Ursula's decision to accept it could hardly be believed. She had read out the letter at breakfast one morning and Melanie, on her way out of the room to fetch more milk, had simply said, 'How extraordinary,' her light, scornful voice dismissing the subject. Only a sense of time passing and middle age approaching had given Ursula the courage (or effrontery) to renew the subject. For the first time that either she or Melanie could remember, her energy and enthusiasm overcame the smothering effect of her sister's lethargy.

She means to go, Melanie told herself. Her sensation of impotence was poison to her. She had a bitter taste in her mouth, and chafed her hands as if they were frozen. If Ursula were truly going, though, Melanie determined that the departure should be made as difficult as possible. Long before she could set out for the station she should be worn out with the obstacles she had had to overcome.

'You can't expect me to stay here on my own just in order to look after your cat.'

And lest Ursula should ask where she was going before she had had time to make her plans, she got up quickly and went upstairs.

The cat was to stay in kennels and Ursula grieved about it. Her grief Melanie brushed aside as absurd, although she was at the same time inclined to allow Ursula a sense of guilt. 'A dog one can at least take with one,' she told her. She had decided that the cat reflected something of Ursula's own nature – too feminine (although it was a tom); it might be driven, though not led, and the refusal to cooperate mixed, as it was, with cowardice resulted in slyness.

The weather had not improved. They could remember the holidays beginning in this way so often, with everything – rain, flowers, bushes – aslant in the wind. It will be pretty miserable at Pamela's, Melanie thought. She could imagine that house and its surroundings – a parade of new shops nearby, a tennis club, enormous suburban pubs at the corners of roads. She was for ever adding something derogatory to the list. 'Dentists' houses always depress me,' she said. 'I don't think I could stay in one – with all that going on under the same roof.'

What awaited herself was much vaguer.

'It will be like being at school – though having to run to the bell instead of ringing it,' Ursula said, when she had picked up the prospectus for the Summer Lecture Course. 'A pity you can't just go to the discussions and not stay there. Breakfast 8.15,' she read. 'Oh, Lord. The Victorian Novel. Trollope. 9.30.'

Melanie, in silence, held out her hand for the prospectus and Ursula gave it to her. She did not see it again.

'Will you want Mother's fur?' she asked, when she began to pack. 'I just thought . . . evenings, you know, it might be useful . . .'

'I shall have evenings, too,' Melanie reminded her.

Their mother could not have guessed what a matter of contention her ermine wrap would turn out to be when she was dead.

'How is Melanie?' Pamela asked.

'Oh, she's well. She's gone on a little holiday, too.'

'I'm so glad. I should have liked to have asked her to come with you,' Pamela lied. 'But there's only this single bed.'

Ursula went over to the window. The spare room was at the back of the house and looked across some recreation grounds – a wooden pavilion, a bowling-green; and tennis courts – just as Melanie had said there would be.

That evening, there was the pub.

All afternoon the front-door bell had rung, and Pamela and Ursula, sitting in the drawing-room upstairs, could hear the crackle of Miss Potter's starched overall as she crossed the hall to answer it. Patients murmured nervously when they entered, but shouted cheerful goodbyes as they left, going full tilt down the gravelled drive and slamming the gate after them.

'I'm sorry about the bell,' Pamela said. 'At first, I thought it would send me out of my mind, but now it's no worse than a clock striking.'

Ursula thought it extraordinary that she had changed so much since their schooldays. It was difficult to find anything to talk about. The books they had once so passionately discussed were at the very bottom of the glass-fronted case, beneath text-books on dentistry and Book Club editions, and Ursula, finding Katherine Mansfield's *Journal* covered with dust, felt estranged. Perhaps

Pamela had become a good cook instead, she thought, for there were plenty of books on that.

Melanie would have scorned the room, with its radiogram and cocktail cabinet and the matching sofa and chairs. The ash-trays were painted with bright sayings in foreign languages; there were piles of fashion magazines that later – much later, Ursula guessed – would be put in the waiting-room downstairs. The parchment lamp-shades were stuck over with wine labels and the lamps were made out of chianti bottles. The motif of drinking was prevalent, from a rueful yet humorous viewpoint. When Pamela opened the cigarette-box it played 'The More we are Together', and Ursula wondered if the clock would call 'Prosit' when it struck six.

'That's the last patient,' Pamela said. 'Mike will come up panting for a drink.'

Her full skirt, printed with a jumble of luggage-labels, flew out wide as she made a dash to the cocktail cabinet. She was as eager to be ready with everything as if she were opening a pub.

Panic now mingled with the feeling of estrangement, as Ursula listened to the footsteps on the stairs. 'Hello, there, Ursula,' said Mike as he threw open the door. 'And how are you? Long time, no see, indeed.'

'Not since our wedding,' Pamela reminded him.

'Well, what will you be after taking?' Mike asked. He slapped his hands together, ready for action, took up a bottle and held it to the light.

'I suppose he feels uneasy because I am a school-mistress,' Ursula thought; 'And perhaps also – lest I shall think Pam married beneath her.'

Pamela put out the glasses and some amusing bottle-openers and corkscrews. Ursula remembered staying with her as a girl, had a clear picture of the gloomy dining-room: a dusty, cut-glass decanter, containing the dregs of some dark, unidentified liquid had stood in the centre of the great sideboard, its position never shifting an inch to the right or left. From that imprisoning house and those oppressive parents, Mike had rescued his betrothed and, though she had shed Katherine Mansfield somewhere on the way, she seemed as gay as could be that she had escaped.

Now she kissed her husband, took her drink and went downstairs – to turn the waiting-room back into a dining-room, she said. Mike's uneasiness increased. He was clearly longing for her to return.

'You must be a brave man,' Ursula said suddenly. 'I remember Pam's mother and father and how nervous I was when I stayed there. Even when we were quite well on in our teens, we were made to lie down after luncheon, in a darkened room for ages and ages. "And no reading, dears," her mother always said as we went upstairs. At home, we never rested – or only when we were little children, but I pretended that we did, in case Pam's mother should think badly of mine. They seemed so very stern. To snatch away their only daughter must have needed courage.'

For the first time, he looked directly at her. In his eyes was a timid expression. He may have been conscious of this and anxious to hide it, for almost immediately he glanced away.

'I girded on my armour,' he said, 'and rode up to the portcullis and demanded her. That was all there was to it.'

She smiled, thinking, *So this room is the end of a fairy tale.*

'Astonishing good health, my dear,' Mike said, lifting his glass.

Melanie took her coffee and, summoning all her courage, went to sit down beside Mrs Rybeck, who gave her a staving-off smile, a slight shake of her head as she knitted, her lips moving silently. When she came to the end of the row, she apologized, and jotted down on her knitting-pattern, whatever it was she had been counting.

'What a stimulating evening,' Melanie said.

'Have you not heard George Barnes lecture before?' Mrs Rybeck was obviously going to be condescending again, but Melanie was determined to endure it. Then – what she had hoped – Professor Rybeck came in. She felt breathless and self-conscious as he approached.

'Darling!' he murmured, touching his wife's hair, then bowed to Melanie.

'Miss Rogers,' his wife reminded him quickly. 'At Saint Winifred's, you know, where Ethel's girls were.'

'Yes, of course I know Miss Rogers,' he said.

His dark hair receded from a forehead that seemed always moist, as were his dark and mournful eyes. As soon as they heard his voice – low, catarrhal and with such gentle inflections – some of the women, who had been sitting in a group by the window, got up and came over to him.

'Professor Rybeck,' one said. 'We are beside ourselves with excitement about your lecture tomorrow.'

'Miss Rogers was just saying that she thought highly of George's talk this evening,' said Mrs Rybeck.

'Ah, George!' her husband said softly. 'I think George likes to think he has us all by the ears. Young men do. But we mustn't let him sharpen his wits on us till we ourselves are blunt. None the less, he knows his Thackeray.'

Melanie considered herself less esteemed for having mentioned him.

'How I love *Middlemarch*,' some woman said. 'I think it is my favourite novel.'

'Then I only hope I do it justice tomorrow,' Professor Rybeck said. Although he seemed full of confidence, he smiled humbly. Nothing was too much trouble.

Pamela had insisted that the three of them should squeeze into the front of the car and Ursula, squashed up in the middle, sat with rounded shoulders and her legs tucked to one side. She was worried about the creases in her skirt. The wireless was on very loud and both Pamela and Mike joined in the Prize Song from *Die Meistersinger*. Ursula was glad when they reached The Swan.

The car-park was full. This pub was where everybody went, Pamela explained; 'at the moment,' she added. In the garden, the striped umbrellas above the tables had been furled; the baskets of geraniums over the porch were swinging in the wind.

'Astonishingly horrid evening,' Mike said, when some of his acquaintances greeted him. 'This is Pam's friend, Ursula. Ursie, this is Jock' – or Jean or Eve or Bill. Ursula lost track. They all knew one another and Mike and Pam seemed popular. 'Don't look now, the worst has happened,' someone had said in a loud voice when Mike opened the door of the Saloon Bar.

Ursula was made much of. From time to time, most of them were obliged to bring out some dull relation or duty-guest. ('Not really one of us'), and it was a mark of friendliness to do one's best to help with other people's problems – even the most tiresome of old crones would be attended to; and Ursula, although plump and prematurely grey, was only too ready to smile and join in the fun.

'You're one of us, I can see,' someone complimented her.

'Cheers!' said Ursula before she drank. Melanie would have shivered with distaste.

'We are all going on to Hilly's,' Pam called to Mike across the bar at closing time.

This moving-on was the occasion for a little change round of passengers and, instead of being squeezed in between Pamela and Mike, Ursula was taken across the car-park by a man called Guy.

'Daddy will give you a scarf for your head,' he promised, opening the door of his open car. The scarf tucked inside his shirt was yellow, patterned with horses and when he took it off and tied it round Ursula's head, the silk was warm to her cheeks.

They drove very fast along the darkening roads and were the first to arrive.

'Poor frozen girl,' said Guy when he had swung the car round on the gravelled sweep in front of the house and brought it up within an inch of the grass verge. With the driving off his mind, he could turn his attention to Ursula and he took one of her goosefleshy arms between his hands and began to chafe it. 'What we need is a drink,' he said. 'Where the hell have they all got to?'

She guessed that to drive fast and to arrive first was something he had to do and, for his sake and to help on the amiability of the evening, she was glad that he had managed it.

'You're sure it's the right house?' she asked.

'Dead sure, my darling.'

She had never been called 'darling' by a man and, however meaningless the endearment, it added something to her self-esteem, as their arriving first had added something to his.

She untied the scarf and gave it back to him. He had flicked on his cigarette lighter and was looking for something in the dash-pocket. For a moment, while the small glow lasted, she could study his face. It was like a ventriloquist's dummy's – small, alert, yet blank; the features gave the appearance of having been neatly painted.

He found the packet of cigarettes; then he put the scarf round his neck and tied it carefully. 'Someone's coming,' he said. 'They must have double-crossed us and had one somewhere on the way.'

'You drove fastest, that's all,' she said, playing her part in the game.

'Sorry if it alarmed you, sweetheart.' He leaned over and kissed her quickly, just before the first of the cars came round the curve of the drive.

'That's the first evening gone,' Ursula thought, when later, she lay in bed, rather muzzily going over what had happened. She could remember the drawing-room at Hilly's. She had sat on a cushion on the floor and music from a gramophone above her had spilled over her head, so that she had seen people's mouths opening and shutting but had not been able to hear the matching conversations. In many ways the room – though it was larger – had seemed like Pamela's, with pub-signs instead of bottle-labels on the lamp-shades. Her sense of time had soon left her and her sense of place grew vaguer, but some details irritated her because she could not evade them – particularly a warming-pan hanging by the fireplace in which she confronted her distorted reflection.

There had seemed no reason why the evening should ever end and no way of setting going all the complications of departure. Although she was tired, she had neither wanted to leave nor to stay. She was living a tiny life within herself, sitting there on the cushion; sipping and smiling and glancing about her. Mike had come across the room to her. She turned to tilt back her head to look up into his face but at once felt giddy and had to be content with staring at his knees, at the pin-stripes curving baggily, a thin stripe, then a wider, more feathery one. She began to count them, but Mike had come to take her home to bye-byes he said, stretching out a hand. If I can only do this, I can do anything, Ursula thought, trying to rise and keep her balance. I was silly to sit so low down in the first place, she decided. 'I think my foot has gone to sleep,' she explained and smiled confidingly at his knees. His grip on her arm was strong; although appearing to be extending a hand in gallantry, he was really taking her weight and steadying her, too. She had realized this, even at the time and later, lying safe in bed at last, she felt wonderfully grateful for his kindness, and did not at all mind sharing such a secret with him.

Pamela had put a large jug of water by her bed. An hour earlier, it had seemed unnecessary, but now water was all she wanted in the world. She sat up and drank, with a steady, relentless rhythm, as animals drink. Then she slid back into the warm bedclothes and tried to reconstruct in her mind that drive with Guy and became, in doing so, two people, the story-teller and the listener; belittling his endearments, only to reassure herself about them. The sports car, the young man (he was not very old, she told herself), the summer darkness, in spite of its being so windy, were all things that other young girls she had known had taken for granted, at Oxford and elsewhere, and she herself had been denied. They seemed all the more miraculous for having been done without for so long.

Of recent years she had often tried to escape the memory of two maiden ladies who had lived near her home when she and Melanie were girls. So sharp-tongued and cross-looking, they had seemed then as old as could be, yet may have been no more than in their fifties, she now thought. Frumpish and eccentric, at war with one another as well as all their neighbours, they were to be seen tramping the lanes, single file and in silence, with their dogs. To the girls, they were the most appalling and unenviable creatures, smelling of vinegar, Melanie had said. The recollection of them so long after they were dead disturbed Ursula and depressed her, for she could see how she and Melanie had taken a turning in their direction, yet scarcely anything as definite as this, for there had been no action, no decision; simply, the road they had been on had always, it seemed, been bending in that direction. In no time at all, would they not be copies of those other old ladies? The Misses Rogers, the neighbours would think of them, feeling pity and nervousness. The elder Miss Rogers would be alarmingly abrupt, with her sarcastic voice and old-fashioned swearwords. They won't be afraid of me, Ursula decided; but had no comfort from the thought. People would think her bullied and would be sorry. She, the plumper one, with her cat and timid smiles, would give biscuits to children when Melanie's back was turned. Inseparable, yet alien to one another, they would become. Forewarned as she was, she felt herself drifting towards that fate and was afraid when she woke at night and thought of it.

Her first drowsiness had worn off and her thirst kept her wakeful. She lay and wondered about the details of Pamela's escape from her parents' sad house and all that had threatened her there – watchfulness, suspicion, envy and capricious humours; much of the kind of thing she herself suffered from Melanie. Pamela's life now was bright and silly, and perhaps she had run away from the best part of herself; but there was nothing in the

future to menace her as Ursula was menaced by her own picture of
the elderly Misses Rogers.

'But *surely*,' insisted the strained and domineering voice. The
woman gripped the back of the chair in front of her and stared up
at Professor Rybeck on the platform.

At the end of his lecture, he had asked for questions or
discussions. To begin with, everyone had seemed too stunned with
admiration to make an effort; there were flutterings and mur-
murings, but for some time no one stood up. Calmly, he waited,
sitting there smiling, eyes half-closed and his head cocked a little as
if he were listening to secret music, or applause. His arms were
crossed over his chest and his legs were crossed too, and one foot
swayed back and forth rhythmically.

The minute Mr Brundle stood up, other people wanted to. He
was an elderly, earnest man, who had been doggedly on the track
of culture since his youth. His vanity hid from him the half-stifled
yawns he evoked, the glassy look of those who, though caught,
refused to listen and also his way of melting away to one victim any
group of people he approached. Even Professor Rybeck looked
restless, as Mr Brundle began now to pound away at his theory.
Then others, in disagreement or exasperation, began to jump to
their feet, or made sharp comments, interrupting; even shot their
arms into the air, like schoolchildren. World Peace they might
have been arguing about, not George Eliot's Dorothea Casaubon.

'Please, please,' said Professor Rybeck, in his melodious
protesting voice. 'Now, Mrs Thomas, let us hear you.'

'But *surely*,' Mrs Thomas said again.

'Wouldn't it be time to say?' asked Mrs Wetherby – she sounded
diffident and had blushed; she had never spoken in the presence of
so many people before, but wanted badly to make her mark on the
Professor. She was too shy to stand upright and leaned forward,
lifting her bottom a couple of inches from the chair. Doing so, she
dropped her notebook and pencil, her stole slipped off and when
she bent down to pick it up she also snatched at some large,
tortoise-shell pins that had fallen out of her hair. By the time she
had done all this, her chance was gone and she had made her mark
in the wrong way. The one and only clergyman in the room had
sprung to his feet and, knowing all the tricks needed to command,
had snatched off his spectacles and held them high in the air while,

for some reason no one was clear about, he denounced Samuel Butler.

'I think, Comrade . . . Professor, I should say,' Mr Brundle interrupted. 'If we might return but briefly to the subject. . . .'

Melanie closed her eyes and thought how insufferable people became about what had cost them too much to possess – education, money, or even good health.

Lightly come or not at all, is what I like, she told herself crossly and, when she opened her eyes, glanced up at Professor Rybeck, who smiled with such placid condescension as the ding-dong argument went on between clergyman and atheist (for literature – Victorian or otherwise – had been discarded) and then she looked for Mrs Rybeck and found her sitting at the end of the second row, still knitting. She gave, somehow, an impression of not being one of the audience, seemed apart from them, preoccupied with her own thoughts, lending her presence only, like a baby-sitter or the invigilator at an examination – well accustomed to the admiration her husband had from other women of her own age, she made it clear that she was one with him in all he did and thought; their agreement, she implied, had come about many years ago and needed no more discussion, and if the women cared to ask her any of the questions he had no time to answer, then she could give the authorized replies. With all this settled, her placidity, like his, was almost startling to other people, their smiling lips (not eyes), their capacity for waiting for others to finish speaking (and it was far removed from the act of listening), is often to be found in the mothers of large families. Yet she was childless. She had only the Professor, and the socks she knitted were for him. She is more goddessy than motherly, Melanie thought.

'We are summoned to the banqueting-hall,' said the Professor, raising his hand in the air, as a bell began to ring. This was the warning that lunch would be ready in ten minutes, the Secretary had told them all when they arrived, and 'warning' was a word she had chosen well. The smell of minced beef and cabbage came along passages towards them. To Melanie it was unnoticeable, part of daily life, like other tedious affairs; one disposed of the food, as of any other small annoyance, there were jugs of water to wash it down and slices of bread cut hours before that one could crumble as one listened to one's neighbour.

One of Melanie's neighbours was an elementary school-teacher to whom she tried not to be patronizing. On her other side was a Belgian woman whose vivacity was intolerable. She was like a bad caricature of a foreigner, primly sporty and full of gay phrases. 'Mon Dieu, we have had it, chums,' she said, lifting the water-jug and finding it empty. The machine-gun rattle of consonants vibrated in Melanie's head long after she was alone. 'Oh la la!' the woman sometimes cried, as if she were a cheeky French maid in an old-fashioned farce.

'You think "Meedlemahtch" is a good book,' she asked Melanie. They all discussed novels at mealtimes too; for they were what they had in common. Melanie was startled, for Professor Rybeck had spent most of the morning explaining its greatness. 'It is one of the great English novels,' she said.

'As great as Charles Morgan, you think? In the same class?'

Melanie looked suspicious and would not answer.

'It is such a funny book. I read it last night and laughed so much.'

'And will read *War and Peace* between tea and dinner, I suppose,' the elementary school-teacher murmured. 'Oh dear, how disgusting!' She pushed a very pale, boiled caterpillar to the side of her plate. 'If that happened to one of our little darlings at school dinner, the mother would write at once to her M.P.'

At Melanie's school, the girls would have hidden the creature under a fork in order not to spoil anyone else's appetite, but she did not say so.

'A *funny* book?' she repeated, turning back to the Belgian woman.

'Yes, I like it so much when she thinks that the really delightful marriage must be that where your husband was a sort of father, and could teach you Hebrew if you wished it. Oh la la! For heaven's sake.'

'Then she did read a page or two,' said the woman on Melanie's other side.

A dreadful sadness and sense of loss had settled over Melanie when she herself had read those words. They had not seemed absurd to her; she had felt tears pressing at the back of her eyes. So often, she had longed for protection and compassion, to be instructed and concentrated upon; as if she were a girl again, yet with a new excitement in the air.

As they made their way towards the door, when lunch was over, she could see Professor Rybeck standing there talking to one or two of his admirers. Long before she drew near to him, Melanie found another direction to glance in. What she intended for unconcern, he took for deliberate hostility and wondered at what point of his lecture he had managed to offend her so.

In a purposeless way, she wandered into the garden. The Georgian house – a boy's preparatory-school in the term-time – stood amongst dark rhododendron bushes and silver birches. Paths led in many directions through the shrubberies, yet all converged upon the lake – a depressing stretch of water, as bleary as an old looking-glass, shadowed by trees and broken by clumps of reeds.

The pain of loneliness was a worse burden to her here than it had ever been at home and she knew – her behaviour as she was leaving the dining-room had reminded her – that the fault was in herself.

'Don't think that I will make excuses to speak to you,' she had wanted to imply. 'I am not so easily dazzled as these other women.' But I wanted him to speak to me, she thought, and perhaps I only feared that he would not.

She sat down on the bank above the water and thought about the Professor. She could even imagine his lustrous eyes turned upon her, as he listened.

'I give false impressions,' she struggled to explain to him. 'In my heart . . . I am . . .'

'I know what you are,' he said gently. 'I knew at once.'

The relief would be enormous. She was sure of that. She could live the rest of her life on the memory of that moment.

'But he is a fraud,' the other, destructive voice in her insisted, the voice that had ruined so much for her. 'He is not a fraud,' she said firmly; her lips moved; she needed to be so definite with herself. 'Perhaps he cannot find the balance between integrity and priggishness.'

'Is that all?' asked the other voice.

The dialogue faded out and she sighed, thinking: I wish I hadn't come. I feel so much worse here than I do at home.

Coming round the lake's edge towards her was the atrocious little Mr Brundle. She pretended not to have seen him and got to her feet and went off in the other direction.

By the afternoon post came a letter from Ursula, saying how dull she was and that Melanie had been so right about it all – and that comforted her a little.

Ursula was polishing a glass on a cloth printed with a chart of vintage years for champagne. Although she was drunk, she wondered at the usefulness of this as a reference. It would be strange to go home again to a black telephone, white sheets and drying-up cloths on which there was nothing at all to read, not a recipe for a cocktail or a cheerful slogan.

On the draining-board two white tablets fizzed, as they rose and fell in a glass of water. The noise seemed very loud to her and she was glad when the tablets dissolved and there was silence.

'There you are,' Guy said, handing the glass to her. The water still spat and sparkled and she drank it slowly, gasping between sips.

'Pamela will wonder where I am,' she said. She put the glass on the draining-board and sat down with a bump on one of the kitchen chairs. She had insisted on washing the two glasses before she went home, and had devoted herself to doing so with single-mindedness; but Guy had been right, and she gave in. Everything she had to do had become difficult – going home, climbing the stairs, undressing. I shall just have to sit on this chair and let time pass, she decided. It will pass, she promised herself, and it mends all in the end.

'Where did we go after that Club?' she suddenly asked frowning.

'Nowhere,' said Guy. 'On our way back to Pamela's we stopped for a drink. That's all.'

'Ah, yes!'

She remembered the outside of this bungalow and a wooden gate with the name Hereiam. It had been quite dark when they walked up the stony path to the front door. Now, it seemed the middle of the night. 'I think you gave me too much whisky,' she said, with a faint, reproachful smile.

'As a matter of fact, I gave you none. It was ginger-ale you were drinking.'

She considered this and then lifted her eyes to look at him and asked anxiously: 'Then had I had . . . was I . . . ?'

'You were very sweet.'

She accepted this gravely. He put his hands under her arms and

brought her to her feet and she rested the side of her face against
his waistcoat and stayed very still, as if she were counting his
heartbeats. These, like the fizzing drink, also sounded much too
loud.

'I didn't wash the other glass,' she said.

'Mrs Lamb can do it in the morning.'

She went from one tremulous attempt at defence to another,
wanting to blow her nose, or light a cigarette or put something
tidy. In the sitting-room, earlier, when he had sat down beside her
on the sofa, she had sprung up and gone rapidly across the room to
look for an ash-tray. 'Who is this?' she had asked, picking up a
framed photograph and holding it at arm's length, as if to ward
him off. 'Girl friend,' he said briefly, drinking his whisky and
watching her manœuvres with amusement.

'Haven't you ever wanted to get married?' she had asked.

'Sometimes. Have you?'

'Oh, sometimes . . . I daresay,' she answered vaguely.

Now, in the kitchen, he had caught her at last, she was clasped
in his arms and feeling odd, she told him.

'I know. There's some coffee nearly ready in the other room.
That will do untold good.'

What a dreadful man he is, really, in spite of his tenderness, she
thought. So hollow and vulgar that I don't know what Melanie
would say.

She was startled for a moment, wondering if she had murmured
this aloud; for, suddenly, his heartbeat had become noisier – from
anger, she was afraid.

'You are very kind,' she said appeasingly. 'I am not really used
to drinking as much as people do here – not used to drinking at all.'

'What *are* you used to?'

'Just being rather dull, you know – my sister and I.'

His way of lifting her chin up and kissing her was too
accomplished and she was reminded of the way in which he drove
the car. She was sure that there was something here she should
resent. Perhaps he was patronizing her; for the kiss had come too
soon after her remark about the dullness of her life. I can bring
some excitement into it, he may have thought.

Without releasing her, he managed to stretch an arm and put out
the light. 'I can't bear to see you frowning,' he explained. 'Why
frown anyway?'

'That coffee . . . but then I mustn't stay for it, after all. Pamela will be wondering . . .'

'Pam will understand.'

'Oh, I hope not.'

She frowned more than ever and shut her eyes tightly although the room was completely dark.

Melanie sat on the edge of the bed, coughing. She was wondering if she had suddenly got T.B. and kept looking anxiously at her handkerchief.

The sun was shining, though not into her room. From the window, she could see Professor Rybeck sitting underneath the Wellingtonia with an assortment of his worshippers. From his gestures, Melanie could tell that it was he who was talking, and talking continuously. The hand rose and fell and made languid spirals as he unfolded his theme, or else cut the air decisively into slices. Mrs Rybeck was, of course, knitting. By her very presence, sitting a little apart from her husband, like a woman minding a stall on a fairground, she attracted passers-by. Melanie watched the Belgian woman now approaching, to say her few words about the knitting, then having paid her fee, to pass on to listen to the Professor.

Desperately, Melanie wished to be down there listening, too; but she had no knowledge of how to join them. Crossing the grass, she would attract too much attention. Ah, *she* cannot keep away, people would think, turning to watch her. She must be in love with the Professor after all, like the other women; but perhaps more secretly, more devouringly.

She had stopped coughing and forgotten tuberculosis for the moment, as she tried to work out some more casual way than crossing the lawn. She might emerge less noticeably from the shrubbery behind the Wellingtonia, if only she could be there in the first place.

She took a clean handkerchief from a drawer and smoothed her hair before the looking-glass; and then a bell rang for tea and, when she went back to the window, the group under the tree was breaking up. Mrs Rybeck was rolling up her knitting and they were all laughing.

I shall see him at tea, Melanie thought. She could picture him bowing to her, coldly, and with the suggestion that it was she who disliked him rather than he who disliked her. I could never put things right now, she decided.

She wondered what Ursula would be doing at this minute. Perhaps sitting in Pamela's little back garden having tea, while, at the front of the house, the patients came and went. She had said that she would be glad to be at home again for Pamela had changed and they had nothing left in common. And coming here hasn't been a success, either, Melanie thought, as she went downstairs to tea. She blamed Ursula very much for having made things so dull for them both. There must be ways of showing her how mistaken she had been, ways of preventing anything of the kind happening again.

'Miss Rogers,' said the Professor with unusual gaiety. They had almost collided at the drawing-room door. 'Have you been out enjoying the sun?'

She blushed and was so angry that she should that she said quite curtly, 'No, I was writing letters in my room.'

He stood quickly aside to let her pass and she did so without a glance at him.

Their holiday was over. On her way back from the station, Ursula called at the kennels for the cat and Melanie, watching her come up the garden path, could see the creature clawing frantically at her shoulder, trying to hoist himself out of her grasp. The taxi-driver followed with the suitcase.

Melanie had intended to be the last home and had even caught a later train than was convenient, in order not to have to be waiting there for her sister. After all her planning, she was angry to have found the house empty.

'Have you been home long?' Ursula asked rather breathlessly. She put the cat down and looked round. Obviously Melanie had not, for her suitcase still stood in the hall and not a letter had been opened.

'Only a minute or two,' said Melanie.

'That cat's in a huff with me. Trying to punish me for going away, I suppose. He's quite plump though. He looks well, doesn't he? Oh, it's so lovely to be home.'

She went to the hall-table and shuffled the letters, then threw them on one side. Melanie had said nothing.

'Aren't *you* glad to be home?' Ursula asked her.

'No, I don't think so.'

'Well, I'm glad you had a good time. It was a change for you.'

'Yes.'

'And now let's have some tea.'

She went into the kitchen and, still wearing her hat, began to get out the cups and saucers. 'They didn't leave any bread,' she called out. 'Oh, yes, it's all right, I've found it.' She began to sing, then stopped to chatter to the cat, then sang again.

Melanie had been in the house over an hour and had done nothing.

'I'm so glad you had a good time,' Ursula said again, when they were having tea.

'I'm sorry you didn't.'

'It was a mistake going there, trying to renew an old friendship. You'd have hated the house.'

'You'd have liked *mine*. Grey stone, Georgian, trees and a lake.'

'Romantic,' Ursula said and did not notice that Melanie locked her hands together in rather a theatrical gesture.

'Pam seems complacent. She's scored over me, having a husband. Perhaps that's why she invited me.'

'What did you do all the time?'

'Just nothing. Shopped in the morning – every morning – the housewife's round – butcher, baker, candlestick maker. "I'm afraid the piece of skirt was rather gristly, Mr Bones." That sort of thing. She would fetch half a pound of butter one day and go back for another half-pound the next morning – just for the fun of it. One day, she said, "I think we'll have some hock for supper." I thought she was talking about wine, but it turned out to be some bacon – not very nice. Not very nice of me to talk like this, either.'

However dull it had been, she seemed quite excited as she described it; her cheeks were bright and her hands restless.

'We went to the cinema once, to see a Western,' she added. 'Mike is very fond of Westerns.'

'How dreadful for you.'

Ursula nodded.

'Well, that's their life,' she said, 'I was glad all the time that you were not there. Darling puss, so now you've forgiven me.'

To show his forgiveness, the cat jumped on her lap and began dough-punching, his extended claws catching the threads of her skirt.

'Tell me about *you*,' Ursula said. She poured out some more tea to sip while Melanie had her turn; but to her surprise Melanie frowned and looked away.

'Is something the matter?'

'I can't talk about it yet, or get used to not being there. This still seems unreal to me. You must give me time.'

She got up, knocked over the cream jug and went out of the room. Ursula mopped up the milk with her napkin and then leant back and closed her eyes. Her moment's consternation at Melanie's behaviour had passed; she even forgot it. The cat relaxed, too, and, curled up against her, slept.

Melanie was a long time unpacking and did nothing towards getting supper. She went for a walk along the sea road and watched the sunset on the water. The tide was out and the wet sands were covered with pink light. She dramatized her solitary walk and was in a worse turmoil when she reached home.

'Your cough is bad,' Ursula said when they had finished supper.

'Is it?' Melanie said absent-mindedly.

'Something has happened, hasn't it?' Ursula asked her, and then looked down quickly, as if she were confused.

'The end of the world,' said Melanie.

'You've fallen in love?' Ursula lifted her head and stared at her.

'To have to go back to school next week and face those bloody children – and go on facing them, for ever and for ever – or other ones exactly like them . . . the idea suddenly appals me.'

Her bitterness was so true, and Ursula could hear her own doom in her sister's words. She had never allowed herself to have thoughts of that kind.

'But can't you . . . can't he?' she began.

'We can't meet again. We never shall. So it *is* the end of the world, you see,' said Melanie. The scene gave her both relief and anguish. Her true parting with Professor Rybeck (he had looked up from *The Times* and nodded as she crossed the hall) was obliterated for ever. She could more easily bear the agonized account she now gave to Ursula and she would bear it – their noble resolve, their last illicit embrace.

'He's married, you mean?' Ursula asked bluntly.

'Yes, married.'

Mrs Rybeck, insensitively knitting at the execution of their hopes, appeared as an evil creature, tenacious and sinister.

'But to say goodbye for ever . . .' Ursula protested. 'We only have one life . . . would it be wicked, after all?'

'What could there be . . . clandestine meetings and sordid arrangements?'

Ursula looked ashamed.

'I should ruin his career,' said Melanie.

'Yes, I see. You could write to one another, though.'

'Write!' Melanie repeated in a voice as light as air. 'I think I will go to bed now. I feel exhausted.'

'Yes, do, and I will bring you a hot drink.' As Melanie began to go upstairs, Ursula said, 'I am very sorry, you know.'

While she was waiting for the milk to rise in the pan, she tried to rearrange her thoughts, especially to exclude (now that there was so much nobility in the house) her own squalid – though hazily recollected – escapade. Hers was a more optimistic nature than Melanie's and she was confident of soon putting such memories out of her mind.

When she took the hot milk upstairs, her sister was sitting up in bed reading a volume of Keats' letters. 'He gave it to me as I came away,' she explained, laying the book on the bedside table, where it was always to remain.

We have got this to live with now, Ursula thought, and it will be with us for ever, I can see – the reason and the excuse for everything. It will even grow; there will be more and more of it, as time goes on. When we are those two elderly Miss Rogers we are growing into, it will still be there. 'Miss Melanie, who has such a sharp tongue,' people will say. 'Poor thing . . . a tragic love-affair a long way back.' I shall forget there was a time when we did not have it with us.

Melanie drank her milk and put out the light; then she lay down calmly and closed her eyes and prepared herself for her dreams. Until they came, she imagined walking by the lake, as she had done, that afternoon, only a few days ago; but instead of Mr Brundle coming into the scene, Professor Rybeck appeared. He walked towards her swiftly, as if by assignation. Then they sat down and looked at the tarnished water – and she added a few swans for them to watch. After a long delicious silence, she began to speak. Yet words were not really necessary. She had hardly begun the attempt; her lips shaped the beginning of a sentence – 'I am . . .' and then he took her hand and held it to his cheek. 'I know what you are,' he said. 'I knew at the very beginning.'

Although they had parted for ever, she realized that she was now at peace – she felt ennobled and enriched, and saw herself thus, reflected from her sister's eyes, and she was conscious of Ursula's solemn wonder and assured by it.

Dick Francis

Twenty-One Good Men and True

Arnold Roper whistled breathily while he boiled his kettle and spooned instant own-brand economy pack coffee into the old blue souvenir from Brixham. Unmelodic and without rhythm, the whistling was nonetheless an expression of content, both with things in general and the immediate prospect ahead. Arnold Roper, as usual, was going to the races: and as usual, if he had a bet, he would win. Neat, methodical, professional, he would operate his unbeatable system and grow richer, the one following the other as surely as chickens and eggs.

Arnold Roper at forty-five was one of nature's bachelors, a lean-bodied, handy man accustomed to looking after himself, a man who found the chatter of companionship a nuisance. Like a sailor, though he had never been to sea, he kept his surroundings polished and shipshape, ordering his life in plastic dustbin-liners and reheated take-away food.

The one mild problem on Arnold Roper's horizon was his wealth. The getting of the money was his most intense enjoyment. The spending of it was something he postponed to a remote and dreamlike future, when he would exchange his sterile flat for a warm, unending idyll under tropical palms. It was the interim storage of the money which was currently causing him, if not positive worry, at least occasional frowns of doubt. He might, he thought, as he stirred dried milk grains into the brownish brew, have to find space for yet another wardrobe in his already crowded bedroom.

If anyone had told Arnold Roper he was a miser he would have denied it indignantly. True, he lived frugally, but by habit rather than obsession: and he never took out his wealth just to look at it, and count, and gloat. He would not have admitted as miserliness the warm feeling that stole over him every night as he lay down to sleep, smiling from the knowledge that all around him, filling two oak-veneered sale-bargain bedroom suites, was a ton or two of negotiable paper.

It was not that Arnold Roper distrusted banks. He knew, too, that money won by betting could not be lost by tax. He would not have kept his growing gains physically around him were it not that his unbeatable system was also a splendid fraud.

The best frauds are only ever discovered by accident, and Arnold could not envisage any such accident happening to him.

Jamie Finland woke to his customary darkness and thought three disconnected thoughts with the first second of consciousness. The sun is shining. It is Wednesday. They are racing today here at Ascot.

He stretched out a hand and put his fingers delicately down on the top of his bedside tape recorder. There was a cassette lying there. Jamie smiled, slid the cassette into the recorder, and switched on.

His mother's voice spoke to him. 'Jamie, don't forget the man is coming to mend the television at ten-thirty and please put the washing into the machine, there's a dear, as I am so pushed this morning, and would you mind having yesterday's soup again for lunch. I've left it in a saucepan ready. Don't lose all that ten quid this afternoon or I'll cut the plug off your stereo. Home soon after eight, love.'

Jamie Finland's thirty-eight-year-old mother supported them both on her earnings as an agency nurse, and she had made a fair job, her son considered, of bringing up a child who could not see. He rose gracefully from bed and put on his clothes: blue shirt, blue jeans. 'Blue is Jamie's favourite colour,' his mother would say, and her friends would say 'Oh yes?' politely and she could see them thinking 'How could he possibly know?' But Jamie could identify blue as surely as his mother's voice, and red, and yellow, and every colour in the spectrum, as long as it was daylight. 'I can't see in the dark,' he had said when he was six, and only his mother, from watching his sureness by day and his stumbling by night, had understood what he meant. Walking radar, she called him. Like many young blind people he could sense the wavelength of light, and distinguish the infinitesimal changes of frequency reflected from coloured things close to him. Strangers thought him uncanny. Jamie believed everyone could see that way if they wanted to, and could not himself clearly understand what they meant by sight.

He made and ate some toast and thankfully opened the door to the television fixer. 'In my room,' he said, leading the way. 'We've got sound but no picture.' The television fixer looked at the blind eyes and shrugged. If the boy wanted a picture he was entitled to it, same as everyone else who paid their rental. 'Have to take it back to the workshop,' he said, judicially pressing buttons.

'The races are on,' Jamie said. 'Can you fix it by then?'

'Races? Oh yeah. Well . . . Tell you what, I'll lend you another set. Got one in the van . . .' He staggered off with the invalid and returned with the replacement. 'Not short of radios, are you,' he said, looking around. 'What do you want six for?'

'I leave them tuned to different things,' Jamie said. 'That one,' he pointed accurately, 'listens to aircraft, that one to the police, those three are on ordinary radio stations, and this one . . . local broadcasts.'

'What you need is a transmitter. Put you in touch with all the world.'

'I'm working on it,' Jamie said. 'Starting today.'

He closed the door after the man and wondered whether betting on a certainty was in itself a crime.

Greg Simpson had no such qualms. He paid his way into the Ascot paddock, bought a racecard, and ambled off to add a beer and sandwich to a comfortable paunch. Two years now, he thought, munching, since he had first set foot on the Turf: two years since he had exchanged his principles for prosperity and been released from paralysing depression. They seemed a distant memory, now, those fifteen months in the wilderness; the awful humiliating collapse of his seemingly secure pensionable world. No comfort in knowing that mergers and cutbacks had thrown countless near-top managers like himself on to the redundancy heap. At fifty-two, with long success-strewn experience and genuine administrative skill, he had expected that he at least would find another suitable post easily; but door after closed door, and a regretful chorus of

'Sorry, Greg,' 'Sorry, old chap,' 'Sorry, Mr Simpson, we need someone younger,' had finally thrust him into agonized despair. And it was just when, in spite of all their anxious economies, his wife had had to deny their two children even the money to go swimming, that he had seen the curious advertisement.

Jobs offered to mature respectable persons who must have been unwillingly unemployed for at least twelve months.

Part of his mind told him he was being invited to commit a crime, but he had gone nonetheless to the subsequently arranged interview, in a London pub, and he had been relieved, after all, to meet the very ordinary man holding out salvation. A man like himself, middle-aged, middle-educated, wearing a suit and tie and indoor skin.

'Do you go to the races?' Arnold Roper asked. 'Do you gamble? Do you follow the horses?'

'No,' Greg Simpson said prudishly, seeing the job prospect disappear but feeling all the same superior. 'I'm afraid not.'

'Do you bet on dogs? Go to Bingo? Do the Pools? Play bridge? Feel attracted by roulette?'

Greg Simpson silently shook his head and prepared to leave.

'Good,' said Arnold Roper cheerfully. 'Gamblers are no good to me. Not for this job.'

Greg Simpson relaxed into a glow of self-congratulation on his own virtue. 'What job?' he said.

Arnold Roper wiped out the Simpson smirk. 'Going to the races,' he said bluntly. 'Betting when I say bet, and never at any other time. You would have to go to race meetings most days, like any other job. You would be betting on certainties, and after every win I would expect you to send me twenty-five pounds. Anything you made above that would be yours. It is foolproof, and safe. If you go about it in a businesslike way, and don't get tempted into the mug's game of backing your own fancy, you'll do very well. Think it over. If you're interested, meet me here again tomorrow.'

Betting on certainties . . . every one a winner. Arnold Roper had been as good as his word, and Greg Simpson's lifestyle had returned to normal. His qualms had evaporated once he learned that even if the fraud were discovered, he himself would not be involved. He did not know how his employer acquired his infallible information, and, if he speculated, he didn't ask. He knew him only as John Smith, and had never met him since those

first two days, but he heeded his warning that if he failed to attend
the specified race meetings or failed to send his twenty-five-pound
payment, the bounty would stop dead.

He finished his sandwich and went down to mingle with the
bookmakers as the horses cantered down to the post for the start of
the first race.

From high on the stands Arnold Roper looked down through
powerful binoculars, spotting his men one by one. The perfect
workforce, he thought, smiling to himself; no absenteeism, no
union troubles, no complaints. There were twenty-one of them at
present on his register, all contentedly receiving his information,
all dutifully returning their moderate levies, and none of them
knowing of the existence of the others. In an average week they
would all bet for him twice; in an average week, after expenses, he
added a thousand in readies to his bedroom.

In the five years since he had begun in a small way to put his
scheme into operation, he had never picked a defaulter. The
thinking-it-over time gave the timid and honest an easy way out; and
if Arnold himself had doubts, he simply failed to return on day two.
The rest, added one by one to the fold, lived comfortably with quiet
minds and prayed that their benefactor would never be rumbled.

Arnold himself couldn't see why he ever should be. He put
down the binoculars and began in his methodical fashion to get on
with his day's work. There was always a good deal to see to in the
way of filling in forms, testing equipment, and checking that the
nearby telephone was working. Arnold never left anything to
chance.

Down at the starting gate sixteen two-year-olds bucked and
skittered as they were fed by the handlers into the stalls.
Two-year-old colts, thought the starter resignedly, looking at his
watch, could behave like a pack of prima donnas in a heatwave in
Milan. If they didn't hurry with that chestnut at present squealing
and backing away determinedly, he would let the other runners off
without him. He was all too aware of the television cameras
pointing his way, mercilessly awaiting his smallest error. Starters
who got the races off minutes late were unpopular. Starters who
got the races off early were asking for official reprimands and
universal curses, because of the fiddles that had been worked in the
past on premature departures.

The starter ruled the chestnut out of the race and pulled his lever at time plus three minutes twenty seconds, entering the figures meticulously in his records. The gates crashed open, the fifteen remaining colts roared out of the stalls, and along on the stands the serried ranks of race-glasses followed their progress over the five-furlong sprint.

Alone in his special box, the judge watched intently. A big pack of two-year-olds over five furlongs were often a problem, presenting occasionally even to his practised eyes a multiple dead heat. He had learned all the horses by name and all the colours by heart, a chore he shared every day with the race-reading commentators, and from long acquaintance he could recognize most of the jockeys by their riding style alone, but still the ignominy of making a mistake flitted uneasily through his dreams. He squeezed his eyeballs, and concentrated.

Up in his eyrie the television commentator looked through his high-magnification binoculars, which were mounted rocksteady like a telescope, and spoke unhurriedly into his microphone: 'Among the early leaders are Breakaway and Middle Park, followed closely by Pickup, Jetset, Darling Boy and Gumshoe . . . Coming to the furlong marker the leaders are bunched, with Jetset, Darling Boy, Breakaway all showing . . . One furlong out, there is nothing to choose between Darling Boy, Jetset, Gumshoe, Pickup . . . In the last hundred yards . . . Jetset, Darling Boy . . .'

The colts stretched their necks, the jockeys swung their whips, the crowd rose on tiptoes and yelled in a roar which drowned the commentary, and in his box the judge's eyes ached with effort. Darling Boy, Jetset, Gumshoe and Pickup swept past the winning post in line abreast, and an impersonal voice over the widespread loudspeakers announced calmly, 'Photograph. Photograph.'

Half a mile away in his own room Jamie Finland listened to the race on television and tried to imagine the pictures on the screen. Racing was misty to him. He knew the shape of the horses from handling toys and riding a rocker, but their size and speed were mysterious; he had no conception at all of a broad sweep of railed racecourse, or of the size or appearance of trees.

As he grew older, Jamie was increasingly aware that he had drawn lucky in the maternal stakes, and he had become in his teens protective rather than rebellious, which touched his hard-pressed mother sometimes to tears. It was for her sake that he had welcomed the television fixer, knowing that, for her, sound without pictures was almost as bad as pictures without sound for himself. Despite a lot of trying he could pick up little from the screen through his ultra-sensitive fingertips. Electronically produced colours gave him none of the vibrations of natural light.

He sat hunched with tension at his table, the telephone beside his right hand and one of his radios at his left. There was no telling, he thought, whether the bizarre thing would happen again, but if it did, he would be ready.

'One furlong out, nothing to choose . . .' said the television commentator, his voice rising to excitement-inducing crescendo. 'In the last hundred yards, Jetset, Darling Boy, Pickup and Gumshoe . . . At the post, all in line . . . perhaps Pickup got there in the last stride but we'll have to wait for the photograph. Meanwhile, let's see the closing stages of the race again . . .'

The television went back on its tracks, and Jamie waited intently with his fingers over the quick easy numbers of the push-button telephone.

Along on the racecourse the crowds buzzed like agitated bees round the bookmakers who were transacting deals as fast as they could. Photo-finishes were always popular with serious gamblers, who bet with fervour on the outcome. Some punters really believed in the evidence of their own quick eyes: others found it a chance to hedge their main bet or even recoup a positive loss. A photo was the second chance, the lifebelt to the drowning, the temporary reprieve from torn-up tickets and anti-climax.

'Six-to-four on Pickup,' shouted young Billy Hitchins hoarsely, from his prime bookmaking pitch in the front row facing the stands, 'Six-to-four on Pickup.' A rush of customers descending from the crowded steps enveloped him. 'A tenner, Pickup, right sir. Five on Gumshoe, right sir. Twenty Pickup, you're on sir. Fifty? Yeah, if you like. Fifty at evens, Jetset, why not . . .' Billy Hitchins, in whose opinion Darling Boy had taken the race by a nostril, was happy to rake in the money.

Greg Simpson accepted Billy Hitchins's ticket for an even fifty on Jetset and hurried to repeat his bet with as many bookmakers as he could reach. There was never much time between the arrival of the knowledge and the announcement of the winner. Never much, but always enough. Two minutes at least. Sometimes as much as five. A determined punter could strike five or six bets in that time, given a thick skin and a ruthless use of elbows. Greg reckoned he could burrow to the front of the closest of throngs after all those years of rush-hour commuting on the Underground, and he managed, that day at Ascot, to lay out all the cash he had brought with him; all four hundred pounds of it, all at evens, all on Jetset.

Neither Billy Hitchins, nor any of his colleagues, felt the slightest twinge of suspicion. Sure, there was a lot of support for Jetset, but so there was for the three other horses, and in a multiple finish like this one a good deal of money always changed hands. Billy Hitchins welcomed it, because it gave him, too, a chance of making a second profit on the race.

Greg noticed one or two others scurrying with wads to Jetset, and wondered, not for the first time, if they too were working for Mr Smith. He was sure he'd seen them often at other meetings, but he felt no inclination at all to accost one of them, and ask. Safety lay in anonymity; for him, for them, and for John Smith.

In his box the judge pored earnestly over the black-and-white print, sorting out which nose belonged to Darling Boy, and which to Pickup. He could discern the winner easily enough, and had murmured its number aloud as he wrote it on the pad beside him. The microphone linked to the public announcement system waited mutely at his elbow for him to make his decision on second and third places, a task seeming increasingly difficult. Number two, or number eight. But which was which?

It was quiet in his box, the scurrying and shouting among the bookmakers' stands below hardly reached him through the window glass.

At his shoulder a racecourse official waited patiently, his job only to make the actual announcement, once the decision was made. With a bright light and a magnifying glass the judge studied the noses. If he got them wrong, a thousand knowledgeable photo-readers would let him know it. He wondered if he should see about a new prescription for his glasses. Photographs never seemed so sharp in outline these days.

Greg Simpson thought regretfully that the judge was overdoing the delay. If he had known he would have had so much time, he would have brought with him more than four hundred. Still, four hundred clear profit (less betting tax) was a fine afternoon's work; and he would send Mr Smith his meagre twenty-five with a grateful heart. Greg Simpson smiled contentedly, and briefly, as if touching a lucky talisman, he fingered the tiny transistorized hearing aid he wore unobtrusively under hair and trilby behind his left ear.

Jamie Finland listened intently, head bent, his curling dark hair falling on to the radio with which he eavesdropped on aircraft. The faint hiss of the carrier wave reached him unchanged, but he waited with quickening pulse and a fluttering feeling of excitement. If it didn't happen, he thought briefly, it would be very boring indeed.

Although he was nerve-strainingly prepared, he almost missed it. The radio spoke one single word, distantly, faintly, without emphasis, 'Eleven'. The carrier wave hissed on, as if never disturbed, and it took Jamie's brain two whole seconds to light up with a laugh of joy.

He pressed the buttons and connected himself to the local bookmaking firm.

'Hullo? This is Jamie Finland. I have a ten pound credit arranged with you for this afternoon. Well . . . please will you put it all on the result of the photo-finish of this race they've just run at Ascot? On number eleven, please.'

'Eleven?' echoed a matter-of-fact voice at the other end. 'Jetset?'

'That's right,' Jamie said. 'Eleven. Jetset.'

'Right. Jamie Finland, even tenner on Jetset. Right?'

'Right,' Jamie said. 'I was watching it on the box.'

'Don't we all, chum,' said the voice in farewell, clicking off.

Jamie sat back in his chair with a tingling feeling of mischief. If eleven really had won, he was surely plain robbing the bookie. But who would know? How could anyone ever know? He wouldn't even tell his mother, because she would disapprove and might make him give the winnings back. He imagined her voice if she came home and found he had turned her ten pounds into twenty. He also imagined if she found he had lost it all on the first race betting on the result of a photo-finish that he couldn't even see.

He hadn't told her that it was because of the numbers on the radio he had wanted to bet at all. He'd said that he knew people often bet from home while they were watching racing on television. He'd said it would give him a marvellous new interest, if he could do that while she was out at work. He had persuaded her without much trouble to lend him a stake and arrange things with the bookmakers, and he wouldn't have done it at all if the certainty factor had been missing.

When he'd first been given the radio which received aircraft frequencies he had spent hours and days listening to the calls of the jetliners thundering overhead on their way in and out of Heathrow; but the fascination had worn off, and gradually he tuned in less and less. By accident one day, having twiddled the tuning knob aimlessly without finding an interesting channel, he forgot to switch the set off. In the afternoon, while he was listening to the Ascot televised races, the radio suddenly emitted one word. 'Twenty-three.'

Jamie switched the set off but took little real notice until the television commentator, announcing the result of the photo-finish, spoke almost as if in echo. 'Twenty-three . . . Swanlake, number twenty-three, is the winner.'

How *odd*, Jamie thought. He left the tuning knob undisturbed, and switched the aircraft radio on again the following Saturday, along with Kempton Park races on television. There were two photo-finishes, but no voice-of-God on the ether. Ditto nil results from Doncaster, Chepstow and Epsom persuaded him, shrugging, to put it down to coincidence, but with the re-arrival of a meeting at Ascot he decided to give it one more try.

'Five,' said the radio quietly; and later 'Ten'. And, duly, numbers five and ten were given the verdict by the judge.

The judge, deciding he could put off the moment no longer, handed his written-down result to the waiting official, who leaned forward and drew the microphone to his mouth.

'First, number eleven,' he said. 'A dead heat for second place between number two and number eight. First Jetset. Dead heat for second, Darling Boy and Pickup. The distance between first and second a short head. The fourth horse was number twelve.'

The judge leaned back in his chair and wiped the sweat from his forehead. Another photo-finish safely past . . . but there was no doubt they were testing to his nerves.

Arnold Roper picked up his binoculars the better to see the winning punters collect from the bookmakers. His twenty-one trusty men had certainly had time today for a thorough killing. Greg Simpson, in particular, was sucking honey all along the line; but then Greg Simpson, with his outstanding managerial skills, was always, in Arnold's view, the one most likely to do best. Greg's success was as pleasing to Arnold as his own.

Billy Hitchins handed Greg his winnings without a second glance, and paid out, too, to five others whose transistor hearing aids were safely hidden by hair. He reckoned he had lost, altogether, on the photo betting, but his book for the race itself had been robustly healthy. Billy Hitchins, not displeased, switched his mind attentively to the next event.

Jamie Finland laughed aloud and banged his table with an ecstatic fist. Someone, somewhere, was talking through an open microphone, and if Jamie had had the luck to pick up the transmission, why shouldn't he? Why shouldn't he? He thought of the information as an accident, not a fraud, and he waited with uncomplicated pleasure for another bunch of horses to finish nose to nose. Betting on certainties, he decided, quietening his conscience, was not a crime if you come by the information innocently.

After the fourth race he telephoned to bet on number fifteen, increasing his winnings to thirty-five pounds.

Greg Simpson went home at the end of the afternoon with a personal storage problem almost as pressing as Arnold's. There was a limit, he discovered, to the amount of ready cash one could stow away in an ordinary suit, and he finally had to wrap the stuff in the *Sporting Life* and carry it home under his arm, like fish and chips. Two in one day, he thought warmly. A real clean-up. A day to remember. And there was always tomorrow, back here at Ascot, and Saturday at Sandown, and next week, according to the list which had arrived anonymously on the usual postcard, Newbury and Windsor. With a bit of luck he could soon afford a new car, and Joan could book up for the skiing holiday with the children.

Billy Hitchins packed away his stand and equipment, and with the help of his clerk carried them the half mile along the road to his betting shop in Ascot High Street. Billy at eighteen had horrified his teachers by ducking university and apprenticing his bright mathematical brain to his local bookie. Billy at twenty-four had taken over the business, and now, three years later, was poised for expansion. He had had a good day on the whole, and after totting up the total, and locking the safe, he took his betting-shop manager along to the pub.

'Funny thing,' said the manager over the second beer. 'That new account, the one you fixed up yesterday, with that nurse.'

'Oh yes . . . the nurse. Gave me ten quid in advance. They don't often do that.' He drank his scotch and water.

'Yeah . . . Well, this Finland, while he was watching the telly, he phoned in two bets, both on the results of the photos, and he got it right both times.'

'Can't have that,' said Billy, with mock severity.

'He didn't place other bets, see? Unusual, that.'

'What did you say his name was?'

'Jamie Finland.'

The barmaid leaned towards them over the bar, her friendly face smiling and the pink sweater leaving little to the imagination. 'Jamie Finland?' she said. 'Ever such a nice boy, isn't he? Shame about him being blind.'

'What?' said Billy.

The barmaid nodded. 'Him and his mother, they live just down the road in those new flats, next door to my sister. He stays home most of the time, studying and listening to his radios. And you'd never believe it, but he can tell colours, he can really. My sister says it's really weird, but he told her she was wearing a green coat, and she was.'

'I don't believe it,' Billy said.

'It's true as God's my judge,' said the barmaid, offended.

'No . . .' Billy said. 'I don't believe that even if he can tell a green coat from a red he could distinguish colours on a television screen with three or four horses crossing the line abreast. You can't do it often even if you can see.' He sat and thought. 'It could be a coincidence,' he said. 'On the other hand, I lost a lot today on those photos.' He thought longer. 'We all took a caning over those photos. I heard several of the other bookies complaining about the run on Jetset . . .' He frowned. 'I don't see how it could be rigged . . .'

Billy put his glass down with a crash which startled the whole bar.

'Did you say Jamie Finland listens to radios? What radios?'

'How should I know?' said the barmaid, bridling.

'He lives near the course,' Billy said, thinking feverishly. 'So just suppose he somehow overheard the photo result before it was given on the loudspeakers. But that doesn't explain the delay . . . how was there time for him . . . and probably quite a lot of others who heard the same thing . . . to get their money on.'

'I don't know what you're on about,' said the barmaid.

'I think I'll pop along and see Jamie Finland,' said Billy Hitchins. 'And ask who or what he heard . . . if he heard anything at all . . .'

'Bit far-fetched,' said the manager judiciously. 'The only person who could delay things long enough would be the judge.'

'Oh my God,' said Billy, awestruck. 'What about that? What about the judge?'

Arnold Roper did not know about the long fuse being lit in the pub. To Arnold, Billy Hitchins was a name on a bookmaker's stand. He could not suppose that brainy Billy Hitchins would drink in a pub where the barmaid had a sister who lived next door to a blind boy who had picked up his discreet transmissions on a carelessly left-on radio which, unlike most, was capable of receiving one-ten to one-forty megahertz on V.H.F.

Arnold Roper travelled serenely homewards with his walkie-talkie-type transmitter hidden as usual inside his inner jacket pocket, its short aerial retracted now safely out of sight. The line-of-sight low-powered frequency he used was in his opinion completely safe, as only a passing aircraft was likely to receive it, and no pilot on earth would connect a simple number spoken on the air with the winner of the photo-finish down at Ascot, or Epsom, or Newmarket, or York.

Back on the racecourse Arnold had carefully packed away and securely locked up the extremely delicate and expensive apparatus which belonged to the firm which employed him. Arnold Roper was not the judge. Arnold Roper's job lay in operating the photo-finish camera. It was he who watched the print develop; he who could take his time delivering it to the judge; he who always knew the winner first.

Note on the Notes

The earliest of these stories was first published over a century ago, and a good half of them are more than fifty years old. It is not surprising that in that sort of time some references will have become obsolete and some verbal usages and expressions obscure. In that time, too, the general reading public have become less knowledgeable and less disposed to clear up such problems for themselves. Recently, for instance, readers of a quality newspaper troubled to write in to grumble that a columnist had left a French phrase untranslated and a mention of the Greek Calends unexplained. In the years when the bulk of the material gathered here was written, you were expected to have access to a standard French dictionary and to, say *The Concise Oxford Dictionary*, and to use them as a matter of course. Should you need them.

Accordingly, I have tried to explain some words and references that may cause contemporary readers difficulty. I have ignored those that seem to me merely uncommon or not immediately clear, partly to strike a small blow for the use of dictionaries and encyclopedias, partly to save what would be quite a lot of space. I have added a few comments and personal remarks, but I have kept critical observations to a minimum.

Notes

Rudyard Kipling (1865–1936) *Beyond the Pale*

Written as a 'turnover' piece for the Lahore English-language paper, *The Civil and Military Gazette*, of which Kipling was assistant editor, and first published there in 1888. Reprinted in the same year with others of the same provenance in *Plain Tales from the Hills*.
bustee: suburb, village.
dhak: a jungle bush of the Punjab.
boorka: a native robe.
the vernacular: Hindustani, the lingua franca of northern India.

Ambrose Bierce (1842–?1914) *An Occurrence at Owl Creek Bridge*

Bierce enlisted in the Union forces at the outbreak of the American Civil War in 1861 and served through to its end in 1865, being twice severely wounded. He began writing his stories about that war in the 1880s and collected them in 1891. He went to Mexico in 1913, a time of civil commotion there, and disappeared.

M. R. James (1862–1936) *'Oh, Whistle, and I'll Come to You, My Lad'*

Most of James's stories were originally written to be read at Christmas-time to friends at King's College, Cambridge or at Eton. This one, his best known, was collected in *Ghost Stories of an Antiquary* in 1904. James said that in its writing he had Felixstowe in mind. The title, embodying an old catch-phrase, alludes to a poem by Burns, ironically since the Burns character is offering friendship – 'whistle and I'll be there'. To 'whistle for a wind' is also what becalmed sailors were said to do and there is or was a superstition that excessive whistling will produce a storm, though I can produce no definite reference.
the Long: i.e. long (summer) vacation.
ferae naturae: of wild nature, i.e. a wild animal. It is not quite clear whether James means to say that a human boy is a wild animal.
The legends on the whistle. The first one, rearranged, gives

FLABIS – FURBIS – FLEBIS: you will blow [the whistle] – you will be raving mad – you will weep. The second legend is translated in the text. At this date the swastika had no Nazi connections, but was an ancient good-luck symbol traceable to medieval times and to modern Japan and Tibet. Irony again.

G. K. Chesterton (1874–1936) *The Blue Cross*

This story, the first in which Father Brown appeared, was first published in 1910 and collected the following year in *The Innocence of Father Brown*. As often, Chesterton telescoped the time of the action. Even by horse-bus, with the last bit on foot, it could not have taken an able-bodied man *all day* (from 'half-way through the morning' to the time of the appearance of the first stars) to cover the seven or eight miles from Victoria to Hampstead Heath. But I suppose it is more fun in compressed form.

colossus of crime: not then the cliché that it has become.

shovel hat: broad-brimmed, favoured by some clergymen. By synecdoche, shovel hat = clergyman.

'The Private Secretary': a three-act farce of this title by the actor Charles Hawtrey opened in London in 1884 and was popular for many years. The eponymous figure is a dim, golosh-wearing clergyman.

spiked bracelet, Donkey's Whistle, the Spots: invented terms.

James Joyce (1882–1941) *A Painful Case*

This appeared in the volume *Dubliners*, published in 1914 before its author turned to modernism in his more famous *Ulysses* and *Finnegans Wake*.

desk: here, a box with a lid designed for reading and writing upon.

Maynooth Catechism, more normally Maynooth catechism: authoritative compendium of religious instruction emanating from the seminary of Maynooth near Dublin.

Hauptmann: German writer Gerhart Hauptmann (1862–1946), author of a series of 'naturalistic' dramas depicting the life of the working classes or the poverty-stricken, published *Michael Kramer* in 1900. Joyce also translated his work.

Bile Beans, or Bile Beans: a patent digestive preparation.

exotic: a delicate plant from abroad.

W. Somerset Maugham (1874–1965) *The Door of Opportunity*

From a collection published in 1933. Like other Far Eastern tales
of Maugham's, this contains a number of native terms whose
meaning can be obtained from the dictionary, or inferred,
approximately at least, from the context.
Sondurah: evidently a fictitiously named one of the native States of
the Malay peninsula under British protection at this time. Such
States became part of the Federation of Malaysia in 1963.
half-a-crown (2s.6d), florin (2s.) = 12½p, 10p, at today's values
£3.00–£2.50.
interest: personal influence.
Smerige flikkers! Vervloekte ploerten!: Dirty buggers! Bloody
peasants!

P. G. Wodehouse (1881–1975) *Jeeves and the Song of Songs*

This story was first collected in 1930. As is customary in the
Jeeves-Wooster stories, the author introduces references to and
quotations from authors well known in his time. These allusions
are often in concealed form and modern readers can miss them. So
in this story there are fragments from the works of Charles
Kingsley, Shakespeare, Bismarck, Kipling (twice), the Book of
Daniel, John Bright and very likely others. It would be tedious to
descant on them all in turn, but I will say something of the last-
named when I come to it, if only because it carries some of the
mocking spirit occasionally to be found in the master's works.
half-past two: sixty-five minutes, including time for a cocktail and
a few songs, seem jolly few for an entire socializing lunch. I only
mention it.
Oddfellows: a mutual-help association.
chi-yiking: making a row; originally a gipsy word, in general use
among coster-mongers and others after about 1880.
the bird was hovering in the air, etc.: refers to 'The angel of death
has been abroad throughout the land: you may almost hear the
beating of his wings.' From a once-famous and passionate speech
against the Crimean War delivered in the House of Commons,
February 1855, by John Bright the Liberal politician.

Irwin Shaw (born 1917) *Act of Faith*

Best known for his first novel, *The Young Lions*, 1948, also concerned with the Second World War. This story was first collected in 1946.

C.O.: commanding officer of the company – not, as in the British army, that of the battalion.

Vladimir Nabokov (1899–1977) *First Love*

The author is best known for his novel *Lolita*, first published Paris, 1955. This story is dated 1948. It contains a number of French expressions of which it could perhaps be said that they look and sound better in a foreign language than in the cold light of English, as the example I give is meant to show.

geminate: double, twin in the adjective sense.

nictitating: my text reads nicitating. This is not a word at all, whereas to nictitate is to wink, not easy to fit into this context. Nabokov's penchant for obscure words sometimes over-reached itself.

cacahuètes: peanuts.

Angus Wilson (1913–1991) *Fresh Air Fiend*

This story was the first printed in Wilson's first book of stories, *The Wrong Set* (1949). It contains a number of allusions to the cultural life of that period or the one before, a couple of which I have detailed. The idiosyncratic punctuation and paragraphing of the original are retained here.

W.V.S.: Women's Voluntary Services, organization of voluntary workers.

(Lady) Ottoline Morrell (1873–1938): patroness of Henry James, Lytton Strachey, T. S. Eliot, W. B. Yeats and others.

Grouper: member of Oxford Group Movement (later Moral Rearmament), calling for moral and spiritual renewal and going in for public confession of supposed faults.

'Anthony Boucher' (W. A. P. White) (1911–1968) *The Quest for St Aquin*

First published in 1951. Like H. Beam Piper below, 'Boucher' was well known in his time as a writer of science fiction in magazines and elsewhere.
fish: an early Christian symbol derived from the letters of the Greek word for fish, *ikhthus*, taken to stand for Jesus Christ.
Retro me, Satanas!: (get thee) behind me, Satan, a rejection of devilish temptation. From Matthew xvi 23, where Christ answers Peter's attempt to talk him out of going to Jerusalem to face his destiny.
Ashtaroth (or Ashtoreth, etc.): heathen goddess corresponding to Venus.
Screwtape: the eponymous devil in C. S. Lewis's work of religious controversy, *The Screwtape Letters* (1940).

Brian Aldiss (born 1925) *Outside*

This story, one of the first its author published, first appeared in 1955.

H. Beam Piper (1904–1964) *He Walked Around the Horses*

Elizabeth Taylor (1912–1975) *Summer Schools*

First collected in 1958.

Dick Francis (born 1920) *Twenty-One Good Men and True*

This story was first published in 1979, though in its periodic style it recalls the author's novels of the earlier 1960s, a date also suggested by one or two plot details.
crescendo: a vulgar error surprising in a normally scrupulous writer. A crescendo is not loudness itself but a gradual increase in loudness. A climax is what is meant.